THE
OTHER SIDE
OF THE
BRIDGE

THE
OTHER
SIDE

ALSO BY MARY LAWSON

Crow Lake

MARY LAWSON

OF

THE

BRIDGE

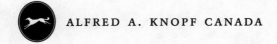

ALFRED A. KNOPF CANADA

PUBLISHED BY ALFRED A. KNOPF CANADA

Copyright © 2006 Mary Lawson

www.randomhouse.ca

Library and Archives Canada Cataloguing in Publication

Lawson, Mary, 1946–
The other side of the bridge / Mary Lawson.

ISBN-13: 978-0-676-97746-2
ISBN-10: 0-676-97746-4

I. Title.

PS8573.A9425O84 2006 C813.'6 C2006–902588–6

Text design: CS Richardson

First Edition

Printed and bound in the United States of America

2 4 6 8 9 7 5 3 1

FOR MY BROTHERS, GEORGE AND BILL,
WHO LOVE THE NORTH.

THE

OTHER SIDE

OF THE

BRIDGE

PROLOGUE

~

There was a summer back when they were kids, when Arthur Dunn was thirteen or fourteen and his brother, Jake, was eight or nine, when for weeks on end Jake pestered Arthur to play the game he called knives. Jake had a great collection of knives at the time, everything from fancy little Swiss Army jackknives with dozens of attachments to a big sleek hunting knife with a runnel down one side for blood. It was the hunting knife that was to be used in the game because according to Jake it was the best for throwing.

"Just once, okay?" Jake would say, dancing about barefoot in the dust of the farmyard, tossing the knife from hand to hand like a juggler, leaping back quickly if it decided to fall blade-first. "Come on, just once. It'll only take a *minute.*"

"I'm busy," Arthur would say, and carry on with whatever task his father had set him to. It was the summer holidays and the list of tasks was unending, but it was better than going to school.

"Come on," Jake would say. "Come *on*. You'll *love* it! It's a really good game. Come *on*!"

"I gotta fix this hinge."

Jake had explained the rules of the knife game to him and it was crazy. You stood at attention facing each other, about six feet apart, and took turns throwing the knife into the ground as close as possible to your opponent's naked foot. You had to be barefoot, Jake explained, or there would be no point to the game. Wherever the knife landed, your opponent had to move his foot alongside it. The idea was to make him do the splits bit by bit, as slowly as possible. The more throws the better. The smaller the distance between the still-vibrating steel and the outer edge of your brother's foot, the better. Nuts.

But in the end, as they had both known he would, Jake wore Arthur down. That was Jake's specialty—wearing people down.

It was a warm evening in July, the end of a long hot day out in the fields, and Arthur was sitting on the back step doing nothing, which was always a mistake. Jake appeared around the corner of the house and saw him, and his eyes started to shine. Jake had dark blue eyes in a pale triangular face and hair the colour of wheat. At nine years old he was slight and reedy (*frail* was the word their mother used) and already good-looking, though not as good-looking as he would be later. Arthur, five years older, was big and slow and heavy, with sloping shoulders and a neck like an ox.

Jake had the knife on him, of course. He always did; he carried it around in its own special sheath with its own special belt-loop, so as to be ready for anything. He started badgering Arthur right away, and eventually Arthur gave in just to get it over with.

"Once, okay?" Arthur said. "*Once.* I play it once, now, and you never ask me again. Promise."

"Okay, okay, I promise! Let's go."

And so it was that on that warm July evening when he was thirteen or fourteen years old—at any rate plenty old enough to know better—Arthur found himself standing behind the line his little brother had drawn in the dust, waiting to have a knife thrown at his bare and vulnerable feet. The dust felt hot, warmer than the air, and soft as talcum powder. It puffed up between his toes every time he took a step and turned them a pale and ghostly grey. Arthur's feet were broad and meaty with red raw patches from his heavy farm boots. Jake's feet were long and thin, delicate and blue-veined. Jake didn't wear farm boots much. He was considered by their mother to be too young for farm labour, though Arthur hadn't been too young at the same age.

Jake had first throw, by virtue of it being his game and his knife. "Stand at attention," he said. His eyes were fixed on Arthur's left foot and he spoke in a hushed voice. He had a great feeling for the drama of the moment, had Jake. "Keep your feet together. Don't move them, no matter what."

He took the knife by the blade and began swinging it loosely between finger and thumb. His forefinger rested easily in the blood runnel. He seemed scarcely to be holding the knife at all. Arthur watched the blade. In spite of himself, he felt his left foot curl inwards.

"Keep it still," Jake said. "I'm warning you."

Arthur forced his foot to lie flat. The thought came into his mind—not drifting gently in but appearing suddenly, fully formed, like a cold hard round little pebble—that

3

Jake hated him. The thought had never occurred to him before but suddenly, there it was. Though he couldn't imagine a reason. Surely he was the one who should have done the hating.

The knife swung for a minute more, and then, in one swift graceful movement, Jake lifted his arm and threw, and the blade circled, drawing swift shining arcs in the air, and then buried itself deeply in the ground a couple of inches from the outside edge of Arthur's foot. A beautiful throw.

Jake's eyes left the ground and he grinned at Arthur. "That's one," he said. "Your turn. Move your foot out to the knife."

Arthur moved his foot outwards to the edge of the knife and drew the blade from the ground. The skin on the top of his left foot was stinging, though nothing had touched it. He straightened up. Jake stood facing him, still grinning, arms at his sides, feet together. Eyes bright. Excited, but without fear. Without fear because—and Arthur saw this suddenly too—Jake knew that Arthur would never risk throwing really close.

Arthur imagined his mother's face if he were to prove Jake wrong and slice off his toe. He imagined what his father would do to him if he were even to catch him playing this stupid game. He couldn't think how he'd allowed Jake to persuade him. He must have been mad.

"Come *on*," Jake said. "Come on come on come *on*! Close as you can!"

Arthur held the knife by the blade, as Jake had done, but it was hard to relax his fingers enough to let it swing. He'd thrown a knife before and he wasn't too bad a shot—in fact a few years back he and his friend Carl Luntz from the next farm had painted a target on the wall of the Luntzes' hay barn and held competitions, which Arthur usually won—but the outcome had never mattered. Now, the chance that he would hit that narrow blue-veined foot seemed overwhelmingly high. And then, all at once, he saw the answer—so obvious that only someone as dim-witted as he must surely be wouldn't have seen it earlier. Throw wide. Not so wide that Jake would guess he was doing it deliberately, but wide enough to bring the game to a safe and rapid close. Make Jake do the splits in three or four steps. Jake would jeer but he was going to jeer anyway, and the game would be over, and Jake would have to leave him alone.

Arthur felt his muscles start to relax. The knife swung more easily. He took a deep breath and threw.

The knife circled clumsily once in the air and then landed on its side eighteen inches or so from Jake's foot.

Jake said, "That's pathetic. Take it again. It's gotta stick in the ground or it doesn't count."

Arthur picked up the knife, swung again, and threw, more confident now, and this time the knife embedded itself in the ground ten inches from Jake's little toe.

Jake made a sound of disgust. He moved his foot out to the blade and picked it up. He looked disappointed and pitying, which was fine by Arthur.

"Okay," Jake said. "My turn."

He took the knife by the blade and swung it back and forth, looking briefly at Arthur, and when their eyes met there was a slight pause—just a fraction of a second—during which the knife hesitated in its lazy swing and then picked up its rhythm again. Thinking back on it afterwards, Arthur was never able to decide whether there was any significance in that pause—whether in that instant of eye contact Jake had seen into his mind and guessed what he intended to do.

At the time he didn't think anything, because there was no time to think. Jake lifted the knife with the same swift movement as before and threw it, but harder than before, and faster, so that it was only a shining blur as it spun through the air. Arthur found himself staring down at the knife embedded in his foot. There was a surreal split second before the blood started to well up and then up it came, dark and thick as syrup.

Arthur looked at Jake and saw that he was staring at the knife. His expression was one of surprise, and this was something that Arthur wondered about later too. Was Jake surprised because he had never considered the possibility that he might be a less-than-perfect shot? Did he have that much confidence in himself, that little self-doubt?

Or was he merely surprised at how easy it was to give in to an impulse and carry through the thought that lay in your mind? Simply to do whatever you wanted to do, and damn the consequences.

ONE

~

Firefighters Battle Bushfire
Lost Bear Hunter Located by Plane: In Bush 40 Hours
—*Temiskaming Speaker*, May 1957

On a small farm about two miles outside Struan there lived a beautiful woman. She was tall and willowy with a lot of fair hair that she drew back into a thick braid and tied with whatever came to hand—a bit of frayed ribbon, an elastic band, an old piece of string. On Sundays she rolled it into a shining ball at the nape of her neck and fastened it somehow so that it wouldn't fall down during church. Her name was Laura Dunn. Laura, her own name, soft and beautiful like she was; Dunn, her husband's name, solid and lumpen like her husband. Arthur Dunn was a farmer, a big, heavyset man with a neck at least twice the width of his wife's, and to Ian, sitting with his parents three pews behind, he looked about as exciting as dishwater.

Ian had first noticed Laura Dunn when he was fourteen—she must have been around all his life but that was the year he became aware of her. She would have been about thirty at the time. She and Arthur had three children, or possibly four. Ian wasn't sure—he'd never paid any attention to the children.

For a year he made do with watching her in church on Sundays—the Dunns came into town for church every Sunday without fail. Then, when he was fifteen, Ian's father said that he should get a job working Saturdays and holidays and start saving up for his further education, the theory being that you appreciated things more if you'd helped to pay for them yourself. Ian couldn't recall anyone asking him if he wanted more education—it was another of the many assumptions people made about his life—but in this particular case he didn't argue. He got on his bike and cycled out to the Dunns' farm.

The farm was an oddity in the Struan area because Arthur Dunn still worked his land with horses. It wasn't because he couldn't afford a tractor—the farm was prosperous enough—and it wasn't through any religious convictions like the Mennonites farther south. When asked about it Arthur would study the ground thoughtfully, as if the question had never occurred to him before, and then say that he guessed he liked horses. No one bought that explanation, though. They all believed that Arthur had been put off tractors years earlier, when his father got one and drove it down to the lower forty, where he rolled it into a ditch and killed himself, all within two hours of its arrival on the farm. Even the youngest and least intelligent of the plow horses would have known better than to fall into a ditch. The day after the funeral Arthur got rid of the tractor and harnessed up the team again and he'd been plodding along behind them ever since.

He was out in the fields when Ian cycled up to the farm. Ian saw him, off in the distance, being towed along by two great heavy-footed animals like a picture postcard of a time gone by. Ian leaned his bike up against the pump, which he guessed would only be used to fill the water trough—all but the most remote farms in the area had running water, and electricity too; they'd been connected up to the grid two years ago, when the power lines were run in for the sawmill.

Ian picked his way between the chickens to the back door. There was a front door on the other side of the house, but he figured no one ever used it. It would lead into the sitting room, where probably no one ever sat, whereas the back door led into the kitchen, which was where life would be lived. He could hear Laura Dunn talking as he climbed the three steps to the door. The inner door was open, letting the sound of voices out, but the screen door was closed, making it difficult to see in. She was scolding one of the kids, by the sound of it, though Ian couldn't make out the words because a baby was crying. Her voice wasn't sharp and sarcastic, as Ian's mother's voice tended to be when she was annoyed about something. It was exasperated, but still gentle and light, or so it seemed to Ian.

There was a lull in the baby's crying and Ian, standing on the top step with his hand lifted, ready to knock on the door, heard Laura Dunn say, "Well for goodness' sake, Carter, couldn't you *share* it? Couldn't you let her have a *turn*?" And a boy's voice said, "She never shares *hers*!"

and a little girl's voice wailed, "I do *so*!" and the baby started to howl again. There was the sound of a chair being scuffed along the floor and then the screen door was flung open, nearly knocking Ian off the step, and a boy charged out. He gave Ian a startled, angry glance before jumping off the steps and disappearing around the side of the house. He looked about eleven or twelve and had the sort of face, Ian thought, that made you want to hit him. The sullen, sulky face of a kid who thinks the world's against him.

The screen door slammed closed again and Laura Dunn appeared behind it. She gave a start when she saw Ian standing there and said, "Oh! Oh . . . hello! It's Ian, isn't it? Dr. Christopherson's son?"

"Yes," Ian said. "Um, yes . . . um, I've come to talk to Mr. Dunn . . . about a job. I wondered if he'd be taking on anyone this summer. I mean, full-time this summer, but maybe Saturdays right away, and then full-time once the holidays start."

He felt himself flushing. He was gabbling, because she was so near, just inches away behind the screen door, and she was looking at him, directly and only at him, with those wonderful soft eyes, eyes that he'd noticed always seemed shadowed, as if they contained deep, unfathomable mysteries, or—the possibility occurred to him now, what with the crying of the baby and the behaviour of the kids—as if she were tired all the time.

"Oh," she said. "Oh, well yes, I'm sure he'd be glad of some help. Just a minute, Ian. . . . I'll come out. Just a minute."

She disappeared. Ian heard her say something to somebody and then she reappeared with a baby in her arms.

A little girl was behind her, but she shrank back when she saw Ian standing there. He moved down off the steps and Laura came out, bouncing the baby gently up and down on her hip. The baby was fat and sexless, like all babies, and had round, unconvincing tears rolling down its cheeks. It and Ian looked at each other and the baby gave a sort of snort, as if it didn't think much of what it saw, and put its thumb in its mouth.

"There, now," Laura said, brushing the top of its head with her lips. "That's better. This is Ian. Say hello to Ian."

"Hi," Ian said. He smiled warily at the baby. It stared back and then curled up and buried its face in the folds of Laura's dress, its free hand clutching possessively at her breast. Ian quickly looked down at his feet.

"The thing is, you'll really need to speak to Arthur," Laura was saying. "He's plowing at the moment." She nodded in the direction of the picture-postcard view of her husband. "If you'd like to go out and have a word with him . . . just along that track there." She looked doubtfully at Ian's bike. "Only I think you'd be better to walk. The horses cut up the path a bit. . . . But I'm sure he'll be pleased— it's so hard to get help. Men nowadays don't know how to deal with horses, you see." She smiled at him. "But maybe you like them. Is that why you've come?"

"Well, sort of," Ian said. He hadn't given the work of the farm—the actual job he was applying for—a thought. Arthur Dunn could have hitched his plow to a moose, for all he cared. At the moment all his attention was taken up with trying not to look at the baby, which had now, unbelievably, wormed its hand inside its mother's dress and was tugging at what it found in there, all the while making fretful smacking noises with its lips.

Laura gently disengaged the small hand. "Shush," she said to the baby. She smiled at Ian again, seeming not to notice his embarrassment. "Come back and let me know what he says, all right?"

Ian nodded, and turned, his mind filled to the brim with the nearness of her, her overwhelming *presence*, and made his way down the muddy track to where Arthur Dunn was plodding up and down the furrows behind his horses. Arthur Dunn, so solid, so dull, so obviously unworthy of such a wife. Arthur Dunn, who, when he saw Ian approaching, halted his team and came across the field to meet him, and said yeah, sure, he could use a hand, and would Ian like to start this coming Saturday?

~

Ian's grandfather had been Struan's first resident doctor, and when he'd answered the "Doctor Wanted" advertisement they'd put in a Toronto medical journal, the grateful townspeople built him a house just a block west of Main Street, a couple of hundred yards from the lake. It was a handsome wooden structure, white-painted and green-trimmed, with lawns on all four sides and a white picket fence surrounding the lawns. In the early days there was a neat white stable for the horse and buggy twenty yards from the house. Later the first Dr. Christopherson acquired a Buick Roadster, which became as much a part of him as his old black leather medical bag, and a garage was added beside the stable. He kept the horse for use in winter, when the back roads around Struan were impassable by anything except a sled. His son, the present Dr. Christopherson (who also drove a Buick, though his was the sedan), was sometimes heard lamenting the absence of the sled even now, given the state of the town's one and only snowplow.

As much as anything else, the building of the house had been a statement of faith on the part of the people of Struan. Until then they'd had to go to New Liskeard if they required a doctor, and if you needed medical help badly enough to make the journey to New Liskeard, the odds were that you were in no state to make the journey. Getting their own doctor was a sign that the town had arrived. In the brief interval between applying the final coat of paint and the arrival of Dr. Christopherson, the people of Struan found excuses to walk past the house and admire it. You looked at that house and you thought, this is no fly-by-night northern settlement sprung up around a sawmill; any town that can afford to build its doctor a house like this is here to stay.

Ian was aware of most of this personal and civic history, and as far as he was concerned his grandfather must have been raving mad. Imagine voluntarily leaving a city like Toronto to come to a hick town like Struan. And though you could excuse his grandfather's mistake on the grounds of ignorance—he couldn't have had any real idea what he was coming to—there was no such excuse for Ian's father. He had been born and brought up in Struan, and had then escaped, but after living in Toronto for almost a decade while he took his medical degree and worked in the Hospital for Sick Children, he had *returned to Struan* to take over his father's practice. Ian couldn't understand it. Why would anyone do such a thing? What was Struan, apart from a sawmill? A sorry bunch of stores lined up along a dusty main street, with nothing in them anyone would want to buy. A couple of churches. The Hudson's Bay Company. A post office. A bank. Harper's Restaurant.

Ben's Bar. A hotel—because, incredibly, some people chose to come to Struan for their holidays—and a little clutch of holiday cottages down by the lake. The lake was the town's only asset, in Ian's opinion. It was large—fifty miles long, north to south, and almost twenty miles across—and deep, and very clear, surrounded on all sides by low granite hills studded with spruce and wind-blasted pines. Its shore was so ragged with bays and inlets and islands that you could spend your life exploring and never find half of them. When Ian dreamed of leaving the town, which he did all the time nowadays, the thought of leaving the lake was the only thing that bothered him. The lake and Laura Dunn.

He parked his bike up against the veranda of the house, climbed the wide wooden steps to the porch, and went in. The door to his father's office was closed and he could hear voices behind it, but the waiting room was empty, so Ian sat down on one of the dozen or so battered old chairs lining the walls and flicked through a two-year-old copy of *Reader's Digest* while he thought about Laura Dunn. The way strands of her hair escaped from their elastic band and drifted around her face. Those shadowed eyes. Her breasts. He'd noticed—he couldn't help noticing—that on the front of her dress there had been two wet circles where her breasts had leaked milk.

The door to the office opened and Ted Pickett, owner of Pickett's Hardware, came out with his arm in a sling. He nodded at Ian and grimaced and Ian grimaced back. Patients entered the house by a side door but both the office and the waiting room were right off the hall, so all his life he'd been used to seeing people going in and out in varying degrees of anguish, and he'd got his responses down pat.

"He doesn't think it's broken," Mr. Pickett said.

"That's lucky," Ian said.

"He thinks it's just sprained. Hurts like hell though."

Ian nodded sympathetically. "Did you fall off the ladder?" There was a ladder on wheels in the hardware store that Mr. Pickett scooted around on, reaching for nails or nuts or brackets or hinges, an accident waiting to happen.

"Yeah," Mr. Pickett said, looking surprised. "How did you know?"

"I just . . . kind of . . . wondered," Ian said politely.

When Mr. Pickett left he knocked on his father's door and went in.

"I've got a job," he said. His father had his back to him. He was rolling bandages and placing them neatly back in their drawer. His desk was littered with papers—patients' notes, medical journals, bills—but the tools of his trade were always properly put away.

"That was quick," he said.

"Arthur Dunn's farm," Ian said. "He said I could start Saturday."

His father turned around and took off his glasses and blinked at him. "Arthur Dunn's farm?"

"Yes, you know . . . doing . . . farm work."

"Farm work." His father nodded vaguely, as if trying to imagine it.

"I thought I'd like something outdoors," Ian said.

Dr. Christopherson put his glasses back on and looked out the window. It had just started to rain. "Yes," he said doubtfully. "Well . . . if that's what you want. Arthur's a nice fellow." He looked dubiously at Ian. "It'll be hard work, you know."

"I know," Ian said.

"Did you see the horses?"

"Yes."

"Magnificent animals."

"Yes," Ian said, though he had barely noticed them. He and his father smiled at each other, glad to be in agreement. They were usually in agreement, unlike Ian and his mother.

Next he went and told his mother, who was watching *I Love Lucy* in the living room. Television had finally—finally!—reached Struan a couple of months earlier, proof, if more were needed, of how backward things were up here. Ian's mother had disapproved of it at first, but now she watched it more than he did. In fact, just lately she seemed to watch it all the time. She was supposed to be in with his father—she was his nurse—but apart from the odd emergency, Ian hadn't seen her in the office for weeks.

"Mum?" he said, standing in the doorway. She was in one of her absent moods—he could tell even though he couldn't see her face. She had two moods nowadays, absent or annoyed, and whichever one she was in he invariably found he preferred the other.

"Mum?" he said again. She turned her head a few degrees, not taking her eyes off the screen.

"I've got a job," Ian said.

She turned a little more and met his eyes, and he saw the glazed look fade as she focused on him.

"What was that?" she said.

"I said I've got a job."

"Oh," she said. She smiled at him. "That's good." She turned back to the television. Ian waited a minute but there was no further response, so he went into the kitchen to get a reaction from Mrs. Tuttle instead. She was breading chicken pieces for supper, dipping each piece in a bowl of beaten egg and then slapping it back and forth in a dish of bread crumbs.

"I've got a job, Mrs. Tuttle," Ian said.

"Have you now?" she said, placing a breaded breast down on the baking tray and taking a pale, slippery-looking chicken leg from the hacked-up carcass on the chopping board. "That's exciting. What is it?"

"Helping Mr. Dunn on his farm."

She paused, then turned her head to look at him. Her glasses were splattered with the day's cooking—a dusting of flour from the tea biscuits, a little smear of butter, a scattering of crumbs—even what looked to be a shred of carrot peel. "Goodness!" she said, ducking her head in order to look over the top of them. "Whatever did you want a job like that for?" Which was what he'd expected her to say, and therefore satisfying in its way, so he smiled at her and left.

His mother was still in front of the television when he passed the living room door on his way upstairs; *I Love Lucy* had finished and she was watching a program in French. It struck Ian as strange, because she didn't speak French. He wondered if anyone else's mother watched television during the day. It was hard to know. The mothers of most of his friends were farmers' wives and didn't have time to sit down, much less watch TV. But his mother had never been like other people's mothers. She didn't come from the North—she was an outsider, from Vancouver originally. She wore smart shoes with heels, even around the house, and skirts with sweaters that matched, and had her hair set in loose waves instead of tight little corkscrews like the mothers of his friends. In the evenings, she and Ian and his father ate formally in the dining room, instead of at the kitchen table. They used napkins—proper white linen ones, washed and starched and ironed by Mrs. Tuttle every Monday. Ian suspected that no one else in the whole of Struan would have the first idea what to do with a napkin.

~

One good thing about his mother's moods of late was that suppers were fairly brief and painless affairs. In the past they'd been hard work because she would insist on having what she called a "civilized conversation" while they ate. That was what evening meals were for, according to her—they were for families to get together and exchange views and experiences in a pleasant environment. Maybe that would have been okay if he'd had half a dozen brothers or sisters to share the burden of thinking up something to say, night after night, but there was only him. He didn't see why they couldn't read at the table. He would have preferred it and he knew his father would as well—you could tell by the wistful, unfocused look in his eyes. He was longing to immerse himself in an article on the renewed threat of polio in rural areas or the latest wonder drug or a new type of surgical dressing that didn't stick to wounds. In Ian's case it would be fishing magazines: a fifty-five-pound muskie caught down in French River, the pros and cons of trolling versus casting, the last word in fishing tackle. He pictured himself and his father, shoulders hunched, chins six inches from their plates, absently forking in their dinners, happily absorbed in the printed word. His mother could look at one of her Eaton's catalogues. Why not? It would be much more relaxed and at least as companionable as the performance they had to go through every night in the name of family togetherness.

But in the last little while she seemed to have lost interest in conversation, civilized or not. Sometimes she still made a half-hearted attempt to get things rolling by saying something like, "So, what has everybody been doing today?" but this evening she didn't even do that. The three of them ate more or less in silence (he and his father both gazing into the middle distance as they chewed, thinking about the things they would have liked to be reading) and then they all excused themselves from the table and went their separate ways.

Ian got on his bike and set off for the reserve. It had rained hard for ten minutes or so while they were eating but now it had cleared and the evening air was cool and fresh. The clouds were drifting away out over the lake and the pale sky shone in the puddles at the sides of the road. Main Street—the only road out of town—was deserted. The stores closed promptly at half past five and the entire population of Struan went home for supper. That was one of the things about the town that exasperated Ian—the way it died in the evenings. The only places that stayed open were Harper's, which served meals until half past six—seven o'clock on Fridays—and Ben's. Ben's Bar was the nearest thing Struan had to a den of iniquity. Every Saturday night it filled up with men from the logging camp upriver who came into town to spend their week's wages on liquor. They'd get completely hammered, cause Sergeant Moynihan and Ian's father between them no end of trouble, and then go back to the camp and the town would settle back into its usual dull predictable self for another week.

For many years Ian hadn't given the town a thought, because it was all he knew, but the previous summer his mother had taken him to Toronto for a week and his eyes had been opened. What had impressed him most had not been the size of the city or the noise or even the buildings– he'd been expecting all of that. What had struck him most forcibly was the fact that when he walked down the street he hadn't known anyone. Thousands upon thousands of strangers. He'd found it amazing. Liberating! Contrast it with Struan, where everyone had known everyone else since the day they were born. And it was worse for him than it was for most people because of his father being public property–"our doctor," people called him–and having his office at home. Ian noticed that they didn't call his mother "our nurse," though. They called her Mrs. Christopherson and left it at that. People were a little bit afraid of her–he knew that. She could be sharp. She could say, "The doctor is a busy man, Mrs. Shultz. Use your common sense."

But they seemed to claim Ian's father as their own, and his home, too, and maybe–in the past year or so he had started to feel this–even Ian himself. Virtually everyone in Struan had sat in his father's waiting room at one time or another, waiting to have their sore throats looked at or bits of their fingers sewn back on, and while they sat they had watched Ian grow up. Many of the older ones must have watched his father grow up as well; they would have seen him crawling around on the same wooden floor-boards that Ian crawled around on, getting bigger by the day and gradually turning into their doctor. Ian was starting to suspect that they thought of him in the same way. Increasingly he got the feeling that people looked at him and automatically thought, Here comes another one. The next Dr. Christopherson.

In fact, the previous week old Mr. Johnson, who'd had his toes shot off forty years ago at the Somme and shuffled along with the help of two sticks, had stopped him in the street and asked if he could have "more of them pills." Ian had said, "I think you should talk to my dad, Mr. Johnson," and the old man looked bewildered. He stood in the middle of the road, blinking up at Ian, his mouth hanging open with the effort of trying to make sense of what he was saying. Ian thought, Oh, come on! I'm only fifteen! But everyone said he looked just like his father, the same big-boned, loose-knit Scandinavian frame, the same pale hair. Maybe if your eyesight was poor it was hard to tell the difference. In the end he took pity on the old man and guided him back onto the sidewalk before he got flattened by a logging truck, and said he'd have a word with his father about the pills.

But the incident irritated him. In Mr. Johnson's case it might have been just a matter of confusion and poor eyesight, but it brought home to him the assumption—unspoken, but suddenly clear—that he would follow in his father's and grandfather's footsteps. As if he had no say in the matter, no ideas of his own.

He imagined living in Toronto, or Vancouver or New York. Think of the freedom. You could be whoever you wanted to be. No one expecting anything of you, no one knowing who your parents were, no one caring if you were a brain surgeon or a bum. Only wherever he ended up, there would need to be a lake or at least a river nearby. He couldn't live far from the water.

He cycled down Main Street to the outskirts of Struan, which took all of three minutes, and then out along the road to the Ojibway reserve, which took a further five. The reserve was spread along the shore of a bay, with a point of land jutting out into the lake between it and

Struan, a symbolic barrier as well as a geographic one. The road ran out of pavement half a mile before it reached the reserve, and the land itself was so low it would grow nothing but bulrushes and bugs—blackflies by the million in early summer, then mosquitoes big enough to pick you up and carry you away. The reserve store, though, where Pete Corbiere lived, was situated right down by the lake, which meant it got the benefit of the wind and was less buggy than the rest. Pete's grandfather was sitting on the steps when Ian arrived, smoking and staring off into the woods. He had scars on his fingers from letting cigarettes burn down too far.

"Hi," Ian said, leaning his bike against a tree.

Mr. Corbiere nodded in greeting.

"You look busy," Ian said. He liked the old man but was never sure how to approach him and several years ago had settled on an uneasy jocularity that he now wasn't happy with but couldn't seem to stop.

Mr. Corbiere nodded again. "Workin' my butt off," he agreed. "Your rod's inside. Put it there to be safe. Kids were playin' with it."

"Oh," Ian said. "Thanks."

"How's your dad?"

"He's fine, thanks, Mr. Corbiere." He looked around for some sign of Pete. "Is Pete out already?"

The old man jerked his head towards the lake.

"Thanks," Ian said again. "Where's the rod?"

"Pete's room."

Ian stepped delicately around Mr. Corbiere's broad rump and went up the steps into the store. It was dark and smelled of mould. A gigantic chest freezer hummed to itself against one wall. At certain times of year the freezer was full of game—rabbits, sometimes still unskinned, hunks of venison, ducks, geese, once a whole beaver, its tail stretched out flat. Beside the huge freezer was a smaller one full of fish, and beside that a smaller one still, given over to ice cream and Popsicles. Along the back wall there were a few shelves with tins on them—Heinz beans, tinned peaches, Irish stew. On a bottom shelf were three loaves of packaged sliced bread. At the other end of the room were hardware items—matches, fishhooks, batteries, snare wire, flyswatters, axes, woollen socks. No beaded moccasins. Beaded moccasins were sold by the roadside at rustic wooden trading posts, along with quill boxes and miniature birch-bark canoes and totem poles six inches high. The trading posts themselves were advertised by large billboards portraying stern-looking Indian chiefs in war paint and full headdress. The Ojibway had never gone in for headdresses and the totem poles belonged three thousand miles away on the west coast of Canada, but the tourists liked them so the band went along with it. "Wouldn't want to disappoint anybody," as the old man said.

Ian pushed aside a row of plastic strips hanging in a doorway and went into the back of the store. Pete and his grandfather lived here. The store was owned by a Scotsman—according to Ian's father, every reserve in the country had a store owned by a Scotsman—who let Pete and his grandfather live there in return for minding the store. There were two bedrooms, a bathroom, and a kitchen that consisted of a sink and a stove at one end of the hall-way. Pete's room was small and square and stupendously untidy—clothes and gum wrappers and schoolbooks and snowshoes not put away since March and girlie magazines left lying open as if the old man wouldn't mind, which he probably didn't. Ian's fishing rod was standing in a corner, looking new and shiny and very out of place. He retrieved it and went back outside. Mr. Corbiere had started on another cigarette. Ian stepped past him.

"Thanks, Mr. Corbiere."

"Catch a big one."

Ian grinned. "I'll try."

Once he got down to the shore it took him only a few seconds to spot the _Queen Mary_. She was across the bay by the sand bar at the entrance to the river—a good spot for pike, especially in the spring. By some trick of the light the old rowboat seemed to be hovering just above the surface of the water, as if it were a ghost ship or something out of a dream. He watched it for a moment, and Pete's motionless shape within it. The evening was very still and the water gleamed a dull silver.

He cupped his hands to his mouth and yelled. The sound flew out across the water and the figure in the boat moved, and lifted a hand in acknowledgement. Then there was a distant _putputput_ from the little outboard and the boat turned towards him. Ian walked out to the end of the dock.

"How's it going?" he said when Pete was close enough. The smell of gasoline and fish rose up from the boat, luring him in.

"So-so," Pete said.

The boat sidled up alongside the dock and Ian jumped in, avoiding half a dozen glistening trout in the bottom. Pete pushed off and headed back across the bay. When he reached the sand bar he cut the engine. The smooth swells of their wake caught up with them, rocked the boat gently, and moved on.

"I can't stay long," Ian said absently, picking through

the tackle box for a suitable lure. "I should study. We've got that biology test tomorrow."

Pete stuck a mayfly on his hook and dropped it over the side of the boat. He said, "You got your priorities wrong, man."

"I know, I know." The tackle box was in a similar state to Pete's bedroom, lures and weights and hooks and bits of fur and feathers all over the place, with the odd dead bug tossed in for good measure.

"It could be a hundred years," Pete said, giving his line a sharp jerk and hauling in a perch, "maybe two hundred, before you get another night as perfect as this for fishing. But there will always, always, be another test."

"Too damned true," Ian said. He was still going to have to go back in time to have a look at the textbook though. He and Pete shared the same policy, developed and fine-tuned over the years, of working just hard enough to keep out of trouble; but in Ian's case, being the doctor's son, the teachers' expectations of him were irritatingly high.

They fished. Pete used a jigger—a stick with fishing line attached and minnows or bugs for bait, or sometimes just a weighted hook with a bit of deer fur on it. Ian used his fishing rod, which was a good one, a birthday present from his parents. If tonight was like other nights, and it would be, he would catch one fish for every four or five caught by Pete. If they swapped equipment, Pete would continue to pull them in and Ian would continue to get next to nothing. It was a fact of life and he had accepted it long ago.

They'd met through fishing—Ian wasn't sure if he actually remembered it or if his father had told him the story at some later date. It was before they'd started school, so they would have been about four or five. Ian's father had been teaching him how to fish and had taken him around to Slow River Bay, and over by the sandbar at the mouth of the river they'd seen another boat, which had turned out to contain Pete and his grandfather, also in the middle of a fishing lesson. Ian's father knew Pete's grandfather the same way he knew everybody within a radius of a hundred miles, and he drifted over to say hi, and the two men started talking. Pete and Ian had eyed each other up and down, their fishing lines hanging in the water, and while they were busy doing that both lines were grabbed. There had been a few minutes of chaos—Ian did remember that— spray flying, boats rocking wildly, both men trying to help without looking as if they were helping, and when the fish were finally landed and held up to be admired, Pete's was a fourteen-inch pike and Ian's was a four-inch sunfish. Neither boy had been able to figure out why the two men laughed so hard—Pete's grandfather had tears running down his cheeks. But the boys held up their catches tri- umphantly, grinning at each other across the gunwales of the boats, two skinny kids with their bellies sticking out, fishermen for life. The fact that from then on Pete had continued to pull in the big ones and Ian had continued not to was just one of those things.

Ian reeled in his line, checked the lure, and stood up to cast again. He whipped the rod back and forth, listening to the hiss of the reel as the line played out, and let it fly. The lure sailed out over the water and then dropped down, light as a raindrop. Not a bad cast. He began slowly reeling it in, the line drawing a delicate V-shape across the surface of the water.

"Got a job today," he said after a while.

"Yeah?" Pete said.

"Yeah. My dad said I should work this summer. Saturdays too."

"You still have time to fish?"

"Oh sure. I'm working eight till six. I'll still have evenings free."

Pete nodded. He looked after the store in the summer while his grandfather acted as a guide for tourists who fancied themselves as woodsmen and loved the idea of a real, live Indian guide. "Found this old Injun up in the woods in Northern Ontario," they'd say to their friends back in the manicured suburbs of Toronto or Chicago or New York, nodding casually at a bear's head nailed to the rec room wall. "Knows the country like the back of his hand."

"I'm working on Arthur Dunn's farm," Ian said offhandedly. He reeled in his line, checked the lure, and cast again. He was aware of Pete looking at him curiously. "I thought it would beat being cooped up in town. There's a job going in the drugstore, but I didn't fancy standing behind the counter all summer long, listening to people complain about their headaches."

Silence from Pete.

"Or listening to women complain about . . . women's stuff," Ian went on, and then paused, suddenly wondering if that could be his mother's problem. The menopause. He'd read about it when looking through his father's books in search of something—anything at all—to do with sex. The whole business had sounded gross. But his mother was too young for that sort of problem. She was nineteen years younger than his father and had produced Ian when she was only twenty. "Or old guys complaining about their in-grown toenails. I get enough medical crap at home."

More silence. The problem with deceiving Pete was that they had known each other too long. A friend who has known you since you were four years old really knows you, whereas your parents only think they do.

They fished. Across the bay they heard the drone of an outboard, the sound gradually dying as it rounded a point of land. Silence settled again. Then two loons started calling to each other, laughing at some melancholy joke of their own, their cries shimmering back and forth across the water. The colour was ebbing out of the trees lining the shore, turning them from sombre green to black.

Pete said, as if ten minutes hadn't elapsed, "Standing behind a counter is just standing, man. Working on a farm is *work*."

He twitched the jig, paused a second or two, and then jerked the line sharply. A trout broke the surface ten feet away. He hauled it in and dropped it in the bottom of the boat. "You could've got a job at the sawmill," he said, rebaiting his hook and dropping it over the side again. "You'd get a job there easy as nothin'. Every guy there's had bits of himself stuck back on by your dad sometime or other. They'd make you foreman in three days flat, you'd be runnin' the place in two weeks. Good money, too. More'n Arthur Dunn can afford."

"Yeah," Ian said, "but who wants to spend the summer working for Fitzpatrick? I'll take Arthur Dunn any day."

Pete hauled in a four-inch perch, too small to keep. He unhooked it and tossed it back into the water. "You could've got a job waitin' on tables in Harper's. Put a cup of coffee down here, pick a cup of coffee up there. Good money, easy work. . . . Or the library. . . . Or the gas station." There was another tug on his line. It was the tiny perch again, the hole in its mouth from last time clearly visible. Pete raised it to eye level and said, "Where's your brains, man?" The fish gaped in astonishment. Pete tossed it back over the side. "Or the hardware store. Woolworth's. The post office. Any of them'd be better than a farm. 'Specially Arthur Dunn's farm."

"The farm's okay," Ian said mildly. "The horses are kind of fun."

"The *horses*?" Pete looked at him, slitty-eyed. Then suddenly he grinned.

"What?" Ian asked defensively.

"Nothin'," Pete said. "Nothin' at all."

They fished for another hour or so but the pike weren't interested, and when Pete caught the little perch for the third time they gave up and went home.

His parents were both in the living room when Ian got back. His mother was sitting in front of the television, though for once she wasn't watching it, and his father was standing in the doorway. When he came in they both looked around. There was a moment's pause, and then his father said, "You're home early. Fish not biting?"

"Nothing worth hauling out of the water," Ian said.

His mother was looking vaguely down at her lap. There must have been a crumb or a bit of fluff on her skirt—she picked it off carefully, studied it for a moment, and then dropped it on the floor.

TWO

~

Toronto Board of Trade Visiting Northern Ontario
Cattle Run Amuck—Men Chased to Lumber Piles—Rifles Used
—*Temiskaming Speaker*, March 1925

Arthur's earliest memory was of standing in the doorway of his parents' room, looking at his mother as she lay in bed. It was the middle of the day but nonetheless she was in bed, and Arthur didn't know what to make of it. The bed was very large and high, and Arthur could only just see her. She had her face turned towards the window. Then Arthur's father called from the bottom of the stairs that the doctor was coming, and she turned her head, and Arthur saw that she was crying.

Then old Dr. Christopherson came, and with him Mrs. Luntz, Carl's mother, from the next farm. Mrs. Luntz

30

patted Arthur on the head and told him to go downstairs and she and the doctor went into his mother's room and shut the door. Later, cries came from the room. During all of this, Arthur's father sat in the armchair in the kitchen with his large lumpy hands spread flat on his knees. His hands looked very strange, lying still like that. Normally if he was sitting down they were busy mending something.

In his memory Arthur had only the one picture of this scene, but from piecing things together later he knew that it must have happened more than once. Three times at least.

Then there was a long spell when his mother was in bed though she didn't look sick, during which time his father got the supper after coming in from the fields in the evening. Most days Mrs. Luntz and other ladies from neighbouring farms dropped by with food in big covered dishes, so all he had to do was heat things up. This wasn't a bad time, as far as Arthur could recall. He remembered his father giving him a dish towel and passing plates down for him to dry, and telling him he was doing a good job. He remembered carrying his mother's supper very carefully up the stairs and taking it in to her, and her smiling at him and thanking him.

He couldn't remember what he did during the day, while his mother lay in bed and his father was out in the fields. He was too young for school so he must have played by himself. But he clearly remembered the day he heard his mother calling him from her room. He would have been just five at the time. He remembered hearing the panic in her voice, and the feeling in his stomach—a cold tightness, like the grip of a hand—as he ran up the stairs. His mother had her knees drawn up under the blankets. She looked afraid. Arthur had never seen fear on an adult's face before,

31

but he had no difficulty recognizing it for what it was. "Go get your father," she had said. "Tell him it's coming! Run!"

Here there was a picture as well as a memory: a picture of himself flying along the edge of the fields, his feet stumbling on the clods of heavy rain-soaked earth. "Dad! Dad!" Terror in his voice. What was coming? Something terrible, terrifying, and his mother all alone in the house with no one to protect her.

And then some hours later, when it was dark and the doctor had come, along with Mrs. Luntz again, and they were with his mother, it became apparent from the screams that echoed down the stairs that they could not protect her any more than he or his father could. Arthur wanted to go to his father and climb onto his lap but he was afraid of the look on his father's face and of the appalled silence between the screams. He wanted to go to his room and get into bed and cower there, but to do that he would have to go up the stairs and pass the door with the dreadful sounds behind it. So instead he curled into a tight ball in the other armchair and stayed there, until many hours later the screaming finally stopped. And then there was another sound, a bawling, like a cross between a crow and a sheep, and he knew that whatever it was had come at last, and had triumphed, and his mother was dead.

Except that in the morning there she was, not dead at all but sitting up in bed, smiling, holding a bundle and saying to him, "Come and see, Arthur! You have a brother! This is your brother! His name is Jacob—isn't he lovely? You can call him Jake."

Was that where it all started, then? Before Jake was even born, with the loss of those other babies? So that when

Jake finally arrived, the outcome of all that pain and fear and grief, he would be so precious to his mother that she could hardly bear it? She carried him around with her all day, holding him tightly, fending off death with the crook of her arm. She loved the new baby—oh, Arthur knew that!—but her love seemed to consist mainly of an agonized anxiety. Arthur would see her looking at Jake with an expression almost of despair, as if she expected him to vanish at any moment, torn from her arms by some dark force. It didn't help that Jake was a sickly child, prone to colds and high temperatures. Or maybe he wasn't really sickly—maybe it was her fear. One cough from the baby and she sent Arthur's father to fetch the doctor, and the doctor's old car would come lurching its way down their driveway, windshield wipers battling against the snow.

"Babies are tougher than they look." That was what Dr. Christopherson said. He said it many times, patiently, attempting to reassure her. But she was not to be reassured. Each new phase of Jake's development brought a whole new host of dangers, so many of them that Arthur wondered how he himself had ever survived. Once Jake started crawling, life became more perilous still. "Did I fall down those stairs, ever?" Arthur asked his mother after she had scooped Jake up from the top of the stairs—he had been some yards away, but from his mother's face Arthur could see that it had been a near thing. But she had her face buried in Jake's neck and didn't hear his question.

But he, Arthur, had probably been a big tough baby. If he had fallen downstairs he'd probably have bounced. Whereas Jake would certainly be killed.

~

The day Jake took his first step, Arthur was formally recruited to the battle against the forces of fate. From now on, and Arthur knew this was a long-term assignment, his first and foremost job in life was to protect his little brother. In fact, he didn't need recruiting. He already knew that his mother's happiness depended on Jake's well-being. Adoring her and needing her as Arthur did, what choice did he have?

Here was another picture: himself and Jake, aged about nine and four, playing in the farmyard. Beside the barn there is a pile of empty boxes, lightweight slatted crates that their father uses for carrying lettuces and tomatoes and other row crops to the market in Struan. Arthur is building himself a castle of crates, an impressive, many-storeyed structure. Jake has dragged one crate away for his own purposes. Something—a sense of unease—causes Arthur to look up, towards the house. He can see the kitchen window from where he is, and he sees that his mother is standing at it, staring out at something. On her face is an expression of horror. Arthur's heart leaps in panic. He looks in the direction of her gaze and sees that Jake has pulled the crate over to the water trough and has climbed up on it in order to see what is inside. Arthur scrambles out of his castle and flies, shouting as he goes, "Get down! Jake! Get down!" Still feet away, he launches himself at his brother, knocking him off the box and sending him sprawling and howling in the dust.

The water in the trough was no more than nine inches deep. A mouse might have drowned in it—in fact, from time to time one did—but surely not a child. That was what Arthur's father said—or maybe didn't quite say, maybe just looked a little puzzled at the fuss—when he heard about the incident that evening. To Arthur, still glowing in the warmth of his mother's gratitude, it was an academic question, since he had acted not to save Jake's life but to rescue his mother from her fear. But in any case it turned out that his father was wrong to doubt the seriousness of the incident. A child could drown in an inch of water; Arthur's mother had read it in a magazine. An inch of water. It had happened.

His father didn't argue, though Arthur could see that he had some difficulty visualizing it. He frowned to himself and narrowed his eyes. An *inch* of water? He studied his boots. But he didn't argue. He bowed to his wife's superior knowledge. Fatal accidents to children fell within her area of expertise, even Arthur knew that. There were subjects his father knew about, such as the farm, and subjects his mother knew about, such as everything else. He knew that his father admired his mother for her intelligence. She read the *Temiskaming Speaker* from cover to cover, every week, and on the rare occasions when the *Toronto Daily Star* made it all the way up to Struan, she bought that too. She was the one who wrote letters if they needed writing, and paid all the bills. Arthur's father could read things provided they weren't too complicated, and he could add up all right, but when it came to writing, his fingers were clumsy and the letters and figures didn't come out as they were supposed to.

Arthur's mother was better at dealing with people, too. The previous spring, when a late frost killed off half the crops and Arthur's father had to go and see the bank manager, she went with him to do the talking. Arthur's father knew what was needed to put things right, how much money he wanted to borrow and how long it would take him to repay it, but he was afraid that in the enclosed space of the bank manager's office the words would refuse to come to him and he'd be left standing there, looking stupid. The Dunn men weren't big on words.

So he relied on his wife. He readily accepted that there were things which she knew that he did not, including how much water it took to drown a child.

~

Despite his mother's fears and Arthur's occasional guilt-ridden, mostly repressed wishes, Jake didn't drown or fall off the roof or get run over by a car, and he grew into a lovely, sunny child. Those were the words Arthur's mother used to describe him. Everyone loved him—she said that too. "It's because he's so cheerful," she said. "So interested in everything and everyone."

Arthur studied his own reflection in the square of mirror in the bathroom. His big plain face and mud-coloured hair. Sunny wasn't the word that sprang to mind. What would the right word be? Not cloudy . . . Overcast? Dull? That was it. Dull. He even felt dull.

As for being interested in everyone and everything—well, he wasn't. Most people and most things were boring, when you got right down to it. But he didn't believe Jake was all that interested either. He just looked as if he was. Even as a small child he had better control over his face than Arthur did: he could make it express anything he wanted, regardless of what was going on beneath the surface. He could make his face shine with interest and enthusiasm when Arthur knew for certain that inside he was wearing either a sneer or a yawn. He only bothered to do it with adults, of course; they were the ones worth impressing. He would greet any adult who crossed his path as if he or she were his favourite person on this earth. He'd say, "Hi, Mrs. Turner!" and his face would light up and glow with warmth as big old, fat old Mrs. Turner waddled up, and then five minutes later, when she'd pressed a nickel into his hand and gone beamingly on her way, he'd be imitating the waddle and trying to persuade you to do "knock-and-run" on her door.

Arthur, on the other hand, was forever being told he looked glum. He wasn't glum; it was just the way his features sat on his face. And when adults crossed his path he kept his head down, because he had no idea what to say.

"You'd better watch out, Arthur," the teacher said. "Your little brother's going to catch up with you."

It was Jake's first year at school. Arthur was in grade six. He had to set off for the two-mile walk to school fifteen minutes earlier than he used to because Jake couldn't walk as quickly and mustn't arrive at school all tired out from running to keep up. Arthur didn't see why they had to go together; there were no hazards to pass on the way to school that he was aware of, no raging rivers to cross, no mountains to climb. Bears ambled through the area from time to time, but no more often than they had when he was Jake's age, and no one had worried about him being eaten by a bear.

But it turned out there was something to worry about after all. In the past year or so, strangers had been wandering up the long road from the south. Hoboes, people called them. They were looking for work, his father said. It seemed that in the world outside there were no jobs anymore. From time to time one of the hoboes would knock at the kitchen door and ask if he could help out in the fields, or chop firewood, or anything else that needed doing, anything at all. Arthur's father felt sorry for them and would have been happy to employ one or two, but he couldn't pay them: money was something farmers—the ones around Struan anyway—had never had much of and nowadays they had even less. Arthur's mother felt sorry for the men too, and gave them food sometimes, but she was also afraid of them. Who knew what a desperate man might do?

So Arthur was obliged to become his little brother's bodyguard, escorting him to school and back, protecting him from . . . what, exactly? What did his mother think a hobo might do to Jake? Eat him? Arthur couldn't imagine, but he knew better than to argue.

Before the end of Jake's first week at school Arthur knew something else, which was that being at school with Jake was not going to be a picnic. All eight grades were taught together—eight rows of desks, grade oners along the wall nearest the door, grade eighters nearest the windows—so comparison of siblings was more or less inevitable, and that Jake would outshine him in every way was inevitable too.

Arthur had suspected for some time that it was his father he took after in the brains department. All his father knew about was farming, and that was all Arthur was ever going to know about too. He was a dunce at school. His mother had told him that book learning was important, so he tried, but none of it made any sense.

Miss Karpinski would ask him a question and he wouldn't have the first idea what she was talking about.

"Can you define an adjective for me, Arthur?" she would say, impatience already licking at the edges of her voice although he hadn't yet had time to fail to know the answer. She was much younger than Arthur's mother and wore dresses with round white collars and belts pulled so tight at the waist that it was surprising she didn't break in half. "Come on, now, we've just done it—haven't you been listening? An adjective is a part of speech that . . . ? What does it do?"

He had no idea.

Jake did, of course. He sat on the far side of the classroom with the youngest kids, smirking at Arthur's stupidity. He'd been born knowing what adjectives did.

So schoolwork was added to the list of things that Jake could do and Arthur could not. The list got added to at regular intervals. Jake could whistle, for instance, while Arthur's mouth was somehow the wrong shape. Jake could ride a bike. The length of time between Jake's first sitting his small neat behind on a bicycle seat and being able to spin off on it, unaided and in control, was about three minutes. Whereas something about bikes eluded Arthur. He knew only one other person who couldn't ride a bike, and that was his father, who had never tried because he said he couldn't see the point.

But Jake's best trick was the way he could make their mother glow. He would wrap his arms around her and hug her with all his might—Arthur wondered why his mother liked it so much, considering how fierce it was, but she loved it, you could tell. So one evening Arthur tried it. He went up to her while she was peeling the potatoes for supper and put his arms around her and squeezed–carefully, because he knew he was much stronger than Jake and didn't want to hurt her. She stopped what she was doing and looked down at him in puzzlement. She said, "What is it, Arthur?" Not unkindly, just perplexed.

He was embarrassed. He thought he must somehow have done it wrong. Squeezed too hard or not hard enough or not in the right place. Then he thought maybe he was just too old, that only little kids could do that sort of thing. But Jake didn't stop doing it as he got older; the hugs got less intense and less frequent but he still hugged her from time to time and it still had the same effect. It was as if he flicked a switch and a light came on inside her. She would glow for half an hour afterwards.

"Time Jake started helpin' out," Arthur's father said when Jake was seven years old.

They'd just finished supper. Arthur's father was sitting sideways in his chair at the table, mending a harness. He had a leather-needle, fearsomely sharp–he'd already stabbed himself with it twice, which was maybe what had given him the head of steam necessary to bring up the subject of Jake–and he was forcing it through the leather with the help of a pair of pliers.

Arthur's mother was washing the supper dishes. Arthur was at the far end of the table cleaning the shotgun, a job his father had entrusted to him on his twelfth birthday and of which he was hugely proud. His father had taught him to use the gun as well, and said he'd give him five cents for any rabbit or crow he shot, rabbits being good for the pot and a real nuisance around the row crops, and crows being just plain evil.

Jake had disappeared the minute his plate was empty, like he always did. They could hear him outside. He'd created so much fuss when Arthur was allowed to shoot the gun and he was not that his mother had bought him a bow and arrow set, a small one, from the Hudson's Bay. He'd painted a big round target on the side of the barn and every now and then there was a *thwack* as an arrow landed. Arthur knew that during the day, when their father was out in the fields and their mother was safely occupied elsewhere, Jake had a different sort of target. He would heap a couple of handfuls of dry grass and twigs around the bottom of a fence post, and half-fill an empty tin can with gasoline from the tank in the barn. Then he'd set the can on top of the fence post, light his heap of dry grass with a match, and attempt to shoot the can off the post. When he succeeded there would be a gratifying *whoosh* and flames would leap up the sides of the post. He was usually pretty quick to douse it with water, but even so a number of fence posts were getting badly charred and one of these days their father was going to notice.

Arthur worried about this. In the past couple of years his role as his brother's protector had widened to include protecting him from the consequences of his own actions. Their father was an even-tempered man and it took a lot to make him wrathful but Jake could provide a lot, and when their father really got going it was an awesome sight. Arthur had been thrashed by him only once, for leaving a stump fire unattended, and he'd taken care not to give him cause again. Jake had been whipped several times. He'd made the most of it, walking with a limp for days, but it had been their mother who really suffered, and so Arthur suffered too. Moreover, he suspected that their father did as well; he had no wish to hurt his wife and would have spared her if he could, and that made him madder at Jake than ever. So Arthur started going out after each of Jake's arson attacks and surreptitiously scraping away the charred wood from the base of the posts. Sometimes he had to sand them down to get rid of the black.

Now Arthur could hear the reluctance in his father's voice as he brought up the subject of Jake helping with the chores. He hated a confrontation with his wife more than he hated crows.

"Oh, I don't think he's big enough yet, Henry." Arthur's mother turned around from the sink. "You only have to look at him."

"I did look at him," Arthur's father said, reluctance dragging his voice down to a mumble. "He looks big enough to do chores. Feed the chickens. Take out the swill bucket. Things like that."

Jake chose that moment to bound in from the farmyard.

"You think you're pretty strong, Jake?" Arthur's father asked. "Or you still just a kid?"

"Sure, I'm strong," Jake said, grinning. "I can beat Arthur."

"Arthur lets you beat him," his father said, "so that don't prove nothin'. See if you can lift that chair." He nodded at a kitchen chair. Arthur's mother turned around to watch, anxious, her hands dripping suds.

Jake grabbed the chair by its back and heaved it off the ground. He swung it back and forth in tight arcs, grinning at the three of them.

"Bet you can't carry it to the door," his father said, and Jake lurched over to the door.

"That doesn't prove anything, Henry," their mother said.

"Sure does. If he can lift the chair he can lift the swill bucket."

"There's a world of difference between lifting something and carrying it all the way out to the barn."

"Not such a big difference as all that." Arthur's father put down the harness and wiped his hands on his shirt-front, then picked up the harness again and stared at it hard. Maybe he was going to have to stab himself with the needle again before he could carry on.

Arthur's mother pursed her lips. She looked at Jake and said, "You go on outside now, Jake. You too, Arthur."

Arthur carefully put the gun down on the table and followed Jake outside. They made a show of going around the corner of the house and then slid back and flattened themselves against the wall by the kitchen door.

"He's just a baby still," their mother was saying.

There was a pause, during which Arthur imagined he could hear his father thinking there was a good reason for that. He said, "Arthur was doin' plenty at that age."

"Arthur's suited to farmwork. Jake isn't. You can see that."

Arthur glanced sideways at Jake. Jake grinned at him. He had great confidence in his mother's ability to win arguments on his behalf.

Their mother said, her voice quiet but full of pride, "Don't you see that Jake is different? He's so clever—he's going to have choices, Henry. He will have something better than this."

Arthur could hear their father's baffled silence. What could be better than this?

Finally he said, "Still won't do him no harm to do his share. Do him good." He sighed, and Arthur imagined him wiping his hands on his shirt again. "He's goin' to grow up soft, Mary, if he don't do no work. He should do his share. Look at Arthur. Didn't do him no harm at all, doin' chores when he was Jake's age. He done them well, and I don't remember hearin' him complain."

Arthur felt the strange sensation of pride swelling in his chest. He had taken the work for granted, it was what people did—the people he knew, anyway. His friend Carl Luntz worked alongside his father and his two elder brothers just the same. Arthur had never questioned it. Certainly never expected to hear praise.

He felt Jake's eyes and turned his head to look at him. Jake's mouth was puckered tight with disgust. His eyes were dark, and Arthur had trouble reading their expression. It wasn't respect or admiration though, that was for sure.

Arthur's mother was wrong when she said that everybody loved Jake. There were exceptions.

"Charlie Taggert threw my schoolbook in the mud," Jake said. He and Arthur were walking home from school. It was September, the worst time of the year as far as Arthur was concerned—endless months of school ahead, cooped up in one stuffy schoolroom at a too-small desk, while outside the maples flamed red and gold and the air was as clear and pure as springwater. Inside was the leaden weight of boredom; outside was the sharp tang of wood smoke and the urgency of shortening days. You could smell the winter coming. You could see it in the transparency of the light and hear it in the harsh warning cries of the geese as they passed overhead. Most of all, you could feel it. During the day the sun was still hot, but as soon as it dipped down behind the trees the warmth dropped out of the air like a stone.

Like the boys on other farms, Arthur headed for the fields as soon as he got home from school in the afternoons in order to get a couple of hours of harvesting in before dark. It had been bone-dry right through June and July, and then just as they were coming up to the corn harvest there'd been a solid week of rain and they'd had to wait for the crop to dry out. Now it was dry and Arthur's father was out in the fields sunup to sundown. He came in at night covered in dust and sweat and tired almost past eating. Arthur would gladly have played hooky and worked beside him all day, but his mother forbade it and his father let on that he agreed with her.

Jake helped when he was told to. Then, and at no other time. And he worked so slowly and ineptly and with so much complaint that his father said it was hardly worth the bother, though he bothered anyway as a matter of principle. Jake might as well have been growing up in the town for all the interest he showed in the farm.

"Dad says do you want to come and help with a calving," Arthur said. His father had sent him to fetch Jake, thinking calving at least would interest him. Surely anyone would be interested in a new life beginning.

"Do what?" Jake was playing with a pack of cards he'd found somewhere. His hands moved swiftly, fanning the cards out and folding them together again. They made Arthur think of birds' wings.

"Come and help. Jessie's having her calf."

"Can't she do it herself?" Jake asked. "She must be able to or there wouldn't be any cows in the world, they'd all have died out like the dinosaurs."

It was a good thing it was Arthur that Jake said it to, and not their father. Arthur knew that Jake was just being logical, and meant the comment seriously, but their father would consider it a smart remark and Jake's smart remarks made him mad.

"Dont'cha want to come and watch, even?"

"Not right now." Jake slipped all the cards with faces into a certain order so fast you could hardly see his hands move. "I'm kind of busy. Later, maybe."

It was school he lived for. School and all the goings-on there, triumphs and disasters, friends and enemies. Especially enemies.

"Look at it!" Jake said as they walked home together. He pulled a book out of his schoolbag and brandished it at Arthur. It was covered in mud. Under the mud you could just make out a dark green cover and the title, in gold print. *English History.* Arthur remembered it, dimly. Kings and queens, dozens of them. Wars, dozens of those too, and all of them with dates, as if anyone cared. Miss Karpinski said the purpose of studying history was that if you didn't you were doomed to repeat it, but as far as Arthur could see the history books proved that you were doomed to repeat it anyway, so what was the point?

"Look at the state it's in!" Jake opened the book more or less in the middle. It looked as if someone had placed it facedown in a puddle and leapt up and down on it half a dozen times. "Miss Karpinski's going to kill me." He sounded really worried.

"No she won't," Arthur said. Miss Karpinski loved Jake. He was the last person in the school she would kill.

"She will! You know what she says about books!"

"What?"

"That they're sacred! That you're supposed to treat them with respect and stuff, because they're the keys that unlock doors."

Arthur couldn't remember Miss Karpinski saying those things, but it sounded like her all right. He must have been not concentrating at the time. A failure to concentrate was apparently one of his problems. He was fourteen now and still in grade eight—he should have gone up to the high school, on the other side of Struan, with Carl and the rest of his class a year ago, but he'd failed the exams. Jake, on the other hand, had skipped a year, so now he and Arthur were separated by only two rows of desks. Arthur found this state of affairs almost unendurable, and the worst of it was that it looked set to go on forever. His father would have been happy for him to leave school as soon as the law allowed, which was the day he turned sixteen, but his mother had been so upset by his last report card that she'd said he was going to get his grade twelve if it took him the rest of his life. The fact was, it was going to take him the rest of his life. To start with, to pass grade eight he would have to please Miss Karpinski, who was both judge and jury when it came to the exams. He couldn't imagine ever pleasing Miss Karpinski.

Jake was still waving the book at him. "What am I going to say to Miss Karpinski?" he asked. His voice was shrill with what appeared to be real anxiety, though with Jake you could never be sure.

"Just tell her it was an accident."

"But Charlie Taggert says he's going to do it again! He says he's going to do it to every single one of my books unless I give him my milk money."

Arthur looked at him uneasily. Jake was a liar—you couldn't believe a word he said—but if by some unlikely chance he was telling the truth this time, and if he did get into trouble, and if Arthur were discovered to have known about it but not helped, his mother would never forgive him.

"What do you want me to do about it?" he said reluctantly.

"Beat him up," Jake said promptly. "He's a bully."

Arthur's brow furrowed. Charlie Taggert was smart and had glasses and Arthur didn't like him, but he didn't look like a bully. On the other hand, Jake didn't look like a bully either but he was. Jake was a subtle bully, a devious bully. He specialized in getting people into trouble. Maybe he simply wanted to get Charlie into trouble. Or maybe Charlie wanted to get Jake into trouble. Or maybe Charlie did want Jake's milk money. Or maybe Jake had done something to Charlie and Charlie threw the book into the mud to get even, and it had nothing to do with milk money. Where Jake was concerned, Arthur always felt he was in over his head, floundering in a sea of unknown possibilities.

"I can't just go beat him up," Arthur said. Charlie was a little kid, and in any case, Arthur wasn't the beating-up sort. He was peaceable, given the choice. Even among his own friends he didn't go in for the rough-and-tumble most of them engaged in.

"You *have* to," Jake said. "It's the only thing that will stop him."

"You can beat him up yourself," Arthur said.

Jake gave him an exasperated look. "He's bigger than I am." The truth was, they were about the same size, but Jake never fought physically. Not that he was peaceable, but fighting was the one thing he wasn't good at. Not with his bare hands, anyway. This was the year of Jake's obsession with knives, but Miss Karpinski didn't allow knives at school, which was a good thing in Arthur's view. His foot still hurt him sometimes, where Jake had thrown the hunting knife into it, and the incident had involved him in all kinds of trouble because he'd had to make out that he'd done it himself—they'd both have been skinned alive if their father had discovered the truth. Arthur had to pretend that he'd accidentally put the prong of a pitchfork through his foot while he was mucking out the barn, a lie that had required him to ruin a perfectly good boot, because no one would be fool enough to use a pitchfork with bare feet.

"Why don't you just tell Miss Karpinski?" he asked.

Jake looked shocked. "You mean *tell* on him? You want me to *tell* on him?"

It was impossible, of course. Jake was right about that. To tell on someone was the one unforgivable sin.

Arthur thought about it. "I'll warn him," he said.

"You can't just warn him! He won't pay any attention to a stupid warning!"

"I'll warn him that if he doesn't pay attention to the warning I'll beat him up."

Jake kept at him the rest of the way home but Arthur didn't budge. He had to keep out of trouble this year or Miss Karpinski would keep him in grade eight until he had a long grey beard.

He approached Charlie Taggert in the schoolyard the next day—went up to the group of boys he was with and stood right in front of him so he had to stop talking to the others and pay attention. Charlie looked up at him, his eyes large spooky ovals behind his thick glasses.

"What?" he said.

"Leave my brother alone," Arthur said.

"What?" Charlie said again, looking puzzled.

"You heard me," Arthur said. The words sounded pretty good. For a minute he considered a new image of himself—a champion of rights. "I'm warning you," he said ominously.

"I haven't done anything," Charlie said. He looked apprehensive but stubborn.

"You threw my brother's book in the mud," Arthur said. "If you do it again I'll beat you up."

"I never touched your brother's book."

"You did so," Arthur said.

"I never touched anybody's stupid book."

Arthur felt a shadow of doubt pass over him, like a crow flying in front of the sun. He looked around for Jake, but Jake had vanished. He looked back at Charlie.

"You did so," he said again, louder, trying to keep the doubt out of his voice. Other kids were standing around watching. "You said if he didn't give you his milk money you'd do it to all his books."

Charlie said, "I didn't. I don't want your brother's stupid milk money. My dad runs the bank—I don't need your brother's stupid money. Your brother bet me his stupid money I couldn't tell how he did that stupid trick with those two cards, and I did, and I didn't even take his money because I don't need it and my mum says you farm kids are poor. I'm going to tell my dad you threatened me."

"I didn't threaten you," Arthur said. "I only said if you did it again I'd threaten you."

"I'm going to tell my dad," Charlie said. And he did. And Mr. Taggert, who happened to be chairman of the school board that year, phoned Miss Karpinski, who sent a letter to Arthur's mother requesting that she come and see her, and Arthur's mother had to go and apologize for Arthur and was ashamed and humiliated to the soles of her shoes.

There had been many times in the past when Arthur had wanted to give Jake a bloody nose, but never more than this time. He fantasized about it for days—saw his fist make contact, the lovely rich blood running down—but whenever and however he pictured it, his mother's face slid into the frame as well: the horror in her eyes, her bitter disappointment in him. So he didn't do it.

The fact was, giving Jake a bloody nose wouldn't have answered the question that Arthur wanted answered. What had Jake been trying to achieve? A suspicion came to him after the event—a possibility that he hadn't considered at the time—and it bothered him, and he would have liked to be able to dismiss it. The suspicion was this: that Jake had no real quarrel with Charlie Taggert, beyond a casual dislike and a resentment at having his card trick undermined, and that he'd never intended Arthur to beat Charlie up, and knowing Arthur so well had never really thought he would. Because Charlie had never been Jake's target. It was Arthur he'd wanted to get into trouble all along.

Was that possible? Could he have made up the whole business with the history book, muddied it himself, maybe, or dropped it accidentally and then decided to put the accident to use?

Arthur worried at the idea, chewed at it. Finally, and with relief, rejected it. Because there was no sense in it. Jake had no reason to do such a thing, and even Jake wouldn't get his own brother into so much trouble for no reason at all.

THREE

~

Rains Douse Bushfires
No. 11 Highway Washed Out
—*Temiskaming Speaker*, May 1957

If he had thought about it properly, Ian would have realized that working on the Dunns' farm was not going to bring him all that close to Laura Dunn. Close to Arthur, yes, but that wasn't what he'd had in mind.

Saturday morning at eight o'clock, as he leaned his bike against the side of the barn, Laura came out and said, "He's down at the ten-acre, Ian. He said to go straight down." She pointed at the hedge running alongside the track. "Third field along on the left. It's down a bit of a hill—that's why you can't see him from here. I think he said you're doing the potatoes today."

"Okay," Ian said.

"We have dinner at noon. I'll see you then."

"Okay."

And that was that. She went back inside. Contact time just less than a minute. Still, it was a minute more than he would have had otherwise. And he would see her at noon.

It was a great morning: a pale blue sky, feathers of cloud off in the distance. A light breeze, still cool—it was only May after all—but bearing the smell of summer to mingle with the smell of fresh manure. Manure was a bit of a problem underfoot—it seemed both horses and cows used the track. He was wearing his oldest shoes but boots would have been better. In between watching his step he looked at the fields. First on the left: pigs, rooting about under a clutch of very old apple trees; first on the right: plowed, the dark soil freshly turned. Second on the left: plowed; second on the right: pasture, and about thirty cows, heads down, munching. They were getting a mixture of young and old grass—you could make out small bright green shoots poking up through the dry yellow of last year. From what he could see, the more distant fields were either plowed or turned over to grass. Some of them were fenced with old zigzagged railings, others were edged with rocks and tree stumps, some fairly new, some so old that they had all but rotted away. Beyond the fields the trees stood dense and dark, their tops tinged with the pale, indistinct green of new growth.

When he reached the boundary of the third field, Ian could see Arthur and the horses, as Laura had said. The horses were standing idle at one side of the field, unhitched from their wagon, heads together as if they were plotting something behind Arthur's back. Arthur himself was out in the middle of the field, walking backwards down a furrow. He was holding a bucket and kept picking stones out of it and dropping them into the furrow. Ian slowed down, mystified, wondering if maybe Arthur was soft in the head and no one had thought to tell him. Then he got it. Not stones, potatoes. Seed potatoes.

Arthur abruptly left the furrow and trudged to the side of the field. There was a large sack standing there, and now that Ian looked he could see that there were more sacks positioned around the field and more still on the wagon. Arthur bent and began to fill his bucket from the sack. When he straightened up he saw Ian and put the bucket down and made his way up side of the field to greet him.

"Mornin'," he said.

Ian gave him what he hoped was an enthusiastic grin. "Morning."

"Potatoes today," Arthur said.

"Great!"

Arthur was wearing muddy overalls and heavy work boots clogged with mud, and what with his solid shape and mud-coloured hair Ian thought he looked pretty much like a giant potato himself. He knew women were supposed to be attracted to powerful-looking men and Arthur definitely filled the bill on that score, but still, it was hard to imagine what Laura had ever seen in him.

"Got you a bucket," Arthur said, and plodded back to the sack of potatoes, behind which, Ian saw, there was a second bucket.

"Fill it up," Arthur said. "Drop 'em in. 'Bout a foot apart. Like this, see." He took a potato out of his bucket, dropped it into a furrow, took a step back, dropped another one, and looked hopefully at Ian. Ian nodded, glad that none of his friends could see him. He imagined Pete saying, very, very slowly, You take the potato out of the bucket, man. And then you drop it into the furrow. Then you take a step backwards. Then you take another potato out of the bucket. . . .

"You finish this row," Arthur said. He took his own bucket and headed off to the start of the next row.

They planted seed potatoes for four hours. There was more to it than Ian had expected. In particular, more pain: pain from the stress of walking backwards without collapsing the furrows as you went; pain from the weight of the bucket; pain from the curious posture required, head down, shoulders hunched. Well before the first hour was up his muscles—all of them, in every part of his body—reminded him of the diagrams of human musculature in his father's textbooks: the muscles were drawn in red ink and looked raw and stretched to breaking point.

He kept himself going with thoughts of Laura. He thought about dinnertime. Arthur would be there, which was a pity, but maybe after dinner he would go off for a nap, and the two of them would be left alone. He imagined them sitting in the shade of an old apple tree, one without pigs around it, talking about this and that, enjoying the peace and each other's company while Arthur snored in a room upstairs.

At twelve o'clock Arthur finally set down his bucket and trudged across the furrows to announce that it was time to go in. Ian followed him gratefully back to the house. They washed at the pump, the icy water numbing their hands and arms, two rangy dogs sniffing around Ian's ankles, the chickens clacking and strutting about. There was a towel hanging outside the back door. Arthur dried his hands on it and passed it to Ian, smiling shyly, looking as if he wanted to say something but couldn't think quite what it might be, and while he was thinking about it Laura went past the screen door carrying a stew pot. She saw them and paused.

"Oh, good," she said. "You're here. Come in and sit down. Ian, I've set a place for you beside Arthur." She gave them a rather harried smile and disappeared.

Ian followed Arthur inside. The kitchen was like the kitchens of other farmhouses he'd been in, large and square, serving the function of living room as well. The cooking area was at one end of the room and at the other was a wood-burning stove with a couple of armchairs crouched around it. The centre of the room was taken up with a long wooden table. It was set for seven and four of the places were already occupied.

All morning he had been imagining that dinner would be a quiet, intimate affair—just Laura, Arthur, and himself, with Arthur not really counting. He'd entirely forgotten about the kids. There they were, all three of them—the boy who'd nearly knocked him off the steps, the small girl, and the baby in its high chair. There was also a very old man, propped up on cushions and so bent over that his chin nearly rested on the table.

Laura was ladling stew into the girl's bowl and the girl was complaining about it.

"Well just leave them," Laura was saying. "Just pick them out and put them on one side."

She smiled at Ian. "You're there, Ian." She pointed with her elbow, both hands being occupied with the stew pot. "Arthur's at the head of the table and you're between him and Carter. Oh, I haven't introduced you: Carter, Julie, March"—she indicated the children in descending order of age—"and this is my father—you may remember him, he was minister at the church for years. No, maybe you're too young. Grampa"—she leaned towards the old man and spoke loudly—"this is Dr. Christopherson's son, Ian. He's come to help Arthur."

"Hello," Ian said uncertainly. Laura hadn't told him her father's name, but maybe it didn't matter because the old man gave no sign that he'd heard a word she'd said.

"But, Mummy," the little girl said, her voice reduced to a whisper by Ian's presence. "They're all mixed up."

"You can pick them out," Laura said. "Look. Like this . . ."

Ian followed Arthur down to the end of the table, trying to quell his disappointment. He sat down beside the boy, Carter, who was tapping the table with his knife, a complex rhythm of dots and dashes like Morse code, and didn't acknowledge Ian's presence by so much as a glance. He looked like Arthur, Ian thought, but not as nice.

"Ian," Laura said. Suddenly she was standing so close to him that the sleeve of her dress nearly touched his arm. "You'll be hungry, would be my guess. How did it go this morning?" She began ladling stew onto his plate, not waiting for an answer. "Say when."

"When," Ian said politely. "Thanks, Mrs. Dunn. It looks wonderful." It was worth all the agony of the morning to be this close to her.

She gave him her lovely smile. "Laura. You don't need to call us Mr. and Mrs., does he, Arthur?" She had an apron on over her dress, which was pale blue with tiny white flowers on it. It had a V-neck, which was always a good thing because of where the V led to, but he couldn't see how low it went because it disappeared under the apron.

She moved on swiftly, doling out everybody's stew. Finally she went to her own place at the other end of the table. Miles away from Ian.

The baby was waving its arms about and making threatening noises. "Shush," she said to it. "Are you going to eat nicely with us? Would you like a piece of carrot?" She fished a bit of carrot out of the stew pot with her fingers and put it on the baby's tray. The baby threw it on the floor.

"I still haven't heard how it went this morning, Ian," Laura said, retrieving the carrot and putting it back on the baby's tray. The baby picked it up and threw it on the floor again and Laura sighed and left it there. She smoothed down the skirt of her dress as if in preparation for sitting down; Ian saw the swell of her hips and looked away. "How was it? Did you find the work terribly hard? It won't be the sort of thing you're used to. Oh, Grampa, hang on—that's a big piece. I'll just cut that up for you." She was off again, moving quickly around to her father's place to cut up his food. The old man watched her hands, mumbling to himself.

"Um," Ian said. "No, it was fine. Very interesting."

"Oh good." She went back to her place and finally sat down. A strand of hair had escaped from the ribbon at the nape of her neck and she pushed it off her face with the back of her hand. If only she would stay seated now. He wanted to savour her presence, but it was difficult to savour something that was continually flying about.

"Will you get as far as plowing them in this afternoon, Arthur?" she said. "Because what Ian's really interested in is the horses."

Carter said, "Isn't there any milk?"

He was at least eleven years old; you'd have thought he could walk to the refrigerator and get himself some milk, but Laura said, "Oh dear, of course there is."

Up again, over to the refrigerator, back with the milk, moving around the table, pouring it for everyone instead of letting them do it themselves.

"Really, I'm interested in everything," Ian said. "Not just the horses. You know, whatever needs doing is fine by me."

"You forgot the bread, too," Carter said.

Ian was sitting beside him, quite close. Close enough that he could easily reach over and thump him without even fully extending his arm. Or just slide a foot around the leg of the chair and flip it out from under him. But Arthur was the one who should be sorting him out. If Laura was too kind and too soft-hearted to discipline her kids—and in Ian's view that was the problem—it was up to their father. But Arthur was busy eating. He ate like he did everything else; slowly, methodically, head down. When he did look up, Ian noticed, it was his wife his eyes rested on, not his children.

Laura said, "What's the matter with me today?" Up again. Down again with the bread.

The baby screwed up its face, waved its arms about, and yelled. The little girl said, "But Mummy, I can still *taste* it."

Carter belched, and grinned sideways up at Ian.

None of them deserved her.

~

There was someone in with his father when he got home, and Becky Standish was in the waiting room. In theory his father dealt only with emergencies on the weekends, but the people of Struan had never paid too much attention to that, and there were always a couple of them who "took advantage," as his mother called it.

"Hi," Ian said to Becky. They were in the same class at school and she was nice enough, though a bit dim.

"Hi," she said, but she blushed and looked away, which meant she had a gynecological problem and was afraid he might ask her what was wrong. So he said, "See you later," and went down the hall to the kitchen. He'd left his mud-caked shoes outside on the porch but his socks were leaving impressive footprints on their own—his mother was going to have a fit when she saw them. He'd say, "Well, I've been working, Mum. Dirt goes with the job."

She was peeling carrots when he came in. Mrs. Tuttle didn't come on the weekends.

"I'm back," Ian said cheerfully. He hurt everywhere and he hadn't had a single moment with Laura to himself, but he felt unaccountably good.

"Fine," his mother said. She didn't turn around. "We'll eat as soon as your father's finished. Is there anyone in the waiting room?"

"Just one." He was trying to assess her mood from the sound of her voice. It sounded different, somehow. Neither angry nor absent, but something else that he couldn't identify.

"Fine," she said again.

"Do I have time for a bath?"

"If you're quick."

He waited for her to ask him how his first day at work had gone, but she just kept scraping carrots. After a minute he said pointedly, "How was your day?"

"Fine." For a moment she paused, her hands in the sink, and he thought she was going to turn around. But she didn't, so he left and went upstairs.

He had a bath, let all the water run out, and had another one, which dealt with the worst of the grime. Given all the aches and pains, it was hard to say quite why he felt so elated. It wasn't as if he had found his true calling as a farmhand. In fact he'd been embarrassed when, as he was leaving, Arthur had said, "Oh . . . uh . . . just a minute," then dug around in the pockets of his overalls and pulled out a handful of coins. Ian didn't think he'd earned them and had wondered if he should say so, but then Arthur said, "See ya next Saturday?" with his vague, uncertain smile, and Ian had felt a rush of pride and gratitude. Arthur couldn't consider him too useless or he wouldn't have asked him to come back. He'd done his first day's work—his first *real* work ever—and the quarters lying in the pocket of his mud-encrusted jeans were the proof of it. And he would do better next Saturday. He'd be a good worker. He imagined Laura saying to Arthur, "How did he do, Arthur?" And Arthur would think about it and then say, "All right. He's a good worker." You could take pride in that, no matter what the job.

He wrapped a towel around his waist and went back to his room. It was tidy, everything in its place, the bed neatly made. His mother had always insisted on order. He'd tried rebelling once or twice, but it wasn't worth it. He wondered what Laura's kids would have been like if his mother had been their mother. Well, not their mother, because then they wouldn't be the same kids, but if by some fluke she'd been responsible for their upbringing. They'd be unrecognizable. Even the baby would be sitting up straight and eating with a knife and fork, a crisp clean napkin tucked under its chins.

He heard the clack of his mother's shoes as she walked down the hall to the waiting room. The sound disappeared for a moment and then she came back and called him from the foot of the stairs.

"Supper, Ian."

"Okay."

He went downstairs stiffly, his muscles protesting. His father was in the dining room already, standing by his chair.

"Hi," Ian said. He put the quarters Arthur had given him on the table beside his father's place. "My first wages," he said proudly.

His father looked at him. It seemed for a moment as if he didn't recognize him. Then he smiled faintly and said, "Very good."

Ian was disconcerted. He studied his father more closely. He looked strange.

"Are you okay?" Ian said.

"Yes," his father said. "Of course."

His mother came in and set a covered serving dish on the table. The vegetable dishes were already there. "We should sit down," she said. She seemed strange as well. Her eyes were red and he noticed that her hands were trembling.

They sat down. Ian looked from one to the other. His mother began serving the meal. The scrape of the spoon on the side of the dish seemed to echo back from the walls.

"Is something wrong?" Ian said.

"Is this enough meat?" his mother said.

"Mum? Is something wrong?"

She put down his plate. She studied it for a moment and then looked down the table at his father. "I have something to tell you," she said finally. "Your father and I have something to tell you."

Afterwards, Ian excused himself from the table, leaving his meal untouched—none of them had eaten anything—and went outside. At first he just stood on the porch, not knowing what to do or where to go. It was getting dark. Bats were flicking back and forth above the houses across the street. One of the Beckett kids from next door raced past on his bike, his crouched-over body a grey blur in the dusk. Ian stepped off the porch and started walking. He gave no thought to the direction. He wanted to walk, and not to think. He walked fast, head down.

His mother had done most of the talking. She'd started off by saying that she was leaving. He hadn't understood at first—leaving what?—and when he'd finally understood, he hadn't believed her. He'd thought she must be upset about something he or his father had done and was saying it to punish them. He'd looked to his father for help, and it was his father's face that told him she was serious.

She said that she and his father no longer loved each other, hadn't loved each other for years. His father tried to protest at this but she stopped him. Actions speak louder than words, she said. She had loved him once, and the proof of it was that she had given up eighteen years of her life for him. She'd given up everything to come with him to this—she searched for the right words—this godforsaken place. This wasteland. She had done all the giving.

After the first couple of sentences Ian had gone temporarily deaf; his mother carried on speaking and he'd been able to hear the sound of her voice, but the words meant nothing. Then his father broke in. It seemed to Ian that his father had aged twenty years since they'd sat down. His face seemed to have caved in. He said, "Beth, for the love of God." To Ian he said, "I'm sorry. We're both very sorry. Your mother is upset; she needs a little time away, that's all."

His mother said—now he could hear her again—"Your father is still trying to pretend."

By now two clear lines of tears were running down her cheeks. Ian was so stiff with shock he could scarcely draw a breath.

His father said, "Beth, please. Please." He looked at Ian and said, "Don't be too upset. We hope very much that this will sort itself out."

"It has sorted itself out," Ian's mother said, the shaking of her voice breaking the words into ragged syllables. "This is how it has sorted itself out."

Ian couldn't look at either of them; his eyes were focused on the fine weave of the tablecloth in front of him. He hadn't even known they were unhappy. Or at least, with hindsight he could see that his mother was unhappy, but he'd thought that was just how she was, her natural state. He had taken it for granted that they loved each other; he'd assumed it the same way that he'd assumed they loved him. Now, suddenly, it came to him that that must be in doubt as well. Surely his mother wouldn't do this if she loved him.

They'd been saying something and again he hadn't heard it. His mother's voice had risen almost to a shout. There was a short silence, and then his father said, "Excuse me," and got up and left the room.

Ian's mother stayed where she was, the tears shining on her cheeks. She was staring at the serving dish. After a minute she took a deep breath and said, "That is typical. His leaving the room at a time like this is typical. But I am glad, because I have other things to say to you. He knows about them—your father knows about them—but I wanted to tell you privately, by ourselves."

She went on to say them, these other things. She said she hadn't fully realized how little she'd had in life until she fell in love with a man who was in love with her. Genuinely in love. A man who was prepared to give things up for her. She said she and Robert Patterson were in love and were going to get married as soon as their respective divorces came through. In the meantime, they were leaving Struan as soon as possible. Robert had already identified a teaching job in Toronto.

Here she looked up; Ian didn't look at her but he could feel her gaze. She said, "I want you to come with us, of course. Robert will be happy to have you; he thinks you're a very fine boy. His children will stay with their mother, but we hope you will come with us. Will you? Will you come with us to Toronto?"

Robert Patterson taught geography at the high school. Ian was in his class. He was a newcomer to Struan, having come from somewhere down south three or four years ago. He had a wife and two young children. He was tall and thin and had wire-rimmed glasses and a sarcastic manner. There was no way *anyone* could love him.

Ian's mother said, "I am sorry to give you so little time, but we wanted to have everything settled, Robert and I, before telling you. I know it will be hard for you at first, leaving your friends and so on. But we'll be able to give you so much more. You know what Toronto is like."

His incredulity and confusion were so great he was unable to think. He struggled to find some order within himself, some coherent thought. After a few minutes, during which his mother waited silently, it came to him that there was one question he needed the answer to straight away. Maybe there were other questions, but they were unimportant compared to this one. He tried to assemble it in his mind, to think how to phrase it, but when at last he managed to gather together the words and tried to voice them, he found he couldn't speak. His jaws felt wired together with tension. Finally he managed. He said, aiming the words at the table-cloth because he could not look at her, "If I won't go, will you go anyway?"

There was more silence, during which he tried to breathe normally. When she finally spoke, what she said was, "Ian, I want you to come with me. With us."

Which was not the answer to his question, so he asked it again. He weighed out the words to make sure that she would understand, and that he himself would understand, their full meaning, now and forever.

"If I won't go with you, will you go anyway? Will you go without me?"

This time, struggling with the shaking of her voice, she said, "Darling, you do not know what it has been like, all these years."

By which he understood, finally, that he was not important to her. Not that important.

Afterwards he was impressed by his response—how calm it sounded. How polite. He said, "I'll stay here with Dad, if that's all right. But thank you for asking me."

And then he excused himself and left the room.

~

The dogs barked when they first got his scent, but then they remembered him from earlier in the day and came to greet him, wagging their tails. He stepped off the driveway when the dogs came up, into the shadow of the trees. He didn't know why he was here. The last thing he wanted was for Laura to see him and come out and start talking to him. The thought of her knowing what had happened filled him with shame almost beyond endurance. What would she think—what would anyone think—of a boy who meant so little to his own mother that she would walk off and leave him? In all his life he had never heard of such a thing. He'd heard of men abandoning their families, but never a woman. Never a mother.

He stood uncertain in the shadows for a few moments and then cautiously moved towards the house. He went around to the back, where the kitchen was. He wanted to see her, that was all. He just needed to know she was still there.

The farmhouse seemed bigger in the darkness than it had during the day. The house and the barn and sheds were solid blocks of night against the blue-black of the sky. The kitchen light was on and there were lights in two of the bedrooms upstairs. Laura was in one of the bedrooms; he saw her moving back and forth, folding things, hanging things in the cupboard in the corner of the room. He could tell she was talking to someone, though he couldn't hear her voice or see anyone else. Probably the little girl. Julie. She must be putting Julie to bed. The boy, Carter, was in the other lighted bedroom—Ian had seen him cross the room. The baby must be asleep somewhere else.

Arthur and the old man were downstairs in the kitchen, Arthur at the table, the old man huddled in a chair by the stove. Arthur was working on something, but Ian wasn't close enough to see what it was. He could have moved closer, but then he wouldn't have been able to see into the upstairs rooms. Anyway, he didn't care what Arthur was doing. It was only Laura he wanted to see. The dogs, who had followed him around to the back of the house, waited curiously beside him for a while and then wandered off. From within the barn he could hear the heavy, quiet movements of the horses.

After some time—he didn't know whether long or short—the light in Julie's bedroom went off. He felt a sudden clench of anxiety, as if a life raft had slipped out from under him, but a minute later Laura appeared in the kitchen, carrying the baby. He could see her better than when she was upstairs: the line of sight was more direct.

She was still wearing the pale blue dress she had worn earlier and her hair was still tied back, but it was looser, as if she allowed it its own way at the end of the day. She said something to Arthur and he looked up at her and nodded, and then returned to his work. Laura went over to one of the big armchairs by the fire, lowered herself and the baby into it, and then, quietly, discreetly, undid her dress and put the baby to her breast.

Ian watched. It was more erotic, and at the same time more painful, than anything he had ever known.

The day his mother left, he would not look at her. She left after breakfast, but he skipped breakfast. He stayed in his room. It was Sunday, but no one had suggested church. She came up to his room. He heard her footsteps, heard her stop at the closed door. He imagined her, facing the door.

After a minute she knocked. He waited a bit, and then said, "Yes?" in a tone completely devoid of interest.

"May I come in?"

"If you want."

He heard the door open, heard her cross the room. He was at his desk, with his books spread out as if he were studying. He didn't turn around. She came to a stop behind him. He began to copy a section out of a book.

She said, "Ian?"

He waited a minute, as if he'd been concentrating and it had taken time for her interruption to filter through to him. "Yes?"

"Aren't you going to come down and say goodbye?" Her voice was shaking.

"I have work to do."

She was crying. He couldn't see her and she made no sound, but he knew. He didn't care. He imagined what tomorrow was going to bring, and the next day, and the next, as the people of Struan heard the news.

She said, struggling to control her voice, "Darling, how can I go if you won't say goodbye?"

"Goodbye," he said.

FOUR

~

Wheat Crop Is Biggest Since 1932
The Average Production of a Cow
—*Temiskaming Speaker*, September 1938

All the way through high school Arthur didn't have a girlfriend. There were plenty of girls in his class at school and
he liked the look of many of them, but he didn't know
how to approach them. What were you supposed to say?
Hello, my name's Arthur? They already knew his name!
He should have approached them back in grade nine,
when some of them—the ones from the small communities out in the sticks—were still strangers. But back in grade
nine he hadn't been interested.

Sometime during his first year in grade ten that had
changed almost overnight. One minute girls were irrelevant,

and the next, he couldn't stop looking at them. He and his friends would hang about during recess and lunch hour, watching the girls walk by in little gabbling groups. That was one of the problems—females didn't come individually, they came in packs. You'd have to walk up to a whole pack, which was out of the question.

By the time he was sixteen (legally old enough to leave school, but of course his mother wouldn't let him) most of the boys he knew had worked it out and were at least able to talk to girls, if nothing more. Some of the more advanced, more confident ones even professed to be fed up with "wimen" already. "They ain't worth the trouble, Art. Take it from me, they just ain't worth the trouble."

Arthur would have liked the chance to find that out for himself, but there was no way. His friend Carl urged him on. "Go on, Art, what you waitin' for? Just go up and ask her." But it was no use. He didn't know how.

Jake, on the other hand, was born knowing. As with schoolwork, Jake had no trouble with girls at all.

When Arthur was seventeen and just entering grade eleven (having taken two years over grade ten), Jake started high school. He was twelve. Five years behind Arthur in age, two years behind him in school, ahead of him already in the matter of girls. Arthur would see him chatting to them in the schoolyard, easily, casually, as if they were friends instead of a different species. In fact, Jake had more friends who were female than male. Other boys were a bit suspicious, maybe even a little afraid of him. He had the ability to get people into trouble—anyone who had been through primary school with him knew that.

Arthur had forgotten how bad it was having Jake in the same school. When he started high school he'd had two glorious years without him, and now, looking back, he saw that he hadn't appreciated those years enough. Jake took to high school as if it had been invented just for him—all those new subjects to excel in, all those new teachers to impress! He talked about the things he was learning at the supper table every night. "They don't teach you arithmetic anymore, they teach you *mathematics*, and there are *three different mathematics*. There's algebra, and geometry, and trigonometry. Geometry's all about lines and stuff. And trigonometry's about triangles and how to work out angles and stuff. And algebra's where you use letters instead of numbers. . . ."

Arthur was sure Jake's enthusiasm was fake, put on to impress their parents, but still it stuck in his throat and made it difficult for him to swallow his supper.

"See, in Latin, nouns have different forms and they have different endings—*loads* of different endings—and we have to learn them all. So I wondered if someone could test me after supper?"

Jake kept slipping sideways looks at their father as he said all this. Their mother would be hanging on every word, her face pink with pleasure, but it was their father's reaction he seemed interested in. But his father just chewed silently, pushing down the food.

"I want to quit school," Arthur said.

He and his father were examining the boarding on the north side of the barn. Some of the planks were starting to rot and would have to be replaced. And it needed to be done soon. Winter was coming and a drafty barn could result in a whole herd of cattle coming down with pneumonia.

His father straightened up and looked at him.

"It's a waste of time," Arthur said. "I want to quit."

His father dug around in his ear with a dirty finger. "Better speak to your mother," he said at last.

"I already did."

"Yeah?"

"Yeah."

It had taken him weeks to work up the courage to approach her, and even more weeks to work out which words were the right ones, the ones that would convince her. How could he explain to her the pointlessness of carrying on? The futile years he had spent sitting at a desk. The endless exams, and his failure to pass them, and the fact that he didn't care. In the end, all the reasons and all the words he could think of added up to just one sentence.

"It ain't teachin' me nothin' I need to know," he'd told her. He'd stood awkwardly in the kitchen, six foot two in his socks, two hundred and forty pounds, a man, not a boy, *aching* to do a man's work. If one of the plow horses had dropped in its tracks, Arthur could have slung the great leather collar around his own neck and finished the job himself, no trouble at all. At school he could hardly squeeze his body into the space between the desk and the seat. He wanted to say, Look at me, Mum! Look at me! I shouldn't be sittin' at those desks anymore. But he knew that argument would cut no ice.

His mother was chopping onions, wiping the tears away with the back of her wrist. Her mouth was a straight white line. She said, "Arthur, you don't know what you're going to need to know in the future."

Maybe she was right about that, but he was pretty sure he knew what he was not going to need to know, namely Latin, chemistry, physics, math, French, history, geography, and Charles Dickens. It was true that there was a machine shop at school that had some handy tools in it, but even there he hadn't learned anything that his father hadn't taught him already.

"If they could teach you how to predict the weather," he said, "that would be good. But they don't teach stuff like that. *Useful* stuff. *They don't teach useful stuff.*"

She looked at him uncertainly. "Don't they?" She'd only been as far as grade eight herself.

"No."

She hesitated for a moment and he held his breath. But then her mouth went tight again.

"They taught you to read and write," she said. "You didn't think that was useful at the time, but everyone needs to know how to read and write."

"Yeah, but I can!" Arthur said. "I know all that stuff! And adding and subtracting and multiplying and that other one—dividing. I don't need more than that, Mum. All the rest I need to know, Dad can teach me. And he needs me on the farm. He needs help. He's got too much work to do on his own."

He felt exhausted. He'd never strung so many sentences together in his life. Surely she must see that he was right.

But she pressed her lips together and shook her head. "Your father's managed just fine all these years; he can manage a few more." She sighed and turned to face him directly, holding the onion knife out to the side, and he knew that he had lost. "A man without an education is at a disadvantage, Arthur. Your father is at a disadvantage.

He's a good farmer, but he's at a disadvantage with edu-
cated people." She smiled at him. "You'll thank me one
day. I promise you. When you have your grade twelve,
you'll thank me."

His father, still waggling his finger in his ear, looked at
him helplessly. "What did she say?" he asked.

"She said I'd thank her one day." Arthur's voice was so
dragged down by misery it was hardly audible, even to him.

"Oh," his father said. "Yeah, well . . ." He took the nail
he'd been using to test for rot and pressed the point of it
into another plank of wood. It sank in ominously. "Gotta
get at this quick," he said. His voice was sad, apologetic.
He'd have liked to help, but he couldn't.

~

November. Arthur and Jake trudged to school each day in
the dark and trudged home again in the dark, and one
thing to be grateful for was, at least now that Jake was older
they didn't have to go together. Most days Jake went in
early to meet with his friends and Arthur went at the last
possible moment, sliding in the door just as the bell rang.
He and Jake were in separate classrooms—something else to
be grateful for—and they didn't see each other during the
day except at lunchtime. He sat at his too-small desk in an
ill-lit classroom and looked out the window at the grey,
snow-heavy sky, and endured. All his friends had left
school now, to take jobs at the sawmill or in the silver
mines or on their fathers' farms. He got to see them only
on Saturday nights. He and Carl Luntz, his best friend,
would walk into town together with Carl's older brothers

and meet up with Ted Hatchett and Jude Libovitz and the rest, and they'd go and hang about down by Ben's Bar. They weren't old enough to go inside, but the liquor generally found its way out, and every Saturday night without fail there would be a fight about something or other and someone would go home with a broken nose or a couple of black eyes. Arthur mostly didn't take part in the fighting. He could never get that worked up about things and the only person he'd ever wanted to hit was Jake. But he was happy enough just standing on the sidelines, watching.

Carl and his brothers were on the peaceful side too, but Ted Hatchett and Jude Libovitz were both enthusiastic fighters. Especially Ted. Ted loved fighting—any excuse would do. He also loved liquor, so one way or another Arthur and Carl generally ended up carting him home between them, each with one of Ted's arms across his shoulders, back to where he lived with his mother on Crow River Road. Ted worked in the silver mine. His father had been killed in an accident at the sawmill when Ted was small and his mother wouldn't let him near the place. She insisted that he work in the mine instead, which involved two hours' walk, morning and night. But Ted didn't seem to mind. He had no brothers or sisters, so he and his mother were on their own and Arthur got the impression they were pretty close.

"I'm an only child," Ted wailed mournfully one night as Arthur and Carl dragged him along through the darkness. "Half an orphan, and an owowownly child. So sad, so sad."

"Sad for your mum, all right," Carl muttered breathlessly. Ted was even bigger than Arthur, so he was quite a load. "If she could only have one she sure deserved better than you."

"That's unkind." Ted was exhaling alcohol fumes powerful enough to melt the snow under their feet. "Isn' he unkind, Art?"

"Dunno about that," Arthur said, grinning to himself in the darkness. "Could be right."

Ted's mother would greet them grimly at the door on each occasion, survey Ted's bloody nose or half-torn-off ear, and say, "Take him upstairs. I don't know why you bother with him. Just leave him in a ditch next time." Though she would thank them both on their way out.

If it was raining or snowing too hard to go into town, Arthur usually went over to the Luntzes' farm and sat on Carl's bed and watched him whittle antlers out of driftwood. Carl's parents, Otto and Gertie Luntz, had immigrated from Germany and still spoke with funny accents, but the boys had all been born in Canada. Their farm was bigger than the Dunns', big enough that it would support all three boys and their families in due course, and the farmhouse was bigger too, so each boy had a good-sized room of his own. Walking into Carl's room was like walking into a forest. He had antlers on his wall that any stag would have been proud to own. He'd pick up bits of driftwood on the beach and whittle them into prongs and then glue the prongs together at exactly the right angle and sand them down until you couldn't find a join if your life depended on it. His walls were covered with antlers—moose, caribou, white-tailed deer—and every now and then he'd stick a real set up there in the midst of them and ask Arthur or whoever happened to be passing his bedroom door to pick it out, and nobody ever could.

"But vy doss he do it, Artur?" Mr. Luntz would whisper—loudly—his brow furrowed in mock perplexity. "Dat is wot

I asks. Der is so many deers in dis country, der is so many, many antlers, so vy 'e makes more? You are a friend of him, so maybe you know?" Carl, without looking up from his whittling, would say mildly, "A friend of *his*, Dad, not a friend of *him*," and Mr. Luntz would wink at Arthur and Arthur would grin shyly back.

He loved Saturday nights. The rest of the week had nothing going for it whatsoever. The kids he sat beside at school—those who had stayed on after they were sixteen—were mostly nice enough, but he didn't belong with them. They were the brainy ones, most of them town-bred, like Steve Williams, whose father ran the Hudson's Bay store, or John Adams, whose father was the minister at the Presbyterian church. All of them were younger than Arthur. They would nod at him when he came in to take his seat; he was a fixture, like one of the desks. The teacher would start talking and Arthur's brain would shut down automatically—there wasn't a thing he could do about it. He would stare out the window at the road and at the fields behind it, and the at dark, silent trees behind the fields, and his brain would just sit there like a lump of cold pudding. Once, in the middle of a history lesson—it was Canadian history, which turned out, incredibly, considering how little of it there was, to be more boring than the history of any other country on earth—a timber wolf slid out of the shadows, head low, body crouched, yellow eyes fixed on the school. No one else noticed it. The teacher's voice droned on. Arthur watched the wolf. The silver-grey of its coat against the silver-grey of the birches behind it. The stillness, as if time itself had paused for a moment. The pale, watchful eyes. You could see how it belonged where it was, how it was meant to be in that landscape.

You could imagine that it and the shadowed trees behind
it were waiting for humans to move on, or die out, so that
they could reclaim the land. Watch out for the traplines,
Arthur thought, though his father wouldn't be pleased to
see it so close to the farms. As if it had heard him, the wolf
turned and melted back into the woods.

The moment the bell rang at the end of the day, Arthur
was off, stamping through the snow, back to the farm to
help his father with whatever needed doing. And lots
needed doing, even in winter—repairs they hadn't had
time for during the summer months, maintenance of the
buildings, care of the livestock. The cattle were all in the
barn now, the pigs in the shed tacked onto the side of
the barn, the horses in their stable. All of them needed to
be fed and watered and have the muck cleared out and
fresh bedding put down. They needed their feet inspected
and their ears looked into and the occasional pat on the
nose to encourage them through the long dark winter days.

Jake was meant to go straight home too, to do his share,
but it seemed there was always something that kept him
at school late. Arthur didn't care, but his father did.

"Where you bin?"

"At school." Jake's face shining with innocent enthusiasm. He was thirteen now, and sometime during the last
year his looks had turned the corner from being sweet to
being handsome: all planes and angles, and that wheat-
coloured hair.

"You come straight home after school. You got work
to do."

"But I can't, Dad! We're putting on a play—a *real* play, by
Shakespeare. It's called *Romeo and Juliet*, and I'm Romeo.
He's the hero. He commits suicide."

Arthur paused in his task of cleaning a sore on a cow's udder and considered the idea of Jake committing suicide. He turned it over in his mind a couple of times, resting his head against the cow's warm belly. Jake dead and gone. The idea had appeal all right.

"We're putting it on at Christmas, so we have to practise every night. It's really good and everybody in town is going to be invited, and we're going to make posters and send them to all the stores, and they'll put them in their windows so everyone will know."

"You come home straight after school. You got work to do."

"But Dad . . ."

"You come home straight after school."

And then in the evening, when supper was over and Jake was in his room doing his homework, and Arthur was in his room not doing his, Arthur would hear their mother's voice, arguing gently for Romeo.

"It's so nice that he enjoys school, Henry, and that he's doing so well. They must think he's very talented to ask him to be the hero. I think we should let him do it. I think it would be good for him."

There was silence for a minute. Then Arthur's father, sounding like a man who knew he was going to lose the argument but had to make his point just the same, said, "They should know better. They should know better than to make farm kids do things after school."

"It's only until Christmas, Henry. I think it would be wrong to stop him. After Christmas he will be able to do his fair share of the work again. You and Arthur could manage up till then, couldn't you?"

Arthur imagined his father's big heavy face. Imagined

him thinking that to say Jake would do his share of the work "again" implied that he had ever done it. But their mother had had a dose of flu a month ago from which she still hadn't fully recovered, and Arthur knew that his father was worried about her and wanted to cause her as little anxiety as he could. And never could resist her anyway.

~

Arthur didn't hate his brother, or not very often. Mostly he just didn't understand him. How did they get to be in the same family? What did Jake want? Because Arthur definitely got the feeling Jake wanted something; you could see it sometimes: there was a fretfulness, a frustration—something indefinable behind the eyes.

Christmas came and went. Romeo died for love and was a triumph, according to his mother. Arthur had to take her word for it. He and his father missed the performance—they were supposed to go but they were in town buying supplies at the hardware store and lost track of the time. Worse still, they had the truck, so Jake and his mother had to hurry the two miles to the school through the snow with Jake's fancy costume wrapped up in a paper bag. They arrived with only five minutes to spare and found Mrs. Castle, the English-teacher-turned-director, almost wringing her hands. When they got home, driven by Otto Luntz (it turned out the whole Luntz family had been there, as had practically every other soul in Struan), Jake went straight to his room without speaking.

"He so badly wanted you to come," Arthur's mother said to them, tight-lipped with disapproval. "It was so important to him, and he wanted you to see it. You most of all, Henry. You more than anybody."

"Since when is a damn-fool play so important?" Arthur's father said sharply, stung by guilt and his wife's reproach. Arthur couldn't remember her ever reproaching his father before. "Farming's important. Work's important. Time he knew what matters and what doesn't."

~

January and February passed, and were easier to get through than usual because the weather was so bad that the school was closed more often than it was open. At the beginning of March there was a blizzard that blew for ten straight days, and doing the most basic farm chores was so difficult and so unendurably cold that Arthur almost—though not quite—thought that being at school might be a nice rest. Snow piled up against the north side of the house and barns until it reached the roofs, which at least gave them some protection against the howling and demented wind. It buried the pig shed altogether, not once but again and again. Every morning they had to dig down to find it, as if the pigs were victims of an avalanche. It felt like an avalanche, felt as if the entire North Pole was sliding down to bury them.

They were prisoners in their own home and their jailers were the wind and the snow. A couple of times a day they shovelled out a trench from the house to the barn and stable, and another trench to the woodpile, and that was as far as anyone dared to go. Arthur's mother was anxious about Gertie Luntz, who had had her appendix out on her own kitchen table at the end of February, but it was too dangerous to snowshoe over to check that she was all right.

The blizzard would swallow you up within seconds. You could be walking in circles for hours and never know it.

They spent the days huddled around the kitchen stove, mending everything in sight, all except Jake, who spent most of his time in his bedroom, doing whatever it was that Jake did. It was freezing up there—Arthur put off going to bed as long as possible—but still that was where Jake chose to be. The company of his family bored him—that was plain as day. Even his mother seemed to bore him. And it was true that their conversation wasn't all that stimulating.

"Better get up on that roof." (This from their father after a groan from the roof timbers.) "Take a shovel. Too much weight on it."

"Okay." (From Arthur.)

That would be it for an hour.

"Would anyone like some tea?" (Their mother, cheerfully.)

"Sure."

Another hour.

Just once, Jake seemed to liven up a bit. It was right after supper—a whole evening of doing nothing lay ahead—and Jake suddenly said, "We should play cards! I'll go get my pack of cards, okay?"

"I got better things to do with my time than play cards," their father said.

"You do?" Jake said, looking around the room. They'd run out of things to mend days ago.

"Biggest damned time-waster ever invented," his father said sharply, suspecting impudence. Jake got up and went to his room.

~

Near the end of that week one of the horses took sick. They had four shire horses—huge animals, intelligent and willing, whose forebears had been shipped over from the old country by a farmer in New Liskeard twenty years previously and bred by him ever since. This one was a two-year-old gelding called Moses. They had had him nearly a year and he was working out well. But on this dark, snow-driven, sub-zero morning, when Arthur and his father battled their way out to the barns, they found him restlessly knocking about in his stall. He was off his feed, couldn't seem to stand still. There was a vet in New Liskeard but he might as well have been on the moon. The nearest phone was in Struan, and even if they got through to him all the roads were blocked. By the afternoon, the blizzard still screaming around the sides of the barn, the horse was worse. By evening he was frantic with pain, throwing himself at the sides of the stall, eyes rolling, froth flying from his mouth.

"Colic," Arthur's father said. Arthur wanted to ask, Is he going to die? but couldn't bring himself to say the words. There was nothing they could do to make things easier for him: he was so crazy with pain they couldn't even get into the stall to try to quiet him with their hands. One ton of horse, like a freight train out of control. They stood by his stall, stamping their frozen feet, wretchedly keeping him company, until finally, about eight o'clock, they couldn't stand it anymore, and Arthur's father went back to the house and got the rifle and shot him.

Jake was in the kitchen when they finally went in, curled up in a chair by the stove, reading a book. He looked up and raised his eyebrows at the sight of the rifle. "You guys hunting in this weather?" he said.

Their father paused. Stood in the middle of the room, head down, studying the floor. Then he went and hung the rifle on its rack over the door, and left the room.

"What did I say wrong now?" Jake asked. Suddenly he was furious, close to tears with rage. "What did I say wrong *now*?"

Arthur, his mind filled with the image of that great still body on the frozen floor, could think of nothing to say.

~

April. The wind turned around and blew from the south and like magic the snow sagged, collapsed on itself, and melted away. The air smelled of damp earth and things trying to grow, trying to force their way up out of the still-frozen ground.

"Those two there," Arthur's father said, nodding at two heifers over by the fence. "Told Otto I'd send 'em over this morning. Simplest thing is, you two take 'em over. Just walk 'em around."

Arthur nodded. It was Saturday, the best day of the week. Sunday would have been just as good if it weren't for the fact that it was followed by Monday.

Jake said, "When?"

"Now," their father said.

"Can't Art take them?" Jake said. "I have to go into town."

Their father was in the middle of harnessing the team. He turned slowly and looked at Jake. Arthur felt a prickle of apprehension, and also of annoyance. Sometimes he got the feeling that Jake was *trying* to provoke their father. Yesterday he had forgotten to feed the pigs. How could you forget to feed the pigs—something that had to be done every day, something that was *always* done? It was as if he wanted to see just how far he could push their father before he snapped. Arthur couldn't understand it; it was like deciding to stir up a nest of rattlesnakes or prod a hive of bees: maybe you didn't know the exact details of what would follow, but you did know that it wasn't going to be nice. So why do it? Why didn't Jake just shut up and do what he was told?

Their father looked at Jake in silence; Jake shrugged and turned away. Arthur relaxed. He went over to the cows and took their tethers and handed one to Jake. The two of them set off down the track between the fields, leading a cow apiece.

There was still snow lying in the furrows, streaking the fields black and white like giant lengths of corduroy. The road was muddy and slippery with patches of ice hidden under the slush, and the heifers were slow.

"I don't know why it takes two of us," Jake said when they were out of sight and earshot of the farm. "Can't you manage two cows by yourself?"

"No," said Arthur.

"Why not? You're so good with cows."

"'Cause of the bridge."

"What about it?"

"They don't like it. Scares 'em. Moves too much. We'll have to take 'em across one at a time."

"Okay, but once we get them across the bridge, will you take them on? 'Cause I've got to get into town. I'm meeting someone."

Arthur shrugged. "Okay."

"Great!" Jake said. "Don't tell Dad, all right?"

Arthur shrugged again. They slogged on, Jake trying to speed things up, eager to be gone, pulling the reluctant heifer behind him. She swung her head unhappily. "Come on, come on, come *on*!" Jake said.

"Slow down," Arthur said. He felt as if it was him Jake was yanking at.

"She can go faster than this when she wants to," Jake said.

"She doesn't want to."

"Maybe you've got all the time in the world," Jake said, "but I've got things to do."

"The bridge is just up there."

Farther into town there was a proper bridge across the river that separated the Dunns' and the Luntzes' farms but this one was a shortcut and saved more than a mile. It was roughly made with poles and ropes and wooden planks, sturdy enough, but the poles were long and had a fair bit of spring in them. Fifteen feet below, Crow River boiled its way over the rocks. It was a pale icy green, swollen with runoff. Arthur's father and Otto Luntz between them kept the bridge in good order but the cows didn't know that and Arthur didn't blame them for their unease.

"Jeez, it's really raging," Jake said, peering down into the foaming water.

Arthur tied his heifer to the handrail of the bridge. "We'll take yours first," he said.

It needed two people all right. Arthur pushed from one end and Jake pulled from the other, Arthur saying, "Okay, girl, okay. It's okay," Jake saying, "Come on, you stupid cow!" They got her over in the end and tied her to the rail, then started back across the bridge. Jake stopped in the middle and bounced experimentally. The bridge replied in slow motion, heaving under their feet. Arthur grabbed the handrail.

"What you *doin'*?" he said. Mostly he just ignored Jake's behaviour—it wasn't worth getting worked up about—but today Jake really did seem to be hell-bent on getting whacked.

"I forgot this was so good," Jake said, letting the motion subside and then leaning over the rail. "It really dances." He leaned over further, trying to see the underside of the bridge. Arthur reached the other end and stepped onto firm ground.

"See that pole?" Jake said. "The one underneath? Bet you couldn't go hand over hand—you know, hanging from it. All the way across."

Arthur didn't bother replying.

"Bet you couldn't," Jake said, grinning at him.

"Let's get the cow across," Arthur said. "You got things to do, you said."

"Bet I could go across, if you're scared to," Jake said. "Bet you."

"Bet you." His favourite phrase since the day he was born. He turned everything—*everything*—into a competition. It seemed so pointless, since he was better than Arthur at everything anyway. But he just had to keep proving it. "Bet you."

"Yeah," Arthur said. "Bet you could. Let's get the cow across. I gotta get back to the farm. Thought you were in a hurry, anyway."

"Bet it wouldn't take me two minutes," Jake said, peering over the side again. "Maybe five. Five minutes."

He ran to the end of the bridge and scrambled down until he could grab hold of the pole. The sides of the gorge were steep; once you left the edge they fell away into a sheer drop—not all that far, but at the bottom were great slabs of granite with water foaming over them. In places the water was deep, maybe deep enough to provide a cushion, but in other places the rocks broke through the surface, glistening, pink as salmon in the sunlight.

"Should I do it?" Jake said, grinning up at Arthur.

Arthur untied the second cow, wondering if he could get her across by himself. She wasn't happy about it. She put one foot on the bridge, then took it off again and looked longingly over her shoulder, back at the farm.

"I'm going to do it," Jake said. The bridge gave a little shudder as he grabbed the pole with both hands and swung himself out. "It's easy," he shouted from under the bridge. "You're so yellow. Yellow-bellied. Chicken-livered."

"Come on," Arthur said to the heifer. "It's okay. Just wobbles a bit." He pulled gently and she tried again, one foot, then the other. "'Atta girl," he said. She stepped forward, all four feet on the bridge now, and Arthur kept moving, walking slowly backwards, encouraging her. "See? It's okay, isn't it?"

"This is great!" Jake said from underneath them. His voice broke up each time he moved his hands. "I'm nearly . . . in the middle . . . already. I told you . . . I could do it. . . . It's great!"

Arthur and the cow were nearly in the middle too, but the motion was worse now, and Jake's hand-over-hand movements were adding to it. The cow staggered. The bridge swung sharply in response and she staggered again. Arthur cursed his brother. "Damn you!" he said. "Damn you!"

"Art!" Jake said, his voice suddenly different. "Don't shake the bridge. It's slippery. It's wet here!" Arthur ignored him. The cow was really scared now, pulling back against the rope, her eyes rolling.

"Come on now," Arthur said, gently as he could. "Nearly there. Come on." She tried another step, managed it, took another. They were right in the middle now.

Jake didn't seem to be moving at all. They were ahead of him, the bridge at its maximum swing.

"Art! Stop walking! I can't hang on!"

He must think there was no limit to Arthur's gullibility. "Come on, girl," Arthur said. "Come on."

"Art!"–panic in his voice–"I mean it! I can't hang on!"

Arthur stopped. He hated his brother. At that moment, he truly did hate him. This love he had for getting himself into situations that might or might not be dangerous and yelling for Arthur to rescue him, and Arthur never knowing whether to believe him or not, and finally having to believe him for their mother's sake, only to find that Jake had been kidding once again. Jake *loved* that. Loved proving to Arthur and the world just how stupid Arthur was. How gullible. He never got tired of proving it.

"Art!"–his voice a shriek–"I'm going to fall!"

"Good," Arthur said. A word that would haunt him for the rest of his life.

He felt Jake fall. Felt his weight leave the bridge. Just like that.

For a moment he was paralyzed. Disbelieving. He couldn't even draw a breath. He stood in the middle of the bridge, staring at the cow, his eyes wide. Then his breath came in with a rush and he grabbed the rail and looked over. For a moment he couldn't see Jake because he expected him to have been washed downstream, whereas in fact he was almost directly under the bridge. He was face up, wedged between two rocks. Water was streaming around and over him. Over his face.

Arthur didn't remember afterwards how he got down to the riverbed. He must have slid down the bank or jumped. He waded out into the icy surge of the river, the breath shocked out of him by the cold. He grabbed Jake under the arms and dragged him to the shore. For one ridiculous moment he wondered if this could be another trick, if Jake could have planned the fall and was playing dead or unconscious for fun—one further, final, joke. But Jake's head lolled to the side, and the water streamed out of his nose and mouth in a way that made Arthur cry out with fear.

He couldn't get up the bank the way he had come down. It was too steep to climb unencumbered, let alone carrying a body. He waded along the edge of the river, sometimes thigh deep, the water boiling around him, stumbling over the rocks, feet and legs numb and unresponsive as tree trunks, looking for a way up. He carried Jake in his arms at first, and then, once he found a way up, slung him over his shoulder, panting with fear. He thought Jake was alive, was pretty sure he'd felt him cough, but he couldn't stop, there in the middle of the river, to be sure. And who knew what injuries he might have or what further damage he, Arthur, might be doing by heaving him up and over his shoulder. But what else could he do? He could not carry him in his arms up the bank, and he could not leave him in the water.

At the top he lowered Jake carefully to the ground to check that he was breathing, and he was, so he picked him up again and ran. All the way across the fields he could see nothing but his mother's face. How could he walk into the house like this, carrying his brother's body? How could he face her? It was impossible to just walk in on her, unannounced. She would die from the shock of it. He prayed that his father would be in the farmyard or in one of the nearest fields. Please God. Please. Sobbing the words as he staggered along.

His prayer was answered. His father saw him coming—Arthur saw him straighten up and stand for a minute, wondering what it was that was heading towards him over the fields, and then start towards them, slowly, and then abruptly at a run.

"Tell Mum," Arthur shouted when his father was close enough. He was crying and found it hard to get the words out. "Tell Mum. Get the doctor."

In nightmares, in years to come, scenes from that day came back to haunt him. Jake's face, under water. That image most of all. But also Jake laid out on the kitchen table, his legs at an angle no legs could possibly assume, and their mother bending over him, literally wringing her hands, her worst nightmares come true. She kept sobbing, "What happened? Oh, Arthur, what happened?" and he should have told her then—told her everything—but he couldn't do it, so he said, "He slipped, he just slipped," and kept saying it, every time she asked, trying to make it true.

Just before his father arrived with the doctor—followed by the hearse, which doubled as an ambulance—Jake opened his eyes. Arthur could see him trying to focus on the ceiling. Then, with a huge effort, he turned his head a fraction and his eyes moved slowly around the room, taking in his mother, and then settling on Arthur. After a moment his lips moved, as if he wanted to say something. To damn Arthur, without a doubt. To accuse him. To tell the truth.

Tell her, Arthur thought, suddenly wishing he would. Tell her what happened. He deserved it, he just wanted it over with.

But Jake said nothing. Maybe he couldn't get the words out. He closed his eyes again, and shortly after that Dr. Christopherson arrived, and examined him briefly—Arthur's father standing flat against the wall as if pinned there by shock—and then with the help of Mr. Leroy, the undertaker, carefully shifted Jake onto a stretcher and took him away.

Arthur was still standing in the middle of the room, going over and over those final seconds on the bridge, trying to change them: trying to replace what happened with what should have happened, what he should have done. Worse still, going over and over what he had said, that one unbearable, unforgivable word. Trying to unsay it. Desperate to find a way around the unalterable fact that once you have said something, it is said. Once it has left your lips, you cannot take it back.

FIVE

~

Town Lights Out: Air Rifles Banned
50 Years of Silver Production
—*Temiskaming Speaker*, May 1957

Mrs. Christopherson had been Dr. Christopherson's nurse as well as his wife, so when she left, Ian's father was in a fix. After a week or two of chaos he seemed to realize that he was going to have to do something about it, even if only (as he told Ian) for the short term. At that stage, it was clear to Ian that his father still believed his wife was going to come back.

In the meantime, the doctor placed an advertisement in the *Canadian Medical Association Journal*. *RN wanted*, he wrote, *for small northern town*. He should have left out *northern*. And maybe *small*, as well. There were only two

94

replies and one of those dropped out when she realized just how far north Struan was. The other one, Jessie Armitage, came out of ignorance.

By then it was summer, and the lake was at its most benevolent. The sun shone every day. It had been a dry spring and there were remarkably few mosquitoes. The nurse—twenty-two years old, Toronto-born and -bred—was enchanted. "It's so beautiful up here," she said to the patients as she changed a dressing or gave an injection or extracted a pea from a child's ear. "I had no idea there was someplace so beautiful in my own country!"

But then came autumn and the equinoctial gales began to blow, stripping the trees of their leaves as if they were disgraced. The lake turned grey and sullen and the swells weren't gentle anymore: they heaved ominously, and tattered rags of spray blew off their tops. The wind barrelled down from the north, driving before it clouds as dark as slate. Pale curtains of rain swept across the lake. Someone in the town said to Jessie Armitage, "This is nothin'. You wait till it's snow 'stead of rain out there. Then you'll see somethin'. Then you'll learn what cold is."

Jessie Armitage went back to Toronto.

Ian found his father down at the lake one evening, watching the waves hurl themselves at the shore. It was working up to a major storm.

"I can't understand how anyone can fail to love it," Dr. Christopherson said. His tone was almost apologetic, as if he were making a confession. Then he added—and Ian saw that it was a confession, in a way—"Your mother hated it. The North, I mean. I thought in time she would come to feel the same about it as I do. But she didn't."

Ian said nothing. His father made a lot of excuses for

his mother in those early days, as if he were trying to convince Ian that she was justified in deserting them. The night after she left he had said, with a wretchedness that brought Ian close to despising him, this man whom he had always admired above all others, "You mustn't blame her. It is my fault, really. She was bored here. It wasn't fair to bring her here." Ian had stared at him, sick with disgust. Was that supposed to be an excuse for deserting her family and running off with another man? That she was *bored*? He thought of Laura, who never stopped working from the moment she got up in the morning and whose companion in life was the most boring man on the planet. You didn't hear her moaning about it. She would have said, if you had asked her—Ian was convinced of this—she would have said that her place was with her husband and children, and that was all there was to it.

In the spring Dr. Christopherson placed another ad in the medical journal and got no replies at all.

"How would you like to be a nurse?" he said to Ian, and Ian said, "Very funny," though he knew his father was only partly joking. What choice did he have, after all? If he really needed help, who else was there to give it? Mrs. Tuttle would faint dead away if she were asked to so much as put on a Band-Aid.

A new teacher, Stanley Bannister, came to take the place of the geography teacher Ian's mother had run off with, and brought with him his new wife, Margie, who happened to be a nurse, and Ian thought he was safe. But after about six months the Bannisters built a house out on Crow River Road, too far away for Margie to be of any help if there were an emergency outside of office hours.

And a surprising number of people managed to have their emergencies outside of office hours.

Ian resented being called on. He knew his father had no option, but he still resented it. It wasn't the work itself he minded; blood and gore didn't bother him, and it turned out that he was good at calming kids—maybe even better than his father. So it wasn't that he particularly disliked the things he was asked to do. What he minded was the fact that he had to do them. The reason behind it.

"Getting a little bit of practice, are you?" the patients would say. Or, "You'll have a head start, when you get to medical school." Ian, helping to hold a struggling child, or preparing the mask for chloroform, would nod and say nothing, because it wasn't worth denying it.

But as time passed, the patients got used to him filling in for Margie out of hours, and no longer commented on it, and Ian got used to it too. He still felt resentful whenever he thought about it, but he didn't think about it much anymore.

~

The day before his seventeenth birthday was a Saturday, and Laura baked Ian a cake. It had pride of place on the kitchen table when he and Arthur came in from the fields at dinnertime.

"It's not really a birthday cake," Laura said, "because it's bad luck to celebrate your birthday early. That's why there aren't any candles. It's just a cake."

It was huge and round and covered with gooey choco-late icing—a kid's cake, but it did look good. They had some for dessert, and then later in the afternoon, when Ian and Arthur took their tea break, there was more cake to go with the tea. They sat on old burlap potato sacks that Arthur tossed down on the tall grass at the edge of the field. Robert and Edward were behind them, still harnessed but unhitched from the plow, cropping grass with a sound like tearing bedsheets. It was hot, and the grass smelled sweet and new, and the bees were droning around as if it were high summer, though it was still only May.

The tea came out of a Thermos but was still hot enough to take the roof off your mouth. The cake—two great slabs of it—was carefully wrapped in waxed paper.

"So what you doin' for your birthday?" Arthur said. His voice, breaking in on the quiet, made Ian jump. Days spent with Arthur consisted of vast rolling plains of silence with the odd half-dozen words dropped into them like stones, and the stones always took him by surprise.

"I haven't really thought about it," he said.

Arthur was trying to shake the icing back onto one of the wedges of cake—it had glued itself to the waxed paper. He shook it violently and it sagged in the middle and then dropped down onto the cake with a nearly audible thud.

"Here you go," Arthur said, passing him a slab.

"Thanks," Ian said. "It's great cake." They were practically having a conversation! When he'd first started working for Arthur, the silence had seemed spooky. Whole days with scarcely a word. He didn't mind—in fact, at the time he was relieved not to have to make conversation. He could absolutely rely on Arthur not to ask how he and his father were making out.

In any case, it wasn't really silence. There were plenty of sounds, mostly from the horses—the heavy, regular thud of their feet, the powerful sawing of their breath, the clanking and creaking of their harnesses. And there were birds and cicadas, and the buzzing of insects and the barking of the dogs and the odd woodpecker hammering away in the distance.

He'd tried having silence at home once or twice. For years he'd automatically switched on his radio when he walked into his bedroom, but after working for Arthur for a while he tried leaving it off. The quality of the silence at home was different, though. It seemed to make his mother's absence more noticeable. And the sounds that broke it were anything but restful—babies howling in the waiting room, sometimes yells from his father's office, the phone ringing, Mrs. Tuttle answering it and muttering anxiously as she made her way along the hall to his father's office. She hated answering the phone: What if someone died while she was talking to them? What if someone was having a heart attack and breathed his final words down the phone line? In the evenings, if there were no calls for his father and genuine silence descended on the house, it had a heavy quality, as if it were laden with the depression which had settled on Ian's father since his mother left. So Ian switched his radio back on, and let Elvis and Chuck Berry and Buddy Holly fill the silence for him.

Now he sat beside Arthur and listened to the bees and the tearing bedsheets and Arthur, slurping his tea out of a chipped enamel mug. There were half a dozen heavy, lumbering footsteps behind them and Edward's gigantic nose appeared over Arthur's shoulder. He was intrigued by the cake.

"Geddoff," Arthur said, and smacked him with a backward sweep of his hand. Edward tossed his head and backed away, then paused, and Ian felt his gaze. He hunched his shoulders and curled himself over his cake.

"Geddoff!" Arthur said again, threateningly. Edward gave up and thudded back to Robert, and blew petulantly into his ear. Robert shook his head violently. Edward was the younger of the two and Robert had no patience with him.

"Aren't you havin' a party? A few friends around?" Arthur said, breaking all records in the conversation stakes.

"I don't think so. I've got an exam on Monday. I'm going to have to study tomorrow."

Arthur nodded sympathetically and slurped his tea, and Ian was swept by a wave of shame. Because Arthur, whatever his limitations, was a really nice guy, and he still didn't have a clue that Ian was only there because he was in love with his wife. And even less of a clue that sometimes, after dark, Ian returned to the farm. Returned, and stood silently within the black shapes of the trees at the edge of the farmyard, like some dark ghost, haunting her.

~

"Do you have a girlfriend, Ian?" Laura had asked a few months ago, and he'd been momentarily gripped by panic. Why did she ask? Had she noticed how he watched her? Did she know how he felt about her? Maybe she could see through him, maybe she had known from the very first time he had come to the farm, asking for a job. But she looked merely interested; not mocking or teasing him. And so he mumbled yes, sort of, he did.

He wasn't quite sure how he'd managed it, but he had a girlfriend all right. He'd acquired her about a year ago, when a whole group of them from his class went out to Low Down Point the night after their last exam for a little end-of-year celebration. They'd made a fire on the beach and roasted hot dogs and marshmallows, and a couple of the guys had smuggled in some hooch, and they all got drunk. They went swimming in the dark. Some of them had had the foresight to wear their bathing suits under their clothes and the others, Ian included, swam in their underwear. A few boys—the ones who spent their entire lives showing off—and a couple of girls—the ones you'd expect—went skinny-dipping. There was a lot of splashing and screaming and falling about, but remarkably, no one drowned or fell into the fire or cracked his head open by diving onto one of the rocks off the end of the point. The water was still very cold, and when they got out their teeth were chattering so hard that no one could speak. They threw more wood on the fire and everybody huddled around it—close as they could get without singeing their eyebrows—and passed around the hooch and yelled, "You ain't nothin' but a hound dog" at the cold and distant stars. Every now and then someone threw more wood on the fire and the sparks whooshed up and vanished into the night.

Pete was there to start with but he kept to the fringes, as he tended to do in groups. He wandered off soon after they got out of the water. Ian found himself sitting beside Cathy Barrett, whose dad worked for the hydro company. She was pretty, and nice, and very cold, and he was quite drunk, so he started rubbing her back, vigorously, to warm her up. One thing led to another and in the morning he discovered that they were going steady.

In some ways he was pleased. He hadn't had a girlfriend before, and wasn't sure that not having one was entirely his own choice; ever since his mother left it had been in the back of his mind that where girls were concerned, he might have been tainted by her disgrace. So Cathy's choosing him—it was she who had sat down beside him, not the other way around—was reassuring. Plus he liked the look of her, and the smell of her, and the way she leaned against him and let him slide his arm around her right away.

Compared to Laura, she was nothing special, of course. He knew he shouldn't compare them, but he couldn't help it. Cathy was small and rounded, with clear pale skin and dark shiny hair, whereas Laura was tall and slender and golden, and in another league as far as beauty went. And Cathy was just a girl, whereas Laura was a woman.

They hadn't got much beyond kissing, that first night. Ian would have liked to go further, would have liked to go all the way, come to that. Who wouldn't? But there were two kinds of girls, the "nice" ones and the "easy" ones, and Cathy definitely fell into the first category. Even if she'd been "easy," though, he probably wouldn't have gone all the way. He wasn't drunk enough for that. Lots of other guys his age did, he knew that, but the idea of sex outside of marriage made him think of his mother. Also, he could never rid his mind of the possible consequences. Sometimes he thought that too close an acquaintance with consequences was ruining his youth—though at other times he thought this was just an excuse and the truth was that he was chicken. You were supposed to do crazy things when you were young, but he never could. Like going out onto the ice too soon after freeze-up, for instance. Kids did it all the time, but they hadn't seen the bodies of other kids, who had gone through the ice, whereas he had. It happened practically every winter, and made his father speechless with rage.

The same problem applied to going all the way with girls. He knew with complete certainty that if he "did it" with a girl just once—once!—she'd get pregnant. Even if he managed to get hold of a safe—and how was he supposed to do that in a town where his father and the pharmacist had known each other all their lives?—even if he managed to get hold of one, from a friend, say, it would turn out to have a hole in it.

Still, when he was out with Cathy, he always pushed things as far as he could. Over the past few months he'd managed to persuade her to let him touch her top half, and he kept trying to work his way farther south. It was a long, slow process, though. There seemed to be a number of stages you had to go through. Initally, she let him feel her breasts but wouldn't let him see them, which was strange and frustrating, though better than the other way around. The softness of her breasts astounded him. The way the nipples hardened under his touch. They were incredible. Miraculous. He couldn't get enough of them. Though sometimes, right in the middle of fondling her (these sessions took place at the Jessops', who were friends of Cathy's parents and whose two-year-old Cathy babysat most Thursday evenings), he would find himself wondering what Laura's breasts would feel like. The idea made him breathless, dizzy with lust. Made him try to slide his hand up the warm, silky skin of Cathy's inner thigh and force her down onto the Jessops' sofa, his erection throttled by his jeans. Cathy would push him away, hissing, "Ian, stop it! Stop it!"—though despite her fierce commands Ian was pretty sure she liked it when he got so steamed up. She couldn't know that she wasn't the sole cause. It made him feel vaguely ashamed, though not ashamed enough to stop doing it.

~

His mother sent him a present for his birthday—a large package, wrapped carefully in brown paper, which arrived several days before the event. He opened it at once, to get it over with. *Hope you like it, darling,* his mother's note said. *I'll be thinking of you all day.* It was a jacket, water-proof, lined with some material light and warm as goose down. He would never wear it.

His father gave him a canoe. They already had a canoe that had belonged to Ian's grandfather, but it was broad and beamy and paddled like a pig, whereas this one was long and slender—you could see that it would slide through the water like a knife. It was a cedarstrip and had been var-nished, inside and out, until it glowed like warm honey.

"Where did you get it?" he asked his father. He'd never seen anything so beautiful. It was tied to the dock, resting on the water so lightly you'd think it weighed no more than a leaf. It was their own dock. Ian's grandfather had bought the plot of land between their house and the lake and had cut a path through the trees so that they'd have access to the water. There was a bell on the dock, a large brass one, hanging from a gallows, that could be rung to summon the doctor if he happened to be out fishing when his services were required. Ian's grandfather had been a keen fisherman and so was Ian's father, though nowadays he seldom had the time. They had their own small bay, with a crescent of beach sheltered between two long points of rock. On a rough patch of ground behind the beach they'd built a boathouse, where the old canoe and the rowboat lived. The doors to the boathouse were open and Ian saw that another rack had been fitted for his canoe to rest on.

"Temagami," his father said. "I asked John Raven to keep a lookout for one. He spotted it when he was down there a while back. It's been in the boathouse down by the docks for the past month. Pete brought it over for me last night."

"It's beautiful," Ian said. His father looked at him and smiled, and Ian had to look away. His father so badly wanted him to be happy that it made him sad. I'm fine, Ian wanted to say, which was true, most of the time. You're the one who's not. You should worry about yourself.

"Think I'll go for a little test run," he said, crouching down to unlace his shoes. "Want to come?"

His father shook his head. "Another time. Don't be late for church."

Ian undid the mooring line and stepped delicately, barefoot, down into the canoe. It shivered slightly under his weight but it took him only a second or two to get the balance of it. The floorboards were warm and mellow under his feet.

"Thanks, by the way," he said, looking up at his father. Dr. Christopherson nodded. It was still early morning, not yet eight o'clock, but already the sun was strong. It beat down on them—his father on the dock, himself in the boat. A little band of ripples sprang up out of nowhere and patted the sides of the canoe.

He paddled down the shore, listening to the slippering of the water under the hull, wondering about his father's motives in giving him such a present. It must have cost a lot of money, for a start, and they weren't rich. His father was useless—Ian's mother's word, and he hated to agree, but it was true—at extracting payment from his patients. "In due course," he'd say uncomfortably. "When you feel able." The whole business of money embarrassed him.

But leaving the cost aside, a canoe was a strange gift, when you thought about it, for someone who would be leaving home in a little over a year's time. Hardly something you could stuff in your suitcase and take with you. He wondered if that could possibly be intentional. No, that was stretching things, not intentional. But unconsciously, could his father have sought to give him something that he would love but would have to come back to Struan to use? Could he be trying to plant in Ian's mind a seed of longing for the North that would grow in him while he was away and finally draw him home? His father took it for granted—Ian knew this—that he would go to university, would in fact have pushed him if he'd been unwilling to go. But he also knew his father wanted him to come back. He had never said so, but he didn't need to. Ian knew it in his bones. Deep down, his father hoped that he would go into medicine and join him in the practice. If you confronted him with this, he would look astonished and deny it. He would say that it went without saying that Ian must choose what he wanted to do with his life. But it also went without saying that he hoped Ian would choose medicine, and Struan.

It would have been bad enough, to disappoint him, to leave home with no intention of returning for anything but the odd holiday, if everything had been normal. But in the circumstances? Leaving his father alone, knowing how low he could get? It scared Ian sometimes—the depth of his father's depression. He had always thought of his father as invulnerable, thought he had the answer to everything. That was the impression he gave, not just to his patients but to Ian as well. He looked rock solid. Unshakable. But it wasn't so.

Mostly he seemed to be all right while he was working. He kept his regular office hours with Margie Bannister, his nurse, and did his rounds and listened to his patients and their woes, just as he always had. And he was generally fine in the mornings; at breakfast they both sat in the kitchen and read the paper. They were both early risers, so even on school days breakfast was a fairly leisurely affair.

It was in the evenings that he went downhill. He fought against it; Ian could see that. He tried—in fact, the trying was the most painful thing to watch. Suppertimes, when he was going through a bad patch, were an endurance test, made worse by the fact that his father seemed to think they should eat "properly," sitting at the big polished table in the dining room as they had done when Ian's mother was there. Ian disliked the room. It still reeked of his mother's presence. It and the living room were full of her little touches: the lacy runner on the sideboard, the cut-glass vases (which had never held flowers because there was nothing but weeds, his mother maintained, within four hundred miles of Struan), the low table lamps on each of the side tables. ("Don't they look charming?" he remembered her saying when the lamps first arrived. "You see the way they cast little pools of light? It's so simple. So elegant. Don't you think?" She had moved one of the lamps fractionally to the right. It was one of the few times he remembered her looking happy, which made the memory all the more painful.)

She didn't buy the lamps in Struan, of course. You

could get oil lamps at the hardware store to guard against the possibility (in fact, the certainty) of power cuts during winter storms, but they were functional. Struan hadn't caught up with the idea of a "charming" home yet. Struan had never heard the word "decor." Eaton's catalogue ("the other Bible," Ian's father called it, because in many of the homes he visited it was the only other reading material in the house) hadn't heard of it either, but at least they had proper lamps, and with a little bit of imagination—Ian's mother said wistfully—you could create the sort of look that turned a house into a home.

In Ian's opinion they should have thrown everything out the day she left, cleared the house of the ornaments and knickknacks, the candlesticks and picture frames, but they hadn't, and all of them were still sitting there, covered with dust (dusting wasn't Mrs. Tuttle's forte), waiting to ambush your memory. Why couldn't they eat in the kitchen, which had always been Mrs. Tuttle's domain? Why couldn't they sit in there in the evenings as well as the mornings?

Though the truth was that he knew why. He knew that his father felt the need to maintain a semblance of "normal" family life. So he said nothing, and they sat in the dining room, night after night. Mrs. Tuttle prepared their supper (on Fridays she made things that they could heat up on the weekend) and set the table before she left, and they ate there, formally, and made polite conversation, even when there was nothing to say.

"Loaded with fat," his father would announce, his voice strained with the effort of lightness, helping himself to a piece of Mrs. Tuttle's fried chicken. "Grease coagulating in your gut, arteries clogging up. We'll both be dead within the year."

"Worth it, though," Ian would say, going along with it, playing his part.

His father would nod in agreement. "Oh yes. A fine way to go."

Or they'd discuss their days.

"Joyce Ingrams was in again today."

"Yeah, I saw her sitting there. She should have a chair with her name on it. What was the matter this time?"

"Nothing at all."

"Can't you just say, 'You're imagining it. Go home'?"

His father shook his head. "She needs the reassurance. Hypochondria is a disease, in a way."

Like depression? Ian thought. If so, he did feel sorry for her.

"Maybe what she needs is to actually get sick," he said. It seemed to help his father if you could get him involved in conversation, as if his brain were less vulnerable when it was concentrating. But it was hard work getting him there, like winding up an old gramophone that was forever running down. "Then she'd know the difference. Has she ever had anything really wrong with her?"

"Not that I can recall. Had the flu a few years back. A mild dose, no danger."

"She'll be really pleased when she dies," Ian said. "She can have 'I told you so' carved on her tombstone."

His father smiled. It was a small triumph to make him smile. Laughter, in the evenings, was beyond him.

Ian thought the bad patches were a little farther apart than they had been at first, but there were still times when it seemed almost as if gravity doubled its pull on his father. The skin of his face sagged; his big frame seemed weighed down. He looked exhausted. Was he ever going to get over it? And if he didn't, how could Ian leave him? The thought of it swamped him with guilt, and the guilt made him angry. You shouldn't have to feel guilty about living your own life. You shouldn't have to be responsible for your parents' happiness. It wasn't fair.

The day was warming up and the morning mist was lifting slowly off the surface of the water. He slid through it, the canoe making no more sound than the mist. It was a beautiful craft, and here he was, gliding along in it, stewing about something that was still more than a year away. He was fed up with himself, with the way he worried about everything—he drove himself crazy. He should be enjoying the canoe. It was a great birthday present and the odds were that his father had bought it for him simply because he knew Ian would love it. Just that, no more, no less.

In the wake of the mist a light breeze was stirring and the clean acid smell of the trees drifted across the water. He dipped into Blake's Bay but there was no sign of Pete, so he carried on to Hopeless Inlet and found him anchored in the marshy bit, where the pike liked to hide, hunched over his fishing line like an old troll.

"Well, well. A white man in a canoe," Pete said as he came up. "Whaddaya know."

"Not bad, is it?" Ian said.

"I'll tell you something," Pete said, stretching out one leg, then folding it up again and stretching the other. The thwarts in the *Queen Mary* were very low, and Pete's legs were very long, so his knees were always jackknifed up around his ears. The knees of his jeans had given up the struggle long ago and were split straight across from seam to seam. "When you guys have evolved a bit more, like in a billion years or so, you'll discover the outboard motor and you'll never look back."

Ian grinned. But lately there seemed to be an edge to Pete's jokes, and sometimes it made him uneasy.

"It's a nice canoe, though," he said, trying again. "You have to admit."

"It's nice," Pete said. "But I'd like to see you land a pike in it. Man overboard." At that precise moment his hook was grabbed by something so big that Pete was flung to the side of the *Queen Mary*. The jigger flew out of his hands and he came within half an inch of going overboard himself.

"Holy shit!" he said when he'd recovered himself. "What was that?"

Ian was laughing too hard to answer. Pete took an oar from the bottom of his boat, paddled the *Queen Mary* up beside the canoe, reached out, and before Ian could stop him gave the side of the canoe a little push, and over it went.

The water was so cold Ian's heart almost stopped. He came to the surface gasping with the shock of it, and there was Pete, looking down at him and grinning like a cat.

"You've christened it," Pete said. "It's good luck to dunk your canoe first time out. You're gonna be a lucky man." And he was right, because Ian heaved himself out of the water, made a wild grab at Pete's arm, and by sheerest luck managed to catch it, flung himself backwards, and Pete ended up in the water too. It was just like old times.

~

At church, Ian and his father sat in their usual pew. It was a full house. The summer-like weather had cheered everyone up and made them more willing to sit through a sermon in return for the pleasure of gathering around the church steps afterwards and getting caught up on the gossip. The women were wearing summer dresses and hats with fake flowers. Everybody looked brighter and more alive than they had a month ago, when there was still snow on the ground. Even the children seemed less fractious than usual. Reverend Thomas was the only one out of step. His sermon was on the theme of pain—on accepting that life was full of it, on enduring it cheerfully, on welcoming the closeness to God that suffering could bring. Ian, who was wider awake than usual because of his early-morning dip, heard his father suppress a snort. He'd seen more of pain than Reverend Thomas had.

Arthur and Laura Dunn and the children sat three rows ahead, as they always did. Ian fixed his eyes on Laura, as he'd been doing now for what felt like his whole life. If Cathy had been there he might have felt guilty, but her family went to the Baptist church at the other end of town. Ian was secretly glad; it left him free to concentrate on Laura. He still felt the usual confusion of emotions when he was in her presence. It was like a drink of cool water in the desert, and being eaten alive by army ants, both at the same time.

After church, while Arthur headed back to his truck so that he wouldn't have to talk to anyone, she came up to speak to him.

"Happy birthday," she said. Carter had followed his father, but Julie and March came with their mother. Julie smiled shyly up at Ian. She was shy with him again because she had seen so little of him during the winter. March, the baby, who wasn't a baby anymore, stopped digging a trench in the sand around his mother's feet with the toe of his shoe and looked up at Ian curiously. Laura said to them, "Aren't you going to wish Ian a happy birthday?"

"Happy birthday," Julie said.

"Thank you," said Ian.

March said, "I gotta truck."

"Do you?" Ian said. "Where is it?"

"At home," Laura said. "Or he'd have been running up and down the aisle with it."

"What colour is it?" Ian asked March. He must be almost three by now. In the past two years he seemed to have improved considerably. So had Julie. Ian didn't mind either of them now.

"Blue," March said uncertainly, looking up at his mother for confirmation. She nodded.

"Like your dad's," Ian said, and March looked over to where his father's truck was parked under a tree. He shook his head.

"It's smaller," he said regretfully.

"Maybe it will grow," Ian said, and March frowned at him under his thatch of fair hair.

"Ian's teasing you," said Laura. She touched the side of March's cheek with the back of her hand, making Ian ache with longing.

He watched her make her way slowly back to the truck, Julie and March trailing along behind her like small dinghies behind the mother ship. Carter and Arthur were standing by the truck. Carter was asking his father something; Arthur shook his head and Carter turned away, his shoulders hunched. Typical Carter posture.

But he wasn't really a bad kid, Ian thought. He didn't sass his parents or refuse to do what he was told or throw rocks through people's windows. It was just that he always seemed so moody. Ian would see him in the school playground at lunchtime and during recess, watching while the other boys in his class kicked a ball around. He wasn't good at sports. Not team sports, anyway. The only thing he was really good at, as far as Ian knew, was running: during sports day at the end of the year he usually won every race he was entered for. He'd come flying in, face flaming with exhilaration, twenty yards ahead of the rest. Maybe speed was his thing; he was fast on a bike, too. Sometimes in the evenings Ian would see him streaking down the road, crouched over the handlebars, head down, a long low cloud of dust trailing out behind him.

At home, though, he was one big negative. Sullen and uncommunicative. It was possible, Ian thought, that Arthur had been like that as a kid, but it seemed unlikely. His silence now was companionable, rather than morose. The same with Pete—you wouldn't describe Pete as gabby, but his silence was thoughtful. Carter's silence was resentful.

Maybe he'd grow out of it. Ian found it hard to believe that Carter was only four years younger than him. He seemed such a kid.

Strange, he thought later, how sometimes when you start thinking about a person, you seem to bring them to the foreground of your life. At eleven o'clock that night there was a hammering on the door and when Ian answered it, Sergeant Moynihan was standing on the porch, gripping a boy firmly by the arm. The boy was Carter. He was bleeding from a cut on his forehead, and his face was white and scared.

"Took his father's truck," the policeman said without preamble, propelling Carter into the hall. "Went for a little spin on his own. Left the road, clipped a rock, ended up in the ditch. Lucky he didn't hit a tree. Where's your dad?"

"He's been called out," Ian said, ushering them towards his father's office. "He shouldn't be too long."

"Stick a bandage on him or something," said Sergeant Moynihan. "I'll phone his parents." He prodded Carter's shoulder with his forefinger. "What's your phone number?"

Carter mumbled the number. He was holding a bloody handkerchief to his head and looked unsteady on his feet.

The policeman headed towards the hall. Over his shoulder he said to Ian, "You're getting lots of practice nowadays, I hear. Stitch him up yourself, why don't you? Save your dad the trouble."

"No thanks," Ian said sourly. He led Carter into his father's office and sat him down in a chair. He still looked very white, and Ian wondered if he was going to keel over. He kept a hand on his shoulder for a minute or two until the boy seemed steadier. Then he went over to the medicine cabinet and got a pad of surgical dressing out of the drawer.

"I'm just going to put a dressing on it," he said. "It'll do until my dad gets back." He carefully removed the bloody handkerchief and applied the dressing. Carter flinched but didn't protest.

"Hold it there," Ian said. "I'll put a bandage around it to keep it in place. It's not too bad. It's almost stopped bleeding."

They could hear Sergeant Moynihan on the phone out in the hall. "I'll find out," they heard him say, and he came into the office. "Your mother's worried, of course," he said to Carter. "And they can't come and get you, can they, because you swiped the truck." He turned to Ian.

"She wants to know how bad it is. Is he going to have to go to the hospital?"

"Probably not," Ian said. He was winding the bandage firmly around Carter's head. "My dad will want to make sure he doesn't have a concussion, though. And it will need a couple of stitches. Tell her we'll bring him home."

Sergeant Moynihan nodded and went back to the phone.

"I can walk home," Carter said, his voice shaky.

"I guarantee my dad will veto that." Ian fastened the end of the bandage to the rest with a safety pin. He was dying to know what the story was.

Sergeant Moynihan came back into the room. "Okay," he said. "I'm going to go and help his dad get the truck back on the road." He turned to Carter. "What was it all about, then? You're way underage, aren't you?" He waited a minute, then prodded Carter's shoulder. "How old are you?" Still no reply. He prodded him again. "Come on, how old?"

"Nearly fourteen!" Carter said, coming to life all at once, angrily leaning away from the prodding finger. He didn't seem intimidated, though. Ian was impressed in spite of himself.

"Thirteen, in other words. Three years away from old enough. You could have killed somebody. Killed yourself. Not very smart, was it?"

Carter didn't reply.

Sergeant Moynihan sighed. "Kids," he said. He hoisted his pants; he had a sizable paunch and his trousers fought a losing battle to stay on top of it. "Okay, I'm off. I expect his dad could come and get him when we get the truck out. If it's still driveable. Didn't look like too much damage." To Carter he said, "You'll be lucky if he doesn't take it out of your hide."

He left, and they heard the police car pull away. Ian sat down in his father's chair and studied Carter. Carter was looking at the floor.

"So, did you just want to go for a drive?" Ian said. He remembered nagging his father to take him driving out along the lake road, where you didn't see another car for hours. He couldn't have been more than fourteen at the time.

"Yeah."

"Why didn't you ask your dad? He'd have taken you, wouldn't he?" Most of the farm kids he knew were driving their father's tractors by the time they were Carter's age. But of course the Dunns didn't have a tractor.

Carter looked up. Under the bandage his face was still very pale but his eyes were hot and angry. There were streaks of drying blood smeared down to his chin; if it had been anyone else, Ian would have cleaned them off, but he suspected Carter wouldn't appreciate it.

"I did ask him."

"What did he say?"

"Same as always. 'Not now.' Everything's 'not now.' He won't let me do anything."

"What do you mean?" Ian asked, intrigued. "Like what?"

Carter shrugged and looked away, his mouth set in a bitter line. For a moment Ian felt sorry for him. It was true that Arthur didn't seem to pay much attention to him. Even the chores he was given to do kept him close to the house, under his mother's supervision.

"How about your mother? Wouldn't she teach you to drive?"

"She's too busy," Carter said, his tone flat.

"Well, sometime when she isn't." He imagined Laura in the passenger seat of the battered old truck, calmly and patiently instructing her son. Well, possibly not calmly—he thought of the harried way she rushed around: you wouldn't exactly describe her as calm. And now that he thought about it, she wasn't always all that patient with her kids, especially Carter. But she was still a wonderful mother. Carter had no idea how lucky he was.

"She's always too busy," Carter said, the bitter tone still there. "She's *permanently* busy."

"You probably just got her at a bad time," Ian said. "You should ask her again."

Carter's head came up. "What do you know about it!" he said nastily. "*You* don't live there! She isn't *your* mother!"

Which made Ian want to take him out behind the house and beat him to a pulp.

He went out to the farm the following night. It was late, almost ten o'clock, and he was afraid the Dunns would have gone to bed, but he was in luck and the kitchen light was still on. Arthur was the only one in there, sitting in his usual chair; he and Laura always went upstairs together, so Ian guessed Laura was helping her father get ready for bed. The old man slept in a small room off the parlour so that he didn't have to negotiate the stairs.

Ian stood under the trees at the edge of the farmyard, out of range of the blocks of light cast by the windows. Upstairs the light was on in Carter's room. The truck was parked over by the barn. Ian went over and had a look at it; as far as he could tell in the darkness, it didn't look any worse than it always had.

He went back to his vantage point and waited for Laura

to appear. The night air was still cold—it was only May, after all. He hunched his shoulders and stuffed his hands in his pockets. It was a relief to have the snow gone so he didn't have to worry about leaving footprints. For five or six months of the year it was really too dangerous to come. Now all he had to beware of was Arthur, who sometimes came out to take a leak against a tree rather than go upstairs to the bathroom. Or Carter—the idea of Carter discovering him made Ian's hair stand on end.

He knew what everyone would think if he were caught. There would be scandal. He'd be called a Peeping Tom. A pervert. But that wasn't so. Sure, he fantasized about Laura, but he had never seen her naked, and it was only when she had been breast-feeding March that he'd seen her breasts. If that had been the purpose of his visits he would have given up long ago. But that was not why he came. He wasn't sure exactly why he did come, but it wasn't for that. It reassured him to know that she was there, that was all. He came to check that everything was as it should be.

One of the dogs nuzzled his legs, and he reached down to pat it. When he looked up, Laura was coming into the kitchen. She paused in the doorway and pushed her hair back off her face in a gesture of fatigue, and Arthur, who had looked up when she appeared, stood up, quite quickly for him, crossed the kitchen, put his arms around her, and drew her close. Laura rested her head against his chest, her eyes closed. She rubbed his back, very gently, with her hands.

Ian watched, electrified. After a moment or two they separated, and began turning off the lights in preparation for going up to bed. But Ian stood on, long after the darkness had closed in around him, holding their image in his mind.

SIX

~

Cow Killed on North Road
Canada Extends Heartiest of Welcomes to
Their Most Gracious Majesties
—*Temiskaming Speaker*, April/May 1939

How long would it take to atone? Arthur, watching the repercussions of Jake's accident rippling out across their lives, saw that it was going to take forever.

Jake was in the hospital for three months. At first, until he was well enough to be moved, he was in the hospital in New Liskeard, and then they transferred him to Sudbury, farther south. The transfer was done in a proper ambulance rather than the hearse, and that plus the hospital fees, plus the four operations it took to put Jake's bones back in the right places, plus his mother's few trips to Sudbury to visit her child, cost money they didn't have.

Arthur's father, who in the months since the accident had developed deep grooves down the sides of his face, had to borrow the money from the bank. Debt. They were in debt. The very word made Arthur's guts churn with anxiety.

Until that time he hadn't given money much thought. They'd never had much, but neither had anyone else they knew. Money was something people in the towns and cities had: Mr. Taggert, the bank manager in Struan, or Mr. Fitzpatrick, who owned the sawmill—they had money. Most of the farmers in the area wouldn't see more than twenty dollars from one year to the next. But they didn't consider themselves poor. With the exception of salt and sugar and tea, they grew just about everything they ate, and for the other things they needed—tools, nails, shoes, gas for the truck, the odd bit of farm machinery when the bits they had were past mending—if you didn't have the money you paid in kind. Even the doctor and the vet were happy if you paid them in chickens or ham or a bushel of corn.

But everyone knew about debt nowadays. Even if you couldn't count to ten, you knew about debt. The men—hoboes—wandering up the dusty road to Struan, looking for work, had brought with them tales of horror from all over the country. Terrible droughts on the big farms out in the prairies, people starving in alleyways in the cities, even kids being sold by their parents in the hope that their new "owner" would feed them well and not work them to death. Hair-raising stories that made you grateful that Struan was where it was, though even here things were hard. Alongside "debt" were other words that had come to have a frightening reality, here in the North as well as everywhere else. "Destitution," for instance. "Starvation."

The small farms around Struan had been lucky, compared to many. The drought hadn't hit them so hard and the fields were small and surrounded by woods, so that even in severe dry spells the wind couldn't blow the topsoil away. They weren't totally isolated from what was happening in the world outside, of course—the price of wheat affected them, and the demand for milk—but most of the farms, including the Dunns', were mixed and on a small scale; if they couldn't sell one thing they could sell another, and if they couldn't sell anything at all they could eat it, and sit tight, and wait for better times.

But the hospital wouldn't accept a cow in payment. The hospital wanted money. A lot of money. Arthur heard a sound downstairs one night about three a.m. He got out of bed and crept along to the top of the stairs and saw his father lower himself into the chair by the stove as if he were an old man, and then just sit there, staring at nothing.

One evening he went back to the bridge. He'd been trying to comfort himself with the thought that he couldn't have saved Jake anyway, but he needed to know that for sure. Standing on the bridge, looking down at the surging water, he had a brief moment of hope, because although he'd got to Jake pretty damned fast after he fell, he could see that he would not have been able to get there in time to catch him, even if such a thing were possible. But there might have been another way, a much simpler way. He left the bridge and walked along the bank, studying the structure of it from the side, and felt his innards clench within him. He went back and walked out to the middle of it, where he and the cow had stood, and lay down on his stomach and hung his head over the side and reached under, groping for the pole Jake had been hanging from. He felt his fingers touch it, the cold, slippery smoothness of it. He could have reached Jake's hand, if he had tried. He could have pulled him to safety. But he had not tried. He had done nothing. He had said, "Good."

That word. He tried to tell himself Jake wouldn't have been able to hear it over the rush of the water. He clung to that hope.

Had he known that this time Jake wasn't crying wolf? Sometimes he thought he must have, deep down. Jake had been annoying him so much that day, maybe he had even willed him to fall. Maybe, just for a moment, at the very heart of him, he had wanted Jake dead.

He wished someone would punish him, send him to jail or something, though he knew there could be no worse punishment than watching what his parents were going through. He wanted to confess but couldn't bring himself to do it. He should have confessed at the time. He remembered his mother, bending over Jake's twisted body, crying, "What happened? Oh, what happened?" Remembered himself telling her Jake had slipped. He should have told her the truth then and there. He should have said, "I could have saved him, Mum. But I didn't believe him." He should have done it then, because it was getting harder to do with every passing day. And worse, much worse, one day soon Jake was going to tell their mother himself, and she would tell their father, and then they would truly despise him. After each of his mother's trips to Sudbury, Arthur searched her face to see if she knew. But each time her look was as it always was. What was Jake waiting for? Why didn't he tell her? There were times when Arthur wished he would.

And then, about two months after the accident, he and his father were out in the bush one afternoon cutting poplar saplings for fencing, and suddenly, out of the blue, his father said, "How did he fall?"

They hadn't been discussing Jake. They hadn't been talking at all. It was hot and still, the sky heavy with the threat of rain, and the flies and mosquitoes were driving them crazy. They were just trying to get the job done, fast, so they could get out of the woods.

Arthur straightened up and wiped his mouth with the back of his hand. He should have been glad that now he could get it over with at last, but his insides had turned to jelly.

"He . . . slipped," he said at last. That lie again. He didn't look at his father. To lose his good opinion—suddenly that seemed unendurable, worse than living with the guilt.

"There's a handrail," his father said, not looking at him either. He leaned on the willowy stem of a poplar with one hand, bending it over, ready for the blow.

"Yeah. But he slipped . . . under it."

"Slipped under the rail? That what you're tellin' me?"

"Yeah."

"He was foolin' around," Arthur's father said, splitting the trunk of the poplar with one savage blow. "Just like I thought. Foolin' around, like always."

"Yeah, but . . ." Arthur said. This was a possibility he hadn't thought of, that his father would lay the blame on Jake.

"But nothin'!" his father said, fury in his voice. "But nothin'! Foolin' around, always foolin' around. And now look. Look what's happened."

He picked up the fallen poplar, furiously hacked off the

crown, and tossed it onto the pile of other poles. "How're we goin' to pay it off, eh? You tell me. You know what happens if we can't pay it off? You know what happens? The bank takes the farm. That's what happens."

Arthur's heart was pounding. He felt words like pebbles rolling around in his mouth, so many he was almost choking on them, all of them wanting to come out at once. *It was my fault, Dad. I let him fall. I could have saved him. I could have reached him, but I didn't. I thought he was cryin' wolf again, but I think I knew he wasn't. I think I knew. You know what I said when he told me he was slipping? I said, "Good," Dad. I said, "Good."*

He tried to say it, got as far as opening his mouth, but his father rounded on him, pointed at him with the head of the axe.

"Don't you damn well make excuses for him! Don't you damn well do that ever again! You and your mother." He shook the axe at Arthur. He was so mad spittle was flying from his mouth. "Fourteen damned years old, never taken responsibility for a single damned thing he's ever done. A baby's what he is. A big useless nuisance of a baby. And now look." The still air echoed with his rage.

All summer long, while the sun beat down on the ripening crops, turning them from green to dusty gold, Arthur worked off his guilt in the fields. Sunup to sundown he was out there. There was comfort in the labour, but no absolution.

Jake came home at the end of July. An ambulance brought him all the way from Sudbury. More debt, though when you looked at him it seemed disgraceful to think about money. He was in plaster from head to toe; both of his legs were in casts from his feet to his hips and another cast encased him from his hips to his armpits. His face, which was practically all of him that you could see, was so thin the bones seemed about to split the skin.

The ambulance men carried him into the kitchen on a stretcher and put him on the bed Arthur's mother had made up for him there. When they had gone, and when Arthur's mother, practically torn asunder by the mixture of anxiety and joy, had gone upstairs to get some further item for Jake's comfort, and when his father, who hadn't said a single word since the ambulance arrived, had gone outside again, Arthur went up to Jake's bed. His mouth was so dry he could hardly speak.

"How ya doin'?" he managed finally.

"Okay," Jake said.

The two of them looked at each other. Arthur was no more capable of reading his brother's expression than he had ever been, but he knew he had to say what needed saying right now, before another moment passed. He licked his lips. "About what happened . . ." he said.

Jake watched him.

"I'm sorry," Arthur tried to say, but his voice cracked. He swallowed and tried again. "I'm sorry about it."

It sounded so stupid he almost expected Jake to laugh. You cripple your brother for life and all you can say is "sorry"? But if there were other words he didn't know what they were.

Jake turned his head away for a minute, gazing at the door their father had gone out of. He looked about six years old lying there, and at the same time about sixty. After a minute he looked back and said, "Did you mean what you said, Art? When we were on the bridge? Did you want me to fall?"

The breath came out of Arthur in a rush, as if he'd been hit in the stomach. He'd been prepared for shouts of accusation or savagely whispered threats of revenge, or for Jake to say he'd hate him for the rest of his life, but not this direct, simple, unbearable question. When he was finally able to speak, all he could say was, "Jesus, no, Jake. Oh, Jesus, no," the words coming out between a croak and a sob.

Jake studied him for a while. Then he said, "How's Dad?"

"What?" Arthur said, wiping his nose with the back of his hand. He could hear their mother walking around upstairs. If she overheard them it would kill her.

"Was Dad very upset?"

"Jesus, Jake! What are you talking about?"

Jake looked at him steadily. "Was he upset?"

"Jesus!" Arthur said, in agony all over again. "Of course he was!" It was the simplicity of the questions he couldn't bear, and the knowledge that Jake must have been lying on a hospital bed, unable to move, asking himself those questions for three whole months.

"He didn't come and see me," Jake said. "Not once."

"Mum wanted to!" Arthur said in anguish. "It cost a lot of money for someone to go. They couldn't both go."

Jake looked away. Finally, without looking back, he said, "Anyway, I guess it doesn't matter." He seemed about to say something else, but they heard their mother's footsteps on the stairs.

How do you go about making amends for something like that? A lifetime wouldn't be long enough.

~

That summer it seemed to Arthur that his life had changed forever—it was inconceivable that things could ever return to how they had been before. And yet they did. Labour Day came, the end of the summer holidays, and his mother made him go back to school. It was incredible. There he was, nineteen years old and the size of a truck, every last vestige of childhood wrung out of him by five months of anguish, sitting at a desk like a little kid, back in grade eleven for the second time.

His friends, when he saw them—Carl, Ted, and the others—couldn't believe it either. They didn't exactly say so, but Arthur knew they found the idea downright embarrassing. None of them was the type to give unasked-for advice but Carl said once, in an undertone, speaking out of the side of his mouth and looking off into the woods, "Why don't you just stop goin', Art? She can't make you. You're bigger'n she is." Arthur thought about it. Imagined himself standing in the kitchen, saying, "I ain't goin', Mum. That's all there is to it. I just ain't goin'." But he could never get the picture to come clear. He had never defied her and guessed he never would.

The ridiculous thing was that Jake, who was longing to get back to school, was nowhere near strong enough, and was probably going to miss a whole year. At the end of August, Dr. Christopherson had come out to the farm and cut the casts off him and helped him to his feet and supported him while he took his first steps, and then broke it to them that, although Jake was healing well, one leg was now shorter than the other, and he was going to have a limp for the rest of his life.

Arthur took the news a lot harder than Jake did. Jake looked as if he thought a limp might be kind of interesting.

Arthur, on the other hand, knew that if they both lived to be a hundred years old, every time he looked at Jake he was going to see that limp.

But still, he almost forgot about it with the agony of being back at school. The first few days went by in a haze of disbelief. He sat at his desk like a sack of cement, hearing and seeing nothing. Then, on the Monday morning of the second week, they were herded off to the gym for assembly, all the classes jammed in together, and Mr. Wheeler, the principal, came in and got up on the little stage at the end of the room and said he had an important—no, a momentous—announcement to make.

Arthur stopped listening. The gym had high windows that you couldn't look out of, like a prison, so he looked at his feet instead and thought that he would rather be dead than be here. After a minute or two, though, he became aware of a stir in the room—kids were looking at each other, some of them were grinning and looking excited—and then he caught a word or two of what Mr. Wheeler was saying. "Duty" was one of the words, and "patriotism" was another. And it turned out that his momentous announcement actually was quite momentous. Canada was at war.

There had been rumours for quite a while about a war coming. In fact, there had been something about England being at war with Germany in the *Temiskaming Speaker* the previous week, but it hadn't meant much to Arthur and wouldn't have even if he hadn't been preoccupied by guilt. There was a joke that the only news that mattered in the North was the weather, but he couldn't see what was supposed to be funny about it. It was true. His father would say the same. His mother was the only one in the family who was interested in what was going on in the world outside. She read the paper and would have liked a wireless, too–the *Speaker* came out only once a week, so the news was always out-of-date by the time they got it. But when Arthur and his father got in from the fields in the evening, they were so tired they wouldn't have cared if half the world had been wiped off the map.

But now it seemed the world had come to Struan. Mr. Wheeler, standing on the rickety little stage at the front of the gym, was reading to them from the speech that the prime minister himself, Mr. Mackenzie King, had broadcast to the nation. "*The forces of evil have been loosed in the world,*" Mr. Wheeler read. He looked out at his audience, a gymful of schoolchildren, graded by age and size, the youngest sitting on the floor at the front, the older ones standing at the back. His face was grave. "*The forces of evil,*" he repeated. Maybe he liked the sound of it, because he repeated it again, in capitals this time. "*THE FORCES OF EVIL!*" He let the words echo around the gym. "And every able-bodied man"–he dropped his voice and looked slowly around the room, not reading anymore, making his own speech now–"every able-bodied man will be anxious to go to the defence of our mother country. Those of you who are not old enough as yet should not despair." He looked gravely at the younger children seated on the floor at his feet. "Your turn will come." He lifted his head and smiled at the older boys. "Those of you who *are* old enough will be proud, I know, to serve your country, and will do so *valiantly.*"

School was dismissed for the day. Arthur started to walk home but then changed his mind and went back into Struan. He guessed that when the other guys heard the news they'd probably come into town. It was full of people already–Arthur had never seen so many people all together before. They were gathered in little clutches around the front of the post office and on the steps of the bank. The older ones mostly looked worried and serious, the younger ones excited. Half a dozen boys were laughing and shrieking and pushing each other off the steps of the drugstore. While Arthur watched, Mr. Phillips, the druggist, came out and told them it was no day for behaviour like that.

Arthur hung around on the outskirts of a group of men by the post office. They were saying that it would all be over in a matter of weeks, that this Hitler guy was full of gas. Arthur listened to them, head down, but keeping an eye out for Carl or one of the others. Finally he saw Carl and Ted coming down the road and went to meet them.

"Hi," Ted called. "You heard, eh?"

"Yeah."

"Whaddaya think?" Carl said. "You going to join up?"

"Yeah," Arthur said again. He saw that it was the answer to everything. He'd sign up and go to the war, and even if it lasted only a couple of weeks, his mother would never be able to send him back to school. No one, not even his mother, could send someone who had been in uniform back to school. He would fight for his country. That would be a good thing to do, something he could set against the terrible events of the summer.

He didn't discuss it with his parents. They had heard the news by the time he got home but if the idea of him joining up had crossed their minds they didn't say so. He guessed they'd be hoping it wouldn't occur to him. His mother would try to stop him going and his father might too. His father didn't approve of war. He'd been in the last one and it had put him off wars for good. Arthur felt bad about deceiving them but he didn't know what else to do.

He met up with Carl and Ted and a couple of others that evening after supper. Carl had heard that there were enlistment teams travelling around the North signing people up, but they decided they wouldn't wait for that. What if the teams had never heard of Struan? It wasn't very big and might not even be on the map. It would be safer to go down to North Bay—that was where most men were going. They agreed to give it a couple of days just in case the *Speaker* had got it wrong and there wasn't a war after all, but by the following day it was clear that it really was happening.

The next morning the whole bunch of them—Arthur and Ted and Jude Libovitz and Carl and Carl's two older brothers and a couple of guys from the sawmill and two Indian guys from the reserve—set out together. Arthur left home at the usual time, as if he were going to school. It made him sweat to think what his parents would say when they found out, but by then it would be done. Once you had enlisted, that was that.

He'd been so busy worrying about his parents' reaction that it wasn't until he was in the back of the truck—they had borrowed Carl's father's old flatbed—that he started to think about what it was going to mean for his father in practical terms. Then he felt so bad he almost jumped out. How could he walk off and leave his father to man- age the farm on his own with debts up to his ears? But then he reasoned that there were still men roaming the country looking for work, and though his father couldn't afford to pay them, many of them were so desperate that they were prepared to work for three square meals and a bed in the barn. And anyway, the war would be over in a few weeks and then he'd be free to work with his father all day and every day for the rest of his life, so it was going to work out for the best all around.

They had a good day for the trip. Warm and sunny. They'd all thrown their coats on the floor of the truck and they sat on them and watched the trees and the rocks and the fields go by. They got to New Liskeard and then headed south, through Temagami. Already Arthur was farther from home than he'd ever been in his life. Carl had brought a big bag of apples and they sat there munching on them, talking about what was to come. They decided they were all going to join the army. Ted said he didn't like the sound of the navy—what happened if your ship went down?—and as for the air force, forget it. None of them had any faith in those parachute things; they all had done a fair bit of hunting and they'd seen the way birds came hurtling to the ground when they'd been shot. "And they're mostly feathers," Carl said. "They don't weigh nothin'. Think how fast we'd fall. Man, we'd make such a hole in the ground they wouldn't have to dig us a grave."

They talked a bit about the war but nobody had much idea what it was about. There was this German guy, Hitler, and he was trying to take over the world, that was all they knew. There was an awkward spell then because they all suddenly remembered that the Luntz brothers' parents were German. But then Gunter, who was the eldest, must have realized what the silence was about, because he suddenly got mad and said they were as Canadian as anyone else in the truck, as Canadian as anyone else in the whole damned country: they'd been born here, and their parents had given them their blessing to go off to fight for Canada—not England, mind you, they weren't fighting for England, but for Canada—and had told them to take the truck to go and join up, and what more proof did any-body want? Which made them all feel ashamed.

After that they were quiet for a bit. The countryside was still pretty wild. Arthur wondered what Germany would look like, or wherever they ended up. Not as beautiful as Canada, that was a safe bet. He got a kind of ache mid-chest at the thought. Homesick already, and he was only fifty miles from home.

And then suddenly they were in North Bay. It was a big town, way bigger than Struan, buildings everywhere, the roads jammed with cars and trucks and army vehicles. The whole place was swarming with men and boys, hun-dreds of them, it seemed to Arthur, and all of them wanting to sign up. Some seemed to be straight out of the woods, tough-looking guys with beards down to their bellies and clothes that looked like they'd been through a couple of wars already. They would be trappers or hunters or lumberjacks; most of them carried rifles as if they thought the army would expect you to bring your own. It was a mystery to Arthur how they could have heard the news so fast, but there they were. He thought he wouldn't mind being drafted into the same outfit as some of them . . . them and the Indian guys. They looked as if they could take care of themselves all right, and you could bet they were pretty damn good shots.

It wasn't until he had this thought that it came home to him that war was about killing people. He might even get killed himself. The idea struck him as funny. Just a couple of days ago he'd been standing in the school gym-nasium, thinking that he'd rather be dead than be there, and now it looked as if maybe God was going to take him up on it. He didn't believe it, though. Couldn't imagine himself dead. Also couldn't imagine killing anyone, couldn't imagine aiming a gun at someone, far less pulling the trigger. But maybe you could just fire to one side of them and hope they'd do the same for you.

They had parked the truck by this time, and joined the lineup of men, and all the time Arthur was thinking these things they were being herded around like cattle, people asking them questions and filling in forms. Eventually Arthur found himself standing in a big tent, stark naked, being examined by an old guy in uniform who turned out to be a doctor. The doctor asked him more questions, about illnesses he might have had and such things, most of which Arthur didn't know the answer to, and what with that and the embarrassment of standing there in the buff, he couldn't concentrate on what the doctor was saying, and it took him a while to realize that he was being rejected.

"Why?" he said, bewildered, when it finally sank in. "What's wrong with me?"

"Flat feet," the doctor said, scribbling on a form. "Flat as pancakes. Never seen a flatter pair of feet in my life." He looked up at Arthur. "You know they say an army marches on its stomach? It's a lie, son. An army marches on its feet, and those feet wouldn't be up to the job." He leaned back in his chair and guffawed as if he'd cracked a really good joke, and then started scribbling again.

Arthur looked down, flattening his privates with one hand so they wouldn't obscure the view. His feet looked flat all right, but so what? They worked. All the thousands of miles he had trudged across the fields of home, lugging sacks of potatoes, bales of hay, bushels of wheat, and the army thought he wouldn't be able to carry a rifle and a little knapsack across some field in Europe?

"They don't hurt," he said to the doctor. "They've never hurt at all. Except once when my brother threw a knife into one of them."

"Go home, son," the doctor said, without looking up at him. "Next, please."

They gave him a little button to wear on his lapel, to show that he was medically unfit and not a coward. But no one would know what it meant. People didn't come up to you to read what was written on a button before making up their minds about you.

His mother forgave him. When she knew he had been rejected her relief was so great that she forgave him for trying to sign up. His father sat there, shaking his head; Arthur saw that his hands were trembling, but he was past caring. Jake was at the table too. He was up and about now, hobbling around the kitchen. Arthur reckoned he must think being turned down because of flat feet was pretty funny, considering his own injuries, but at least he wasn't smirking. He was just listening, saying nothing.

"You tried, Arthur," his mother said soothingly, her voice full of sympathy now that he was safely home. "You tried your best to serve your country. No one can do more."

Her voice grated on him. It made him want to shout at her, which he had never done. He kept his head down and shovelled in his dinner. Flat feet. He felt sick with humiliation and disappointment. All of his friends were going, of course. It was a repeat of when he was sixteen and they had all left school except him. He was like some poor bloody bullock with its head permanently stuck in a fence, watching the rest of the herd amble off to greener pastures.

"You tried," his mother said again. "No one can help having flat feet, Arthur. There's nothing you can do."

"Sure there is," his father said. He seemed to have recovered from his shock and there was something in his voice—a winding up, a digging in, like a man girding his loins for battle—that made Arthur pause with his fork halfway to his mouth.

"What do you mean, Henry? They've turned him down."

"All those boys," his father said. "All those boys. Otto Luntz? All three boys goin'. How's he goin' to run that farm? Jim Collins? Both his boys gone. Frank Libovitz? Same. They're gonna need men to work in the fields. Country's gotta eat. The army's gotta eat."

"What are you saying, Henry? Arthur tried to go. He offered and they turned him down. They can't ask more of him than that. He's free to carry on with his education."

Arthur's father put down his fork and wiped his hands on his shirt a couple of times, then looked straight down the table at his wife. "Arthur's not sittin' in school when other boys are off fightin' for their country. That's what I'm sayin'. If he can't fight, he has to farm."

His mother said, "Henry, there's no—" but his father raised his hand and cut her off.

"That's the end of it," he said. "I'm tellin' you, Mary. That's the end of it." He picked up his fork and went on with his dinner.

And that was the end of it.

Freedom. Nineteen years old, flat-footed and riddled with guilt, but free at last.

SEVEN

~

Speckled Trout Season Starts on Saturday
Compare Three Ways of Pasturing Cows
—*Temiskaming Speaker*, April/May 1960

When he was younger, Ian had assumed that as you got older things became clear. Adults had seemed so sure, so knowledgeable, not just about facts and figures but about the big questions: the difference between right and wrong; what was true and what wasn't; what life was about. He'd assumed that you went to school because you had to learn things, starting off with the easy stuff and moving on to the bigger issues, and once you'd learned them that was it, the way ahead opened up and thereafter life was simple and straightforward.

What a joke. The older he got, the more complicated

and obscure everything became. He understood nothing anymore—nothing and nobody, including himself.

Cathy broke up with him in April. She said their relationship wasn't going anywhere. He hadn't realized it was supposed to. Where did she want it to go? When he asked her that, she burst into tears. Now she avoided him, turned her back on him, walked off if he tried to talk to her. He felt bad about it. He still liked her and would have preferred to remain friends.

And then there was the equally complicated business of what he was going to do with his life, in terms of a career. A couple of months ago, Mr. Hardy, the history teacher, had asked him to stay behind after school for "a little talk." There were nine of them taking grade thirteen, six boys and three girls, and Mr. Hardy was having little talks with each of them in turn, so Ian had known it was coming.

"Well then," Mr. Hardy had said, closing the door behind Ian and motioning him towards a chair. "What's it to be?" They were in the history classroom. A map of the world hung on the wall behind him, with the British Empire coloured pink. A cartoon was pinned up beside the map—gigantic Canadian soldiers looming over a terrified little Hitler—and beside the cartoon was a newspaper headline, yellowed with age, that read, SUCCESS OF OPERATION PROVIDES JOLT FOR NAZIS. Both cartoon and headline referred to the battle of Dieppe in the Second World War, and Mr. Hardy, who'd had his leg shot off there, had printed a caption for the cartoon in neat black letters that said, THE FIRST CASUALTY OF WAR IS TRUTH. His classes knew more about the battle of Dieppe than they knew about all the other battles in history put together.

Mr. Hardy sat down behind his desk and raised his

eyebrows at Ian. "Am I right to assume I'm speaking to the next Dr. Christopherson?"

He had smiled, and Ian had felt irritation rising up in him like a wave. "I've decided I'd like to study agriculture," he said.

He'd had no idea he was going to say such a thing until the words came out of his mouth, but it was satisfying to see his teacher's reaction.

"Agriculture," Mr. Hardy said slowly, as if he hadn't heard the word before and wasn't too sure what it meant.

"Yes," Ian said. "I'd like to be a farmer."

Mr. Hardy picked up a pencil and doodled a little square on the blotter on his desk. He nodded thoughtfully. Then he looked across at Ian. "You've thought seriously about this, have you, Ian?"

"Yes," Ian said.

"Have you discussed it with your father?"

"Yes." Which was a lie. He hadn't discussed it with any-one, because he had no intention of becoming a farmer. He had spent enough time with Arthur to know that farm-ing was not an easy option. It was just that he seemed to have become allergic to the question. It felt as if people had been asking him that question twice a day since the day he was born. Though maybe it wasn't so. Maybe he just kept asking it of himself.

"Well," Mr. Hardy said after another pause. "There's an excellent school of agriculture in Guelph. Would you like to apply to that?"

Ian's heart started to thump. Was this it, then? Had he just decided his future in a single spasm of irritation?

"Where is . . . Guelph, exactly?" he said, as if that had anything to do with anything.

"Southern Ontario. Not far from Toronto."

There was a long silence. The teacher doodled another square. Ian cast about in his mind for a way out. Finally he said, "Can I think about it?"

Mr. Hardy nodded. "I think that would be a good idea." He looked up and smiled again, and his smile suggested that he knew Ian was bluffing, which irritated Ian so much that he almost decided to become a farmer after all, out of spite.

But here he was, months later, still thinking about it, or to be accurate, still avoiding thinking about it, and the final exams were upon him. Each year the teachers implied that the exams you were taking now were the most critical ones you would ever face, and each year the moment you'd finished you could see the next lot looming. It was like climbing a mountain—it wasn't until you reached the top that you realized it wasn't the top, it was merely a foothill. To add to it all, for some unaccountable reason, in the past year he had started creating hurdles for himself, mini-peaks within the overall mountain range. He'd be annoyed with himself if he didn't achieve an A. He had no idea why. He envied Pete, who seemed to be less concerned about the future with every passing day.

It was math he was studying when his father called him. Math was one subject he'd never worried about. He'd always thought you could either do it or you couldn't, so there was no point in studying for it, and he'd continued to believe that right up until he'd flipped open the textbook earlier in the evening and seen the chapter on differential equations and integration. He'd understood it fine when they'd studied it in class, but now it looked like Greek—in fact, parts of it were—and the exam was tomorrow.

He'd been working for a couple of hours when there was a commotion in the hallway downstairs. Loud voices and scuffling. A moment later his father called him from the foot of the stairs in the calm but very definite tone he used when he needed help now, this minute. Ian got up from his desk and went down the stairs fast.

There was a trail of blood leading from the side door to his father's office, and when he got inside there was a sizable pool of blood on the floor. The room was crowded with people. His father and Sergeant Moynihan were trying to lift a struggling man onto the examination table, and there was another man standing against the wall. Most of the blood was coming from the first man, from a wound in his thigh. Ian stepped forward, grabbed a flailing leg, and helped heave him onto the table. He didn't know the man, but guessed from his accent—not French, but something European—and from the stink of alcohol that he was a logger. He was swearing in fractured English, and Sergeant Moynihan was swearing back. "Just shut up, for Christ's sake," he was saying. "You've caused enough trouble for one night, we don't need to listen to you as well."

"Bloody bastar'," the man said, trying to lunge at the man against the wall. "Stinkin' bloody bastar'."

He was young, early twenties at most, and strongly built, and Sergeant Moynihan had to lean hard on his shoulders while Ian lay across his legs. The second he was on the table Ian's father jammed his hand into the man's groin to stop the bleeding. It had been spurting out, bright red blood. That spurting, pumping action and bright red blood was bad news, Ian knew. His father tapped the man's chest sharply with his free hand and said, "Listen to me. You've got a bad cut here. If you don't let us see to it you're going to be in real trouble. Do you understand?"

"Bastar'," the man said, but he did stop thrashing about. His face was very pale and his forehead was beaded with sweat. A belt was cinched ineffectually around his thigh a couple of inches above the wound—his own belt, evidently; his trousers were sagging down. Below the belt his trouser leg was soaked with blood. A rag had been wrapped around the wound but it had slipped down. "I'm going to need you to do this, Ian," his father said. Ian let go of the man's feet—he was quiet now anyway—and stepped up beside his father. Dr. Christopherson took his hand and wedged it in hard to the groin. "Keep it there," he said. To the policeman he said, "How long has it been since you got to him, Gerry?"

"Fifteen minutes, maybe. Had to get the both of them into the car."

"And how much blood was there when you arrived?"

"Fair-sized pool. All of them crowded around outside Ben's, no one doin' a damn thing to stop it."

Dr. Christopherson was slicing the man's trousers with a pair of scissors, upward from the tourniquet.

"What you *doin'*?" the man said, lifting his head and craning to see. Suddenly he seemed terrified. "What you bloody *doin'*?"

"It's okay," Dr. Christopherson said quietly. "Don't worry. What's your name?" He was working fast; Ian could feel the urgency in his movements. He slit the man's trousers right up to the waist, then slit the underwear too.

"Right," he said to Ian. His voice was calm and quiet; if you didn't know him, you wouldn't realize there was any cause for concern. "Now we can see what we're doing. Your job is to shut off the femoral artery. I'll show you exactly where in a sec. Don't let up the pressure with your hand just yet."

Ian nodded. His own heart was pumping hard. He'd seen plenty of blood before, but never like this. He was standing in blood; there was a thick pool of it spreading out under the table. His father pulled the man's trousers aside as far as Ian's hand would permit, exposing the groin. The man's genitals flopped out and the doctor tucked them back under the torn trousers. The man didn't seem to notice. He'd stopped resisting in any way. "What's your name?" Dr. Christopherson asked again, sparing a moment to glance at his face, but he didn't respond. It was scary how fast he'd gone from fighting to apathy. He lay still now, staring vaguely at the ceiling. His mouth was open and he was panting: short, shallow breaths.

"Okay," Dr. Christopherson said to Ian. "Now I want you to press right there. Use both thumbs. Press hard."

Ian pressed down, trying to identify the artery with his thumbs. He found it, felt the man's pulse throbbing, and flattened it hard against the bone beneath. The man's genitals spilled out again and he couldn't avoid touching them with the edge of his hand. "Sorry," he said, but the man didn't care.

His father was watching to see that the bleeding had stopped. "Good," he said. "You've got it. Keep it like that." He pulled on the belt to undo the tourniquet and the man gave a high thin scream and arched his back.

Ian struggled to keep his thumbs in position. "Okay," his father said gently. "It'll only take a minute. Just hold on." He removed the belt and started cutting off the bandages around the man's leg.

"Any idea what made the cut?" he asked Sergeant Moynihan. "Knife? Broken glass?"

"Knife. Both of them had knives."

Ian glanced over at the man against the wall. He hadn't even looked at him before, but now he saw that it was Jim Lightfoot, who lived near Pete on the reserve and who had been a year ahead of them in school until he left to work at the lumberyard. He was bleeding from a cut running down the side of his face from forehead to chin. He was moving his head in an odd way, raising his shoulder to wipe the blood away instead of wiping it off with his hand, and Ian realized with a shock that his hands were tied behind his back. Jim felt his glance and looked at him, and Ian gave him a swift, embarrassed nod. Jim looked away.

Dr. Christopherson was peering at the wound in the other man's leg. "We could be in luck," he said. "It's not quite severed. I think we can deal with that. You're going to have to play anesthetist, Gerry, but we have to get some blood into him first."

He glanced at Jim Lightfoot. "You know your blood group, Jim?" Jim looked at him but didn't reply. Dr. Christopherson went over to his desk and opened one of the file cabinets in which he had the medical records, including the blood group of every person in Struan and the surrounding area, plus a list of those who would act as donors in an emergency. He flicked through it for Jim's card, looked at it, and shook his head.

"Group B," he said. "It's going to be you, Gerry." He got two sawhorses from over by the wall and set them beside the examination table.

"Jesus," Sergeant Moynihan said. "It's always me! Why not Ian?"

"Ian is group B too, and we don't know this man's group, and you're group O, which is the best bet. We've been through all of this before. Help me set up the table, please."

"How about your volunteers?" Gerry said. "Get one of them for a change."

"We don't have time," Dr. Christopherson said. "Help me with this, please."

"I hate those bloody needles! How many bastards have I given my own blood to over the years?"

"Gerry, we're in a hurry."

Still grumbling, the policeman helped him put the old door they used as a transfusion table onto the sawhorses.

"Roll up your sleeve and lie down, please." Ian's father was already back at his cabinet, taking things out of the drawer, moving fast.

Ian felt the man give a kind of shudder, then draw in his breath and let it out in a long, slow exhalation. He was still staring at the ceiling. Ian waited for him to take another breath. His father was preparing the transfusion tubing and had his back to them. Sergeant Moynihan was rolling up his sleeve. Ian watched the man's face. Breathe, he thought. The man stared at the ceiling, unblinking. Ian said, "Dad?" His own heart was suddenly thumping so hard he could hardly breathe himself.

His father looked around. He dropped the tubing and came over, put his hand on the side of the man's neck. He shook his head, then raised his hand, fist clenched, and hit the man hard on the chest, over the heart, hard enough that Ian jumped.

"Keep up the pressure." He checked again for a pulse. "Don't let up. We'll try it again."

Again he hit the man, harder this time. Ian felt the shock of it through the man's body. His own hands and shoulders and neck were almost seizing up with the strain of holding the same position, but he scarcely noticed. All of his concentration was taken up with willing the man to breathe. Breathing was so simple—surely he could do it if only he'd try. Ian found himself taking deep breaths to demonstrate how simple it was.

His father checked once more for a pulse and shook his head. "One last time," he said.

He hit the man again. Felt for a pulse. "Poor lad," he said. "Poor lad."

Ian stared at his father. He couldn't believe it. It couldn't be over as quickly, as simply, as that.

Gerry Moynihan said, "That's it?"

"Yes." The doctor sighed, and stepped back. "You can let go, Ian. It's no good."

Ian looked down at the man, who was still staring at the ceiling, who surely in a moment would blink, and finally draw a breath.

"You can let go," his father said again. "He's gone." He went over to the cupboard by the window, got out a sheet, brought it back to the table, and started to unfold it. He said gently, "Let go, Ian." Ian looked down at his hands, his thumbs still pressed into the man's groin. "Come on, now," his father said. Ian made himself take his hands away. A thin stream of blood ran out from the wound. He stepped back from the table, clutching his aching hands in his armpits, and watched his father close the man's eyes and cover him with the sheet. Sergeant Moynihan was whistling between his teeth, looking at Jim Lightfoot. Ian's father went over to the sink and washed his hands, scrubbing them hard, his face grim. He drew a chair out from the wall and positioned it so that it faced the light.

"Come and sit down, Jim," he said. "Let's have a look at you. Take off his handcuffs, Gerry."

Sergeant Moynihan shook his head. "As of right now this boy's on a murder charge."

"This boy's injured. Take off his handcuffs, please, so I can treat him."

"You can treat him just like he is. He's on a murder charge and I'm not taking any chances."

"I'm not going to argue with you, Gerry. I don't treat patients with their hands tied behind their backs."

Ian still couldn't take it in. The way it had happened so fast, between the letting out of one breath and the drawing in of the next. He couldn't comprehend it. He watched the standoff between his father and Gerry Moynihan, but it had no interest for him. In any case, his father would win. With some detached corner of his mind he wondered if the two of them had been classmates at school. They were about the same age. There must be dozens of people in Struan who had been all the way through school with the boy who was now their doctor. One day you'd be gouging each other's eyes out in the schoolyard and the next you'd be obediently saying "aahhh" so he could look at your tonsils, or pulling down your pants so he could stick a needle in your ass.

Gerry Moynihan was digging in the back pocket of his trousers. He pulled out a set of keys. "It's on your head if he runs for it," he said flatly.

"I accept full responsibility," Ian's father said. "Come over here, Jim."

The chair was only a couple of feet away from the table where the dead man lay. Did Jim realize yet that he had taken someone's life? The phrase had a meaning now that it had not possessed before. To take a life. Ian watched while his father cleaned the long, jagged wound and began to stitch it up. Jim gripped the edges of his chair. "Won't take long," Dr. Christopherson said. His stitches were small, precise, perfectly placed. He was proud of his stitching, Ian knew. His one vanity. The scars his patients had were fine, faint lines that faded to nothing in a matter of weeks. With the lumber camp out in the bush and the sawmill down the road, he got a lot of practice.

"Could you phone Reverend Thomas for me, Ian," he said. "Tell him we have a dead man here."

Ian nodded. He went out into the hall and made the phone call. Then he came back into the office. His father was still stitching. He looked up. "You can go, if you like," he said.

On his way out Ian noticed that he had tracked blood into the hall. His footprints merged with the trail of blood the man had left on his way in. A life, spilled on the floor. He took off his shoes and put them down by the wall, neatly, side by side. Then he went up to his room. His math books were still spread out on his desk. He sat down and stared at them for a while. They were monumentally unimportant. At about eleven o'clock he heard a car pull up, and voices in the hall. They would be taking the body to the church for the night.

Shortly after the car drove off, his father came upstairs and stuck his head around the door.

"You okay?" he said.

"Sure," Ian said, half turning in his chair.

"Don't stay up too late."

"No."

His father hesitated. "You did well tonight."

"Thanks," Ian said.

"Sometimes there's nothing we can do."

"No."

His father went back downstairs and Ian heard him moving around down there. At about midnight his father went to bed.

Ian sat on at his desk, thinking about the cold, hard fact of death. "He's gone," his father had said. One moment there had been a man lying on the table, and the next, only a body. They didn't even know the man's name. Didn't know where he had come from. The loggers came and went; many of them were recent immigrants and spoke next to no English. When the trees in one area had been felled, the logging camp would move on and start again. The men had little to do with the town except on the weekends, when they came in to get drunk. The townspeople considered them foul-mouthed and lawless. Their work was dangerous, far more dangerous than working at the sawmill—at least at the mill the saws were fixed and you didn't have to work at terrifying heights. There were no steel cables whipping around, or dead branches hurtling down on you, or sudden shifts of wind toppling trees in the wrong direction. Floating logs didn't roll over and trap you beneath them.

Did the loggers know how suddenly death could over-take them? How it could come upon you out of nowhere? Maybe they did. But it seemed to Ian, alone in the silence of his room, that it made life pointless. What was the sense in making plans, in striving for things, if it could all end like that, in an instant? It felt like a betrayal. Like a monstrous joke on the part of God.

~

The strange thing was, when he woke up in the morning nothing had changed. His first thought was not about the dead logger, or even death in general, it was about the math exam. It seemed shameful, almost indecent. He tried telling himself that the exam didn't matter, since he could be dead by lunchtime, but the fact was, he was unlikely to be dead by lunchtime and the exam mattered a lot. He took the textbook downstairs with him to look at over breakfast.

His father was sitting at the kitchen table eating toast and reading the *Globe and Mail* from the previous Saturday—it still took a couple of days for the papers to make it as far as Struan. He looked up and smiled vaguely as Ian came in. Ian poured himself a bowl of cornflakes and sat down across from him.

"Math, is it?" his father said from behind the paper. He was blotting up toast crumbs with his finger, licking them off and blotting again. Just recently he'd taken to dabbing his finger in the butter first and using the butter to blot up the crumbs. Ian had been disgusted initially, but then he tried it and got hooked, so now both of them did it.

"Yeah."

"You can either do math or you can't." His tone was absentmindedly reassuring.

"Yeah," Ian said. "Question is which."

His father lowered the paper and smiled.

He didn't show any sign of wanting to discuss the events of the night before. There was no trace of the mess in the hall, apart from a suggestion of damp on the dark wood floor. Ian's shoes, carefully cleaned, were standing by the front door. Everything seemed normal. The fact was—Ian saw this suddenly—everything *was* normal. His father was so familiar with death that it didn't warrant discussion. It wasn't a shocking or unusual occurrence, it was commonplace. Which was the most shocking thing of all.

"I'm off," Ian said when he finished his cereal.

"Good luck."

Good luck. Maybe that's all it was. Maybe the whole of life depended not on how hard you tried, how determined you were, how sensible, how smart: maybe the whole shooting match depended on luck.

There were seven of them taking the exam. Cathy had dropped math at the end of grade twelve—she said it made her sick to her stomach—so at least Ian didn't have to face her bitterly turned back. Five of the others were standing in the hall outside the classroom when Ian arrived, waiting for Mr. Turner to show up. They all looked jittery. Fats Fitzpatrick was leaning up against the wall, chewing gum so fast his chins wobbled. Ian looked around for Pete but he hadn't arrived yet.

"How's it going, Fats?" Ian said. Fats nodded and kept chewing. There was something about him that always cheered Ian up. Maybe it was just the fact that he always looked so oppressed that you were bound to feel on top of things by comparison. His father owned the sawmill and Fitzpatrick's Hotel and the holiday cottages down by the lake, which made him the richest man in town. Worrying about all that money had made him bad-tempered and mean, especially with his kids. You could tell just by looking at Fats that his father had told him he'd skin him alive if he failed these exams.

Ron Atkinson and Susan Jankowitz were sitting on a table beside the door. They shifted over to make room for Ian. "I'll be glad when this one's over," Ron Atkinson said. "It's the worst."

Ian nodded.

Susan Jankowitz said, "It's okay for you guys. You're both so brainy." She was hugging herself with nerves. She was a big-busted girl and the hugging did astonishing things to her breasts. *Ma-mas,* Pete called them—"Man, would you look at those ma-mas." They bunched together now and quivered like racoons in a sack. Ian found it almost impossible to keep his eyes off them. "I couldn't sleep last night," she said. "I know I'm going to fail."

"You'll be okay," Ian said, though she wouldn't. He caught a disconcerting echo of his father in his own voice, mindlessly reassuring. "Anyone seen Pete?" He leaned forward around Susan's ma-mas to look down the hall.

Ron said curiously, "What's he taking the exams for?"

"What are you taking them for?" Ian asked, but it came out ruder than he'd intended, so he added, "What are any of us taking them for?"

Ron said, "Does he want to go to university or something?"

"Why not?" Ian said. Back in public school both he and

Pete had skipped a year, while Ron had failed one, so Ron was two full years older than they were but in the same class. He must know how smart Pete was, and yet somehow he *didn't* know it. It was incredible the way people managed to hang on to their prejudices even when the evidence that they were wrong was staring them in the face.

"Is he thinking of leaving the reserve? Having a career?"

"Why not?"

Ron shrugged.

"Here comes Mr. Turner," Susan said. There was still no sign of Pete.

Mr. Turner loped up, a bundle of examination papers clutched to his chest. "My, my, aren't we all looking bright and eager today," he said. "Budding Einsteins, every one. Come in, come in."

He opened the door of the math room and they trooped in behind him. "If you want to sharpen your pencils, do it now. Go to the john, do it now. Say your prayers, do it now. The end is nigh. Judgment Day has dawned. I've had a look at the paper and you're all going to fail." He was grotesquely cheerful.

They milled about for a bit, went to the toilet, came back. They settled reluctantly into their seats. Mr. Turner was ticking off their names on the register.

"Corbiere is missing," he said. "Anybody seen Corbiere?" He looked at Ian and raised his eyebrows. Ian shook his head.

"He's got two minutes," Mr. Turner said. "Time, tide, and exams wait for no man. Fitzpatrick, you're chewing gum. Get rid of it."

Ian rolled his pencil between his fingers. Come on, come on, he said to Pete inside his head. He admired

Pete's nonchalance, but this was going a bit far. Right now it amounted to added stress, and he had more than enough already.

"No Corbiere," Mr. Turner said, looking at his watch. "Time's up."

He went over to close the door. Pete shambled in.

"You're late, Corbiere. For two bits I'd shut the door on you. Take your seat."

Pete nodded at Ian and sat down at his desk. Ian felt a surge of relief mixed with irritation.

"Remember," Mr. Turner said. "Show your working out. I'll say it again: show your working out. There are marks for working out. Okay, everybody ready? Turn your papers over . . . now!"

Ian turned the paper over and looked at the first question. It was a cinch. You could either do math or you couldn't.

"Why were you late?" he said to Pete afterwards.

"I wasn't late."

"He could have kicked you out. You know what he's like."

"He didn't though, did he?" Pete said. They were out by the bike racks, around the back of the school. Pete had turned his bike upside down to adjust the chain and was turning the pedal with his hand. The wheel sang as it spun in the late-morning air.

"If you miss an exam, that's it," Ian said, resentment stirring. Pete's attitude was starting to annoy him.

"You worry too much, man."

With an effort, Ian bit back a retort. Abruptly, it occurred to him that Pete's behaviour might have something to do with the events of the night before—Jim

Lightfoot and the logger. He saw his father, spreading the sheet over the silent figure. Gerry Moynihan, whistling through his teeth. Jim would have spent the night—the first of many nights—in a police cell, and there would be some angry people on the reserve.

"Is this something to do with what happened last night?" he said. In all the years of their friendship, all the thousands of hours of fishing, side by side in Pete's battered old boat, they had never once talked about the tensions between their two communities. The older they got and the more they understood, the less point there seemed to be in talking about it. But now he wanted to know what was going on inside Pete's head. It seemed to him that, of all the kids in the class, Pete was the one who had the most to gain by leaving Struan behind, and the exams were his passport.

"Is what something to do with what?" Pete asked.

"Would you cut it out?" Ian said snappishly. "Is the fact that you nearly missed a final exam connected with the fact that Jim Lightfoot was in a fight last night and a man died and Jim is in jail? That's what I'm asking."

"Oh, that," Pete said. He turned his head up towards the sun and closed his eyes, still spinning the bicycle wheel with his hand. "That's nothin' to get worked up about, man. That's just another Indian in jail, accused of somethin' he didn't do. Nothin' new in that. Happens all the time."

Ian managed—just—not to yell at him, not to say, What are you acting like this with me for? I didn't do anything! He swallowed the words and studied Pete's profile in silence.

"What happened last night is nothing to do with you," he said finally.

"Oh, right," Pete said.

"It goddamned well isn't!" Ian said, suddenly enraged by his tone. "You have a choice, whether or not you let yourself get drawn into all that crap! It's history! Some people are stuck in it, but *you* have a choice!"

Pete, his eyes still closed, his face still turned to the sun, said, "You know what I like about you, man? You have such a simple view of life."

Ian cycled home, anger and frustration gnawing at him. He wished he could withdraw from everything—go and live in a cave. He couldn't imagine how mankind had managed to make such a mess of things. He threw his bike down by the porch, climbed the steps, flung open the door, and found himself staring at a trail of blood on the floor. His heart gave a jolt, but then he saw that relative to the night before it wasn't much—just smears and splatterings at regular intervals leading from the side door to the waiting room. He peered into the room. Office hours were over for the morning and Margie, the nurse, had gone home for lunch. There was no one there except Fats Fitzpatrick, who was sitting on one of the chairs. His foot, wrapped in something strange—maybe a shirt: there seemed to be a couple of sleeves sticking out of the bundle—was resting in a small puddle of blood.

"You're bleeding on my floor," Ian said. He could feel the tension inside him easing already. Any distraction would have been good right now, but Fats in the waiting room was excellent.

"Sorry," Fats said. "I can't help it." His large moon-face was even paler and more doleful than usual, but he'd looked like that when he came out of the exam.

"If you were trying to commit suicide," Ian said, "it's your wrist you want, not your foot."

"I cut it on a tin can," Fats said.

"No kidding?" Ian said. "How did you manage that?" He dragged one of the other chairs over in front of Fats, took half a dozen *National Geographic*s and Eaton's catalogues from the pile on the table, put them on the chair, reached down and lifted Fats's foot onto the pile.

"I don't want to talk about it," Fats said. "This has been the worst goddamned day of my life."

"You sure didn't waste any time," Ian said. "We haven't been out of the exam an hour." He was watching the foot. Blood was still leaking out, though more slowly. Now it was ruining the magazines. He looked at the door to his father's office. "You checked that there's someone in there with him, did you?" he said.

Fats nodded. "What'll he do? Like, what do you do with a cut?"

"You don't want to know," Ian said. "Take my word for it."

"You're a real bastard, Christopherson, you know that?"

Ian nodded. "So's my father. It runs in the family." The cut was still leaking. He should press on it, direct firm pressure on the wound, but Fats would yell and possibly hit him—he was their star quarterback and could pack quite a punch. Ian got some more magazines and added them to the pile. At least it was just seeping, not spurting. He didn't fancy jamming his hand into Fats's meaty groin.

"Will he put stitches in it? I mean, he doesn't normally do that, does he? He doesn't stitch every little cut a person comes with."

"I don't think that's a little cut," Ian said. He went over and tapped on the door to his father's office. His father said, "Come in." Ian opened the door and stuck his head around it. Mrs. Jenner was sitting beside his father's desk with her sleeve rolled up, displaying a monstrously swollen elbow.

"Hello, dear," she said. "How are you?"

"Hi, Mrs. Jenner. I'm fine, thanks." He looked at his father and said, "Fairly urgent," in an undertone, hoping Fats wouldn't hear. His father nodded. "Okay. Be with you in a minute."

Ian went back and sat down beside Fats. "So tell me how you managed to cut it on a tin can," he said. "Was the can on the table at the time? And was it tuna, or beans, or peaches, or what?"

"Piss off," Fats said.

"It makes a difference to the treatment," Ian said. "If it was tuna he'll do one thing, because it's fish, and if it was beans or peaches he'll do another. For your sake I hope it was beans or peaches." He thought for a moment. "The worst one's corned beef, actually. That's a real nightmare. Was it corned beef?"

"Piss off."

He left Fats with his father and went out in the canoe. There'd been an east wind blowing for days, which normally meant rain, but it hadn't materialized yet. The lake was choppy, little scuds of wind ruffling the water, and he had to work at keeping the canoe steady. The sky was grey on grey—low dark clouds hanging under higher paler ones, the whole lot moving slowly across the sky.

Without thinking, he'd automatically turned west towards Hopeless Inlet. It was where Pete had nearly been

pulled out of his boat a year ago and ever since then
Pete's mission in life had been to get even with whatever
it was that had grabbed his line. Normally Ian would
have joined him, but Pete's comment still rankled. They
seemed to have reached an impasse, and he didn't know
why, or what to do about it.

He turned the canoe into the wind and paddled hard.
The cool air felt good on his face—he imagined it filling
his lungs, flowing through his whole system. It was hard
going, though—the wind gusting against the canoe, swinging the bow around. When he reached the mouth of Slow
River he turned into it for a rest. Rounded humps of pink
granite rose out of the water on either side, forming
shields against the wind, and between them the river
flowed smooth as syrup. Ian paddled slowly, trying not
to disturb the stillness, trying instead to absorb it. He
needed to clear his mind of the tangled mess that seemed
to occupy it nowadays—exams, death, the future, the past,
his father, women, his friend. He craved stillness, the
mental equivalent of the river's flow.

He concentrated on the movement of the water, the
small tight whirlpools left by his paddle, the smooth curve
of water over rocks beneath the surface, the narrow V-shape
fanning out from the bow of the canoe, but thoughts kept
crawling back in. He slid the canoe up beside a low bank
of rock and climbed out. As soon as he stood up he was
battered by the wind again so he sat down on a shelf of
rock, low down by the water, and watched the river drifting
by, and gave himself over to worrying.

He was getting good at it, that was for sure. If there were
an exam in worrying he'd top the class. Earlier he had
been looking around his room, wondering which of his

possessions he should take with him to university: a few books—*Moby-Dick, The Last of the Mohicans, The Catcher in the Rye*—his radio, his camera, a photo of himself and Pete holding up a pike, twenty-six pounds, thirty-four inches long, their biggest ever. That had started him worrying about Pete again, and had also made him realize that he didn't have a photograph of his father without his mother, which had set him thinking about her. He wanted no reminders of her cluttering up his new life.

He wished he could prevent his mother from getting hold of his address, wherever he ended up, but he knew his father would give it to her. She still wrote every week and in three years he had not opened a single letter; they went straight into the wastepaper basket, envelopes intact. Even so, from the envelopes themselves, he knew more about her life than he wanted to know. Her last name was no longer Christopherson, for instance: she had married the geography teacher. And they had moved to Vancouver a year ago. She phoned him on his birthday and at Christmas, and for his father's sake he didn't hang up on her, but once he left home he reckoned he would be able to sever that contact as well.

The pain of what she had done no longer filled the whole of him, but what was left was a hot, glowing coal of bitterness that flared up whenever he thought about her. He wanted to get rid of that as well. He wanted to be—to have been—untouched by her betrayal, as if she were nothing to him and never had been. Just a casual visitor who had stopped for a while and then moved on. He had a fantasy that in a few years' time they would pass on a street somewhere and not recognize each other. That would be good. That was what he was aiming for.

There was something in the water: the movement caught his eye. It was heading directly towards him. It wasn't until it was about ten feet away that he was able to work out what it was—a water snake, with a frog in its mouth. It kept coming towards him; presumably it thought he was part of the rock. When it reached his feet, it slid the first eighteen inches or so of its length out of the water, drawing a smooth, glistening S-shape on the pale rock, and then, to Ian's consternation, rested its sleek, dark head—plus frog—on the top of his shoe. Then it yawned hugely and began to eat.

Ian, holding himself rigidly still, watched with fascination and disgust. The frog was headfirst inside the snake's mouth but very much alive. It was at least twice the diameter of the snake's head and fought hard, legs thrashing, toes scrabbling for purchase, pulling backwards with all its might—he could feel the struggle through the leather upper of his shoe. His impulse was to try to rescue the frog, but he could see the absurdity of that. The frog was the snake's dinner, after all. And he himself had eaten beef last night.

The snake, having moved its jaws about until the frog was in exact alignment, began to swallow, slowly—the lack of haste was the most disconcerting thing about it. Waves of contractions flowed along its body, sucking the frog down. The frog fought furiously. It managed to hook the toes of its left hind foot into the hard edge of the snake's lower jaw and set its right hind foot against the side of Ian's shoe and pushed for all it was worth, muscles swelling and straining with the effort. The fight went on and on. Sometimes it almost seemed that the frog would win its freedom, but blood was making a red slick on its back now and there was no real doubt about the outcome. This is how it goes, Ian thought. Like it or not, this is how it goes.

It was nearly dusk by the time he turned back. The wind was increasing and the waves were building up. They weren't big yet but the water was choppy and the canoe bounced around like an eggshell. As Ian neared the dock he saw that there was someone sitting on it, a dark figure, with knees drawn up, arms clasped around knees. Cathy.

She watched him silently as he manoeuvred the canoe alongside. He put down his paddle and grabbed the dock to stop the canoe smacking against it.

"Hi," he said cautiously.

"Hi."

He got out of the canoe and hauled it up, then flipped it over, belly down, in case of rain. "You been here long?"

"A while." Her voice was muffled by her arms, which were still wrapped around her knees. She was wearing a light jacket that made a ruffling sound in the wind. When he sat down beside her, he noticed that she'd been crying, and his heart sank.

"You okay?" he said. She put her head on her arms and began to cry. "Hey," he said, his heart sinking lower still. He put his arm around her. "Hey, Cath, what's wrong? What's happened? Has something happened?"

He pulled her closer, searching guiltily through his mind for something he might have done to upset her further—apart from not missing her all that much, which she couldn't have known about. She was leaning against his shoulder now and he could feel his shirt getting wet.

"Hey," he said softly. "Come on. Tell me what's happened."

She lifted her head, finally, and looked at him. She was very pretty when she cried. Her eyes became luminous pools and when the pools spilled over, the tears traced clear silvery lines down her cheeks. He wondered if she would have cried so much if she'd been made ugly by tears, if her nose became red and swollen and her eyes puffed up.

"Nothing's happened," she said. "Not really. It's just that I've discovered . . . how much I love you. I've just wanted to . . . *die*, Ian. These past few weeks, I've just wanted to die. I just . . . don't care about . . . anything anymore. About the exams or anything else. I'm going to fail, and I don't care. I just need to be with you. I've just realized that it's the only thing that matters."

Oh God, he thought. He looked out over the lake. Whitecaps were starting to appear; a last lone gull was skimming the tops of them, graceful as a skater. He felt bowed down under the weight of her love. He wanted to say, Look, I'm sorry, but I'm just too tired to think about this at the moment, could you come back next week? But he couldn't say that, and anyway, next week he still wouldn't know how to reply.

And then, to complicate things still further, the thought slid into his mind that, given how Cathy was feeling, he could almost certainly persuade her to have sex with him, right now, right here on the dock. He was sure of it. He started to get an erection just thinking about it. He shifted his position, drew her closer to him, and with his free hand unzipped her jacket. She was wearing a sweater over her blouse; he slid his hand up underneath it, cupped her breast for a moment, then began undoing buttons. Cathy turned her face towards him and lifted her mouth to his, willingly, trustingly, and he knew she was going to let him, and simultaneously, with a feeling close to despair, knew that he couldn't go through with it. Not because of his principles, not because it would be taking advantage of her, but because, when it came right down to it, he was chicken. Too scared of the consequences to take the risk.

Cathy was still looking up at him, her eyes questioning now. He had to say something. He whispered, "I respect you too much, Cath. We should wait."

It sounded so false, so unbelievably corny, that if he had been her he would have got up and walked off and never spoken to him again. But Cathy smiled, and curled up against him, and whispered back, "I'm so lucky to have found someone like you. I can't believe how lucky I am."

~

It was a relief when Saturday came. There was a simplicity about his work on the farm that seemed to be the perfect antidote to everything else. He envied Arthur the smooth pattern of his days. Sure, he had worries, but in many ways there just couldn't be a more perfect life than plodding up and down a field all day, under the pure, uncomplicated sky.

That morning he began plowing the ten-acre, which bordered the northernmost edge of the farm. The Dunns' boundary was marked by the Crow River, and when you were working on the ten-acre you could hear it in the background all day, the smooth cold rushing of it filling the gaps between the clinking of the horses' harnesses and the bickering of crows. It was his favourite field. More than in the others, which were so well tended, so tamed, you could see the history of the farm in this field.

Needless to say, it wasn't Arthur who had told him its history: it was Laura. Details came out from time to time, generally at dinner. "It was a bush farm, wasn't it, Arthur? Just a small clearing hacked out of the bush. By your grandfather?"

A nod from Arthur. "Yeah."

"Most of the farms up here started off as bush farms, Ian. Sometimes they didn't even bother felling the trees to begin with, they just planted turnips and potatoes in among them, to tide them over the first winter. And then when they did cut down the trees, they had to wait years for the stumps to rot enough to dig them out. How many years does it take, Arthur? Five? Or even more than that?"

"Kinda depends."

"And the rocks—getting the rocks out. You've seen the size of some of them, Ian. Can you imagine the work?"

Down at the ten-acre he could imagine it. Just yards away, on the other side of the river, it was wilderness still.

He liked plowing. He was getting good at it, too. When he first started he'd been astoundingly bad. He had thought there was nothing to it, that you lined up the horses and leaned on the plow and off you went—Arthur made it look that easy. His furrows were so straight they looked as if they'd been drawn with a ruler. And the horses were every bit as good; you didn't have to tell them a thing. They lined themselves up, side by side, one standing in the latest furrow, the other on unplowed land, and then they set off, the one in the furrow placing each huge, dinner-plate-size foot exactly in front of the last.

When they got to the end they turned themselves around, stepping sideways, precisely in time with each other, big as buses, delicate as dancers, sidling around until they were lined up again, facing the other way. A tractor couldn't have turned that tightly in a million years. Ian never got tired of watching them.

His own first furrow had looked like the path of a drunk on a Saturday night. Arthur had set him up with Robert and Edward because they were the more experienced team, and Ian had thought he was doing fine until they got to the end of the field and turned around. The horses had practically recoiled with shock—certainly they both took a step backwards. Robert had looked at him over his shoulder as if to say, What the *hell* is that? It had taken Ian months to get the hang of it. But he took pride in his fields now. They were nothing compared to Arthur's, but they were no longer a total disgrace.

Carter had a row with his mother over dinner.

"I told you I was goin'!" He was red in the face and his voice was shrill. "I told you Lucas said to come on Saturday afternoon, and you said okay!"

"Carter, I can't believe I said you could be away for the whole of a Saturday afternoon. I need you to do the row crops. I haven't been able to get at them all week."

"You did!" Carter was so outraged that Ian decided he was telling the truth. "I told you he's got these steer-horn handlebars, and he doesn't like them, so he said we could swap and I should come out to his place today! I told you!"

"Why can't you both bring your bikes to school?" Laura said, slapping a great mound of mashed potato onto his plate, spilling half of it onto the table in her exasperation. "Why can't you swap there?"

"He can't cycle to school!" Carter said. "He lives miles away! He gets the bus! That's why I have to go today—it'll take me hours! I *told* you, Mum! I told you on Monday! You *never listen!*" He pushed his chair back from the table and slammed out of the house. A moment later they heard the crunch of bicycle wheels on the drive.

"I do remember something about it," Laura said wearily. "But I'm sure I wouldn't have said he could go today."

The truth was, Ian admitted to himself, she didn't listen. Sometimes it was as if she was in a world of her own. A quieter one, presumably. One where there weren't unceasing demands on her time. He tried to imagine her sitting on a sofa with her feet up, but abruptly he was reminded of his mother, so he pushed the thought away.

"The thing is," Laura was saying, "Betty Hart is sick. Your father said she'd end up in the hospital if she didn't stay in bed, Ian, so I've been looking after her little one all week. I'm taking him again this afternoon. He's a good child, but clingy, you can't put him down, and the row crops are in such a state."

"Would you like me to do them?" Ian asked. The vegetable garden was just around the side of the house. He looked at Arthur. "Or do you want me to carry on with the plowing?"

Arthur chewed, considering. "Guess you'd better do the row crops."

"That would be wonderful," Laura said. "Just wonderful."

Which was great. The garden would get done, and maybe Laura wouldn't go on at Carter when he got back, and he, Ian, would be less than a hundred yards away from her for the whole afternoon.

Julie and March came with him when he went out to start on the row crops. They announced that they were going to help.

"I had a feeling you might," Ian said resignedly. "Do you help your mum when she does the weeding?"

"No," Julie said. "She doesn't need help."

"I see," Ian said. He rummaged around in the toolshed and found a couple of hand forks. "Here you go. Do you know which ones are weeds?"

"The green ones," March said.

"Well, yes and no," Ian said. "The big green ones are vegetables. See this?" He pointed to the feathery top of a carrot. "This is a carrot. You don't want to dig it out, it needs to grow some more."

March looked at him suspiciously. "That's not a carrot," he said.

"Yes it is." Ian eased enough soil back from the carrot to show its root. "See?"

March looked flabbergasted. "It's a carrot!" he said. The good thing about kids, Ian thought—one of the few compensations for them being such a pain in the neck—was how astonished they could be by things you completely took for granted.

"He didn't even know!" Julie said, doubling over with mirth.

"Get weeding, you," Ian said. "You're wasting time being mean to your brother. These little green things are the weeds, March, and you don't pull them out, you dig them out. Everybody okay with that?"

March dug furiously for a minute and a half and then wandered off, back to the house. Julie carried on for a while, carefully digging out each weed and placing it neatly on the grass at the edge of the vegetable patch, all the little thread-like roots pointing in the same direction. After a while she got tired of that and just scratched around with a stick. Then she got tired of that too and sat down on the grass to watch Ian.

"Having a break *already*?" he said.

She nodded. She was looking quite a bit like her mother today, Ian thought. One day she might be almost as beautiful.

There was a call from the house—Laura's voice, calling Julie. Julie narrowed her eyes, wondering whether to hear it or not.

"Your mum's calling," Ian said firmly. "Go and see what she wants."

She ran off and disappeared around the side of the house. A minute or two later March appeared, carrying something—a plate of cookies. He was walking very carefully, holding the plate in both hands, concentrating hard.

"That's very nice of you," Ian said when March came up. He put down his hoe and rescued the plate, which was listing dangerously. "Are they all for me?"

"No," March said.

"Oh. Right. Are any of them for me?"

"I can have *one*," March said, his tone of voice showing what he thought of that.

"You'd better choose which one you want first, then." Ian squatted down and held out the plate so that March could see the options. March picked up a cookie, hesitated, put it back. Picked up another one, put it back. And another.

"What exactly is it that you're looking for?" Ian asked when they didn't seem to be getting anywhere. "The biggest one or the one with the most chocolate chips?"

March twisted the bottom of his T-shirt in both hands and hoisted it up and down over his smooth round belly.

"Oh, I get it," Ian said. "You want the biggest one *and* the most chocolate chips. Tricky."

A movement at the edge of his field of vision caused him to look up. Julie had appeared around the corner of the house, carrying a tray of glasses. Behind her was Laura, with Mrs. Hart's baby in her arms. Ian felt a surge of pleasure.

"Here comes your mum," he said. March quickly crammed a cookie into his mouth and chewed fast.

Laura frowned at him as she came up. "Now that's the last one," she said. The baby was covered in chocolate from ear to ear.

Julie held the tray of glasses out to Ian. "It's lemonade," she said.

"Thank you," Ian said, taking one and putting the plate of cookies down on the grass. If only the kids would go now, and take the baby, and leave Laura and him alone, just for two minutes. Just two minutes of her uninterrupted presence, on this beautiful warm afternoon.

There was the sound of a car and they all looked up. It was coming along the track from the main road, trailing a cloud of dust. Ian didn't recognize it—it didn't belong to anyone in the area. As it got closer he saw that it was a Cadillac, two-tone, red and cream, big wings at the back, shiny chrome trim. Ian watched it admiringly—he'd never seen one like it.

"Who could this be?" said Laura, swinging the baby over to her other hip. "Someone must be lost."

The car pulled into the farmyard and they all started walking towards it. March ran ahead, Julie hung on to her mother, Ian followed on behind, intrigued. The car came to a stop and the dust caught up with it and settled slowly. The door opened and a man got out. Laura stopped so suddenly that Ian bumped into her.

"Sorry," he said.

She didn't reply. She stood there, motionless. Across the farmyard, the stranger leaned back comfortably against the car, folded his arms, and smiled at them.

Afterwards, looking back on that first meeting, trying to remember what his initial reaction had been, searching through his memory for any clue, however small, to what was to come, all Ian could remember was the smile.

EIGHT

~

Only One-fifth of Seeding Completed Prior to Downpour
Premier King Gives Parliament Outline of War Programme
—*Temiskaming Speaker*, May 1940

"Listen, Artur," Otto Luntz said. "Sit down, listen. I read you."

He fumbled around in his shirt pocket for his spectacles and grimly set them on his nose. "*It is still raining,*" he read. He made his voice deep and slow, the way Gunter's was, so that was who the letter was from. Every couple of weeks Arthur went over to the Luntzes' farm after supper to see if there were any letters from the boys; none of them was what you'd call a born letter writer, but something generally arrived from one or another of them about twice a month.

Otto Luntz looked up. "Dey are in England still. Still! Doing nutting! Sitting around all day, fat as pigs!"

"Read the letter, Otto!" Mrs. Luntz said, setting a cup of tea and a plate of cookies in front of Arthur. He could always tell if a letter had arrived the minute she opened the door. She was a big, heavy woman, somewhat stern, unleavened by the humour her husband had in such abundance, but when she'd heard from her boys it seemed to Arthur that her whole body got lighter; she positively floated around that kitchen.

In the early days he had felt ashamed and embarrassed to be there when their sons were not, but both Mr. and Mrs. Luntz seemed so genuinely glad to see him that he had stopped worrying about it. He saw that, apart from anything else, it gave them an excuse to read the letters yet again, to hear the boys' voices in the words they wrote. The letters were just about in shreds from being folded and unfolded so often.

"*You never seen so much rain,*" Mr. Luntz read on. "*It's been raining for weeks, everything's soaked. No action yet and nobody seems to know when there will be. We went on a training course, pretty good, except we already knew it all. Eric and Carl doing fine, send their love. Well, no more news. Hope you are both doing okay.*"

He put the letter down and looked at Arthur with mock severity. "Vot sort of letter, eh? *It's raining.* So vot! It is raining here! One, two, tree . . . five sentences, an' den dey say, *No more news.* I tell you, Artur, Gertie and me, ve give our farm to you, okay? In our vills, ve leave everyting to you. Our boys don't deserve it."

But the relief showed plain in his face. No news was good news.

~

Month after month, the letters kept coming from England. Practically the whole Canadian army seemed to be stuck there, sitting on its hands. *Went to London last week on leave,* Carl wrote. (The best letters were from Carl, in Arthur's opinion.) *You never seen such a town, it'd take you days just to walk across it. Saved up our pay, went to see a show—you wouldn't approve of the women, Ma. Tarts on the street, too, all made up like I don't know what. If you see Art, tell him he's missing out on a real education.*

Everybody's real fed up with doing nothing, though. They've got us in these stupid little tents, whenever the wind blows they collapse. They keep sending us on training courses—we must be the best-trained army in the whole damned war. We just want a chance to show what we can do.

1940 came and went, and still none of the boys from the Struan area had seen a single minute of action. Arthur stopped feeling quite so guilty about being at home. No one had handed him a white feather or crossed the road to avoid speaking to him—everyone knew he had tried to enlist. It seemed he was doing more to support the war effort than his friends were. At least he was producing food. In fact, he was probably feeding them. Carl and the others could be eating a ham sandwich right this minute: ham, bread, and butter, all thanks to him. He imagined the whole crowd of them, Carl, Eric, Gunter, Ted, Jude, and the rest, squatting on their haunches in their useless little tents while they ate their sandwiches. He missed them, all of them, but especially Carl. The country seemed empty without them.

People at home, farmers in particular, were having a tougher time than their troops were. The Dunns didn't fare badly—with Arthur still being at home they were no worse off than before the war—but many were having a real struggle. Otto and Gertie, for instance: when they gave the boys their blessing to go off to war the country was crawling with out-of-work men looking for farm labouring jobs, but then, almost overnight, the men were gone. They'd all enlisted too, or gone to war-related jobs that paid real money.

Otto had a tractor, which meant he could cover a fair amount of ground, but the Luntzes' farm was bigger than the Dunns' and was more than one man could manage, even if he had a whole fleet of tractors. Gertie couldn't help; she had a big vegetable plot and chickens and pigs and a few cows for milking—there just weren't any more hours in her day. So Otto was on his own, out there in the fields. Early mornings, if the wind was in the right direction, Arthur could hear the tractor, and it seemed to him it had a lonely sound.

He and his father helped out as much as they could, but even with the three of them working together, stooking at ten o'clock at night sometimes, the stooks throwing huge spooky shadows in the narrow beam of the tractor's headlights, they couldn't get it all in. Waste. It was frustrating. For the past ten years there had been no market for anything and cheap labour to burn, and now, suddenly, there was a market for everything but no one left to gather it in. And the government kept on at them about increasing their production. Grow more food! Mother England needed food! She needed ham and cheese, millions of pounds of it, and eggs (powdered) and milk (condensed), and wheat and flour and just about everything else you could think of.

In the spring of 1941 Otto came over one night with a proposition. The boys were still in England, going crazy with boredom, and Otto had spent the winter thinking things over. It looked as if the war might drag on for a while and even with help from Arthur and his father there was just no way he could work all his fields. He was anxious not to let them go to ruin. He wanted the farm to be in good shape for the boys when they got home.

"I vunder if you take some of my fields?" he said. He was sitting at the kitchen table. Arthur's mother had given him a mug of tea and he wrapped his big red hands around it, the fingernails so split and blackened they looked like chips of wood. What he wondered, he said, was if they'd like to take on some of his land and turn it over to pasture so that they could increase their dairy herd. He was going to concentrate on pigs. He'd keep about half his acreage for barley for the pigs—he could manage half of it all right. The Dunns could make proper use of the rest and keep it in good order by doing so, and maybe pay him a bit of rent if they were able. Then, when the war was over and his boys came home, everything could go back to normal. If Arthur and his father found at that stage that they had too many heifers, they could sell some and make a tidy profit, or maybe even buy some more land. What did they think?

Arthur and his father looked at each other. They'd been wondering if they should buy a few more heifers. Two years ago it would have been out of the question, but thanks to the war they had a little money now. Not much, grant you—the government gave it with one hand and took it back in taxes with the other—but still, for the first time ever, they had a little real cash. Cash, which you could hold in your hand, and count, and use to pay off the debt from Jake's medical bills, which they had now almost done. If the war lasted, and there was no sign that it was going to end anytime soon, they would be able to sell any amount of milk. There would be money enough to rent some of Otto's land and buy a few heifers. Maybe even their own bull. And when the war ended, well, they would see.

Otto was looking from one to the other of them. Arthur couldn't help noticing, couldn't suppress a small surge of pride that Mr. Luntz recognized that he was part of the picture now. His mother was sitting in the chair by the stove knitting socks for the boys overseas, listening, but staying out of it. Not too long ago she would have been at the table herself, but she seemed happy now to leave things to the two of them. Jake had come into the room at some stage—Arthur noticed him, leaning against the wall, watching them—but he didn't stay long. He was not part of the picture, needless to say. But then, Arthur reasoned, trying to quell the guilt that the mere sight of Jake always raised in him, he had never wanted to be.

"You vant to tink about it?" Mr. Luntz said anxiously.

"Guess we're done thinking," Arthur's father said, and Arthur nodded, and Otto smiled, and the three of them finished their tea and pulled on their boots and went out to look at Otto's land, which was lying pale and peaceful in the moonlight.

August 1942. Otto and Gertie Luntz received two telegrams in one day.

Arthur's mother was beside herself. "How can I face Gertie?" she said, fiercely brushing away the tears she felt she had no right to shed. "What can I say to her? What can I possibly say?"

Arthur's stomach had gone cold when he heard the news and he was ashamed of his relief when it turned out that Carl was okay, it was Eric and Gunter who had been killed. Fighting for Canada, the home of their birth. They'd finally left England, all the boys from Struan together, as part of the Royal Regiment of Canada assault force. They landed on the beach at the German-held port of Dieppe and Gunter and Eric were killed the moment they set foot on the ground. They were not the only casualties, by any means. Nearly half the households in Struan got a telegram that day, and many others across the country. The papers were full of it. COURAGE UNDER FIRE! VALUABLE LESSONS LEARNED. OUR GLORIOUS BOYS!

The following day the Luntzes received another telegram, informing them that Carl was missing. The day after that a fourth arrived, saying that he was dead.

Arthur's mother, now beyond tears, went over to the farm again. There was smoke coming from behind the barn so she went to check on it before going into the house. Otto was there. He had made a big pile of driftwood sticks and was burning them. He didn't look around as she approached. She said, "Otto?" and then realized that the sticks were not just sticks but the antlers Carl had spent his childhood carving. Her horror was so great that she could not speak. She turned and went home, out to the fields, and found her husband and dragged him back to the Luntzes' farm, to stand beside Otto and help him watch the antlers burn. Then she went into the farmhouse to look for Gertie. She found her sitting in a kitchen full of smoke— a rhubarb pie was burning in the oven; she must have put it in just before the final telegram arrived. Arthur's mother took the blackened pie out of the oven, put it outside the back door and then sat down beside Gertie, who looked at her without recognition and said, "Tell them."

"Tell them what, Gertie?" she said fearfully, her voice a whisper.

"Tell them no more telegrams. I don't vant more telegrams."

"No," Arthur's mother said. "No, Gertie. There will be no more telegrams."

There were thoughts that wouldn't leave Arthur alone. He would wake in the night wondering if Carl had known, before he died, that Eric and Gunter were dead. Had he seen them fall? Or had he been ahead of them, maybe, and looked back, and found they were no longer there? Run back for them. Tried to drag them to safety. Then Arthur would start wondering how Carl himself had died. Whether someone had been with him at the end, one of the other guys from Struan, or a friend he'd made in the army. Or if he had died alone, lying on a beach, or in some field that had been pounded to paste, a swamp of mud and bodies like in the photographs you saw of the Great War. Died at night, maybe, in agony, with no one around. Stupid, pointless thoughts that didn't help anybody, but he couldn't get them out of his head.

Then at other times—and this was almost worse—he'd forget. He'd be out in the fields working away, and he'd think, It's Friday, it'll be good to go into town with Carl tomorrow night, see all the guys.

~

Reverend Gordon, the Presbyterian minister, went off to be with the troops. He had a young family and there was his flock in Struan to consider, many of whom were grieving for lost fathers and sons, but with such carnage overseas his conscience would no longer permit him to stay at home. Across the country, churches were appealing to old ministers to come out of retirement and fill the empty spaces, but in the meantime the church elders did their best, labouring over sermons into the night and reading them out at the Sunday service.

The government decreed that older students at the country's secondary schools would be released from their studies to help on farms, especially during the harvest. (At last, in Arthur's opinion, they had their priorities right.) The problem was, most of them were town boys who didn't know one end of a cow from another, and anyway there weren't enough to go around.

Arthur and his father joined forces with Otto, as they had agreed. The purpose behind their agreement—to keep the Luntz farm in good order for the boys—had died with Carl and his brothers, but it went against nature to neglect a farm. Otto worked like an automaton, as if someone had wound him up and set him running. Arthur and his father feared for him. Feared he would kill himself with work. Feared that was his goal. But still there was much that needed doing that didn't get done.

Jake didn't help, of course. Jake was exempted from farmwork. From any work, in fact. His limp excused him from everything. There were a thousand chores he could easily have done, but somehow there was no question of him doing them. He had changed since his accident. Or maybe it was the rest of them: Arthur and his father, and even his mother—maybe they were the ones who had changed. Whichever, it was understood that Jake no longer owed anybody anything. His broken bones had paid for all his sins—past, present, and future—and from here on he was a free agent.

In some ways it made things easier. If Jake wasn't expected to do anything, there was no friction with his father when he failed to do it. He seemed more cheerful than he used to be, though he didn't spend any more time at home than he had to. "How's everyone?" he would say when they sat down for supper. "Everyone had a nice day?" It was clear that he didn't expect an answer and wouldn't have cared what it was, but at least he asked the question. Arthur would nod and their mother would start prattling away about the local gossip and their father, though he didn't respond, at least didn't give him a sharp look. It was as if Jake were a guest, someone who didn't intend to stay long but was prepared to be polite while he was there. Just don't interfere with his life, that was all. It was clear to Arthur that their mother hadn't quite grasped that yet.

"Jake, honey, I've had a letter from Mr. Wheeler."

Arthur, sitting outside on the back doorstep searching through a jar of nuts and bolts, heard the anxiety in her voice. Mr. Wheeler was the school principal.

"He wants me to come and see him. Do you know what it's about? Is everything all right at school?"

Silence. Probably a shrug from Jake.

"But what would it be about, Jakey?"

"Dunno. Wheeler's an old fool. Just don't bother going, Mum."

"Oh, but Jake . . ." her voice trying for a firmness she no longer seemed to possess.

"Gotta go, Mum. See you later."

It turned out that Jake had cheated on a test. How could he do such a thing? Why *would* he do such a thing, when he was so clever that he didn't need to? That was what she couldn't understand. Mr. Wheeler said gravely that because of Jake's accident they would be lenient this time, but if it happened again he would be expelled.

Jake denied it, of course. He said a boy in his class had made it up, a boy who had it in for him.

He was nearly sixteen now, almost as tall as Arthur but thin as a rake, and better-looking than ever. His limp did him no harm with girls; Arthur knew that for a fact. No harm at all. It didn't matter who they were, how old, or where they came from, Jake could make them light up like candles. Arthur saw him after church one Sunday, chatting to the Miller girls and their mother. Mr. Miller was manager of the Hudson's Bay store, and he and his wife, who was blond and plump and still pretty, though she must have been nearly forty, had three daughters, ranging in age, Arthur guessed, from about ten to eighteen. Jake was standing with them on the church steps, talking to them, making big gestures with his arms. Arthur heard him say, "And if I hit it, it would fall off and douse the grasses, and there'd be this great *whoosh* of flame. . . ." And Mrs. Miller and all three girls started laughing, their eyes fixed raptly on Jake's face. It was only the eldest girl that Jake was interested in, but he was busy charming all of them, just because he could.

Not just charming them, either. Arthur went into the barn late one afternoon and heard a sound, and paused, trying to identify it. Hot dusty light slanted through cracks in the boards and the air was thick with the smell of cattle. He heard the sound again: Jake's voice, very low. He was up in the loft and the words sifted down with the sunlight. Low though they were, Arthur could hear them plain as day.

"Put your hand there." You could even hear the smile in his voice. "There. That's right." His voice became thick as the dust.

Arthur stood rooted to the floor of the barn. He couldn't understand what he was hearing. Or rather, he understood it perfectly, but he couldn't believe it was Jake. That Jake could say such things to a girl. He felt suddenly sick with lust and longing. He was twenty-one and hadn't touched a girl in his life.

Jake still suffered pain sometimes. Usually in the evening. Arthur could tell by the way he kept shifting his position, trying to get comfortable. He would stand up, walk around, sit down again. Move his shoulders restlessly. He never complained about it though. Arthur almost wished he would. Jake's stoicism made him feel worse.

He was no longer waiting, hour by hour, for Jake to tell their parents what had happened on the bridge. He didn't know why the axe hadn't fallen, but it hadn't, and it didn't feel imminent. Maybe Jake was biding his time. Hoarding the revelation, like money in the bank. Or maybe he didn't intend to tell them directly, maybe he had decided that it was more valuable to have something to hold over Arthur. A debt that he could call in when the time was right.

~

"The Jackson boy is home," Arthur's mother said, piling potatoes onto her husband's plate. "But he's lost an arm, according to Annie. And Stan and Helen Wallace's boy is still not well enough to travel." She piled the beans and carrots high—one good thing about living on a mixed farm was that food rationing didn't affect them. But her lips were tight. Arthur noticed that little lines radiated out around them as if she'd pursed them too often lately, at too much bad news. "The thing is, you get used to it. We're all getting used to it. Is this enough, Henry?" A nod from Arthur's father. "To hearing these things, I mean. No one takes any notice anymore. It's as if all these deaths and all these horrible injuries are . . . normal. You hardly even feel shocked anymore. It's terrible. You should at least feel shocked! Pass me your plate, Arthur." She began forking fat slices of beef onto Arthur's plate.

"And you know what else? They're turning Hamborough—what used to be Hamborough—into a prison for prisoners of war. They're sending German prisoners all the way over here and putting them in special camps. Some of them are being sent to the prison in Monteith. Jake, how much meat would you like?"

"Just a slice," Jake said. "Hamborough? You mean the old ghost town?"

"Yes. Some of the buildings are still good, apparently. So they're putting the prisoners there. I don't think it's a good idea. What if they escape? Are you *sure* you can't eat another slice, Jakey?"

Jake flinched. He hated it when she called him that.

"Yes, I'm sure."

"Well, have lots of potatoes." She ladled potatoes onto his plate. "I don't think having escaped prisoners roaming around the woods is a good idea."

"Won't there be guards?" Jake said. "That's too much, Mum. I can't eat all that."

"Try," his mother said, gently urging. She worried about him all the time, Arthur knew. Every minute of the day. The war, the death of the Luntz boys, hadn't changed that. In fact, it had made things worse: with boys dying by the thousands, how could hers be spared? Fate must have something else in store for them. Specifically for Jake: Jake was the one she worried about. Arthur understood that. It had always been so, and now more than ever. He didn't blame her. Jake was always in the background of his mind too. A shadow, tinged with guilt.

"The Veterans Guards are going to guard them," their mother said. "But they'll fall asleep. They're old men."

Jake gave a snort of laughter. He ate a slice of beef, one potato, and about half a carrot, and then pushed back his chair.

"I'm off," he said. Sometimes Arthur wondered if he ate so little because he knew how it distressed her.

"Aren't you having dessert? It's pie."

"I'll have some later."

"Where are you going?"

"Out." He patted her head and was gone. The screen door slammed behind him.

Into the silence of the room his mother said, "Do you think he's happy? With us, I mean. Is he happy, here, with us?"

Arthur looked at her, and saw desolation in her eyes.

~

One evening at the beginning of May, Otto Luntz came over to tell them that he and Gertie were going away.

"I don't know how long," he said. He sat down at the table and accepted the cup of tea Arthur's mother set down before him. "Maybe a vile. Gertie's sister in Oshawa, ve go stay vid her. Maybe ve sell de farm, I don't know." He looked from one to the other of them. His expression was so bleak that it was hard not to look away. "I be glad you look after tings," he said. "I pay, of course."

"We don't want no money from you, Otto," Arthur's father said. "We'll be happy to look after things as much as we can." He sounded anxious though. There was a limit to how much they could do.

But Otto understood that. He said, "Important ting is de pigs. I know you can't do more land, but I tink maybe if you usse my tractor you can do some liddle more? You get my fuel ration too. Den you got horses and a tractor?"

Arthur and his father looked at each other doubtfully. They had never wanted a tractor, didn't care how fast it was, how efficient. They'd told themselves it wasn't worth the money—Otto had borrowed heavily from the bank to buy his and in the early stages it kept breaking down, costing him even more—but the simple truth was that they hadn't liked the idea of it. Hadn't wanted a big, ugly, noisy machine crawling across their land. If you compared it to the horses, who knew their work so well, who were quiet and companionable, and fertilized the land as they went instead of compacting the soil or churning it into a sea of mud every time it rained, the horses won hands down. But now, if they had Otto's land to consider as well as their own . . .

"We ain't neither of us driven a tractor before," Arthur's father said, as if hoping that would excuse them.

"I show you tomorrow," Otto said. "It iss not difficult."

So the next day he showed them, and it wasn't difficult. Both Arthur and his father had a turn driving it up and down the Luntzes' driveway and it seemed pretty straightforward. Like a truck but bigger. So it was settled. The Dunns would look after the farm as well as they could and keep a share, unwillingly, of the profits, and Otto and Gertie would take their time over deciding what to do next—though they all knew they were saying good-bye for good, that the next time the Luntzes came to Struan it would be merely to clear out the house.

Otto brought the tractor over on the morning he and Gertie left. What with the strain of the farewells nobody paid it any attention, but after the Luntzes had gone they all went and had a closer look at it, even Jake. It might be for farm work but it had wheels, and Jake liked wheels.

"It just makes me think of those boys," Arthur's mother said. She was red-eyed and her voice was clogged as if she had a cold. "I'll never see it without thinking of them."

"No point dwellin' on it," Arthur's father said. "It don't help."

"I know it doesn't help." Her voice was sharp with unhappiness. "But it's a fact."

"Doesn't look as strong as two horses," Arthur said, to change the subject, though it did look pretty strong. It didn't look as friendly as the horses, though, that was for sure.

Jake was wandering around it, patting the huge tires, drawing a line along the dusty flanks with his finger. "I'm glad it's red," he said with satisfaction. "Red's the right colour for a tractor." He climbed up and sat on the seat and grinned down at them. "Bet it's fun to drive," he said. "Wonder how fast it can go. Whoo! We should take it out on the road and see what it'll do!"

"It's not a toy," his father said sharply, in the voice he used to use with Jake, and Jake flushed.

He said, "That was a joke, Dad. I was making a joke."

"It's dinnertime," his mother said. "Maybe after dinner you can all try it."

But maybe Jake guessed he wouldn't get to drive it, because after dinner he wandered off, like he always did. Arthur's mother did the dishes as usual, and Arthur and his father retired to the armchairs for a few minutes like they always did to let the food go down, though maybe for a little less time than usual because, although they wouldn't have admitted it even to each other, they were both quite excited about the tractor.

"Looks bigger'n it did before dinner," Arthur said, when they went out to it again.

"Won't look no smaller tomorrow," his father said. "Might as well give 'er a go."

He climbed up stiffly, placing his feet on the plates with deliberation, and made to sit down. Then hesitated and looked down at Arthur. "You wanna go first?"

Arthur shook his head.

"You sure?"

"Yeah."

"Okay. Here goes." He started the engine as Otto had shown him and it fired up with a roar. He and Arthur grinned at each other. He put it into gear and the huge wheels started turning. He grasped the steering wheel tightly with both hands and yelled, "I'll take her down to the lower forty!"

Arthur nodded and watched him drive off.

"I hope he's careful," his mother said. Her voice made Arthur jump. He hadn't heard her coming up behind him.

"I'll follow him down," he said. "See how he's makin' out."

"Tell him not to go so fast," his mother said. "I'm going over to the Luntzes to look at Otto's pigs. Just to make sure they're all right. If you drive it, Arthur, you be careful."

He set off, following in the tread marks of the tractor. His father was out of sight already—he did seem to be driving kind of fast. But then, that was the thing about tractors: they were fast. Otto reckoned he could plow four to five acres in the time it took a team of horses to do one. Maybe they would end up buying it, when Otto came to sell things off. It was noisy, though. He wasn't keen on the noise. His father must be three fields away by now but you could still hear the roar. And then all at once the pitch changed. The roar wavered and then rose, and kept climbing until it was more like a scream. Arthur frowned, wondering what his father was doing. Did he have it in the wrong gear? Suddenly uneasy, he walked faster, then broke into a run. The scream went on. He'd passed the tractor many times when Carl or one of the others was plowing and he'd never heard it make that noise before.

When he got to the brow of the hill he couldn't see it at first. He stopped and looked around. He could hear it louder than ever, the high scream kept on and on, and the tread marks were there, running fairly straight down the side of the field, but there was no sign of the tractor, just some big brownish-black thing sticking up out of the ditch at the bottom of the field. And then he realized what it was and started running and shouting at the same time—"Dad! Dad!"—just as he had shouted all those years ago when the baby was coming and his mother was in danger, running and shouting, now as then, with fear clutching his heart.

The tractor had rolled right over so that the wheels were spinning in the air. His father was underneath it. All Arthur could see was his head and neck. He was face up and his face was purple and his eyes were bulging and his mouth was gaping wide. Arthur leapt down into the ditch and grabbed hold of the side of the tractor, keeping clear of the monstrous wheels, and braced his legs and heaved with all his strength. The tractor did not move one fraction of an inch.

"Hold on, Dad! Hold on!" Arthur yelled, his voice cracking with disbelief and terror. The tractor was still screaming like an animal; he turned so that his back was against it and reached behind himself and braced his legs against the side of the ditch and *lifted*, put all of his huge strength into it, and lifted, roaring with the effort. Was there a movement? He didn't know but he thought there might have been, and he couldn't let the tractor down again because then all of that weight would be back on his father. He roared, "Jesus! Jesus!" and as if in answer there was a movement at the top of the ditch and Jake was there, white and staring with shock. Jake jumped down and reached up swiftly and turned off the engine and the silence screamed as loud as the engine had. Jake grabbed hold of the tractor and tried to lift as well, but his strength was nothing and made no difference at all.

"Get the horses!" Arthur roared at him. His legs were shuddering with the strain. What if he could not keep it up? What was the point of his size and strength if he could not keep the weight of the tractor from crushing his father?

Jake nodded and scrambled up the side of the ditch as fast as his limp would allow, and at the top spared a fraction of a moment to look back. He stopped. Arthur roared, "*Get the bloody horses!*" but Jake slid back down the slope and put his hand on Arthur's arm. He said, "Art, he's dead." His voice was shaking and his lips were bluish with shock.

Arthur glanced down and saw the dreadful colour of his father's face and the way his eyes bulged, and saw now that blood was running from his mouth. But that did not mean he was dead, none of it meant he was dead—it just meant they had to get the weight off him so that he could breathe.

"Get the bloody horses!" he bellowed again, and Jake hesitated, then nodded, and scrambled up the side of the ditch once more, and disappeared. Arthur waited, sweat pouring down him, shoulders, back, and legs trembling violently, saying over and over again, "Hold on, Dad. Hold on. He'll be right back. Just hold on."

Then Jake was there again, with two of the horses and their harnesses and ropes and all that was needed—grant him that, in this one instance Jake did all that was needed, and did it fast, and did it well—and they hauled the tractor off their father's broken body, and Arthur, sobbing now, carried him across the fields and into the house.

~

Arthur's mother said, "I didn't think it would be him. I thought one of you would be taken from me. I never thought it would be him. I thought we would have years and years together. I thought we would grow old together."

Jake said, "I thought when I grew up and got a job somewhere, doing something important, he'd see I wasn't useless. You want to know the truth? I hate him for dying before he learned I wasn't useless. That's the truth."

As for Arthur, he had no words.

NINE

~

May Remove Wolf Bounty
Expert Warns Silage is Tricky
—*Temiskaming Speaker,* May 1960

They had been standing beside the vegetable patch when
the Cadillac pulled into the farmyard. They all started
moving towards it, but then the door opened and a man
got out, and Laura stopped so suddenly that Ian bumped
into her.

"Jake," she said. Just that.

Ian looked from her to the stranger, curiously.

The stranger's smile widened. He was leaning against
his car, arms folded, weight on one leg. He was wearing a
suit, something you didn't see all that often in Struan,
and very clean shoes.

"Hello, Laura," he said. "How are things down on the farm?" It sounded like a joke rather than a question, and maybe that was how Laura took it too, because she didn't answer. The man's eyes moved from her to the baby she was holding and then to Ian, and Julie, and finally to March. "One, two, three, four," he said musingly, nodding at each of them. "You have been busy." His gaze moved back to Ian and he tipped his head to one side. He was still smiling but he looked puzzled. "You're Carter?" he said.

The question seemed to fluster Laura. She switched the baby from one hip to the other and said, "No, no, he's not. . . . I'm sorry, I should have introduced you. This is Ian, Dr. Christopherson's son. He helps Arthur in the summers. And this one isn't mine, I'm just looking after him for the afternoon. Ian, this is Jake, Arthur's brother." She hesitated, then said, "You should have written, Jake. You should have told us you were coming."

"That would have spoiled the surprise." He stepped forward and extended his hand to Ian. "I didn't think there was much family resemblance," he said.

Ian shook hands. "Nice to meet you." Three summers now he'd been working on the farm and never once had anyone mentioned Arthur having a brother.

"Carter isn't here right now," Laura said. "He'll be back soon. And Arthur's out in the fields."

Jake laughed. "Where else?" he said. "How's he doing?"

"Oh, fine," Laura said. "He's doing just fine. We're all fine."

Jake was looking around the farmyard curiously. "The old place isn't looking too bad. Barn looks good. Is that new?"

"About five years old. I think about five years." There

was a pause. Laura said, "You . . . you must be hungry, Jake. How far have you come today? Would you like something to eat? Supper's still a long way off. You'll stay for supper, won't you? But in the meantime . . ." Her voice trailed off. She seemed nervous, Ian thought. She was being polite to Jake in the way that you're polite to a stranger or someone you're uncomfortable with.

Jake was smiling at her again. "I stopped in town and had a look around. Had a piece of pie in Harper's. But sure, I'll stay for supper. In fact, I was hoping you could put me up for a day or two."

"Oh! Of course!" Laura said hurriedly. "Of course you must stay as long as you like. . . ." She looked down at Julie and said, "This is your uncle Jake, honey. Say, 'Hello, Uncle Jake.'"

"Hello," Julie whispered.

"Hi," Jake whispered back. "You look just like your mum, did you know that?" Julie shook her head. "You're a lucky girl," Jake said, and winked at her. Julie smiled shyly, and Jake turned back to Laura. "Maybe I'll just take my suitcases in and then go and find Art."

"Oh, you mustn't go out to the fields," Laura said hastily. "It's very muddy. You'll ruin your shoes. Ian will go and get him, won't you, Ian?"

"Sure," Ian said. He noticed now that Jake had a limp. Polio? An accident? His father would know.

"We'll go together," Jake said cheerfully. "The shoes will survive. I want to surprise Art." He opened the trunk of the car and lifted out two suitcases. Ian stepped forward and took them, feeling like a lackey. Jake grinned at him. "If you insist," he said. "You can charge Art extra. 'Additional services rendered.'"

Ian took the bags into the kitchen and put them by the stairs. Through the window he could see Laura and Jake, still talking. Or maybe Laura was just listening. She was holding the baby in front of her now, and was watching Jake over the top of its head. March was circling her, around and around, eyeing the stranger; as Ian watched, Laura put her free hand on his head and drew him towards her. He put his arms around her knees and she stroked his hair. Julie was still beside her, so she seemed to be wrapped in children. It made quite a picture, Ian thought. It would be called *The Mother*. Though there was something about the scene that wasn't as reassuring as that title suggested.

He went to the door and Jake saw him and jerked his head backwards, meaning "Come on, let's go," so Ian went out and joined them.

"Ian knows which field he's in," Laura was saying as he came up. "He'll be so glad to see you, Jake."

She wasn't all that pleased herself, Ian thought. He wondered if Jake was aware of it. But he looked perfectly at ease.

They started off down the track, Ian being careful not to walk too fast. The limp was quite pronounced.

"So," Jake said. "How long have you been working for my big brother, then?"

"About three years."

"And is he a good employer?" Something about the idea seemed to amuse him.

"Yes, he's great," Ian said. "He's a really nice guy."

"Oh, sure," Jake said, nodding. "Sure. No one could accuse Art of not being nice." He looked sideways at Ian and added, "He's got a nice wife too, hasn't he?" Ian looked at him quickly and Jake laughed. "That's what I figured."

Ian felt his face go hot. He stuck his hands in his pockets, then pulled them out again. "She's a really nice woman," he said, and Jake laughed again and slapped him on the back. "Don't worry," he said. "I won't tell on you. We'll change the subject. You're Dr. Christopherson's son. I don't remember him having kids. How old are you? Seventeen? Eighteen?"

"Eighteen," Ian said.

"Well you were around, then. I've been gone—let's see— about fifteen years I guess."

"Did you leave to go to university?" Ian asked, anxious to keep the conversation on this relatively safe course. Jake looked to be in his mid-thirties now, so he'd have been the right sort of age. It would probably have been unusual for a farm kid to get to university back then, but he could have won a scholarship. You could see he was smart.

"Thought about it," Jake said, "but decided against it. It was a bit too . . . you know." Ian didn't know, but it seemed impolite to say so. "Besides, my father was dead by then and Art was running this place. He was doing all right financially—he had a good war, as they say—but still it didn't seem right to ask him to shell out for me."

They'd come to a gate and he stood back and waited for Ian to open it. The ground was a soggy mix of mud and cow dung and Jake picked his way carefully. Ian squelched through it. His boots were so caked with mud already they couldn't get any worse.

"I've done fine without it," Jake went on. "A formal education's not much use in the real world." He was using little hummocks of grass as stepping stones, searching for the next one, but he spared a moment to glance at Ian.

"But I imagine you're the academic type. You off to university soon?"

"Yes," Ian said, feeling vaguely ashamed of being so
predictable. "In the fall."

"To do what?" Jake asked.

"I'm not sure yet."

"Well, it doesn't make much difference. Just get out of
here, that's the important thing." He waved a hand at the
surrounding landscape. "Out of Struan! Out of the North!
Out of the goddamned *bush*!"

Ian grinned at him and Jake grinned back. "You know
what I mean?"

"Definitely."

There was a big clump of grass beside the path and Jake
stepped onto it and wiped his shoes. "Where are you
thinking of going?"

"Probably Toronto." All these questions. Jake had asked
more questions in ten minutes than Arthur had asked in
three years.

Jake frowned. "Seems a bit of a waste, doesn't it?"

"Um, does it? In what way?"

"Well, it's a bit . . . safe, don't you think? Toronto's
nothing. How about somewhere a little more exciting?
How about New York? Los Angeles? Hell, why not go to
China? They have universities there. See the world!"

Ian stared at him, and Jake laughed. "Got you thinking,
haven't I? I'm serious though. You could go anywhere,
smart kid like you. Grab your chance in both hands,
buddy, and run!"

They'd come over the brow of the hill now and the
ten-acre spread out before them. Arthur was on the far
side of the field. The horses were at a standstill and he was

squatting down beside the seed drill, fiddling with something. Probably it was jammed—you had to keep an eye on it. "The man himself!" Jake said. "And he still has the horses! Incredible!"

Arthur must have heard something, because he straightened up and looked in their direction. He stood for a moment or two, evidently trying to figure out who the stranger was, and then he must have worked it out—maybe he saw the limp—because he started across the field to meet them.

Jake speeded up as much as the limp would allow, hurrying towards his brother. Ian followed slowly, thinking about what Jake had said. It was true: he could go anywhere. No one had ever said that before. The teachers asked such limiting questions and made such limited suggestions. They said, "What do you want to do?" by which they simply meant what subject do you want to study, and when you replied they said things like, "Oh, Sudbury is close, and it has a good course in that," or if you were lucky, "Toronto has a good reputation in that field." In their thinking they never left the province, far less the country. It would cost more to go farther, but probably not that much more. Maybe it took someone from outside to point out that there was a world out there.

Jake and Arthur were walking towards him across the field and Ian realized that he'd missed the reunion. He'd wanted to see Arthur's reaction to this brother turning up out of nowhere, but he'd forgotten to watch. They were walking side by side, Jake talking animatedly, gesturing with his hands, glancing sideways up at Arthur while at the same time picking his way across the muddy field.

He looked very slight beside Arthur, very sharp, in his suit and his city shoes. Sharper than his brother, in every way.

Arthur wasn't saying much, but there was nothing new in that. As for whether he was pleased to see Jake, it was impossible to tell.

~

Ian would have liked to go fishing with Pete that evening—he hadn't spoken to him since their discussion after the math exam and he wanted to get things straightened out. But he and Cathy were back to going steady again and he'd promised her they'd go for a cheeseburger at Harper's when he got back from the farm. So he had a bath and changed into clean jeans and a T-shirt and then got back on his bike.

Cathy was sitting cross-legged on the porch of her parents' house, waiting for him. Her mother was in the kitchen—Ian saw her at the window and waved and she gave him a wave back. She and Cathy's father approved of him, according to Cathy, even though he went to the wrong church, but Ian suspected that was because of who his father was. Being the doctor's son gave you a head start with people's parents.

"What kept you so long?" Cathy said severely. She was wearing a blouse the same pale pink as her cheeks. Each time Ian saw her afresh he was reminded of why the other guys at school envied him. Maybe she wasn't all that deep a thinker, but she made up for it in other ways, like looks, and general amenability.

"Some of us have to work," he said, parking his bike against the side of the porch.

"Did you plant lots of corn?"

"No, but I weeded lots of weeds."

"I'll forgive you, then." She got to her feet and came down the steps and slipped her arm through his. Then she turned and waved to her mother.

"Where should we go?" she said.

Ian said, "I was thinking of the Ritz."

"Oh, I'm tired of the Ritz. Can't we go somewhere else?"

"Well, let's think. There's a place called Harper's that's supposed to be really 'in' at the moment."

"Oh, yes! Let's go there!"

She was so happy since they'd got back together. So easy to please.

"One more exam," she said, taking his hand and swinging it high. "Just one. And then our school days are over forever and our real lives begin! Can you believe it? I can hardly believe it!"

"I know," Ian said. All the exams finished on Monday—geography, which Cathy took, in the morning, and chemistry, which he took, in the afternoon. That was it. Less than two days and they'd be finished. The whole class was going out to Low Down Point in the evening for the celebration to end all celebrations.

"Aren't you excited?" Cathy demanded. "I'm so excited about next year I can hardly sleep anymore."

"Yeah," Ian said. "Me too."

She pouted at him. "You don't sound very excited."

"I am, though." She was so enthusiastic, that was the problem. Her enthusiasm wore him out.

Ron Atkinson and Fats Fitzpatrick were already at Harper's when they arrived, hunkered down in the booth by the door. Fats had his foot up on the opposite bench. He'd tried to pull a sock on over the bandages but they were too fat, so the sock was just crammed over his toes like a little hat.

"It's the man himself!" Ron said. "With the woman herself! Whaddaya know!"

Fats said, "Hey, I'm glad to see you, Christopherson. I need to ask you something. When I want to have a bath or a shower or something, do I take off the bandage or leave it on?"

"Whichever you like, Fats," Ian said. "I don't mind a bit." He steered Cathy towards a booth at the far end of the room.

"But I need to know!" Fats yelled after him.

"Just keep it dry!" Ian yelled back.

"Your dad must get so tired of that sort of thing," Cathy said under her breath, sliding into her seat. "Everywhere he goes, people must ask him questions about their health. I wish there was somewhere else we could go. Somewhere we could be more private."

Susan Jankowitz came over to their table—she worked in Harper's on Saturdays. She had been in tears after the math exam but she seemed to have recovered. "What will it be, children?" she said, her pencil poised over her notepad. She was wearing a white blouse that needed more buttons.

"Are you going to order?" Cathy said, raising her eyebrows at him. He was neglecting his duty.

"Oh. Sure. Two cheeseburgers with everything except onions"—Cathy thought onion breath was revolting—"one milkshake . . ." He looked at her. "Strawberry or chocolate?"

"Chocolate."

"And one Coke. And a double portion of fries."

Susan nodded, scribbling fast. When she left, Cathy looked around as if she'd never been here before. She was wearing a wistful expression.

"We're going to miss it, you know," she said.

"Miss what?"

"All this." She gestured at the dark wooden booths with their stained red plastic-cushioned seats, the red Formica tables, the walls festooned with photos of happy fishermen holding up big fish. Paper placemats with more fish swirling about the edges, fishing lines coming out of their mouths. Above the door to the toilets there was a three-foot-long muskie, stuffed and nailed to the wall.

"When we're older, we'll look back on this place and realize it was beautiful."

"Harper's?" Ian said.

"Even Harper's," Cathy said earnestly. "We'll look back and we'll realize that our childhoods were beautiful, and everything in them was beautiful, right down to"— she looked about her—"right down to the holes in these cushions. We'll realize that Struan was the most wonderful place in the world to grow up in. We'll realize that wherever we go, wherever we live for the rest of our lives, it will never be as perfect as here."

A little worm of irritation rose up in Ian from somewhere about mid-chest. "Maybe we'd better not go," he said, twisting his mouth in a smile. He reminded himself about her looks and her general amenability. It didn't work. The fact was, her sentimentality had really started to get on his nerves lately. It was too much; it struck him as fake. And her expectation that he would feel the same made it more irritating still. It made him want to swing in the other direction, deny feeling things that he actually felt.

"But we have to go." Cathy leaned towards him earnestly.

"We don't have to go. Most of the kids we started school with aren't going."

"Yes, but people like us have to go. You know that."

Susan set down their cheeseburgers and the drinks and Cathy smiled up at her.

Ian bit into his cheeseburger. It was very good. He wouldn't remember Harper's for its beauty, he'd remember it for its cheeseburgers.

"You of all people," Cathy was saying. "You have so much potential, Ian. You couldn't develop it here. You need to spread your wings. We both do."

He wished she would stop talking. If she would just shut up, it would all be fine.

"Don't you think it's amazing that we found each other?" she said. "I mean, what are the chances, really? In a town this size? We're so *lucky!*"

"Um . . ." he said around the cheeseburger. Cathy still hadn't touched hers. "Of . . . finding each other?" Surely it was the chances of missing each other that were remote.

"The chances of finding the person you want to spend your life with! In a little tiny town! Out of all the people in the world, and all the places in the world, *that one person* happens to grow up in the same town as you." She sighed. "You know what my mother said? She said she'd never seen me look so happy as I've looked since we got back together. Don't you think that's lovely?"

Ian nodded. He picked up a fistful of fries and stuck them in his mouth. Cathy leaned across the table towards him. She was looking very serious all at once.

"I had a talk with them last night—with my parents. They were saying they thought it was time I decided where I'm going next year. Which school of nursing. They think I should get my application in." She took his hand and turned it palm-upwards and studied it. It was greasy from the fries and she frowned, and pulled a napkin out of the dispenser on the table and began cleaning each finger in turn.

Ian chewed his fries very thoroughly and swallowed them. The conversation was making him uneasy. "Haven't you decided?" he said. With his other hand he gathered more fries. He had a sudden urge to stuff the whole plateful in his mouth.

"Well, no." She crumpled up the napkin and pulled out another. "I can't, can I? Until you do. Your career is more important than mine. Mum and Dad understand that— they completely understand that. I can do nursing anywhere, so it doesn't really matter. But they think it's time we decided. You know, so we're sure to get our first choice."

Ian paused, the fries halfway to his mouth. He put them down again and looked at them. It was as if she had opened a door in her head and showed him everything that was going on in there. The picture she was working on.

She said, "Ian?" Her voice was puzzled. She released her hold on his hand and he withdrew it carefully. He began aligning the fries in a neat little row on the side of the plate, prodding them this way and that until they were level along the bottom. He pushed one end of the row of fries together so that they made a fan shape.

After a while he heard her get up from the table. He saw the movement at the periphery of his vision. She slid out of the booth and he heard her footsteps receding down the aisle. He got to his feet and dug a fistful of coins out of his pocket and put them down beside the plates—hers still untouched—and followed her out. As he passed their booth, Fats and Ron Atkinson whistled slowly and Ron said, "Hey, lover-boy. What've you done now?"

He followed Cathy down the street at a distance. He didn't want to catch up with her while there were still people about. When she turned down the road she lived on, he caught up with her. She tried to walk away but he got in front of her, saying, "Wait, Cath, wait." She stepped this way and that, trying to get around him, and then gave up and just stood there, her arms at her sides. He took her hand and led her over to the side of the road. A tree had come down in a storm earlier in the year and the trunk was still lying there, waiting to be cut up; he sat on it and gently pulled her down beside him. He told her he wasn't ready to make decisions about his future yet. He said maybe he was very immature or something, but he really wasn't ready for that. So he thought it would be best if they broke it off. She was crying. She asked if it was something she'd done, something she'd said, and he said no, it wasn't her at all, it was him. She said she'd try to be different, she loved him so much that she'd be anything he wanted, and he shook his head, appalled. She said she didn't want to tie him down but couldn't they just go on as they were; and he said no, he was sorry. He was really sorry.

It was a while before she pulled herself together, but finally she did. She took a deep breath and wiped her face with her fingers, looking straight in front of her, chin raised. Then she stood up. Ian stood up too, and asked if she wanted him to walk the rest of the way home with her. She said no, so he stayed where he was and watched her walk away.

~

Once when he was a small child a Sunday school teacher had taught a lesson on being good. She'd said it was sometimes difficult to know the right thing to do; it could be hard to tell good from bad, right from wrong. But, she had added, speaking in the hushed but cheerful voice that Sunday school teachers always seemed to use, there was one foolproof way to tell. All you had to do was ask yourself what Jesus would have done. You worked out what Jesus would do in any situation and then you did it, and it was sure to be right.

He'd forgotten the lesson the minute the class was over, but now it came back to him. He saw that for the past three years he had been working on a variation of that idea: in any tricky personal situation he had asked himself what his mother would have done, and then he had done the opposite. It seemed to him that she was the perfect anti–role model: she hadn't cared how much she hurt the people who loved and depended on her; she had put her own desires above those of everyone else; she had lied and pretended and deceived. He had made it part of his own personal code of behaviour never to behave as she had done, and yet when it came to it, he had treated Cathy much the same. He hadn't exactly cheated on her, unless you counted loving Laura from afar, but he had allowed her to think he loved her when he didn't, which amounted to the same thing.

It scared him that he'd ended up behaving like his mother. It made him wonder if at some deep, unalterable level he resembled her.

He went home. He had left his bike at Cathy's; he'd have to pick it up sometime when she wasn't around. When he got in, there was a note from his father on the kitchen table with the name *Lefebvre* and a phone number—he always left a note in case of emergencies—and the words *yet another* scribbled at the bottom, by which he meant another baby. He seemed to be delivering babies every other night at the moment; it was practically an epidemic.

Ian went down to the dock. It was very peaceful there. It wasn't dark yet and the low clouds gave the lake a metallic sheen. He flipped the canoe over, slid it into the water, and climbed in.

He paddled down the shore, keeping close in, the canoe sliding silently through the water. There was a cold mist stealing across the lake ahead of the night. Ian laid his paddle across the canoe and did up his jacket. The canoe was drifting towards the old beaver lodge at the entrance to Low Down Bay. It had been abandoned for a number of years but the beavers had returned the previous fall and the stark white branches of the birches they'd brought down were sticking up out of the water like bones. He sat motionless for a while, wondering if he'd catch sight of a beaver, but there was no sign of them. Spring wasn't their busy time—they did most of their building in the fall. The females would be having their young about now, curled up safe and dry in the depths of the lodge.

He turned the canoe and paddled out around the point. He thought about the year to come, saw himself walking down a city street, cars roaring past, the stink of exhaust fumes, people jostling against him. No silence, anywhere. He thought about Arthur's brother waving his arm and saying, "Out of Straun! Out of the North! Out of the god-damned *bush*!" On one level he agreed with him completely. On another level he wasn't sure he would survive.

He rounded the point that formed the eastern shore of Hopeless Inlet, and sure enough, the *Queen Mary* was there, Pete hunched over his fishing line like always. Ian came up slowly, careful not to disturb the water.

"How's it going?" he said quietly.

"So-so," Pete said.

There were half a dozen trout in the bottom of the boat. "Doesn't look too bad," Ian said, nodding at them.

"Chicken shit, man."

Ian couldn't assess his tone. He didn't know if he was welcome or not. Until a week ago he wouldn't have given the matter a thought: he'd have tied the canoe to the *Queen Mary* and climbed in. His rod was still where he'd left it, sticking out over the stern. Was that a good sign? Maybe Pete hadn't even noticed it.

"You reckon he's still down there, eh?" Ian said.

"Yup."

"Still think he's a muskie?"

"Yup."

"You actually seen him?"

"Nope."

Ian slid the canoe back and forth with his paddle. He wasn't sure what he was waiting for. An invitation? Pete to say, "Aren't you gonna fish?" Whatever it was, it didn't come.

"Good luck," he said finally.

Pete looked at him for a moment, then nodded. "Thanks."

His father was in the kitchen when he got home, eating a hunk of cheese straight from the fridge.

"Hi," Ian said, grateful that he was back. "How did it go?"

"A bouncing baby boy."

"Are the proud parents happy?"

"Not 'specially. They've got nine already."

"Good grief."

The fridge was wide open. The Irish stew Mrs. Tuttle had left for them was on a shelf beside a very large jar containing one dill pickle.

"We could heat that up," Ian said, nodding at the stew. She made a double dose of it every Friday to see them through the weekend. Sometimes she called it something else—a *casserole,* that was her new word for it—but it was always the same stew.

"We could," his father agreed. "Are you that hungry?"

"Not really."

"Me neither. Have some cheese." His father cut another hunk of cheese and handed it to him, then studied him for a moment. "Everything all right?"

"Yeah. Well, sort of. I broke up with Cathy."

"Oh. That's . . . too bad." He didn't say, "again?" which was nice of him. He was good about things like that.

"Yeah. It wasn't . . . going anywhere. We don't have enough in common."

His father nodded. The absence of Ian's mother drifted into the room.

"Plus there's something wrong with Pete," Ian said quickly. "Not wrong, exactly. Strange. I don't know what it is."

His father said, "This is a tough time for him, you know. It's always difficult having a foot in both camps, but when there's trouble between the camps it's really hard."

"I guess." Though it seemed to him that if you'd been friends for the whole of your life you were entitled not to be seen as part of a camp. He wished he and Pete could talk about it, properly, get it out in the open, but that would never happen. Their relationship was based on things not said, and the more important something was, the less likely they were to discuss it.

"What does his grandfather think about it all? Jim Lightfoot being arrested and everything?" Ian knew his father had a lot of respect for the old man, and guessed they would have talked.

"Joe? He's very concerned. Concerned about Jim and concerned about the damage to relations between the town and the reserve."

"Have you seen Jim?"

His father nodded. "Saw him this morning. He's not in great shape. He's an outdoors kind of guy. Being locked up is pretty much a death sentence for him."

"What'll happen to him?"

"He'll be shipped down to the district jail in Haileybury. I think he's going on Monday. They've got a presiding judge there."

"Who will find him guilty of murder," Ian said bitterly. "In spite of the fact that the logger must have started it. Jim wouldn't pick a fight."

"His case will be put to the court," his father said.

"By who?"

"The court appoints a defence lawyer."

"Oh, right! The court appoints him. Some white guy straight from university who can't get a job anywhere else."

"You're judging them in advance, Ian. You're doing exactly what you're accusing them of doing. Making assumptions based on prejudice."

"I'm making assumptions based on Gerry Moynihan and a million guys just like him."

"Gerry's not all bad. He's just a product of his upbringing."

"Yeah, well, his upbringing stinks."

His father sighed.

The cheese needed something to go with it. Ian opened the cupboard beside the fridge and took out a box of crackers. "Want one?"

They ate side by side, looking into the fridge. Ian's anger slowly subsided. He knew it wasn't fair to take it out on his father. He would be using his influence to do all that he could for Jim.

"We need a dog," he said after a while.

"You're thinking of the stew?"

"Yeah. She's getting worse. Mrs. Tuttle, I mean."

"Oh, well. She does her best," his father said.

"No, she doesn't, Dad." His father was always making excuses for people. Maybe it was a nice fault, but it was irritating nonetheless.

The fridge hummed at them. Outside the wind was picking up. A volley of fat raindrops splattered against the kitchen window. Ian liked the sound: the combination of wind and rain always made the house feel safe.

"Seriously," he said. "I'd like a dog."

"So would I," his father said musingly. "Maybe we should get one."

They had had a dog once, an Irish setter called Molly who'd accompanied his father on his rounds for years and who was so much a part of the family that when she died they hadn't been able to bear the thought of getting another, because it wouldn't be her. But maybe now the time had come. In fact, Ian saw all at once that it would be perfect. A dog, padding gently around the house, accompanying his father on his rounds, lying at his feet in the evenings. He felt a huge lift of spirits at the thought.

"Yeah," he said. "Let's get one."

"All right. We will."

Ian took out the jar of dill pickle in celebration. He unscrewed the lid, picked out the pickle with his fingers, stuck the end of it in his mouth, poured the vinegar down the sink. The smell of it wafted up like ether. He bit the pickle in half and passed the other half to his father.

"Another Irish setter, do you think? To go with the stew?"

His father nodded around the pickle.

The pickle required more cheese and the cheese required more crackers. They ate absently; both lost in thought, crumbs trickling down onto the floor. The various events of the day scrolled backwards through Ian's mind.

"Did you know Arthur Dunn had a brother?"

"Yes," his father said. "Jack. No, Jake. Why?"

"He came today. Rolled up in an amazing Cadillac."

"Did he really? I haven't seen him for years." He took the box of crackers from Ian and reached into it. It was empty. He put it down and opened the bread bin and took out the bread.

"He's not much like Arthur, is he?" Ian said, getting the butter out of the fridge.

"We might as well sit down," his father said. "No, he's a different kettle of fish altogether. I always preferred Arthur, to tell you the truth."

They sat down, bread, butter, and cheese between them.

"He's lame," Ian said. "Was it polio?"

"No, an accident. He fell off a bridge. It was a miracle he didn't break his back."

They finished the cheese. Ian got up and opened the cupboard again and started moving jars around.

"Where's the honey?"

"I believe I may have finished it at breakfast."

"The jar was half-full, Dad. What did you do, eat it with a spoon?"

"Have some jam."

"You're going to get fat," Ian said.

"I'm looking forward to it." His father leaned back and patted his paunch fondly. In truth, there wasn't all that much of it yet.

"That reminds me," Ian said. "I want a picture of you."

"What for?"

"To take with me. You know, to throw darts at when I'm away."

"There are lots lying around," his father said vaguely.

"Yeah, but they're old. And they all have . . . they're all out of date. I want an up-to-date one."

There was silence. His father looked at him. He said gently, "You have to forgive her, Ian."

"What?" As if he didn't know.

"You have to forgive her."

~

On Sunday morning when he woke up he realized that far from having days and days to prepare for the chemistry exam he now had somewhat less than thirty hours. He skipped church and studied all day. He was good at cramming, even enjoyed it to a degree; there was a kind of masochistic pleasure to be found in concentrating so hard for so long. He took an hour off for supper and then worked till midnight. He got up at six, had breakfast, and started in again. By half past ten in the morning he'd finished. The entire chemistry textbook, a whole year's work, was now inside his head, and provided it didn't all fall out between now and the exam, he'd be fine.

He decided to go out and get some air; it would help to consolidate the seething mass of facts inside his head. Then he'd have a sandwich and go and take the exam.

Downstairs, patients were trooping in. Monday was always a busy day for his father (people, the considerate ones, anyway, saved up their illnesses over the weekend) and the waiting room was jammed. Apart from six or seven adults there seemed to be about a dozen babies and every one of them was howling. More were on the way. As he passed the patients' entrance Mrs. Aaronovitch, the wife of the chemistry teacher, came in with her little girl in tow, and the little girl was howling too. She was covered in red blotchy spots and looked sick as a dog. This place is a nightmare, Ian thought, nodding at Mrs. Aaronovitch and heading for the door.

On the doorstep he paused. Red blotchy spots. He turned on his heel and went back in and caught up with Mrs. Aaronovitch just as she was about to go into the waiting room.

He said, "Excuse me, Mrs. Aaronovitch, would you mind waiting in the living room?"

She turned and looked at him in surprise.

Ian said, "Just in case your daughter's got something infectious." He smiled reassuringly at both of them and gestured to the living room across the hall. The little girl stopped howling, which was a relief. Her eyes were so red it hurt even to look at them.

"Oh!" Mrs. Aaronovitch said. "Oh, goodness, Ian! Of course!"

"Just in case," Ian said. "What with all the babies in there." He led them into the living room and moved a couple of books off the sofa. "Have a seat. I'll go and tell my father you're here."

The little girl croaked something to her mother.

"Oh, yes," Mrs. Aaronovitch said. "She wonders if she could have a drink. Could she have some water?"

"I'll ask my dad," Ian said to the child. "I think he'll want to take your temperature first, but then you can probably have one, okay?"

He went through the waiting room, stepping over babies and smiling vaguely at people without meeting their eyes so they wouldn't try to start a conversation with him. Mr. Harper, who owned Harper's Restaurant and who, according to Ian's father, had the highest blood pressure on the planet, came out just as he was about to knock on the door. Ian stood aside to let him pass and then stepped in and closed the door behind him. He said, "Mrs. Aaronovitch's kid has a red blotchy rash. Very red eyes. She looks really sick. I've put her in the living room. It's crawling with babies out there."

His father passed his hand over his face. He looked

beat already and the morning wasn't half over. He said, "Thank you. Good thinking."

"Where's Margie?" Ian said, looking around.

"She has the flu."

"She sure picked a good day, this place is a madhouse. Oh, the Aaronovitch kid's thirsty. Can she have a drink or do you want to take her temperature first?"

His father sighed and looked at his watch. "Are you off to your exam?"

"It's not until one. I was just having a break."

His father looked at him consideringly. Ian said quickly, "I was going out for some air."

"Oh. Okay, fair enough."

Which instantly made him feel guilty, of course. He said resignedly, "What did you want me to do?"

"No, no. Off you go."

"If you just want me to take her temperature or something . . ."

"Are you sure?"

"Dad . . . !"

"Okay. Thank you," his father said, capitulating fast. "And while you're doing it, check the inside of her mouth. If there are white spots it's measles, in which case tell her mother to take her home and give her half an Aspirin mashed up with jam. Tell her I'll come as soon as I've finished here. If there are no white spots I'll see her in the living room."

"Okay."

"Wash your hands."

He washed his hands at the sink in the corner and his father gave him a thermometer. "I owe you," his father said.

"I want a camera."

His father smiled.

"Can she have a drink afterwards?"

"Small sips."

Ian opened the door and it hit a baby squarely in the seat and sent it sprawling. It had been yelling already but now it really roared. Nancy Scholtz, who had been a year ahead of Ian in school and got pregnant at fifteen and now had three kids but still no brains, got up to collect it and smiled winningly at him. He resisted the impulse to say, Nancy, keep your kid out of the doorway, are you dumb or what? because, of course, she was.

He went back to the living room. "Okay," he said to the little girl, squatting down in front of her. "My dad said I should take your temperature and then you can have a drink. But first he wants me to look inside your mouth. Could you open your mouth for me?" She did, and he carefully turned her cheek inside out. White spots.

"Well, there you go!" he said, as if it were really good news. "You've got measles."

"Oh, dear," Mrs. Aaronovitch said. Ian smiled at her in commiseration.

He shook down the thermometer and said to the child, "So what that means is, after I've taken your temperature I'll get you a drink and then you and your mum can go home, and my dad will come and see you there later this morning. That's good, eh? You won't have to sit here anymore."

She looked at him dully. She obviously just wished he would leave her alone. He said gently, "I'm going to put this thermometer under your tongue to see how hot it is in there, okay? It has to stay there for two minutes. You can time it for me—I'll give you my watch . . ." He slid the thermometer under her tongue. "Don't bite it, okay? Just close your mouth around it. That's good, keep it like that." He undid his watch and gave it to her. Was she old enough to know what a second hand was? "See the hand that's moving quite fast? When it's gone all the way around twice, we're done."

They watched the hand go around.

"Don't you have an exam today, Ian?" Mrs. Aaronovitch said, keeping her voice low so as not to distract her daughter.

"Yeah." He grimaced at her. "Chemistry. The last one."

"Well, this is good of you."

"That's okay. Makes a break. Dad will go and see her as soon as he finishes here. He says to give her half an Aspirin mashed up with jam."

"It was her birthday Saturday," Mrs. Aaronovitch said. "She had a party. She didn't look very well then, but I thought it was the excitement."

"Oh, boy," Ian said. It was his father he was thinking of, more than the kids. "Maybe you'd better tell my father who was there."

"Yes, I will."

The little girl was holding his watch and the thermometer out to him.

"Wow!" Ian said, but quietly, because she looked as if a loud noise would make her head fall off. "One hundred and four degrees! That's impressive!"

He might have been mistaken, but he thought she almost smiled.

He went down to the lake and sat on the dock for a while, staring into the water and not thinking about anything much. Around noon his father came down.

"I'm off to see the Aaronovitch child," he said. "Thanks for your help this morning."

"That's okay."

"I guess you'll be gone by the time I get back."

"Yeah, we're all going out to Low Down. I'm not sure when it starts. I probably won't be in for supper."

"That's fine. Have fun. By the way, I heard some news this morning that will interest you. I had a call from Gerry Moynihan. Jim Lightfoot escaped from jail last night."

Ian looked up at him. "You're kidding!"

"Gerry went in this morning to give him his breakfast and the jail was empty."

"How did he get out?' Ian said. 'Does Gerry know?"

"Oh, yes, he knows. Hard to miss it. They cut a hole in the roof."

"The roof?" Ian gave a hoot of laughter. "That's great!"

"It may not end up being so great. The RCMP are involved now. As far as they're concerned, a suspected murderer is on the loose."

"They'll never get him. He'll have lit off into the woods."

"Of course. But they'll be all over the reserve, looking for whoever was involved. Things are going to be pretty unpleasant."

Ian thought about Pete, wondering if he would have been in on it. More than likely. "I still think it's great," he said.

He was half expecting Pete not to turn up for the exam, but he was there, not even late this time, waiting in the hall with everyone else.

"How are things?" Ian said cautiously, leaning against the wall beside him.

"Not too bad."

"I heard about the jailbreak."

Pete looked at him. "Me too."

"The Mounties there yet?"

"They're everywhere, man. Comin' out of the wood-work, crawlin' up the walls, you can't go for a crap without finding a Mountie in there, sniffin' around."

He grinned. He looked as if he'd just won a million dollars.

Mr. Aaronovitch arrived and they filed into the room and sat down. They were pros at this now—it was almost a shame it was all coming to an end. Aaronovitch handed out the papers and said ready, set, go, and they all flipped the paper over and started scribbling. For three hours Ian poured out onto the paper everything he had taken in in the past two days, and when it was over his brain felt as empty as an old boot, nothing in there at all.

Afterwards they milled around restlessly, talking about how great it felt to be finished but how it didn't seem real, and how it was going to take a long time to sink in. Somebody suggested they go to Harper's, but Ian decided against it. You could predict exactly what the conversation would be. They'd do a post-mortem on the exam, question by question, until they'd all con-vinced themselves they'd failed. He didn't fancy it. He caught Pete's eye and nodded questioningly at the door, and Pete nodded in reply. Ian felt a huge relief. Almost as good as Jim Lightfoot getting away was the fact that Pete seemed to be back to normal.

Their fishing tackle was at Pete's, and his grandfather had told him to stay out of the way of the Mounties, so they decided to hike up to the Leap. It had been years since either of them had been there; fishing was so addictive it left time for nothing else.

The Leap was a sheer granite cliff over three hundred feet high, rising up out of the lake. It might have been possible to scale it if you had the right equipment, but as far as anyone knew it had never been done. Instead you approached it from the rear, where the climb was merely steep rather than precipitous.

They went past Cathy's house to pick up Ian's bike, cycled to the point where the road came closest to the Leap, and then abandoned their bikes and set off. The going was easy at first, rising gently across great rounded humps of pink lichen-encrusted granite, bare but for the occasional tuft of grass or rich green pillow of moss. Here and there, in hollows deep enough for a little soil to gather, there was a knotted jack pine, hanging on tight.

Then the rocks got steeper and they had to pick their way, climbing as fast as they could, both feeling the urge to push themselves physically, to get the blood moving again after the concentrated mental effort of the morning. Part way up there was a giant turtle-shaped boulder they remembered sitting on as kids, so they climbed up and sat on it again to get their breath back.

"It was your grandfather who brought us here the first time, wasn't it?" Ian said breathlessly. "Years ago. We were really young."

Pete nodded.

"Was it your birthday or something?"

"Yeah."

Ian had a dim memory of the old man helping him up a rock, saying something encouraging to him in a language he didn't understand, then saying it again in English.

There. Now up this one. Good. Good. He was a great old guy. And now there were Mounties prowling around the store. Asking questions.

"How's he doing? You know—with everything that's going on."

"He's okay. Worried."

"About Jim?"

"About everything, man. About everything."

Below them a couple of crows were bouncing about on a boulder, yelling at each other. Then a third crow joined them and added his opinion, then a fourth. They stood around bickering for a moment and then, abruptly, they seemed to reach agreement and they all flew off.

Ian put his hands flat on the rock and lifted himself fractionally, easing his backside into a more comfortable position. The rock was warm from the sun and under his hands the rough rounded surface felt like the skin of an ancient beast.

"How old are these rocks, do you think?" he said pensively.

"They've been here forever," Pete said. "These are some of the oldest rocks in the world."

Ian looked at him curiously. "Really?"

Pete nodded. "Bits of the Shield are going on three billion years old."

"Three *billion*?"

"This is top-quality rock, man. It was a mountain range once. High as the Rockies. Then it was under the sea . . . then there were glaciers on top of it." He patted the rock approvingly with his hand. "Still here."

They climbed on. The rocks rose up more steeply and sometimes they needed to search for handholds and haul themselves up. And then abruptly they scrambled over a crest of rock and found themselves at the top, the lake spreading out below them, dazzling in the sun.

"Wow!" Ian said. "I'd forgotten how fantastic the view is."

The sun on the surface of the water was so bright that he had to shield his eyes to look at it. In the distance the shoreline looked like lace, hundreds of bays and rivers and inlets running off from the vast pool of the lake itself and disappearing into the wilderness.

"What's that at the edge of the cliff?" Pete said.

"Where?"

"There's something in the air."

They were still thirty feet or so back from the edge, but now, looking more closely, Ian could see that the air appeared to be dancing in a strange way, almost like a heat haze but not quite. At first he thought it was a trick of the light but as they got closer he could see that Pete was right, there was something in the air. Many things, in fact. Thousands of things.

"Holy shit!" Pete said. "They're dragonflies!"

A curtain of dragonflies was hanging in the air at the very edge of the cliff, hundreds upon hundreds of them, like a vast army of tiny helicopters, hovering, almost motionless apart from a slight swaying to maintain their position on the updraft of warm air from the lake. All of them were facing inwards as if they'd been on their way somewhere and had come smack up against a sheet of glass.

"What the hell are they *doing*?" Ian said, getting as close to the edge as he dared. Three hundred feet below, the waves were frothing around the foot of the cliff.

"Dunno."

"Have you ever seen them do that before?"

"Nope."

Pete sat down, cross-legged, at the edge of the cliff, face to face with the dragonflies. He watched them and they watched him. Man and bug, Ian thought, grinning at the sight. Man and bug, eye to eye on the brim of the oldest rock in the world. He sat down beside Pete, edging cautiously closer to the brim, and focused on one individual dragonfly. They were hovering quite close together, not more than four or five inches apart in any direction, but they maintained their positions so well that it was easy to pick out just one. It was less than three feet away—he could have touched it if he'd leaned out over the edge—but it didn't seem in any way perturbed by his presence. They eyed each other, mutually uncomprehending.

"So how old are dragonflies?" he said at last. "Since you know so much."

"You mean these particular ones?"

"No. Like, when did the first dragonfly fly?"

"Two to three hundred million years ago."

"That's not a very satisfactory answer—give or take a hundred million years. Can't you be a little more precise?"

"Two hundred and seventy-six million, three hundred and ten thousand, four hundred and twenty-two years ago on the fourteenth of December."

"Thank you."

"Anytime," Pete said. "If there's any little thing you need to know, just ask." They sat on in silence, or almost silence; if you listened closely you could just hear a faint thrumming from thousands of wings. Beyond the dragonflies the sun was sinking slowly, casting its rays across the lake, and on either side, everything, as far as the eye could see, was slowly dissolving into the haze.

Ian thought, If I live to be a hundred years old, I will always remember this.

~

It was after dark by the time they got to Low Down. Most of the others were there already and had a bonfire going. Cathy was there, huddled in a little group of girls who kept shooting dirty looks at Ian. He avoided looking at them.

Someone had spread a couple of old blankets out on the sand a few feet back from the fire and Ian sat down and stared into the flames. He felt strange, distant and detached. Part of his mind was still back on the cliff and the other part was too tired for a party. He tried to shake himself out of it—this was probably the last get-together they'd have before they all went their separate ways—but the others didn't seem to feel particularly hyped-up either. Someone passed him a Coke and someone else held out a king-size bag of potato chips; he took a handful and ate them slowly. People were standing around in the shadows at the edge of the firelight. Others were down by the water. Pete was down there, looking out over the lake. Maybe he was back with the dragonflies too. Or communing with his mythical muskie. Or wondering what the Mounties were up to on the reserve, and how his grandfather was making out.

It was getting cold. The fire had died down enough to cook the hamburgers and hot dogs people had brought, so they did that and then heaped more wood on the fire and huddled around it. There was a bit of petting going on, but nothing serious. Someone tried to start a singalong, but it petered out almost immediately, and they sat mostly in silence, like a bunch of cavemen, watching the flames.

Earlier they'd talked about staying all night, greeting the sunrise together, but in the end people started drifting away about one in the morning. The goodbyes were quiet and subdued.

Pete had disappeared some time before, so Ian went home alone. He cycled slowly, wanting to hang on to the feeling of detachment that had taken him over. A state of not-being. A state of no-time. No past, no present, no future. No decisions. He thought it would be good to stay like that for the rest of his life.

When he got home the car was gone; his father was out on a call. Ian went up to his room. He lay on his bed, thinking of what Jake had said about leaving the North, then thinking about Jake himself. It must be strange, coming back after a long absence to the place you grew up in. Strange to see again things that were once so familiar they were almost a part of you. Though it was hard to imagine Struan or anything in it being a part of Jake. He didn't look as if he had ever belonged. He was a city type. Sure of himself. Confident. Ian envied him that. He looked like someone who had no doubts about himself or where he was going. Someone who knew exactly what he wanted out of life. Someone who had all the answers.

TEN

~

Victory Loan Nearing Objective
Runaway Truck Finishes Up in Mill Creek
—*Temiskaming Speaker*, May 1943

The cows needed milking, so he had to get up in the mornings. If it hadn't been for that, maybe he wouldn't have. Maybe he would have stayed in bed, sagging into the mattress, too weighed down with loss to move, while the forest crept in and took over the farm. But the urgent lowing of the cows reached him where he lay under his heap of grey blankets, and it wasn't a sound anyone with a heart in him could ignore.

Once he was up, other things couldn't be ignored either. The frosts had gone but until a week ago the soil had been too wet to drill. Now it was ready and the oats and barley—the crops the animals depended on during the long winter months—needed to go in straight away. He was going to need more feed than ever before because they'd increased the size of the dairy herd, thanks to their arrangement with Otto, and if he sold them now he'd take a loss. And then there were Otto's pigs. The piglets could be sold when they reached market weight but he couldn't sell the sows. Otto depended on them for his livelihood.

So there would be the pigs to get through the winter, and the cattle, and the horses. He didn't see how he could manage it. It was only ever going to be possible with the use of Otto's land, and one man alone couldn't work two farms. He and his father had figured out that between them, using the tractor and both teams of horses, they could just do it. The tractor. Whenever Arthur thought of it he saw the giant wheels clawing the air, saw his father's face—purple, eyes bulging out. The day before the funeral he'd driven it, for the first and last time, back to the Luntzes' farm and stuck it in Otto's barn. He didn't want to see it ever again.

But Otto's land was going to be ruined if it wasn't tended properly; that was another worry. He needed to write to Otto and tell him what had happened, ask him to come back and sort things out. Sell the farm, or find someone to rent it to. He knew he had to do it but the thought of putting all that down on paper defeated him. How would you say it? "Dear Otto, Dad was killed your tractor fell on him." How could you write that? His mother would know what to say but she got upset when he asked her to do it. There was no point in pressing her. She wasn't in a state to deal with anything at the moment. He would have liked to talk things over with her, tell her of his worries, but it was out of the question. It would have been a relief to tell someone. To have someone else share his fear that they would end up in debt again. That they could lose the farm.

Some days he felt he didn't care. Let it go. He had no heart for it, now that his father was gone. There seemed no purpose in it anymore. But then he'd think about his mother and Jake. If they lost the farm, what would they do? Where would they go?

So Arthur kept working. In the mornings after the milking was done and he had been over to the Luntzes' to see to the pigs, he harnessed both teams of horses and took them out to the fields and worked them alternately, two hours on, two hours off. They worked sunup to sundown, plowing, harrowing, seeding, up one furrow, down the next. The same thoughts kept going around and around in his head, keeping pace with the heavy footsteps of the horses. Keeping pace with his grief. He ached with grief, felt sick with worry. Once he said aloud, startling himself and the horses, "What am I goin' to do, Dad?" And the silence rushed in so hard, so fast, it knocked the breath out of him. He stopped in his tracks and the horses came to a halt and looked around at him inquiringly. "It's okay," he said, but he was crying all at once and they looked uncertain. "It's okay," he said again, wiping his face with his sleeve. "Move on." They moved on, and he followed along behind, tears running down.

Sticking to the routine was all he knew how to do, but the routine was of his father's devising, and memories ambushed him at every turn. For a few days after the accident the imprint of his father's behind was still visible, alongside Arthur's own, in the long grass bordering the field where they'd been sowing the potatoes. It seemed incredible. Just days ago, so recently that the grasses hadn't straightened up yet, they'd sat together, sipping hot sweet tea, surveying how much they'd done and how much was still to do. Not knowing.

Had they spoken, that last time? He couldn't remember. Probably not. They didn't speak much. There was no need. One of them might say, "Soil's heavy," or "Lookin' pretty good," and the other might nod. Or they might just finish their tea in silence and heave themselves to their feet and go back to the teams.

Now he found he couldn't sit down for his break. He drank his tea standing up, beside whichever team he was using. His father's horses were gentle with him. He'd expected them to play up, unsettled by a strange hand on the plow, but they did not. It seemed to him that they understood. They were the only comfort he had, out there alone in the fields all day.

At dinnertime and again in the evening he'd walk back to the house along the track and for the first couple of weeks the prints of his father's boots were still there, like his signature written on the land. Then it rained and they were gone. That had seemed a treachery, that his footsteps could be erased so easily. How many thousands of times had he walked along that track? All his life. His own father, Arthur's grandfather, had brought the track into being, had cleared the land and plowed the very first furrow behind the broad swaying back of an ox. Their footsteps should have stayed forever.

Last thing at night he went out to the barns for a final look around before bed, as he and his father had always done, just to check that everything was okay. They used to stand for a minute or two in the farmyard afterwards, studying the sky, and Arthur did it still, couldn't break the habit, though of all the moments of his day it caused the greatest pain. He stood alone in the silence of the night, remembering. In his mind's eye he saw the two of them— always saw them the same, standing together, faces turned upwards. Clouds pale against the blue-black of the night. Stars cold and bright. The moon hanging there, pale and brilliant, clouds drifting across it like smoke. The sky and the silent land beneath it stretching on, and on, and on, so that he and his father were shrunk to almost nothing by the vastness of it. Two tiny insignificant specks, side by side, faces upturned, staring at the sky.

~

They had to write to Otto. There was no way around it. It was mid-July now and Otto's fields were a mass of sow thistle. They couldn't keep putting it off.

He said, "Mum, we've gotta tell him. He's gotta sell the land or rent it to someone else, or it's goin' to be ruined."

They were at the supper table. Jake was there, for once. Arthur hardly ever saw him anymore. School had finished for the summer but Jake was always "out." Their mother was in a permanent state of panic about him. "Where could he be, Arthur?" she'd say at five-minute intervals. "Where do you think he is?" As it happened, Arthur knew where he was, some of the time at least. He was very close at hand, in the hay barn, to be exact, with a girl. Not always the same girl—at the moment it was Susan Leroux, a thin, wiry, dark-eyed girl who lived with her drunken bum of a father in a shack down by the sawmill. She was several years older than Jake and had a "reputation," and Jake was busy enhancing it.

Tonight, though, he was at home, in body if not in spirit, sitting at the table with them, reading a comic book while he ate.

"You're gonna have to write to Otto," Arthur said to his mother, trying to speak firmly. He had to make her understand.

She was instantly upset. "But Arthur, they don't know yet what they want to do. They might want to come back. Surely we can keep it in order for them."

Her lips were quivering. You'd have thought that after suffering such a loss nothing else would matter to her but that didn't seem to be how it worked. She was fearful about everything now. It was as if she had finally seen the awful power of fate, its deviousness, the way it could wipe out in an instant the one thing you had been certain you could rely on, and now she was constantly looking over her shoulder, trying to work out where the next blow might fall.

Arthur said, trying to be gentle but still firm, "I can't do it, Mum. I've tried. I just can't cover the ground. Come fall, if Otto doesn't do somethin' I'm gonna have to sell the sows. We're not gonna to be able to feed 'em through the winter. We're not even gonna be able to feed our own cows. Anyway, I can hardly milk 'em all— it's takin' me hours."

She said tearfully, "I'll try to help you more, Arthur. I know I haven't been much help."

That was for sure. She couldn't seem to get herself together. She would start milking and half an hour later Arthur, working his way down the row of patient animals, would find her still in the same place, sitting on the milking stool, face vacant, hands in her lap. Even her own jobs, tasks she'd been doing all her life—the row crops, the farm accounts, the chickens, collecting the eggs—seemed to be beyond her. Even cooking the meals. "Oh, goodness," she would say when Arthur came in at the end of the day. "Goodness, Arthur. Your supper . . ."

She seemed to have lost her mind. That felt like the right expression. She looked permanently bewildered, as if she had just put something down and now couldn't find it. Arthur would get himself bread and cheese. Or not bother. Just go to bed.

If only she would see the truth of what he was saying now, if only she wouldn't argue. He didn't have the strength to argue with her. He was exhausted to the point of despair.

But she was going on. "We can't let them down like that, Arthur. Not after all they've been through. We must find another way."

"There *ain't no other way*!" He stopped. She'd jumped and was staring at him, wide-eyed. He took a deep breath and tried to collect himself. "There ain't—isn't . . . there isn't no other way, Mum. There's only me to do it all, and I can't."

"You should get yourself a POW," Jake said, not looking up from his comic. Superman was raising his fist to the sky.

"What?" Arthur said, impatiently. All he needed was Jake sticking his oar in. There was no reason on God's earth why Jake couldn't help with the milking, but of course he didn't. Jake did nothing. Jake did nothing so consistently, so defiantly, that it was almost as if their father were still alive and Jake was still fighting him, still refusing, as a matter of principle, to do one single thing his father would have approved of.

"A POW," Jake said. "A prisoner of war."

"What about him!" Arthur said, almost shouted, exasperated beyond endurance. What did he care about lousy stinking POWs? They could all drown themselves as far as he was concerned.

Jake looked up at him. "You should get yourself one," he said. "Lots of farms have them—they're all over the place. There are about a dozen of them working at the sawmill. They've got them down the mines and everything." He went back to his comic.

Arthur sat there, staring at him. "They let POWs work on the farms?" he said at last.

Jake flipped a page. He said, "Why don't you ever know what's going on, Art? Are you deaf or blind or what?"

Arthur looked at his mother.

"I don't think it's a good idea," she said instantly. He could tell she'd known about it. Deliberately hadn't told him. "Enemies, working on your farm. It's not safe!"

"They don't let the dangerous ones do it, Mum," Jake said.

"How do they know who's dangerous?" their mother cried. "They wouldn't know until it was too late! Until we're all dead in our beds!"

Arthur was trying to take it in. A prisoner of war, working for you. Helping out in the fields.

"Don't they run away?" he said at last.

"Where to?" Jake said. He tossed the comic aside and reached for the bread. "Anyway, they're too scared of bears." He grinned. "They wear this uniform—blue with a big red circle on the back, like a target—and somebody told them the bears really go for the red circle, like bulls. A couple of them broke out the first week, someone said, and after two days they were back. Asked to be let in."

Arthur turned it over in his mind, looked at it this way and that.

His mother said, "Arthur! I won't have them here! They're Nazis! Murderers!"

Arthur said, "Can you have more than one?"

"Dunno," Jake said.

"Arthur," his mother said, her voice low and trembling, "We are not going to have murderers on our farm."

Their names were Dieter and Bernhard—Arthur didn't catch which was which at the time and never did know for sure—and they were delivered bright and early one Saturday morning, dumped out of the back of a truck like a couple of young bullocks.

"There ya go," the guard said. He was a scrawny little guy with wispy white hair and a rifle bigger than he was. He must be one of the veterans from the last war: they were the ones who guarded the prisoners. "They're all yours. You can keep 'em here, or we can take 'em back to the camp at night, up to you. Course, you lose a couple of hours' work if you do that, so if I was you I'd keep 'em here. They get thirty cents a day, twenty cents bonus if they do a real good job, don't give it to them—give it to us, we keep it for them. They get three meals a day. If you keep 'em here, they can sleep in the barn till it gets cold, then you gotta take 'em into the house. What's it to be?"

They were about sixteen, Arthur guessed. Younger than Jake, but strong-looking, both of them, not thin and weedy like Jake was. They looked scared to death. They were watching him as though they thought he was going to stab them in the belly with a pitchfork. It made him uncomfortable.

"So what's it to be?" the guard said again, sucking his teeth.

Arthur couldn't see them slitting anybody's throat. They were just kids. His mother was hiding in the house, cowering behind the sofa, probably, or crouched inside a cupboard; it troubled him to add to her fears, but it couldn't be helped. Anyway, she'd be okay once she saw them. He wasn't going to waste two hours' working time a day.

"I'll keep 'em here," he said.

"You can't mistreat 'em," the guard said warningly. "Geneva Convention, for one thing; and for another, if you mistreat 'em the Krauts'll mistreat ours. Tit for tat. So don't knock 'em about and don't starve 'em. Somebody'll check up on 'em from time to time, check they're workin' all right and you're treatin' 'em okay."

"I ain't gonna hurt them," Arthur said. "Tell them that."

"I don't speak no Kraut," the guard said, "and they don't speak no English. Some do but these two don't."

That was fine by Arthur; he didn't speak it much himself. Though he would have liked the boys to know that he meant them no harm.

"They know anythin' about farming?" he said hopefully. "Like, do ya know what they did before?" What did people do in Germany? Fought wars, mostly. Probably these two had been in the regular army or a weapons factory or something.

"They were at school," the guard said, consulting a sheet of paper. "But they both grew up on farms. That's what it says here anyways."

"Yeah?" Arthur said, hardly daring to believe it. He looked at the boys, who were watching him apprehensively. He waved his hand at the fields, raised his eyebrows enquiringly. The boys looked at each other, shifted their feet uneasily, whispered together. Then they shook their heads violently.

"Ah," said Arthur. He'd known it was too good to be true.

"They didn't understand you," the guard said. "I reckon they thought you was sayin' were they goin' to try to escape. Try somethin' else."

"Like what?" Arthur said.

"I dunno what. Whaddaya do on a farm? Show 'em a tractor or somethin'. Show 'em a cow."

The boys were looking apprehensively from the guard to Arthur and back again. Arthur pointed to the cows, grazing peacefully two fields away. The boys looked bewildered. Arthur made milking motions with his hands. The boys looked at each other . . . and you could see the light dawn, you could literally *see* it. They both grinned and looked back at Arthur and made milking motions to match his own. Beautiful, firm, graceful milking motions, you could hear the milk hissing into the pails. Arthur felt himself smiling, felt relief flowing through him like a wave of cool cream. He loved those two boys. He even loved the guard. He wanted to fall on his knees and thank somebody, but he wasn't sure who. God? The government? Jake?

They knew how to work, those boys. Up at five to milk the cows (doing the job properly, giving the cows a little something to munch on to keep them happy, washing down their udders well, milking them swiftly, giving them a quick pat of thanks and moving on down the row) then into the kitchen, bright and eager, for a quick breakfast of porridge and bread and butter, then out to the fields till noon. In for dinner, pork from Otto's pigs, or maybe a chicken, with vegetables from the garden (served with much clucking and wordless urging by Arthur's mother, who had been converted within ten seconds of seeing their scared young faces). Back out to the fields until sundown. It turned out that neither of them was all that good behind the plow, but they were trying hard and getting better. They worked as if their lives depended on it. Worked until Arthur wondered if maybe they were still afraid he'd beat them, or maybe afraid he'd say they weren't good enough and send them back to the prison camp, and then they'd be sent somewhere worse. But then, seeing one of them lean his face into the warm neck of a cow one morning and straighten up a minute later with his eyes suspiciously moist, he figured it out: they were homesick. Homesick, and the cows and the pigs and the heavy soil were as near as they could get to home. It was their fathers' fields they were seeing all day as they worked Arthur's land. Arthur could understand that. He'd have been the same.

And in fact, in some vague way quite apart from their usefulness, their presence here on his father's farm was a comfort to him too. Even the fact that they couldn't communicate with words seemed right.

They were definitely good for his mother. She liked having them to fuss over. "Such *nice* boys," she said. She was still anxious and distracted, but she was better than she had been. At least she had meals ready on time. "They're so polite." They said "*Danke schon*" when she set their dinners down in front of them and carried their plates over to the sink when they'd finished. "Their parents must be good people. Like Otto and Gertie. Brought their boys up to be polite and hard-working."

"Yeah," Jake said, tipping his chair back on its hind legs. "They straighten the straw in the barn every morning when they climb out of it. Sweep it into nice straight lines. Polish the cows."

"I wish they'd sleep in the house," his mother said, not noticing Jake's tone. She'd made up beds in the parlour—put pillows on the floor and folded blankets for mattresses—and shown them to the boys, but they'd shaken their heads politely and indicated that they liked the barn.

"Probably used to barns," Jake said. He rocked back and forth, looking vaguely out the window. "Probably live in barns at home. It would be nice if they washed now and then, but you can't have everything."

She noticed that. "Jacob," she said reprovingly. "They wash at the pump every single morning."

Jake kept on rocking, gazing at nothing. "Do they? Must be just part of them, then. Maybe Nazis just stink like that naturally."

Funny how much he disliked them, Arthur thought, when he was the one whose idea it had been to get them in the first place. But who knew what went on inside Jake's head? Arthur had seen him out in the fields one evening—it was such a rare sight that he had stopped and looked again to be sure it was Jake. He was standing at the edge of the ditch where their father had died. Not doing anything, just looking down into the ditch. It had seemed to Arthur that he looked rather a forlorn figure standing there. Which was odd, because the last word you would ever use to describe Jake was forlorn.

~

Arthur took one team of horses and either Dieter or Bernhard over to the Luntz farm. The fields were in a bad state, thick with weeds, but if they plowed them under they might just get a little barley in and hope for a longer than usual summer. It was worth a try. But in the farm-yard Dieter, or maybe Bernhard, suddenly stopped in his tracks, staring at the ground in front of him.

"What?" Arthur said.

The boy pointed down at his feet, looking at Arthur, eyes wide.

Arthur looked down. There was nothing there, not so much as a blade of grass. They were outside the barn where Otto kept the tractor, and the ground was packed hard from the tractor's weight, the tread marks set in there like concrete.

"What?" Arthur said again. The boy knelt down and traced his finger around one of the tractor treads. He looked up at Arthur and pointed to the barn, eyebrows raised in question. He stood up and went to the barn and pulled the door open, the hinges already creaking with rust from lack of use. The tractor was standing where Arthur had left it the day after his father's funeral. The sight of it made him feel sick. The boy climbed nimbly up onto it, sat himself down, and gripped the steering wheel with both hands, grinning from ear to ear.

So. In Germany they had tractors. Probably the other boy drove one too. Which explained why neither of them was much good at plowing with the horses.

The boy pointed past Arthur to the fields beyond, and raised his eyebrows hopefully.

"No," Arthur said. It came out flatter and harder than he'd intended and the boy stopped grinning and got down off the tractor. He came out and closed the door of the barn and stood with his back to it, looking puzzled and a little bit scared.

"It's okay," Arthur said. "We just don't use it, that's all."

The boy nodded vigorously, as if he understood and agreed. He went to the horses and led them over to the gate.

Arthur stood where he was, looking past the boy to the sprawling fields of weeds. He thought of his father, not as he had been in the final, terrible moments of his death but as he had been in life. He'd been stubborn, sure, but not to the point of downright foolishness. Not to the point where he'd allow a neighbour's land to be ruined when it was in his power to save it. Not when there was a war on and the country needed every last mouthful of food it could produce. Using the horses, it would take Dieter/Bernhard, inexperienced as he was, a whole day, sunup to sundown, to plow half an acre of land. Arthur could do double that, but according to Otto, with a tractor you could do four to five acres in that time. And here was a boy who knew how to use it. Arthur could guess what his father would say, up there in heaven, if he happened to be looking down at the moment. "Stoopid," he'd say, spitting the word out like he did when he was really disgusted by something. "Just plain stoopid." If Arthur tried to argue with him, if he said, "But I hate it, Dad," his father would snap, "So what!"

The boy had opened the gate and was leading the horses through. Arthur cleared his throat. "Well, just a minute."

The boy looked around at him.

"Maybe you could use it here," Arthur said reluctantly.

Dieter/Bernhard craned his head forward a little. Both boys did that when they were trying to guess Arthur's meaning.

"Just here, though," Arthur said warningly, spreading his hand across Otto's fields and then bringing it down sharp to mark the boundary between the two farms. "It ain't comin' on our land. I don't want to see it. Just keep it here."

He didn't see it—the boy took care of that—but sometimes he heard it. Sometimes when the wind was in the right direction the heavy growling of it drifted across from Otto's farm. Strangely, though, it wasn't his father Arthur saw when he heard the sound. It was Carl. Carl, sitting high up there on the tractor, eyes narrowed against the sun, churning his way down the field as if the past four years had never been. As if the whole bloody mess of the war and everything that followed from it had been nothing but a bad dream.

~

It was the summer of 1944 when Reverend March and his daughter came to Struan. Reverend Gordon was still overseas with the troops, and in the interim his place had been filled by a succession of clergymen who had come out of retirement to fill the gap, then found the rigours of life in the North too much for them and left again. But Reverend March was from North Bay, so, the people of Struan reasoned, he should know what he was letting himself in for.

He was an old man, going on seventy, stern-looking (but kindly, beneath it, everyone agreed on that), grey-haired and slightly stooped. He was recently widowed—his wife had died of influenza—and had welcomed the move to Struan for his daughter's sake, hoping that a new environment would help her get over her loss. The daughter's name was

Laura. She was seventeen or eighteen, very young to be the child of such an old man. She was in church the first Sunday after they arrived, sitting by herself in the pew at the front. Before the service began her father introduced her, speaking from the pulpit, and she stood up and turned around to smile at the congregation. Arthur saw her and fell in love so hard that he felt bruised all over for a week.

It couldn't have been her beauty that triggered his fall, because she didn't look beautiful that day. Her eyes were red and her face was pale and the smile she gave the congregation was apprehensive and unhappy.

"Poor little soul," Arthur's mother said on the way home. "It's only been a few months since her mother died. I don't think it was right to uproot her so soon."

Arthur wasn't listening. He was busy trying to still the chaos within. He felt as if something huge had grabbed him and swung him around half a dozen times and then dropped him on his head.

"They're staying with Dr. and Mrs. Christopherson until the house is ready," his mother said. "It's a shame they couldn't move straight in when they arrived but they had to wait for Gertie and Otto's permission, and their letter didn't get here till Thursday."

She was taking an interest in things again, sounding almost like her old self. If he'd noticed, Arthur would have been relieved.

She was prattling on. "But Gertie's happy the house won't be standing empty any longer and of course the rent will be helpful for them. It gives them more time to decide whether or not they're going to come back. It's Gertie, you see. She can't bear to sell it, and she can't bear to live in it. They're still with her sister in Oshawa. Anyway, I told her we'd move their furniture into that big bedroom at the back of the house. Reverend March is bringing his own; I don't know why. I said you and the boys would do it, Arthur. Move the furniture. And it would be nice if you could clear up around the yard so that it looks tidy when they move in. Arthur? Are you listening?"

"What?"

"I said I'd like you and the boys to tidy up around the yard before the Marches move in. Get it looking nice for them. And then help them move their things in. Everything's sitting in Dr. Christopherson's garage at the moment; a big truck brought it all up for them last week. Would you have time to do the yard tomorrow? You or one of the boys?"

"What yard?"

"Goodness' sake, Arthur! The Reverend and Laura— don't you think that's a pretty name? They're moving into Otto and Gertie's house, for the time being at least. If they like it here they might stay permanently. Maybe if Gertie and Otto decide not to come back, the Marches will buy their house. It would be handy for everybody, don't you think? Anyway, they want to move in as soon as they can."

They were moving into the *Luntzes'* house? That girl was going to be his *neighbour*? Arthur was stunned. He went over to the Luntzes' farm at least twice a day to see how Dieter/Bernhard was making out. He would see her every day. Every day! He didn't know whether to be over-joyed or appalled. She'd see how stupid he was, how he never knew what to say.

As for helping her and her father move in, that might take *hours*. He wasn't sure he'd survive hours in her company.

~

When it came to it, it was Laura who looked as if she might not survive.

"Over there, I think," Reverend March said. "At an angle, if you follow my meaning, Arthur. Facing the fire, but not head-on. What do you think, Laura?"

"Yes," Laura said. "Yes."

Arthur held the great high-backed armchair in front of him like a shield. He had to peer around the wing of it, like a child afraid of monsters, to see where Reverend March was pointing. He set the chair down carefully.

"Excellent," Reverend March said. "That's perfect. Don't you think, Laura?"

"Yes," Laura said. "Yes, that's nice."

Arthur was bringing their things in on his own. He'd sent Dieter and Bernhard off in the truck to collect more of the Marches' furniture from the doctor's garage. He'd had a moment's unease as he watched the truck rumbling off down the road—two POWs who'd been given the perfect getaway vehicle: if the prison camp guard got to hear about it, he would have a heart attack. But half an hour later they were back. They just plain didn't want to escape.

They'd made three trips already, picking things up from the garage and unloading them in the farmyard: chairs, beds, lamps, a sofa, a dining table, a bureau, a sideboard, chests of drawers—all of it standing with its feet in the dust.

Arthur carted into the house everything he could carry on his own. Reverend March had tried to help but Arthur's mother had forbidden it. "Goodness, Reverend, you mustn't! Or you, Laura! Goodness, no! Let Arthur do it!

You just decide where things should go." She was rushing around polishing things, cleaning things that were already perfectly clean. She kept apologizing for Jake not being there to help. "He so wanted to be here," she said, "but he . . . he'd promised to help a friend today." (Jake had said, "Well I can't. I'm busy.") "He's a little older than you, Laura. But he had an accident and missed a year of school so I expect you'll be in the same class in September."

Arthur brought in a small side table. Most of the furniture was big heavy stuff, made of a rich, dark wood he didn't recognize but feared might be expensive. He was scared he would damage something. He'd given the boys a pile of old blankets to wrap around things when they were loading them, and he brought each piece into the house carefully, easing it through doorways.

Reverend March wanted the downstairs sorted first, which seemed the wrong way around—shouldn't you sort out where you were going to sleep first of all?—but Arthur didn't say so. He was trying to get the job done as quickly as possible, for Laura's sake as well as his own. By then he'd realized the state she was in.

It had been quite a while before he'd noticed. For a start he was fuzzy-headed with lack of sleep. He'd spent the night thinking about her, worrying about making a fool of himself in front of her, worrying that she would not know he'd tried to enlist and would think he was a coward—a zombie, they called them—who had refused to fight for his country. Then in the morning, when he and his mother went over to the Luntzes' farm to open up the house and get it aired, he'd started thinking about Carl again. He kept seeing him coming down the stairs or disappearing around a corner, and it made his insides feel hollow. And then the

Marches arrived and his confusion about Laura came piling back in on top of everything else, and his mind was
just a mess, not a clear thought in it.

He had been out in the farmyard when she and her father
drove up in the reverend's old car. Laura was wearing a big
floppy hat that shaded her face, so maybe he wouldn't have
seen how she looked anyway, but he was afraid to look at
her for fear she would see his confusion. He mumbled his
hellos to her and her father and carried on carting things
into the house. His mother said, "Oh, the poor child," a
couple of times under her breath, but she'd been saying
that all week, so he didn't think anything of it.

He was so *aware* of her, that was the problem. It was
as if she sent out some sort of beam, as if she were surrounded by a light that was denied to everyone else in
the world. And worse than that, being aware of her somehow made him aware of himself as well. He became so
self-conscious he could hardly walk straight. He was terrified he'd trip over his own feet. Drop something valuable.
Fall down the stairs.

But then, about halfway through the morning, he'd
suddenly noticed that she was saying yes to everything.
Absolutely everything, without exception.

"Ah," Reverend March said. "The bureau. Lovely.
Where do you think, Laura? Over by that wall?"

"Yes," Laura said. "Yes, that's nice."

"Maybe you could move that chair, Arthur. To the
right a bit. There! That's excellent, don't you think?"

"Yes. Yes, it is."

"Laura, dear," said Arthur's mother, appearing suddenly
in the doorway. "Laura, would you like me to unpack the
china for you?"

"Oh, yes. Yes, thank you, Mrs. Dunn."

"Should I put it into whatever cupboard I think, dear, just to give you a bit more space? Then you could rearrange it yourself later?"

"Thank you, yes. Thank you, Mrs. Dunn."

Once he'd noticed it, he kept on noticing it, and finally he'd stolen a sideways look at her. They were in the parlour by then. The Luntzes had never used their parlour. Arthur had passed the door countless times but he couldn't remember ever being in it before. Laura was standing beside her father in the middle of the room. She'd taken her hat off when she entered the house so now he could see her face clearly, and he was shocked by the look of her. She was extremely pale, her skin a bruised, bluish white, and her eyes were terribly swollen, the eyelids shiny and red. She looked like she'd been skinned, like you could see the inside of her, all raw and bloody. He saw that she didn't care where anything went or whether it looked better here or there. He saw that he needn't have worried what she'd think of him. She wasn't thinking of him. She hardly knew he was there.

After that, he stopped worrying about himself. He just brought things in and set them down as quickly as he could. It seemed to him that she was holding herself together by a thread and he wanted to get out before the thread snapped.

The boys came back with the final load of furniture and the three of them finished bringing in the pieces for downstairs. Then they all trooped upstairs to sort out the bedrooms. There wasn't much in the way of bedroom furniture—just the two beds and two chests of drawers and a couple of trunks containing bed linen and clothes.

"You've chosen which room you want, haven't you, Laura?" her father said. They were on the landing, Arthur and one of the boys supporting an iron bed frame between them. Arthur was trying to block out thoughts of Carl. Anxiety about Laura had pushed Carl out of his mind while they were downstairs, but now he was back.

"Yes," Laura said.

"Perhaps you'd just show Arthur where you want the bed," her father said. "Oh, excellent. Here comes my chest of drawers." He disappeared into another bedroom.

Laura said, "This room." And in the fraction of a second before she spoke, Arthur knew whose room it would be.

Laura had gone in and was looking around; her footsteps echoed on the bare wooden floor. Arthur stood on the landing, holding up his end of the bed frame, wondering if he could ask her to choose another room. Knowing he couldn't.

"I guess against this wall," Laura said, disappearing behind the door.

Arthur licked his lips. There was nothing he could do. He nodded at Dieter/Bernhard and they turned the bed frame on its side and eased it through the doorway. The antlers were gone, of course. There was nothing to show that they had been there but a pockmarking of nail holes in the slatted wooden walls.

"Over there, I guess," Laura said. "Against that wall."

They put the bed against the wall. Arthur straightened up slowly. There had been no bodies; that was part of the problem. No funerals. Just memorial services. Which meant that it had been possible, some of the time at least, to pretend that Carl and the others were still just "over there." Not really dead, just absent. Now, by the act of putting down someone else's bed in the exact spot where Carl's had been, he had made it real. He, Arthur Dunn, the one who had stayed at home, safe and comfortable, saved by his bloody feet, which had never given him a moment's trouble in his life. And Carl and the other guys he'd grown up with, guys he'd sat beside in that damned school year after year—all but a couple who were in hospitals somewhere overseas with bits of them shot off—all of them dead. Setting down the bed, shoving it up against that terrible, bare wall, it felt as though he were betraying them. Stupid, maybe, but that was how it felt.

Laura was saying something. He pulled himself together.

"Pardon?" he said. He forgot not to look at her and her appearance shocked him all over again.

"Did you know them well?" she said. "The people who lived here?"

It took him a moment to answer, to be sure that his throat was clear. Then he said, "Yeah. Pretty well."

"They had three boys, someone told me," Laura said. "And they've all been killed."

"Yeah."

"Were they . . . were they friends of yours?"

He nodded. "'Specially the youngest one, Carl. We were friends."

Maybe it was that final detail, on top of everything else, or maybe it was just that she was too tired to hold on any longer, but all at once she was crying, silently, still looking at him, not even turning her head away. There was a movement behind him—Dieter/Bernhard abandoning ship, hightailing it out of the room. Arthur stood where he was.

"I'm sorry," Laura said, wiping the tears away with the

flat of her hand. "I heard your dad died too. I'm so sorry. Everybody seems to be dying. Everybody."

"Yeah," Arthur said. "I know." That was how it felt all right.

"I'm sorry," she said again.

"It's okay."

"My dad says it's part of God's plan," she said. "He says we just don't understand. He says everything will turn out for the best because God cares for us. But I don't believe it. I don't believe He cares for us. I don't believe anyone who cared for you would have a plan like that. Do you believe it?"

Arthur shifted his feet uncomfortably. He said, "I don't know much about that sort of stuff."

She wiped her face with her hand again and asked miserably, "Do you think I'm wicked, for thinking that?"

"No." He shook his head. "No."

He heard her father's voice on the landing and held his breath, afraid he might come in, but then there was the sound of footsteps going downstairs.

"Do you wish we weren't here?" Laura said. "In your friend's house?"

"No!" Arthur said. He was dismayed. Had he made her think that? Had his feelings been that obvious?

"Are you sure?"

"Yes! Yes, I'm sure! It's good it isn't empty. It's better than it being empty." And maybe that would be so, in the long run.

"Thank you," she said, as if he'd given her a gift. She dug a sodden handkerchief out of her sleeve and blew her nose. She said, "I didn't want to come here, to this sad house, but there wasn't anywhere else. I didn't want to come here at all, to Struan, I mean. I don't know any-body. At least at home I had my friends." She looked at him out of her sore, red eyes, and said, "But you've been really nice. You and your mum. Thank you."

~

Sitting on his bed that night, looking down at his feet, he went over it again and again in his mind. It seemed to him that something huge had happened, that his life had changed forever. In all his days he could not have imagined having such a conversation with a girl. He mustn't kid him-self that it meant anything, though. He knew it was just luck, though luck seemed the wrong word in the circum-stances. She wouldn't have chosen him to confide in if she'd had any choice. It was just that she was in despair and he happened to be there; if she hadn't been in such a state, the conversation wouldn't have taken place. In fact, if he hadn't been feeling pretty sick about things himself, it wouldn't have taken place, because he'd have fled—he'd have beaten Dieter/Bernhard down the stairs.

But she had thanked him for being nice. That meant something, didn't it? Not much, maybe, but something.

~

The following week a German POW was murdered in the woods down by Crow River. Or at least, that was where his body was found. Arthur was there when they found him; he and the men he was with weren't looking for bodies, they were looking for bears. Five sheep and two calves had been killed in the area in the previous weeks and one farmer, Frank Sadler, had had a visit from a bear while he'd been going about his business in his outhouse.

"Did me a favour, really," Frank said, telling the story afterwards. "I'd been havin' a bit of a problem in that department, bit of a logjam, you might say. I was startin' to think it'd take dynamite to shift it, but he scared the whole lot outta me in two seconds flat. But Lona and the kids, they're all scared to go out there now. Nobody's regular anymore, an' it's makin' them bad-tempered. Somethin's gotta be done."

So half a dozen farmers, Arthur among them, set up a posse and went bear hunting. The truth was, Arthur would rather have gone on his own—that way he would only have the bear to worry about and not half a dozen nervous guys waving Lee-Enfields around as well. But they had asked him along, which was good of them, granted that they were his father's generation; and he hadn't known how to say no.

Having bears on the brain, when they came across the body they assumed at first that a bear had done the killing. Then they saw that there were no teeth or claw marks. And then they saw that the man's hands were tied behind his back. From the look of him, he'd been beaten to death.

"Anybody know him?" Charlie Rugger asked. They were standing in a circle around the body, six burly farmers with their rifles pointing at the ground. It was early morning and the sun was filtering slant-wise through the maples, dappling the body with light. The man was wearing the prison camp uniform—dark blue jacket with a big red circle on the back—and the sun made gently flickering maple-leaf patterns on the circle as if the man was Canadian and proud of it.

"Yeah," Lennie Hogenveld said, squatting down so he could see the side of the man's face. It was a mess, but you could just about make out his features. "He was workin' for Stan McLean."

"Any guesses who might want to do it?"

"Sure," Lennie said. "I could name you two dozen right off the bat. He's a Kraut, isn't he?"

"Yeah, but him in particular," Charlie said.

Lennie shrugged. Every Thursday the *Temiskaming Speaker* carried a list of Northern boys killed, wounded, or missing in action, on its front page and every week the list seemed to get longer. In the follow-up to D-day several families had lost all their sons. If the murder was the work of a madman—and from the state of the body it looked as though it was—well, there were plenty of madmen about nowadays, fathers or sons or brothers driven out of their minds with grief and rage.

It turned out that whoever had done it had gone for the man in the night. There were signs of a commotion in Stan McLean's barn, where he'd been sleeping, straw all over the place. Arthur decided to bring the boys into the house to sleep. It was still warm enough in the barn and they protested, but he wasn't taking any chances. He also didn't like the idea of Dieter/Bernhard being all alone out in Otto's fields during the day but there was nothing he could do about that. Thanks to the driest August for years the barley was ready to harvest, and they had to get it in. At least Otto's place was occupied now and most of the fields were visible from the house.

He'd hoped that Dieter and Bernhard wouldn't learn about the incident, but when the guard from the prison camp made one of his visits to check up on them there were other POWs in the truck, and of course the boys were keen to talk to them. Arthur saw by their faces afterwards that they'd been told.

He'd hoped Laura wouldn't hear about it—another death for her to deal with—but that was a vain hope too; Reverend March was one of the first to be called. Arthur saw her a couple of days after the murder. It was two weeks since the Marches had moved in but he hadn't seen much of her in that time, or at least not close enough to talk to. In the mornings he and Dieter/Bernhard came over at about half past six and though her father was up and sometimes came out to say good morning, and though the tractor must have wakened Laura, she was never around so early. When Arthur came at the end of the day she and her father were usually eating their supper. He'd get the odd glimpse of her as she passed the kitchen window but that was all. At first it was a relief—he was almost as afraid of speaking to her as he had been the first day he saw her. But then he started to think she was avoiding him. Maybe she was ashamed of having broken down in front of him and never wanted to lay eyes on him again. Maybe it was simpler than that; maybe she had realized that he was nothing but a big dumb farmer and not worth the effort of speaking to.

But that morning, two days after the murder of the POW, he was at the farm a little longer than usual. He'd run out of nails (everybody had run out of nails; it seemed every nail in the country had been requisitioned) and it had occurred to him that there might be some in Otto's shed. Which there were, a whole quart pickling-jar full. When he emerged triumphantly from the shed cradling the jar in the crook of his arm he saw Laura at the kitchen window. She saw him too. She raised her hand in a hesitant wave, then disappeared, and the kitchen door opened and she came out onto the veranda. Arthur made his way across the farmyard to her, his tongue drying in his mouth.

"I saw the shed was open," she said as he came up, "and I wondered for a minute . . . you know . . . who it was. But then I saw it was you."

She was wearing a short-sleeved dress, grey-blue with a white collar. Her hair was loose and drifting every which way about her shoulders and her feet were bare. Pale, slender, perfectly unblemished feet.

"Oh," Arthur said. "Yeah. Sorry. It was me. I was lookin' for somethin'. I shoulda told you I was goin' in there."

"I was just being silly," she said.

She still looked unhappy, he thought, but much better than when he'd seen her last. And beautiful. So beautiful. As if her beauty had been hidden under the dark weight of her grief and now was starting to emerge.

There was a silence. Arthur tried to think what else to say. "Found these," he said finally, lamely, holding up the jar of nails.

She leaned forward slightly. "Are they nails?"

"Yeah. It's good, 'cause they're short. I mean, not the nails are short—they're all sizes—just you can't get nails nowhere anymore. *Anywhere* anymore."

He stopped abruptly. What was he *talking* about? She wouldn't care about nails, she'd think he was crazy.

But she nodded. "Like everything," she said. "Shortages."

"Yeah," he said gratefully.

He looked away. The tractor disappeared behind a clump of trees and reappeared on the other side. "Well," Arthur said, but at the same moment she said, "Is he safe out there, do you think? On his own?"

"Should be okay in the daytime," he said, though he still wasn't happy about it. "I bring 'em in at night now though." It sounded as if he was talking about cattle. "Dieter and Bernhard, I mean. They sleep in the house now."

"Yes," she said. "Good." Then she added, "Which is the one who comes here? Is he Dieter? Or Bernhard?"

"I dunno," Arthur said. "I never worked out who's who." He gave her an embarrassed smile and she smiled back.

"They're nice. Both of them. You can tell."

He nodded. They listened to the tractor grinding away. A German boy riding it, like in the days before the war.

"Normally it's real peaceful here," he said, afraid that she'd think Struan was the kind of place that had madmen and murderers in it in normal times. "We never had a murder before. There's been fights and stuff, but never a real murder. Not that I know of."

"I know," she said. "It's the war. It's making people crazy."

"Yeah."

Another silence. He looked out over the fields and cleared his throat. "Well, should be gettin' on."

She said quickly, "Thank you for the other day. I didn't thank you properly. I'm sorry I was . . . upset."

She flushed, and his heart started to thump. But then there was a movement behind her and the screen door opened and her father came out.

"Good morning, Arthur," he said. He smiled and rubbed his hands together briskly. "You're bright and early as usual. You people here put us city dwellers to shame."

"Mornin'." Arthur felt himself go hot. What if Reverend March didn't like him talking to his daughter? He looked friendly enough at the moment, but what if he got the wrong idea? What if he got the *right* idea? Anxiously, he held up the jar of nails as if they were proof of good intentions. "Found these in the shed," he said.

"Nails," Reverend March said. "I hope you're not planning to set up a black market in them, Arthur." He smiled. Then saw his daughter's feet and frowned. "Laura, go and put your shoes on." He spoke gently but you could see he was displeased, as if he thought she wasn't properly dressed.

Laura said, "It's just my feet, Daddy," her tone a little impatient. Maybe they'd had this conversation before.

"Even so," Reverend March said.

She sighed. "Well," she said to Arthur. "Bye."

"Yeah," Arthur said, shifting his feet. "Bye." He and Laura's father were left facing each other with nothing to say. The old man smiled and rubbed his hands together vigorously to show his good will. Arthur smiled back and rattled the nails.

Chopping wood that evening, it came to him that there had been no danger of Reverend March getting the wrong, or the right, idea about his feelings for Laura. The Reverend would have had no fears on that score whatsoever, because the idea was so absurd it would never have entered his head.

It made no difference, the fact that it was absurd. She took over his life anyway. Milking the cows, he thought of her. Repairing the binder. Cutting the corn, threshing the oats, mending the fence. She was with him every minute of the day.

~

How long did it last, that perfect, golden period when he plainly and simply loved her, with no fear of any kind? Two weeks? Three at most. Three weeks lost in love, floating through the days. Not that he wasn't working; it was September now, everyone was working. Every farmer in the province was cloud-watching, working with one eye on the sky, wondering if the rain could possibly hold off until they got the crops in. The whole region was up to its neck in oats; everyone who could be spared was helping with the harvest. So Arthur was living in a haze of work and love, and the weeks slipped by.

~

All this time Jake was busy with his own affairs, whatever they might be. Arthur hardly saw him. If he happened to be home during the half-hour Arthur and the boys took to eat their supper, Arthur would see him then, but that was it. After supper they went out again, worked until it was too dark to see, and then went to bed.

Jake was back at school. The cheating incident of the previous year had been forgiven, and he was now doing his senior matriculation, to their mother's joy. According to her the whole world was waiting for boys who had their senior matriculation. Particularly (Arthur thought but didn't say) if they were excused from going to war. All the jobs that would have been filled by all the boys who were never coming home would be open to Jake.

Arthur suspected that if Jake hadn't had a cast-iron excuse for not signing up he would have concocted one. Fighting for his country wouldn't be Jake's idea of a good time. But there was no comfort in that: no army in the world would accept Jake. If you looked at him from behind, you could see there was something not right about the shape of his spine. The walk to and from school each day was as much as he could manage.

Laura had started school as well. Arthur didn't like to think of her as a schoolgirl, sitting at a desk, sticking up her hand to answer questions. In his mind she was a woman. He wanted her to be at home, and to know that she was close at hand.

"How does Laura seem to be fitting in at school?" their mother asked.

Jake didn't hear her. He was flipping through last week's copy of the *Temiskaming Speaker*.

"Jacob?"

"Yes?"

"How does Laura seem to be fitting in at school?"

"I dunno. Okay, I guess."

"Isn't she in your class?"

"Yes."

"Well, you should help her, Jakey. It must be very difficult, starting at a new school, not knowing anyone. You should introduce her, make sure she gets to know people. She's shy, you know."

"I don't know her, Mum."

"Yes, you do! Of course you do!"

"I've met her once. That isn't knowing her."

"Well, you should get to know her." There was a teasing tone in their mother's voice that Arthur had never heard before. "Don't you think she's lovely? That hair of hers. And she has such a sweet face."

Arthur froze, mid-chew, a lump of potato in his mouth.

"You know," their mother said, "it might be nice if you invited her to come around here after school one day."

Arthur waited, motionless, his eyes on his plate. The potato had glued itself to the roof of his mouth. It, or what his mother was saying, nearly made him gag.

"Don't you think that would be a nice idea?" his mother said.

No reply from Jake. Arthur had to see his expression, so he looked up.

If only he hadn't done that. If only he had just stayed as he was. Swallowed his potato, kept his head down. If only. But he raised his head, just fractionally, just an inch or so, and the movement caught Jake's eye. And Jake, who had been on the point of saying something irritable to their mother—you could see it in his face—paused and looked at Arthur curiously, and said, "What's the matter?"

Right then, as he felt the slow flush spreading over his face, as he saw Jake notice it, saw the light dawn, saw him smile, Arthur knew what was going to happen. He saw the whole thing, right then.

ELEVEN

~

Ontario to Initiate Certified Swine Policy
Youthful Drivers Banned on Tractors
—*Temiskaming Speaker,* June 1960

"Your daddy was the good boy," Jake said. "I was the bad boy."

Ostensibly it was Julie he was speaking to. It was dinner-time. Since Jake had arrived, meals at the farm were a lot more entertaining, there was no denying that.

"I was *always* getting into trouble," Jake said. Julie was watching him from her place across the table and Ian could see that she wasn't sure whether he was being funny or not.

"I wasn't any good at anything—you know, any of the farm jobs. I couldn't have milked a cow to save my life. But your daddy, by the time he was your age, your daddy

264

could milk two cows at once." He stretched his arms out to the side as far as he could without knocking off March's head, clenched his hands around two imaginary teats and pulled down one hand after another, making a hissing noise like milk spraying into a bucket. Julie decided that was funny and giggled. March was looking sideways up at Jake, under the shadow of his arm. "Oops," Jake said. "Gotcha, March. You're all covered with milk." March looked down in consternation.

"He knew every cow by name, didn't you, Art? There was Daisy and Maisie and Millie and Lily and Polly and Dolly . . . dozens of them, and your dad was on first-name terms with every one. Whereas I'd be out behind the barn trying to burn down the fence posts. Remember the fence posts, Art?"

Arthur gave a fractional nod. Jake's presence hadn't noticeably enlivened Arthur. If anything, the reverse. Jake rattled on with his stories of the good old days and Arthur just sat chewing his dinner, his eyes on his plate, saying not a word.

"Your daddy didn't approve," Jake said, winking at Julie. "He'd try to scrape off all the charred bits. He kept trying to save me from myself, didn't you, Art?"

Even Carter was listening, Ian noticed. He didn't slam out of the house the minute he'd finished eating like he used to; he stuck around, listening to whatever Jake might have to say.

"He didn't manage it though," Jake said mournfully. "To save me, I mean. I was a lost cause." He let his voice trail away, sadly, and Julie giggled again.

For the first couple of days Ian had thought it was a real bonus having him there, an emissary from the outside world, proof that it really did exist. But by the end of the week he was starting to feel that he wanted things to be as they'd been before. Jake's presence changed things; the place felt different with him around. More interesting, but less relaxing. Even the routine was altered. Arthur didn't take his full half-hour break after dinner, for instance. Spring was a busy time, of course, but even so, the mid-day break had always been sacred. No matter what, Arthur, Ian, and the old man used to retire to the arm-chairs as soon as they finished dinner, for what Laura called "digestion time." In the early days Ian had tried to help her with the dishes, but she had looked quite shocked, and said that he must sit down and digest his meal. He'd seen that it was part of the natural order of things, and that was how she wanted it.

Now, though, Jake sat with them, leafing through the *Temiskaming Speaker* and reading out the bits he found funny, which was just about everything, and it seemed to get on Arthur's nerves.

"*Cheese factory works three shifts,*" Jake would read. "Now if that isn't earth-shattering news, I don't know what is. Here's another one, this will interest you, Art. *Memorials— mid-June sale. Special ten percent discount till end of June.* Isn't that great? You can stock up on tombstones! *Keep feed racks in your pastures.* Do you keep feed racks in your pastures, Art? And if not, why not?"

After a few minutes of this Arthur would heave himself to his feet and say to Ian, "Well, gotta get back to it. No need for you to come jus' yet, though. You sit for a bit." And off he'd go, back to the fields.

So Ian could have sat on with Jake, but it didn't feel right, having a rest while Arthur was working. And anyway it wasn't restful. When Arthur went out, Laura allowed Julie and March back in—normally they were banished from the room during digestion time—and they wandered around chattering and asking for things and getting under Laura's feet. She was snappy with them, and even more so with Carter. Carter had always gone out to the barn straight after dinner to fiddle with his bike—it spent more time in pieces on the floor of the barn than it did on the road—but now he stayed, listening to Jake, and for some reason this irritated his mother. She'd say, "Carter, would you get on with things, please?" And he'd get up reluctantly and go out to do whatever task he had been given.

As for Jake himself, he seemed perfectly at ease. Ian couldn't imagine what he found to do all day. Mostly he seemed to follow Laura around, talking to her as she fed the chickens or hoed the row crops or made up a mash for a sick calf. It seemed to Ian that his presence flustered her. There was a tension in her movements that he hadn't seen before. And she didn't look at Jake when she replied to his questions, she seemed to keep herself permanently half-turned away from him. The more Ian saw, the more he was convinced that Laura didn't like Arthur's brother.

Ian liked him fine. The only thing he wasn't keen on was the way Jake hung around Laura. That was starting to make him uneasy. He wondered what Arthur thought of it. But Arthur didn't seem to notice. The way he kept his head down nowadays, he probably didn't even see.

Late one afternoon March found a baby rabbit under a bush by the corner of the barn. By some chance the dogs were off on an errand of their own.

"Catch it!" March shrieked. He threw himself at the bush and it exploded with rabbits, baby rabbits everywhere. They leapt about in panic, then headed for the safety of the long grass that bordered the woods. March ran after them yelling, "Wait! Wait!" but they were gone. For half an hour he combed the grasses, searching, calling softly for them. Ian, who was in the farmyard rubbing down Robert and Edward before turning them out to pasture for the night, went out to him.

"They've gone to find their mother," he explained. "They were too small to be without her. She'll have taken them into the woods where it's safe."

March looked at him tragically.

"Don't you want them to be safe?" Ian said, tousling his hair. "If they stayed around here the dogs would eat them. Wouldn't that be terrible?"

Jake watched the whole thing with amusement. "Sentimental little guy, isn't he?" he said when Ian came back. "Must take after his mother. I don't recall Art ever crying over a rabbit. He'd shoot them and stick them in a pot."

He was sitting on the stump they used as a mounting block, swatting flies with a yellow plastic flyswatter. He'd taken to joining Ian there at the end of the day. It was kind of flattering until you remembered that he had nothing else to do.

"Yes," Ian said. "He does seem to take after Laura." He had finished grooming Edward and just started on Robert. Grooming was a long job—like washing a bus—but one of his favourites; there was real pleasure in seeing the rich, dark glow of the horses' coats emerge from under the dust and sweat of the day. And they loved it, and were appreciative, nuzzling him with their noses from time to time.

"Any of the kids going to be interested in taking over the farm, do you think?" Jake said.

"I don't know." He paused, thinking of Carter. "Carter might. Maybe March too. He likes the animals." Robert prodded him with his nose—get on with it.

"Carter?" Jake said. He seemed to find the idea amusing. "Not a chance. I haven't seen him out in the fields once."

Ian didn't reply. He was remembering Carter's comment about Arthur never letting him do anything. He wondered suddenly if Carter would actually have liked to be working out in the fields beside his father. Strange that Arthur always gave him kids' jobs around the farmyard. In a way it was a shame they didn't have a tractor. Carter would have been really good with that, he was good with anything mechanical. He loved Jake's car, though unlike Jake, it was the engine he was interested in. Jake didn't seem to care about engines. It was the style that mattered to him, Ian thought. The image.

"Anyway," Jake went on, "I reckon the communities up here are doomed. They're being drained of their life blood." He swiped the flyswatter at a horsefly and it wheeled away. "Meaning the likes of you and your friends."

"You think they're going to turn into ghost towns?" Ian said. He couldn't imagine it. Couldn't see Struan deserted, stores boarded up, dust blowing down the street like in a Hollywood western.

"Not necessarily ghost towns, but a lot smaller than they are now. Which . . . damn that thing! I'd forgotten how infuriating they are." The horsefly was back, circling around him just out of range of the flyswatter. "Which will mean even fewer jobs, so even more young people will leave, and so on. A slow decline." He ducked down and the horsefly came to Ian instead. Ian manoeuvred himself so that he was within reach of Robert's tail and the fly went back to Jake.

"Struan's still growing" Ian said. "My dad has so many patients, he's going nuts. 'Specially in the summer—tourists rolling in poison ivy and getting fish hooks in their ears and stuff. And during the hunting season—rich Southerners shooting each other in the tail."

Or during a measles outbreak. There were some pretty sick kids in Struan at the moment. Ian kept an eye on Julie and March but so far they'd both escaped.

"Catering to tourists is no kind of life," Jake said. He abandoned the stump and went over to Edward and ducked down beside him. The horsefly landed on Edward's shoulder and Jake brought the flyswatter smashing down on it. Edward swung his head around and gave him a baleful look.

"But it's not only tourists," Ian protested. Suddenly it seemed important to him that Struan continue to exist. He might not want to live in it but he definitely wanted it to be there. "There are other things. Like, people are always going to need lumber, so they're always going to need the lumber mills, and if you've got a lumber mill you need men to work there, so you need the town."

"Somehow, I don't see you working in a lumber mill," Jake said. He sat back down on the stump. "As for your dad, he's way too good a doctor to be stuck up here. He should be down south. He could be earning three or four times what he's earning here, working half the hours."

Ian had thought the same himself, from time to time, but

now that the idea was voiced by Jake he found he didn't agree. His father would not be happy in some city down south, no matter what they paid him. "I think he just likes it up here," he said.

"Well, maybe," Jake said. "But it's kind of a waste, don't you think? Someone with that much ability, treating people's sore throats?"

Ian concentrated on brushing the area of Robert's shoulder where the collar was inclined to rub. He knew Jake meant it as a compliment but he was offended that anyone would see his father's job in such a light. Being the only doctor in a huge area, on call twenty-four hours a day, three hundred and sixty-five days a year, handling every emergency, the nearest hospital hours away–how could anyone consider that a simple job? It took at least as much skill as being a specialist in a big city, with a hospital full of fancy equipment. His father was important to the people up here, he played a big role in their lives. Didn't they deserve a good doctor? The more Ian thought about it the more offended he was.

But Jake must have sensed what he was thinking because he smiled suddenly and said, "Don't get me wrong, I think your dad's admirable, devoting his life to the people up here. He does a great job, I know that. I'm just biased. I've always thought that if God had meant us to live in the North he wouldn't have given us the brains to find our way south."

~

In the evenings Ian and Pete went fishing, like always. Sometimes they explored, testing out the bays along the western shore of the lake, but that wasn't serious fishing, that was to find good spots to take tourists. Pete was having a busy summer. At the beginning of the season a lawyer from New York, who regularly hired Pete's grandfather as a hunting guide, had asked the old man if he would take him and some of his friends pike fishing. Pete's grandfather passed him on to Pete, and now the word had got around and Pete was in high demand. So high, in fact, that he was having to pass on some of the requests to his friends on the reserve, or he'd never have time to fish himself.

The tourists paid good money, which was great, of course, but according to Pete, the main reason he was happy to help them out was that then he could control where they fished. He wanted to keep them away from Hopeless Inlet. Hopeless was where the phantom muskie had his territory and Pete didn't want anyone else to catch it.

He was still after that fish. They hadn't seen a sign of it in more than two years but he was convinced it was there. Ian was starting to doubt it. The two of them had covered every inch of Hopeless—every marshy river-mouth, every point of land, every reef—and had worked their way along the shore for miles in both directions without a whisper of it. In that time Pete had caught several very big pike but he insisted none of them was the fish that had nearly pulled him out of his boat.

"How do you know?" Ian asked, more than once, clambering up onto the thwart, knees around his ears, trying to keep out of range of the teeth of the twenty-pound monster flailing about in the bottom of the boat. "How do you know this isn't him!"

"He's not big enough."

"Not big enough! You're out of your mind!"

Pete was up on a thwart too. He'd tried to subdue the pike with a paddle but it had knocked it out of his hand and now he was fending it off with an oar. There was blood and water flying all over the boat.

"This is just a pike, man. He's not a muskie. He couldn't pull me outta the boat."

"Sure he could!" Ian yelled. "You were off balance!"

"I was sitting down! How can you be off balance sitting down?"

"He's a figment of your imagination!" Ian said. "He's taken over your brain!"

"He's there, man. He's right down there. I can feel him."

In fact, it made no difference to Ian where or why or how they fished. He was in love with fishing, never mind that all he ever caught was snags and sunfish. There was something about being out on the water, the silvery ever-moving surface hiding God knew what life-and-death struggles underneath, the long stretches of peacefulness that might or might not be broken at any moment by a burst of savage excitement. You could think, during those long stretches—or better still, you could not think. Though lately he had to fight to keep the thoughts at bay. Always the same thoughts: his future, what he was going to do with his life. His own indecision was driving him insane.

He wished he could be more like Jake in that regard. Whatever his other failings, Jake did have an admirable philosophy of life. He summed it up in two words: "Don't sweat." His life had been extraordinary, it seemed to Ian. He'd left home on the spur of the moment and with nothing at all: no money, no plans, no high-school certificate—none of the things they told you were essential. He'd bummed his way around, to start with, getting a job when he ran out of money, leaving it when he'd earned enough to move on. He'd picked peaches in California, worked as a blackjack dealer in New Orleans, been a short-order cook, an encyclopedia salesman, the manager of a classy bar in New York. Most recently he'd had his own company, something to do with real estate, and had just sold it for a "tidy sum." He wasn't sure what he was going to do next, he said; he had a couple of ideas he was playing with. His whole life sounded like a fabulous game. And he made it sound so simple. "Just let things happen," he advised, clapping Ian on the shoulder. "It's the only way to live."

As if it were easy to do what he had done, to leave the well-marked path, resist the pressures, defy people's expectations. It took courage to do that. Courage and imagination. Ian was starting to think he didn't have a grain of either.

"Could you get me a rabbit?" he said now to Pete, pushing the thoughts aside yet again. The pike was subdued now, gasping in the bottom of the boat, occasionally smacking its tail against the floorboards. "Preferably a baby one?" Both Pete and his grandfather had traplines so it was feasible.

"What do you want a rabbit for?"

"For March. Arthur's kid. I thought maybe I'd build him a hutch."

Pete twitched the jig, waited a moment, then jerked it hard, and a smallmouth bass broke the water ten feet away, its body arcing gracefully. "I could get you a dead rabbit," he said, hauling in the line. The bass fought furiously, showering them with spray.

"A live one was more what I had in mind."

"If it was dead you wouldn't need a hutch. He could carry it around. Hang it around his neck. It wouldn't ever run away." He caught the struggling bass in his hand, removed the hook, smacked its head on the gunwale, and dropped it into the bottom of the boat. "What did you say his name was?"

"March."

"Is that like 'March, April, May'? Or like 'Forward march'?"

Pete was positively garrulous nowadays. The Mounties had given up trying to find whoever was responsible for Jim Lightfoot's escape, and had finally left the reserve.

"He's named after his grandfather. Laura's dad was—is— Reverend March." The poor old guy was still hanging on. He had everything the matter with him but Laura looked after him so well he was going to live forever.

Pete skewered a minnow on his hook and dropped it overboard. "What's the kid want a rabbit for?"

"A pet."

They fished. High above them four turkey vultures circled slowly on the last thermals of the day, waiting for something to die. The *Queen Mary* rocked gently in a swell that had originated hours ago and miles away, back in somebody's past.

Pete said, "A dead one would be best, man. You could skin it and eat it and then stuff it with feathers. It would look just like the real thing."

"I think he'd know."

The previous night Ian had sat down and drawn up a list of every career he could think of, everything from a geologist to a chimney sweep. Then he started crossing them off, one by one (starting with "doctor"), the plan

being that there would be a few left for him to think seriously about. The problem was, he'd crossed them all off.
Every single one fell into one of three categories: predictable, boring, or ridiculous.

"Have you decided what you're going to do?" he said
to Pete, startling himself because he hadn't intended to
ask until he'd made up his own mind.

"When?" Pete said.

"For the rest of your life."

"Oh. Yeah."

Ian looked at him surprise. "You have? When?"

"A while ago."

"Why didn't you tell me?"

"I've been waitin' for you to make up your mind, man."

"Well, tell me now. Maybe it will help me make up
my mind."

"Naw."

"Why not?"

"You have to make up your mind first."

"Why?" Ian was starting to get annoyed. "Have you
told Mr. Hardy?"

"Nope."

"Look, just tell me, okay?" He didn't want to play
games about it.

"Soon as you've made up your mind."

They fished. Irritation scratched Ian's insides.

There was a faint tug on his line. Pete said quietly,
"You've got somethin'."

Ian held his breath. There was something there all
right. He waited for the count of three . . . then jerked the
rod backwards hard. There was a savage yank from the
other end, the rod arched over, the line screamed out of

the reel, and a second later a long, smooth, streamlined shape shot out of the water twenty yards away, sailed up into the air, twisted right around so that its head was almost touching its tail—and was gone. The slack line drifted on the water like weed.

"Shit," Ian said.

"He was a nice one," Pete said admiringly.

"I didn't set it hard enough. Shit."

"He was smart, man. He knew exactly what to do."

Which was a generous thing to say.

They fished. Ian's heartbeat slowly returned to normal. The evening air was fresh and cool. He felt better, despite losing the pike. That was the thing about fishing—it was almost impossible to stay wound up for long.

The shadow of a vulture sailed across the water. Pete said, "Did you know vultures piss on their legs to keep cool?"

"You're kidding," Ian said.

"Nope. It's a fact."

"How do you know?"

"Ancient tribal lore, man."

"Really?"

Pete twitched his jig. "Naw. I read it somewhere. Some book by some scientist guy."

"Oh," Ian said, disappointed. He would have liked it to be tribal lore. "Well, how would he know?"

"How would he know what?"

"That they piss on their legs to keep cool. Maybe they're just lousy shots. Can't pee straight. He could know that they piss on their legs, but how the hell could he know *why*?"

It was a serious question but it struck Pete as funny. He started to laugh.

"What's funny about that?" Ian said. He looked up at the vultures soaring on the wind and suddenly it came to him—a newly minted thought.

"I've got it!" he said. "Holy shit, I've got it! I know what I'm going to do! At last! I know what I'm going to do!"

Pete stopped laughing. He reached under his seat, pulled out a bottle of Coke, and prized the top off on an oarlock. "What?" he asked suspiciously, taking a swig.

"I'm going to be a pilot!"

It was so perfect that he was astounded that he hadn't thought of it before. He'd never even thought to put it on his list. It was totally different from what everyone expected of him, and on top of that it was a good job—interesting, respected, well paid, the lot. Not the air force, though. He'd be a commercial pilot and see the world. No one—not his father, not his teachers, not even Jake—could disapprove.

Pete choked, and Coke shot out of his nose. He started laughing again.

"What's so funny?" Ian said, but that only made Pete worse. He howled with laughter, rocking the boat, offending the vultures, who wheeled away on the cool evening air.

~

"Think you'll come back here in the summers?" Arthur asked. They were sitting on a granite outcrop in the middle of a field of wheat, drinking tea. The sun was hot but there was a breeze, which made it just about perfect. The horses were standing head to tail under a couple of trees at the side of the field, politely swatting flies for each other with their tails.

It had been so long since Arthur had spoken that Ian looked at him in surprise. He was very quiet these days, even by his standards.

Ian thought about the question. The closer he came to leaving the more he saw that he was going to want to come back fairly regularly, not only for his father's sake, but also for his own. "I think I probably will," he said. "Next summer, anyway."

Both of them were watching the wheat. The breeze brushed over the top of it like a vast and careless hand, making it roll and sway, hypnotic as the sea.

"Don't suppose you'll want to work on the farm, though?" Arthur said.

"Would you have work for me?"

"Sure."

"You don't think you'll want to get someone who could be here weekends as well?"

"Ain't too many people want to work on farms nowadays," Arthur said. "'Specially not too many who're good with horses."

"Do you think they'll remember me?" Ian said. "The horses, I mean?" Such sentimentality. He was glad Pete couldn't hear him.

It was Arthur's turn to look surprised. "Course they'll remember you. They'll remember you same as we will."

Absurd how pleased he was to hear it.

Jake said, "And then there's women. You interested in benefiting from my vast experience?"

Both conversations took place on the same day. If you compared the two brothers physically, Ian reckoned, stood them side by side and studied them, you could just about see that they might have a gene or two in common. Their eyes were the same colour, for instance, and both had quite fair skin. But if you could get inside their heads—tunnel your way into their ears and take a look at what was going on in there—you wouldn't think they were even the same species.

He gave Jake what he hoped was a man-of-the-world grin. (Eighteen years old and still a virgin. If by some terrible chance Jake discovered that, he just plain wouldn't believe it.) "Sure."

"Point one, they're wonderful," Jake said. "You have to give them that: the world would be a boring place without them. But point two, they're out to get you. All of them. They can't help themselves—it's biological. Their goal in life is to tie you down."

Ian nodded, thinking of Cathy. You could imagine Jake having trouble with women. He was a very good-looking guy.

Laura chose that moment to come out into the farmyard. She gave them both a wave and headed for the barn. Jake and Ian watched her.

Jake said thoughtfully, "Though there is the occasional one you might not mind being tied down by, right?" He looked at Ian and raised his eyebrows suggestively.

Ian smiled uncomfortably. He didn't like Jake talking about Laura like that.

"I'll tell you something," Jake said. "As you get older—this is your uncle Jake speaking—as you get older, believe it or not, the idea of settling down starts to have a certain appeal. Like the other evening at supper I was looking at Art, sitting there like a sack of cement like he always does, Laura waiting on him hand and foot, and

I thought, you know, if you look at it a certain way you could say that my dear dumb ox of a brother has it all."

Here was the sum total of what Ian knew about Jake, almost two weeks after he'd arrived at the farm. He was thirty-five. He'd never been married. He'd lived in Toronto, Calgary, San Francisco, New Orleans, New York, and Chicago. He liked New York best and reckoned he'd go back there. He thought Cadillacs were the only cars worth owning. Considering how much he talked, it was remarkable how little he revealed about himself.

But a couple of days later, he said, "Actually, I've just split up with someone. We'd been together three or four years, I guess. She was a looker, and nice enough, but you know . . ." He shrugged. He looked moody, which was unusual. It made Ian wonder if it could have been the girl who had ended things. Maybe that had something to do with why he was here. Maybe he'd come home to lick his wounds.

~

Ian was halfway around the point in the canoe when he heard the bell on the dock clanging wildly. It was Saturday evening and he and his father had just finished supper. He turned the canoe around and paddled back fast. Gerry Moynihan was on the dock, jigging impatiently from one foot to the other. "Car accident," he said, hauling the canoe up on the dock almost before Ian got out of it. "Margie's arrived but your dad needs you too. Four people hurt pretty bad, ambulance in New Liskeard's comin' but it'll take a while."

The two of them were running up to the house. Gerry

Moynihan was panting. His paunch heaved up and down as he ran, not quite in synch with the rest of him.

"Who are they?" Ian said. "From around here?" He could hear screaming now, coming from the house.

"Tourists. Detroit plates. Going too fast. Bull moose on the road, smacked straight into it. Crushed the car."

It was a family, the parents plus two young children. The man was on the examination table and Ian's father was trying to get a tube down his throat. The mother was on the trestle table on the other side of the room, moaning faintly. Margie was bending over one of the children, a little boy, who was spread out on Dr. Christopherson's desk. The other child, hardly more than a baby, was the one making the noise—at least it meant his heart and lungs were working. He was on a pile of blankets on the floor. There was a bandage around his head but blood was leaking through it and his face was covered in blood. He was pulling at the bandage and screaming hysterically.

"Deal with the bleeding," Ian's father said, nodding at the child. "Then see if you can calm him down."

"Is it okay to pick him up?"

"Yes, but support his head. Gerry, I need you here."

It was after midnight by the time the ambulance had taken the children and their parents off to the hospital. Ian and his father sat in the kitchen, listening to the silence. Ian wondered if the baby's screams were going to echo in his head for the rest of his life.

"I think a cup of tea is in order," Dr. Christopherson said after a long while. "By way of celebration. All four of them should make it." He heaved himself to his feet. His face looked drawn, the skin sagging with fatigue. He'd been called out twice the previous night and had been working

THE OTHER SIDE OF THE BRIDGE

sixteen hours straight. The measles epidemic hadn't burned itself out yet and weekends meant nothing.

The little coal of anger, three years old now and lying dormant most of the time, flared up in Ian—amazing how it could still go from barely a glimmer to white-hot rage in a matter of seconds. Anger born of guilt. Anger born of the unjustness of the guilt. In a couple of months' time his father was going to be alone here. What would he do, on a night like tonight?

"You need another nurse."

"You could be right." His father set the kettle on the stove. "You did well with that little lad tonight, by the way. You have a real way with them."

"You need to advertise for another one right now," Ian said. "*Right now*. First thing in the morning."

He was so mad, all at once, he was almost shaking.

His father put a hand on his shoulder. He said quietly, "Ian, things are going to be fine here. You don't need to worry about me. Things are going to be fine."

She had stopped writing to him and he was glad. She had phoned him on his birthday back in May and cried down the phone line so he'd hung up on her. There had been one final letter after that and then nothing. He missed the act of throwing the unopened envelopes away—over the years of her absence he had received one hundred and ninety-two letters from her and the ritual of throwing them away unread had given him great satisfaction—but when they stopped coming, he was glad. He still looked for them in the mailbox, but when they weren't there, he was glad.

~

He had to go to the farm. It was very late but he knew he wouldn't sleep otherwise; he was still too angry, too stirred up. He waited until his father had gone to bed and then got on his bike. The moon was up, and the night had an eerie brightness. The road looked unreal, insubstantial as a ribbon, as if at any moment it might unstick itself from the ground and lift off into the air. When he got to the woods surrounding the farm he left his bike in its usual place and made his way through the woods on foot. While he was still some way off he saw a light flickering, which meant that Jake—it was sure to be Jake—was still up. Ian felt a surge of irritation. He would have preferred him not to be there, not to be in the house at all. It got in the way of the sense of calm he used to find there.

When he got close, though, there didn't seem to be anyone in the kitchen. Ian moved around, trying to see into the corners of the room. He wasn't taking much care to be quiet so he got a serious fright when he suddenly saw the glow of a cigarette outside the back door. Jake must be standing on the doorstep. In fact, now that he knew he was there, Ian could make out his shape.

Jake didn't move, though. The dogs were wandering around—they came up behind Ian waving their tails—so maybe he assumed the noise was them. The cigarette glowed and died a few times and then Ian saw him drop it onto the doorstep, grind it out with his shoe, and brush it over the edge. A moment later Jake turned around and went in.

He didn't seem to be in any hurry to go to bed. In the kitchen he lit another cigarette and sat down in an armchair by the fire. It looked as if he could be there awhile. Ian fidgeted. He was about to give up and go home when Laura appeared.

She didn't come into the kitchen, just stood in the doorway. She was wearing a dressing gown tied tightly around
her waist and was holding it closed at the neck with one
hand. Jake smiled at her and said something. She shook her
head. She said something—something urgent, it seemed to
Ian, because she leaned forward as she spoke.

Jake tipped his head to one side and made some reply.
He looked quite relaxed; whatever Laura had said didn't
worry him. She shook her head again, still clutching the
neck of her dressing gown. She was upset about something, Ian was sure of it. Then Jake stood up. He stubbed
out his cigarette in a saucer on the table, taking his time
over it, mashing the butt into the saucer several times, and
then started to cross the kitchen towards her, smiling, as if
to reassure her. Laura turned abruptly and left the room.

For a moment Jake stood where he was, looking at the
empty doorway. Then he went back to the chair and sat
down. He fished out another cigarette, lit it, and started
smoking, his head resting against the back of the chair.

Ian realized he had been holding his breath. He didn't
know what to make of it. Laura's posture, the way she left
so fast when Jake came towards her—it was as if she was
really upset with him, or even afraid of him. Though that
seemed ridiculous.

He walked back through the woods to his bike, mulling
it over. It made him uneasy. It made him wonder what
Jake was playing at. Why, exactly, he was here.

~

They'd been fishing for a couple of hours when Pete suddenly said, "Oh, nearly forgot." He reached under his seat

and hauled out a small shoebox from among the clutter of fishing tackle and beer bottles. The box was the flimsy sort they put moccasins in to sell to tourists at the trading post. It was soggy along the bottom from lying in bilge water and looked in danger of disintegrating. Ian wedged the handle of his fishing rod into a hole in the *Queen Mary*'s floorboards, took the box, one hand underneath it to stop it from falling apart, and opened it. Inside, crouched down among some dead grass and a little pebbled heap of dung, was a very small grey rabbit.

"Wow!" Ian said. "Is he ever cute! Where'd you find him?"

"Near the trapline."

"He's tiny! Are you sure he's old enough to leave his mother?"

Pete stuck a minnow on his hook and dropped it overboard. "We ate her last night, man, so it's kind of an academic question."

"Oh," Ian said. He stroked the rabbit gently behind the ears. Its fur was so soft he could scarcely feel it. The rabbit quivered and flattened itself against the floor of the box. "Poor thing," he said. "This isn't a big enough box, either."

"What are you talking about?" Pete said. "It's a perfect fit."

'He doesn't even have room to turn around," Ian said. "I thought you guys were supposed to have this special thing with animals. A respectful relationship. Like, asking their forgiveness before shooting them, that sort of thing."

Pete gave him a look. He reached out and took the box, one hand still holding the jig over the side of the boat. He put his head down to the box and said, "Hey, wabbit, forgive me, man. I'm sorry I had to eat your mum and stuff you in a shoebox."

He handed the box back to Ian. "There you go. He feels better about everything now." He bobbed the jig up and down in the water.

Back at home Ian went up to the attic and rummaged around in the clutter. There wasn't anything perfect but he found a box that would do. It was nearly as flimsy as the shoebox and the sides weren't as tall as he would have liked, but the rabbit didn't look like much of an escape artist and at least it would have room to roam around a bit. He took the box outside, put a saucer of water at one end, covered the bottom with a thick layer of grass and leaves, and decanted the rabbit into it. It looked even smaller in there. It flattened itself down and closed its eyes as if it were praying for a speedy end. He was sorry he'd asked for it. March would love it, if it lasted long enough to give it to him, but he'd probably cuddle it to death within a couple of hours. Killed by love. Well, maybe it was better than being eaten.

He decided to delay giving it to March for a few days, though. He'd let it have a little peace before its next adventure; it would be a shame for both the boy and the rabbit if it died on the spot. He would put the box around the back of the house where it would get the morning sun but wouldn't bake in the afternoon. In the meantime, he'd get some chicken wire and work out how to make a run for it. It would need to be a big one, with a hutch the rabbit could hide in. March could help him make it.

"We're going to have a zoo," his father said later that evening. Ian had brought him out to admire the rabbit.

"I had a call from Ernie Schwartz. His bitch had a litter six weeks ago and he said we could come and choose a pup this weekend if we liked."

"No kidding!" Ian said. "An Irish setter?"

"Yes. Ernie says it has a pedigree. I told him that was more than we had and we didn't want to pay a fortune for it, and he said he didn't want a fortune, he wanted me to tear up the bill for setting his daughter's leg."

"Oh," Ian said. "Is that okay?"

"I'd forgotten all about the bill, so I suppose so."

"You need a secretary as well as a nurse."

"I just need to get myself organized."

"Pigs might fly," Ian said.

His father sighed.

"By the way," Ian said. "I've decided what I'm going to do next year." As he said it, he felt a kind of ache, mid-chest.

"Oh, yes?" his father said. "What have you decided?"

"I'm going to be a pilot."

His father looked at him, then looked away. Ian had been half-afraid he might laugh, like Pete, but he didn't. He crouched down and began to examine the rabbit. "A pilot," he said, after a moment. "That's an interesting career. Good for you." He didn't look up.

Ian said, "It's what I really want to do."

"Good," his father said. "Excellent. Then you must do it. It sounds very good." He moved the saucer with the water in it closer to the rabbit.

"I'll have to go and talk to Mr. Hardy about it," Ian said. The ache had spread outwards, filling his entire chest now, tightening his throat. "I don't know how I go about applying, like where you go to train, that sort of thing."

"No," his father said. "No, neither do I. Get Hardy onto it. He'll know." He looked up, finally, and smiled. "It sounds like an interesting career. Good for you."

By rights he should have dreamed about his father that night, but instead, as he slipped down into sleep, Jake's car rolled smoothly into the farmyard and the passenger door opened and Ian's mother stepped out, her legs long and elegant in high-heeled shoes. Ian was standing by the water trough but she paid no attention to him. She picked her way through the dust of the farmyard and went into the house and sat down in the armchair Jake usually sat in. She took a pack of cigarettes out of her purse and lit one. Ian was standing by the table; he must have followed her into the house. She looked at him with a little smile and said, "Tell Laura she doesn't have to worry about Arthur. Arthur will be fine."

TWELVE

~

Sixteen District Men Among Casualties: Community Mourns
District Man Collects $80 on Dead Bears
—*Temiskaming Speaker*, October 1944

October. The skies a pale, lifeless grey, the fields stripped
bare, everything holding its breath, clenched against the
coming cold. Jake's pursuit of Laura was nicely under way
and all Arthur could do was stand and watch.

"He says your father was a wonderful man," Laura said.

They were in Otto's barn. Arthur and the two POWs
were preparing winter quarters for the pigs; it had snowed
the previous night and any day now they'd have to move
all the animals inside. Laura had just arrived home from
school and had brought mugs of tea out for the three of
them. The boys were sitting on bales of straw, warming

their hands on the mugs. Arthur and Laura stood in the doorway, Laura leaning against the door, her arms wrapped tightly around her to keep out the cold. She was wearing an old coat of her father's and had a long red scarf wound several times around her neck. It was coming on for dusk and the light was seeping out of the sky, draining the colour out of everything as it went—everything, it seemed to Arthur, except the bright flame of that scarf.

Laura said, "He says you're exactly like him. He says you've been wonderful since he died, the way you've run the farm—both farms—all by yourself. The way you've provided for him and your mother. He says he's worse than useless, no help to you at all." She smiled to show that she knew that wasn't true, that Jake did everything he could.

Arthur looked at the ground. Sometimes he could hardly bear to be near her.

"He told me how you saved his life, Arthur," she said. "How you risked your own life wading out into the river and then carried him home in your arms."

Had Jake sat down and worked it out, the best way to win her over? Had he studied her, thought about who she was and how she'd been raised and decided on the best strategy? Or was it just another thing that Jake was born knowing? He and Laura walked to and from school together every day now. Half an hour each way. Five hours a week alone in her company, telling her the version of things he wanted her to hear, painting the picture he wanted her to see.

"He says you're the one your mother depends on," Laura said another time, her voice full of pity and admiration for Jake.

It was true, that was what was so clever about it. Arthur had known it for years without ever putting it into words. He was the one his mother depended on; Jake was the one she loved.

Sometimes when he looked at Laura he was almost paralyzed with the fear of losing her. He could hardly get his breath, sometimes. Which was strange: how could you be so terrified of losing something you didn't have?

~

Other things were going on in the world: major, historic things that were of infinitely greater importance than the small matter of one man's love for a woman who was being stolen by his brother. In the middle of November a grainy picture of a battleship called the *Tirpitz* was taped to the window of the post office so that everybody could see it, though you couldn't actually see much for the billows of black smoke pouring out of the belly of the ship. It was the very last German battleship, so they said, and now it was at the bottom of the sea. The war was nearly over and Hitler was on the run. A few months back the RAF had dropped more than two thousand tons of bombs on Berlin in one night; there couldn't be anything left of it but dust. Any day now peace would be declared, and everything would return to how it was before.

Everyone knew, though, that nothing would be as it was before. Not for anyone. The prison camp guard arrived one morning not long before Christmas with letters for the boys. They excused themselves immediately after dinner and took them to the parlour, which was their bedroom, to read. Usually when they got letters they read bits out to each other and if you were in the kitchen you would hear them jabbering away, even laughing some-times at bits of family news. It was Arthur's mother who noticed that there wasn't any jabbering this time.

"They're very quiet," she said suddenly. Arthur looked up from the buckle he was sewing on a harness. It was true, there wasn't a sound from the parlour. He and his mother looked at each other, he with the pliers poised to pull the needle through, she with her hands in the sink.

"Do you think . . ." his mother said, but at that moment Dieter/Bernhard appeared in the doorway. His face was strained.

"Dieter's brudder," he said. "Is *tod*. Dead. He is killed."

"Oh!" Arthur's mother said. "Oh, the poor child . . ." She was already halfway across the room, drying her hands on a tea towel as she went. The boy—Bernhard, this must be, the one who drove Otto's tractor (finally Arthur knew which was which)—stood aside and she went in to the parlour. She'd have her arms around Dieter in a second, Arthur knew. It was so easy for women—their arms opened out instinctively and they gathered in what-ever hurt there was and that was that; they didn't even have to think about it. Arthur and Bernhard looked at each other helplessly, then looked away.

A few lucky men came home on leave for Christmas. You'd have thought that if the war was nearly over, as they kept saying it was, they could call it quits now and let everyone go home for good, but no, the best they could do was give some of them thirty days leave before sending them back to the slaughter. Then, the week before

Christmas, Ted Hatchett did come home for good. Of the truckload of boys who had gone down to North Bay to enlist, he was the only one, apart from Arthur himself, who was still alive.

"You must go to see him, Arthur," his mother said, though he knew that all too well himself. "Apparently he nearly died; he was in the hospital in England for a whole year, but he's well enough to see people now. He'll feel strange, being back. You must visit him."

Arthur went, full of guilt and foreboding. What could he say? What could he say to a friend who had nearly died in battle while he himself had stayed safe and snug at home? Ted had been overseas for nearly five years. Five years of being shot at and bombed, of being soaking wet and freezing cold and having your friends blown to pieces around you. Five years during which Arthur had done what, exactly? Milked the cows. Slept in his own bed every night. Eaten three good meals a day. He trudged through the snow filled with dread.

Ted's mother looked terrible, and he should have been warned by that. Should have realized something was badly wrong when she wasn't dancing with relief and joy that her son had come home from war. She managed to smile at Arthur when she opened the door but didn't say anything. She ushered him into the living room, where a bed had been made up in the corner, and then left him and Ted alone. It was dark in the living room and Arthur couldn't make out Ted's face. He said, "Hiya, Ted. How are ya?" before his eyes adjusted to the light.

There was a scar running down the right side of Ted's face, with a stretch of shiny pink skin covering the eye socket. And as Arthur's eyes adjusted to the dim room, he saw more: saw that the blankets were stretched smooth and flat across the bed, smooth and flat as a tabletop, where Ted's legs should have been. And that where his left arm should have been there was an empty sleeve, folded and pinned across his chest. He was looking at Arthur out of one eye so savagely bright it made Arthur think of an animal caught in a trap, an animal you'd kill as quickly as you could to put an end to its pain. Arthur turned around and left the room.

In the kitchen he stopped, head down, breathing hard. Ted's mother was peeling potatoes and crying into the sink. She looked at Arthur, her face all blotchy with grief, and said, "Talk to him, Arthur. Please talk to him."

Arthur went back to the living room and tried again. He managed to say, "I'm real sorry," but that was it. He stood for a minute with his face averted and then he turned and went home.

He was sick with himself. Sick with the world. He wanted to smash something, anything, cleave something in two. He started clearing land, a couple of acres he and his father had just begun working on when his father died. More land to farm was the last thing he needed right now but hacking down trees was the only job he could think of that was violent enough to ease his feelings. Part way through the first afternoon he looked up from the pit of a root he was digging out and saw Dieter and Bernhard looking down at him. They were carrying axes too—they must have raided the shed—and such was his state of mind that for a moment Arthur thought they had come to kill him. It seemed entirely right; he wouldn't even have resisted. Then they pointed their axes at the nearby trees and raised their eyebrows and he saw they felt the need for a bit of violence too, so he nodded and waved a hand at the surrounding bush—go ahead, hack 'em all down, rip the small ones out by the roots, the more the better. For three days, while snow drifted softly down around them, they attacked the forest like a raging storm, chopped and sawed, then harnessed up all four horses and dragged roots out of the ground like rotting teeth, till the place looked like their very own battlefield, cratered and ruined and smashed to bloody pulp.

At dusk on the third day Jake appeared, limping through the trees like a pale ghost. Arthur saw him coming out of the corner of his eye. He was in mid-swing, about to take another blow at the smooth rounded skin of a beech tree, and suddenly he saw blood on the snow. A big splash of blood, red as Laura's scarf. He closed his eyes for a moment, the axe still raised, and when he opened them again it wasn't blood, it was just a big clod of churned-up earth, black as night, not red at all. He lowered the axe and looked at Jake. The shock of seeing Ted Hatchett had actually succeeded in driving the business of Jake and Laura out of his mind for several days, but now it was back. Jake met his eyes and there was a pause, during which Arthur wondered if maybe Jake had seen blood on the snow as well.

"What?" Arthur said, and Jake said, quietly, that their mother wanted them to stop now and put everything away because tomorrow was not only Sunday, it was Christmas Eve.

There were two services, one in the morning and one in the evening. The church was crammed for both of them; even those who were not normally among the faithful turned out on Christmas Eve. It didn't feel very festive, though. Five years of war had drained the capacity for festive feeling out of people. The war might be coming to an end in theory, but in practice the telegrams were still arriving and peace was just an unreal dream. At the morning service Reverend March did his best, preaching a sermon about the Christmas gift of hope and about giving your pain to God. Arthur would have liked to be uplifted by it but wasn't. He didn't feel hopeful about anything and the bit about giving your pain to God made him think of Ted Hatchett. He imagined Ted holding out his pain to God with the one hand he had left—here you go, God, it's all yours. What happened next, exactly? Arthur couldn't see for the life of him how it was supposed to help. He knew that Reverend March was smarter than he was so he should take it on trust, but he couldn't, so he gave up and watched Laura instead.

She was in her usual pew at the front of the church, and Arthur had positioned himself, as he always did, so that he had a clear view of her back. Her back was very straight and slim and upright. Looking at it calmed him, and after a while the thought came to Arthur that the bit in her father's sermon about hope might have something in it after all. Maybe he could hope, where Laura was concerned. Maybe he had been wrong to be so fearful about her and Jake. Just look at her sitting there, listening so intently to what her father was saying. She wasn't Jake's kind of girl. In fact, if you tried to imagine the absolute opposite of Jake's kind of girl, Laura would be it. Jake would have had no interest in her whatsoever if he hadn't seen that Arthur was in love with her. He liked girls with what he called "a little bit of fun" in them, by which he meant girls who would accompany him to the barn. Laura would never accompany Jake to a barn in a million years.

And he must know that. Jake, sitting on the other side of their mother now, thinking about God knew what, must know that. He was probably tired of her already. He was just doing what Jake had always done; he was saying, "Bet you." Bet you I can take her away from you. Bet you I'm better than you at this, like I'm better than you at everything. When he had tortured Arthur a little more he would drop her and move on. And maybe Laura would be sad for a couple of days but then she'd see Jake for what he really was and be relieved that he was gone.

All day that thought comforted him. He went over to Otto's farm after dinner to see to the pigs—Sunday or not, Christmas Eve or not, the animals had to be fed—and Laura waved cheerily to him from the kitchen window. Pleasure washed over Arthur like sunshine. It was going to be all right.

It was after the evening service, when Reverend March was standing at the back of the church shaking hands with his congregation and wishing them a Merry Christmas, that Arthur saw Jake come up to Laura and whisper something to her. Arthur was standing with his mother, waiting his turn to shake the reverend's hand, so he had a good view. He saw Jake come up behind her and bend his head and whisper in her ear. Laura's eyes widened a little and she flushed, and then she turned and looked up at him, and smiled.

Was it the smile that did it, that caused the cold snake of fear to coil around Arthur's heart? Or the angle of her chin as she turned her face upwards to look at Jake? Or was it simply the light that came into her eyes when she heard his whisper—the brightness, the happiness, the pure and unmistakable yearning in those clear grey eyes.

~

He couldn't look at Jake. Couldn't be in the same room with him. He spent as much time as possible out in the barns, but the weather didn't cooperate; in the middle of January the temperature hit forty below. If you stayed outside for more than a couple of minutes you could feel the marrow freezing in your bones. In desperation Arthur took to visiting Ted Hatchett. He'd go and sit with him for an hour or so in the afternoons. It was impossible to say if Ted welcomed the visits, but his mother certainly did. She was so grateful it made Arthur ashamed. He was there to get away from Jake and to ease his own guilt, and also because in Ted's presence everything, including life itself, seemed trivial, and there was a certain bleak comfort in that.

He could never think of anything to say, of course; he sat there racking his brains for some event he could tell Ted about. Not a whole lot was going on.

"Pigs chewed through the barn door last night."

Ted turned his head slowly and looked at him. It was hard to tell if he was interested. The Hatchetts weren't farmers—Ted's father had worked in the sawmill and Ted himself in the silver mine—so he might not care all that much about pigs. But it was the only thing that had happened all week.

"They ain't hungry," Arthur explained. "Just bored. They hate bein' inside. They like rootin' about in the soil, lookin' for bugs and such. Got to give them lots of straw to root about in in the winter or they go nuts an' start eatin' the barn. Boys didn't put down enough straw yesterday."

Ted said nothing. As far as anyone knew there was nothing physical preventing Ted from talking but apparently he hadn't said a word since he was wounded. He'd been a tank gunner—Arthur knew a few more details now, from his mother—and had been somewhere in Italy. The tank hit a mine and blew up and everyone else in it had died.

"Floor of the barn's concrete, see. Can't root about in concrete."

Ted blinked his one eye. Arthur took it as encouragement.

"Cows don't mind so much. Seem pretty happy just standin' there doin' nothin'." He stopped—it struck him that maybe that was tactless. Even the cows, even the pigs, had more freedom than Ted had now. The problem was, everything was tactless. There was nothing happening anywhere in the world that wasn't irrelevant to Ted.

Arthur thought of telling him what was going on in his mind. Imagined saying, "I'm scared I'm going to kill my brother. He's made this girl I love fall in love with him. He didn't want her, he just took her because he saw I loved her. But now I think he's going to make her, you know, go out to the barn with him, like he does with other girls. I know she'd never do anything like that, but he's awful good at wearin' people down, and she's so much in love with him. . . . And if he did it, if he wore her down . . . I think I'd kill him. I'm really scared I would."

He wondered if Ted's one eye would show any interest if he said that.

He still saw her practically every day. It was a torment, because she looked so happy. She seemed younger than when she'd first come to Struan, more carefree, more like a schoolgirl. She laughed and tossed her head if you said something funny, not that Arthur ever did; it was Jake who could make her laugh. The happier she was, the more fearful Arthur became. He wanted to warn her: don't trust my brother. He imagined himself saying it, saw the disbelief and reproach in her eyes.

Spring came early. By March the snow had gone from the fields, though there were still pockets of it left in the woods. Arthur kept going out to the fields, picking up a little pinch of soil and rubbing it between finger and thumb, looking at the sky, sniffing the air. Should he start the seeding? All the farmers in the area were wondering the same thing. A couple of them had begun already. Arthur was anxious to get started if only to distract himself, but he was cautious. Would his father have started so soon? He picked up another little nugget of soil and rubbed it, seeing his father as he did so, or rather feeling him, feeling the moisture content (a little bit wet) and the soil temperature (a little bit cold) with his father's forefinger and thumb. He saw that his hands were his father's hands, broad and square and powerful. It gave him confidence.

Whenever the boys saw him going out to the fields they came with him; they wanted to get started too. They were very subdued nowadays. Arthur guessed they'd heard on the POW grapevine how the war was going: German armies in retreat, towns and cities bombed to rubble. They must need distracting as much as he did. "Is goot?" they'd say hopefully, copying his gesture, rubbing small crumbs of soil. "Is goot time now?" But Arthur shook his head. He decided to wait till the ground warmed up a little more. A couple of days of strong sunshine should do it.

Then on the first of April there was a heavy snowfall and overnight the temperature plummeted to ten below. The boys grinned at him and bowed, and said, "Goot farmer!"

He was going to miss them when they went home. He couldn't imagine what he'd do without them. What would he do about Otto's land? The thought took him back to Laura, as all thoughts did.

Jake and Laura took to doing their homework together after school. They took their books upstairs to Jake's room. Mrs. Dunn was so delighted that they were "friends" that she didn't even protest.

"She's so good for him, Arthur," she confided in a hushed voice. "She's quieting him down, don't you think?"

Arthur was appalled by her innocence. How could she know her own son so little? He wouldn't have left any girl alone in Jake's presence for ten seconds. He studied Laura surreptitiously for signs that she was being pressured to do things she didn't want to do. He wasn't sure what those signs would be, but he was sure he'd know them if he saw them.

He saw them on a Saturday morning at the end of April. He was in the cow barn—the cold snap had broken and he and the boys were taking the cows out to pasture for the first time—and Laura appeared in the doorway. The minute he saw her, he knew.

"Mornin'," he said, his heart tightening in his chest. And she smiled at him vaguely, and said good morning, and he knew.

She told him that their generator had stopped working and her father wondered if Arthur could have a look at it. She apologized for bothering him, and he said it was no bother, he'd come right now. They walked back to the Luntz farm together and she hardly spoke, and he knew without a doubt.

He had to take the generator to bits to find out what the problem was and he kept dropping things, nuts and screws rolling off into the grass. His head was buzzing like a nest of hornets, thoughts flying about every which way. He kept seeing her and Jake together, Jake whispering to her, touching her. It caused such rage within him that he could hardly breathe. He struggled to calm himself down. He told himself he didn't know anything for sure, but that wasn't true; he knew something for sure, he just didn't know what. He told himself that probably nothing serious had actually happened yet. If anything serious had happened, Laura would be in a terrible state and she wasn't, she simply looked confused and unhappy. He decided, with huge relief, that this must mean Jake was working on her but hadn't got anywhere yet. He would be pushing her in small steps, each one hardly seeming like anything, but keeping up a constant, unrelenting pressure; Arthur had been on the receiving end of Jake's campaigns often enough to know how he worked. She'd be afraid of losing him, afraid he'd think she was a prude. Prude was one of Jake's words—Arthur had heard him say it of other girls he knew. "She's such a prude."

He dropped another screw and had to go searching through the grass on his hands and knees. There was the sound of footsteps and he looked up and saw Reverend March coming around the corner of the house.

"I've come to see how you're getting on," the reverend said jovially. He stood squarely in the light, looking down in bafflement at the dismembered generator spread out on an old tarpaulin on the ground. "Heavens above," he said. "Heavens above. What would we do without you, Arthur?" It was a good question. Reverend March couldn't have hammered a nail into a plank of wood to save his life.

"It's okay," Arthur said, unable to look at him directly because of the images swimming about in his head. "Just dirt in the carburetor, that's all."

"I'll take your word for it," Reverend March said. "It is very good of you to rescue us once again. We always seem to be appealing to you."

Arthur dropped another nut. This time he managed to slam his hand down on it before it could roll off the tarpaulin. He wondered if he could warn the old man that his daughter was in danger. How would you go about saying it? However he put it, Reverend March wouldn't believe him. Jake had charmed him as he charmed everyone else: Arthur had watched him do it and it was something to behold. Jake listened seriously to every word the old man said, deferred to him, asked his opinion, laughed at his jokes. He even asked questions about things Reverend March had said in his sermons. The seriousness, the studiousness with which he asked them made Arthur want to puke, but you could see how impressed the reverend was. If Arthur tried to tell him it was all an act, that Jake was out to seduce his daughter, the old man would think he'd gone mad. The same would be true if he tried to warn Laura herself. She wouldn't believe him either. Jake's lies were far more convincing than the truth.

He was going to have to deal with Jake directly. It made him sweat to think about it but he could see no other course of action. He would tell him straight out that if he touched Laura he would kill him. He would make sure that Jake believed him. He saw himself making sure, slamming Jake's head against a wall. The thought made his hands shake.

A movement caught his eye: Laura, carrying something out to the clothesline. Reverend March saw her too. She began pegging out a tablecloth, stretching the sides so that it would dry flat. Watching her, Arthur felt rage swelling up inside him again, hot and acid as bile. He bent over the generator, afraid that the old man would see the state he was in.

"She isn't quite herself today," Reverend March said absently. "We've been trying to make a decision. We've been trying to decide whether or not to settle here. In Struan, I mean. When this dreadful war is over and Reverend Gordon returns to his flock, we've been wondering whether or not we should stay. It's a decision we have to make, but I'm afraid it is upsetting her."

Arthur paused in the act of threading a screw.

"Personally I am in favour," Reverend March said, watching his daughter walk back to the house. "I have been overwhelmed by the kindness of the people here, the way you have all, in the midst of your own troubles and sorrows, welcomed us into the fold. But it's a difficult decision for Laura. She has friends back home, whom she misses."

Laura disappeared around the corner of the house and the old man sighed. He bent down and picked up Arthur's screwdriver and examined it curiously, turning it over a time or two.

"Initially the plan was simply to come for the duration of the war," he said, testing the sharpness of the screwdriver cautiously with his finger. "To fill a need and to get Laura away from things for a while. We intended to go back. Not to the same house—the memories there are too painful—but back to North Bay. But of course, in the interim she has also made friends here. Very good friends."

He smiled down at Arthur and gave him the screwdriver. "I don't know why I am burdening you with this, Arthur. Burdening you yet more. It's just that Laura seems rather cast down at the moment, and I'm afraid that the issue has brought back both the memories and the sorrow. She was so much better; it is painful to see her unhappy again."

He seemed to expect a comment of some sort. Arthur stood up, wiped his hands on his overalls, and managed to mumble something about everyone being real pleased if they settled here. His head was spinning. He'd been so sure. So sure. And now it seemed it might not concern Jake at all.

Reverend March was thanking him for his kind words. Arthur nodded. He squatted down again and finished cleaning the carburetor. Reverend March kept talking and Arthur nodded from time to time to show that he was listening, although he wasn't. He put the generator back together, reconnected the fuel line to the gas tank, and started the engine. The generator shuddered into life.

Reverend March stopped in midsentence and stared at it. "Miraculous," he said. "Completely miraculous. I don't know how you do it."

After supper he went to visit Ted Hatchett. He sat beside him for an hour, saying nothing. He kept seeing Jake, wedged between the rocks under the bridge, the water rushing over his face. His fault. Arthur's fault. He saw Jake the day he got home from the hospital, lying on the bed in the kitchen. His face, as he asked, "Did you mean what you said, Art? When we were on the bridge? Did you want me to fall?" And then the months during which Arthur had waited, sick with dread, for Jake to tell their parents what had really happened on the bridge. Sure that he would. But he never did.

He saw that it was impossible to be sure of anything, where Jake was concerned. He would never know what Jake was thinking or intending, never know his motives, never understand the first thing about him.

So now he couldn't think what to do. How much to trust his own gut feelings, how much weight to give to what Reverend March had said. He was sure Jake was pressing Laura. Maybe she was upset about the question of where they were going to live, but he was sure there was more to it than that. Almost sure.

What could he do? He could warn Jake off, but that was dangerous because it might backfire. If Jake was playing games, courting Laura just to torture him—otherwise, surely, he would have given up on her by now—then it would definitely spur him on.

A sound, a kind of creaking, near at hand, broke in on his thoughts. He looked around, trying to figure out where it was coming from, and then realized it was Ted. He was trying to say something. Arthur leaned forward to hear him better. Ted had another couple of goes and finally managed to get it out.

"How're the pigs?" was what it sounded like.

"The pigs?" Arthur said, his mind still on Jake.

Ted nodded.

"They're good," Arthur said, sitting back in his chair. "They're real happy. We put 'em out last week. In the orchard. You remember the Luntzes' orchard? Little patch, don't produce much in the way of apples but it looks nice. They're rootin' away there. Look real happy."

Ted nodded again and Arthur suddenly realized that he'd actually spoken.

He said cautiously, "Hey, Ted, you spoke," but that seemed to be it as far as Ted was concerned, and he didn't say anything more.

~

The eighth of May, 1945. Someone got hold of a copy of the *Toronto Daily Star* only one day out of date and stuck the front page up in the window of the post office. You could read the headline from across the street: it said UNCONDITIONAL SURRENDER in letters four inches high. The town was jammed with people: farmers and shop-keepers, men from the sawmill and the lumber camps and the mines, servicemen home on leave, veterans from the last war, mothers, grandmothers, schoolkids, and babes in arms. Finally it was over, or at least the European war was over: there were still the Japanese to deal with, but surely that wouldn't take long.

Flags appeared out of nowhere and so did the hooch. There was no liquor store in Struan, but Ben's Bar was cleaned out before noon and there must have been plenty more stashed away because by midafternoon things were getting a little out of hand. Men were reeling down the street, drinking straight from the bottle, and here and there scuffles were breaking out. Arthur had driven his mother into town for the occasion but when the drinking started he took her home again. She was upset. She didn't hold with liquor at the best of times.

"It's disgusting," she said. "Just disgusting. I can understand people being happy, but carrying on like that isn't right. It's not respectful to the families who've lost their sons. Which is almost all of them. I saw Marjorie Black there and she was crying, and so was Anna Stubbs."

Her mouth was set in a straight line but the soft skin under her chin was trembling. Arthur wondered if she'd seen Jake and if that was part of the reason she was so mad. Jake and Laura had been sitting on the steps of the bank with a group of kids from the high school and Jake was drinking something from a Coke bottle that was the wrong colour for Coke. He wasn't the only one, and Arthur wouldn't have thought anything more about it if he hadn't seen Jake offer the bottle to Laura, and her take a sip before handing it back. Her face was flushed, which caused Arthur to wonder if maybe that wasn't the first sip she'd had. The minute the idea entered his head he felt his guts clench up. Was Jake plying her with drink? Was he seizing the occasion to get her drunk so that he could seduce her? He pushed the thought away, forced it back into whatever dark cave it came from. Probably Jake was simply celebrating, like everybody else, and had no sinister motive at all.

He took his mother home but then came back into town. It seemed important to be there. He parked the truck around the back of the post office and walked through the alleyway to Main Street. Someone had built a bonfire right in the middle of the road outside the post office and there were a dozen or so men gathered around it, their arms wrapped around each other's shoulders, yelling "Roll Out the Barrel" at the tops of their voices. Arthur recognized them as miners. They'd been stuck underground for the past six years: the war consumed so much coal that men who'd been working down the mines when war broke out hadn't been allowed to leave, and there was a resentful tone to their singing, which surged whenever someone in uniform walked by. It looked to Arthur as if all the makings of a brawl were there and he decided to move on.

He made his way along Main Street and then slowly back, pretending to himself that he wasn't looking for Laura. There was no sign of the high-school crowd. Maybe they'd all gone to someone's home, or down to the lake to have their own party on the beach.

He stood by the corner of the bank and watched the crowd. There was a fair number of men in uniform, some of them bandaged up, some on crutches or with an arm in a sling, others just home on leave. They looked so happy. Happy, and proud of their victory. Their victory, not his.

Suddenly he saw himself as others in the crowd must surely see him: a silent, solitary figure, standing apart from the rest. He looked out at the hordes of singing, laughing people and felt more alone than he'd ever felt in his life. Was this how it was going to be, then? Was this who he was? A man apart from his fellows, making the journey through life alone?

Two men in air force uniform supporting a third between them suddenly veered away from the rest, dragged their companion over to the side of the road, and held him while he spewed up into the gutter. "'Atta boy!" one of them said. "Now ya got room for more!"

The one who'd spewed up had only one arm, and abruptly Arthur was reminded of Ted. He turned, disgusted with his own self-pity, and made his way through the crowd back to his truck.

Mrs. Hatchett must have seen him pulling into the drive because she opened the door as he came up the steps. She said, "Arthur," and smiled tremulously, ushering him into the living room. He sat down in his usual chair beside the bed. Ted's one eye was closed and Arthur thought he might be asleep, but after a minute, without opening his eye, Ted said, "You been into town?" He was talking more or less normally nowadays.

"Yeah," Arthur said.

"What's it like?"

"Noisy. Lots of people. Most of 'em drunk."

Ted nodded. After a while he said, "It's just Europe that's surrendered? Hitler and that lot?"

"Yeah," Arthur said. "Japs are still fightin'."

He wondered if Ted wanted to go in to see the celebrations for himself. His mind shrank from the thought of picking up that truncated, mutilated body, carrying it out to the truck, trying to prop it up somehow so that Ted wouldn't fall over. He suddenly saw himself and Carl, carting Ted home between them, one arm each, dragging him along the frozen road. Ted's loquacious, cheerful drunkenness. *An owowownly child. So sad, so sad.* It seemed like another world.

He cleared his throat. "You want to go see what's goin' on?"

Ted opened his eye and looked at him. "No," he said.

Which was a relief.

Mrs. Hatchett brought in two cups of tea and set them down on the table beside the bed and went out again. A minute later she reappeared in the doorway. She said,

"I have to go out for a while." There was something in her voice, and Arthur looked at her and saw that her face was twisted with grief. He looked away quickly. Maybe the ending of the war had brought it all home again.

Ted said, "Okay, Mum."

His mother came over to the bed and kissed his forehead, and then she left. They heard the car pull out of the drive.

"Mothers," Ted said apologetically.

"Yeah."

Arthur picked up his tea. Mrs. Hatchett made it way too weak and didn't put half enough sugar in it, but he didn't like to ask for it different.

"You want your tea?" he asked. He wasn't sure Ted could reach it where it was.

"No, thanks."

They sat in silence, Arthur thinking about nothing much.

"Got a favour to ask," Ted said after a while.

"Sure," Arthur said.

"That chest of drawers?" He nodded at the chest that stood on the other side of the room. "My dad's service revolver is in the top drawer. Check it's loaded and put it in the bottom drawer?"

It seemed an odd request and Arthur nearly asked why, in fact was on the very point of asking when a reason—the only possible reason—occurred to him, and a chasm seemed to open up inside him. He sat motionless, Ted's voice echoing inside his head. He was aware of his own heartbeat. Of the teacup in his hand. He was aware of Ted waiting. Another memory came to him: himself and his father, in the barn one night in the dead of winter, a blizzard howling outside. A horse, frantic with pain. He licked his lips, which had gone dry, and put down the teacup and got up and crossed the room and opened the top drawer of the chest. The gun was lying there as Ted had said. Arthur took it out and checked that it was loaded. Then he bent down and opened the bottom drawer and put the gun inside and closed the drawer again.

"Leave it open."

Arthur opened the drawer. He straightened up, keeping his face turned away.

Ted said, "Somethin' else. Little bit awkward. I could do it but it would take a long time and if I passed out or something an' didn't make it, and my mum came back and things weren't finished with, it would be kinda hard on her. So if you could just give me a hand to get over there on the floor I'd be grateful."

Arthur licked his lips again. In the silence he could hear the birds outside, singing away.

"She won't say you've been here," Ted went on as if they were discussing the weather, "so you won't get in trouble or nothin'. Anyway, they'd see it would be possible for me to do everythin' myself."

Somewhere in the distance Arthur could hear a plane, or maybe more than one. Maybe they were taking part in the celebrations.

Ted said, "Not a great thing to be asked to do, I know that. If you don't want to, that's okay. I could manage myself."

Arthur found he couldn't speak. He couldn't even open his mouth. All he could manage was a nod.

"Thanks," Ted said. "There's no hurry, she'll stay out for a good while. Finish your tea first if you like."

Jake got home very late that night, well after two in the

morning. Arthur was still up, sitting at the kitchen table. His mother had gone to her room at some stage but after a while she came down again and sat at the other end of the table, worrying about Jake.

Arthur was barely aware of her presence. Earlier in the evening Reverend March had called around to tell them that Ted Hatchett had shot himself. Arthur dimly heard him say that Mrs. Hatchett's sister was with her. There was no mention of suspicious circumstances and Arthur wouldn't have cared if there were. He was past caring about anything. He scarcely noticed his mother's increasingly frantic state as the hours ticked by, and when Jake finally rolled in, wreathed in smiles and alcohol fumes, he barely noticed that either. The row between Jake and his mother, her tears, Jake's defiance, raged right over his head and for all he heard of it they might as well have been a hundred miles away.

Even the note of triumph in Jake's voice, which a few hours earlier would have set the alarm bells clanging inside his head, made no impression upon him at all.

~

The boys left three weeks later, at the end of May. It was another loss, in a way. As far as Arthur was concerned they were more a part of the family than Jake had ever been. The two of them began their goodbyes in a properly dignified manner (the prison camp truck had arrived and other POWs were looking on), standing side by side and almost at attention, but then Arthur's mother started crying and undid them both. "Ve tank you very much that you have so much kindness," Dieter said, blowing his nose on a handkerchief ironed lovingly by her the evening before, and Bernhard said, "Ve vill remember always. And Canada always." And they hugged her, and shook Arthur's hand so earnestly that he was almost undone himself.

He missed them badly, for more reasons than one. Reverend March and Laura had decided to stay in Struan and were buying the Luntzes' house; Otto and Gertie had finally decided to sell the farm. The farm land was being sold separately, though, and Arthur had undertaken to look after it until the sale went through. Once again he was trying to run two farms on his own, and there weren't enough hours in the day. It didn't worry him as it had before the boys came though. Ted's death had put things in perspective in a way that the war itself had not: what was the loss of a crop or two beside that? Also, there was a restless, uncertain feel in the air at the time that made everything seem unreal. He noticed it most when he went into town; it felt like the end of something—not just the war, which in fact wasn't over yet, but something more. It was as if the whole country, maybe the whole world, was wondering what came next and didn't know who to ask.

Maybe it was because of this, the feeling of restlessness and change, that he didn't pick up the signs that something was amiss with Laura. Or maybe it was because by then he thought she was safe. Late on a Monday afternoon, shortly after the boys left, Arthur was driving home from the market and saw Jake coming out of Harper's with a girl who wasn't Laura. They were laughing about something, both of them doubled up with laughter. Arthur slowed the truck and saw Jake reach out and punch the girl's shoulder lightly with his fist; saw the girl hit him back, still laughing; saw them scuffle, playful as kids, but nowhere near as innocent. Arthur felt his very soul expanding with relief. It was over. Jake was tired of Laura at last.

He didn't finish with her all at once of course, that wasn't Jake's way. He kept her in reserve, like a nearly stale loaf of bread that you haven't given to the pigs yet in case you decide you want one more slice. The afternoon following the incident in town, Arthur was in the farmyard when Laura arrived with her books under her arm; it was Tuesday, and she and Jake always did their homework together on Tuesdays. She thought she must somehow have missed him after school and had come on alone. A few minutes later Jake arrived, and looked surprised to see her, but he put his arm across her shoulders, the way he did with girls, as if he owned them, and said casually, "Oh, sorry! Should have told you. I had to go into town for something." Arthur saw Laura look up at him, perplexed but hopeful. Almost, but not quite, reassured.

Arthur went out to the barn and shovelled dung. Rage and joy battled within him, along with something less admirable, something he was ashamed of but couldn't deny: satisfaction. Now at least Laura would realize exactly who and what Jake was. Much as he wanted to beat Jake to a pulp, Arthur wanted even more for Laura to see that she was well rid of him.

So he did nothing. He watched Laura's growing bewilderment and distress, as one week gave way to another, and he put it down to unrequited love.

In the middle of July, two things happened in quick succession that should have made him suspicious. The first was that Jake came out to the barn one evening just as Arthur was finishing the milking, and said he needed money.

"Something's come up," he said, looking around at the milking stalls as if he'd never seen them before. "Got to get it sorted out."

"How much?" Arthur asked. He didn't ask what for because he didn't care, and in any case knew Jake wouldn't tell him.

"All you've got." Jake grinned at him, but he looked uneasy. Jake was never uneasy, so that should have been a warning in itself. "I'll pay you back."

Arthur knew he wouldn't, but didn't care about that either. He gave Jake ten dollars, which was all he had in his pocket.

"Is that all you've got?" Jake asked, in a tone of disbelief.

"Yes," Arthur said, and went back to the milking, and didn't give it another thought.

The second thing happened the next morning. Arthur had been hoeing turnips for a couple of hours when his mother came panting down the track that ran between the fields—she was getting a trifle heavy around the hips in her middle age—to tell him that Jake's bed hadn't been slept in. Arthur figured he was in someone else's, but knew better than to say so. His mother insisted that he come back to the house to confirm that Jake wasn't there and sure enough he wasn't, but lying on top of his chest of drawers was a note that their mother in her anxiety had failed to notice. Arthur picked it up and read it, and passed it to his mother. It was short and to the point: *Sorry to go without saying goodbye. Love, Jake.*

Years later, the image of his mother reading that note was to be one of Arthur's clearest and most painful memories of her. He'd be doing something else, repairing a fence maybe, or removing a stone from a horse's shoe, thinking of nothing in particular, and suddenly there she'd be: a brave, loving, foolish woman, a mother above all else, finally defeated, standing in the bedroom of the person she loved best in the world, reading the single sentence with which he said goodbye.

~

It was the end of July when Laura came to him: a warm summer's evening, the sunset filtering through the trees. Arthur was at Otto's farm, checking on the pigs. They were out in the orchard rooting about under the trees and he was watching them and thinking about Ted Hatchett and didn't hear her coming up behind him.

She said, "Arthur?" and he started and turned, and then flushed because she was so close to him, standing right by his elbow.

In spite of having said his name, she wasn't looking at him. She was looking at the pigs as if they were what she had come to see.

She said quietly, "Arthur, did he say anything to you? Do you know where he's gone?"

He didn't understand at first. She was referring to Jake, he knew that, but he saw that she was very upset, very distressed. He thought she must still be pining over him, and felt a pang of disappointment.

She said, "I keep thinking about my father. About what it will do to my father." She looked up at him then and he saw fear in her eyes. That was when he realized what she was saying. He could hardly believe it; it seemed impossible, because what she was saying was that he'd been right all along: his suspicions about Jake had been spot on. He stared at her, incredulous, searching back through his mind, trying to think when it would have happened, and where, and why he hadn't guessed. VE Day. It would have been VE Day. He remembered now. Saw Jake, drunk and triumphant, entering the room.

Laura said in a whisper, "Arthur, is he going to come back?"

He didn't know what to say. No, Jake was not going to come back. Arthur might know next to nothing about his brother but he did know that. Becoming a husband and father before the age of twenty would not be part of Jake's plan.

Laura was watching him fearfully, her eyes searching his face. Her saw her understand. She let her breath out, and drew another in, unsteadily. She said, "Arthur, what am I going to do?"

Silent Arthur. A man uneasy with words. For the first time in his life he knew exactly what to say.

"Marry me."

~

He knew she didn't love him, and that she was still in love with Jake. He knew he only married him because there was no other option. It made no difference. He loved her and he wanted to look after her, and that was all.

He knew that certain things would be difficult, though in fact some of them turned out to be harder than he'd expected. His mother, for instance; he was taken aback by her reaction.

"I know what's going on, Arthur," she said, her voice made harsh by a bitterness he hadn't known she was capable of. "I see what's happened. I wasn't born yesterday, you know. I'm not blind. Though I was blind, I see that now, thinking she was so sweet, when in fact she's the kind who's out to trap boys, out to ruin their lives, boys with their whole futures in front of them. If you think you can bring her back here you're mistaken. I won't have her in the house. That's the end of it. If she comes, I go. You decide."

After a whole lifetime of trying to spare her pain, it hurt him to be the cause of more, but he would marry Laura no matter what the cost. He offered to build his mother a house of her own, closer to town, but she refused even to discuss it. She went to live with a cousin down in North Bay and though Arthur went to see her when he could, she never forgave him.

The wedding night was hard too. He'd thought carefully about what he should do, and when the time came he showed Laura to his parents' room with the double bed in which he and Jake had been born, and said that if she needed anything he'd be in his room just down the hall. She looked up at him, her face white with the strain of the day, and the relief in her eyes was hard to bear. But he dimly feared that once she stopped being grateful to him she might come to hate him for not being Jake, and all he could think to do to avoid that was to demand nothing of her. He promised himself that he would not enter her room unless she invited him and he kept that promise, though it was two long years before she appeared one night in the doorway of his room.

When she gave birth to Jake's son, though, that was the

hardest of all. She was entirely preoccupied with the baby, and although he did not resemble his father, Arthur was sure that she saw Jake when she looked at the child. Arthur saw him too. He found it next to impossible even to look at the boy. He knew it was wrong of him, knew that Carter was not to blame for anything and that if he couldn't love him he should at least try to accept him, but it was beyond him.

None of those things altered how he felt about Laura. All he allowed himself to wish for was that she would be able to accept their life together and not hold the circumstances of it against him. So it was amazing to him when one night, not long after the birth of their daughter, Laura looked up from the chair by the stove in which she sat to nurse the baby, saw him watching her, and smiled, and said quietly, "Thank you, Arthur."

He didn't know what it was that she was thanking him for, but he saw that she was happy, or at least mostly happy. It was more than he had ever hoped for, to have made her happy. He considered himself the luckiest of men.

~

It was fifteen years almost to the day when Jake came back. He shouldn't have let him stay, of course. That very first day, when Jake came limping across the field towards him smiling his famous smile, he should have told him to go. But there was something in Jake's face as they approached each other across the field—not contrition, Jake wasn't capable of contrition, but a kind of ruefulness, a recognition of past history, that had made Arthur think maybe Jake had changed. In fifteen years a man might change, mightn't he? And if he had, wouldn't it be wrong to turn him off the farm for sins committed when he was scarcely more than a child?

And then there was his own happiness—Arthur's happiness. That came into it too. Things had turned out so well for him; he had all that he had ever dreamed of and more. Whereas Jake, he suspected, in spite of or maybe because of the flashy car, did not. Surely that required him to show a little generosity, a little forgiveness?

And then there was the fact that Laura seemed in no way pleased to see Jake. In their bedroom, the night after Jake arrived, she had said, "Arthur, I don't think he should stay long." Didn't this show that, far from needing to do as she asked, there was no need to do anything at all? That was what he told himself. He reassured her that Jake wouldn't want to stay more than a day or two in any case, and reassured himself as well.

And finally, of course, there was, and always would be, that moment on the bridge.

So he did not tell Jake to go, and not having told him to go, he didn't watch him, either. The days passed, but still Arthur told himself that everything was fine, that Jake would leave soon of his own accord. That there was no reason, no need, to tell him to go.

THIRTEEN

~

Tough Times for Dairy Industry
Wean Lambs at Fifteen Weeks
—*Temiskaming Speaker*, June 1960

Late on Saturday afternoon when Ian got home from the farm he and his father drove out to Ernie Schwartz's place and chose themselves a little Irish setter bitch. She slept for most of the trip home on an old towel, on Ian's lap. It was a long drive and they'd forgotten to ask when she'd last had anything to eat or drink, so when they got home they took her into the kitchen and put a bowl of water and the saucepan full of Mrs. Tuttle's Irish stew on the floor for her.

"It's what we got her for, after all," Dr. Christopherson said. "To deal with the stew."

The puppy took her responsibilities seriously. There was more of the stew than there was of her but she polished off most of it. When she had finished she stood rigid for a moment or two, eyes bulging slightly, and then opened her mouth and threw up the whole lot onto the floor.

"I guess that was predictable," Dr. Christopherson said. "We should have given her just a spoonful to begin with."

"It looks exactly the same as when it went in," Ian said. "No better, no worse."

Then the puppy stepped in the vomit and slipped and fell in it, so they had to take her down to the lake and give her a bath. When she was clean they put her down on the warm yellow sand to dry off and watched her try to shake herself. She couldn't seem to get the hang of it—every time she managed to work up a little momentum she fell over—and in the end they had to give her another bath to get the sand out of her coat. Ian's father wafted her up and down in the water, supporting her with a hand under her belly—she was so small his one hand held her like a cradle—and she looked up at him, this giant being who kept baptizing her, her eyes anxious but trusting, her fur, soft as feathers, spreading out around her in the water like a halo.

They carried her, dripping, back up to the house to dry off on the grass, and sat down on the bottom step of the porch to watch her. She tried several more times to shake herself, falling over each time, and then forgot about it and began exploring, staggering around in circles, nose down, tail in the air.

"She's gutsy, isn't she?" Ian said. "Less than two months old, just left her mum, set down in a strange place with people she's never seen before, and she's exploring already."

All he asked of her, this small scrap of wet fur, was that

she be family, friend, and companion to his father for the rest of her days. She just had to go on his rounds with him and lie at his feet in the evenings and protect him from loneliness and unhappiness and old age. That was all.

"The advantage of a small brain," his father said. "She's living in the moment and the moment is good."

"That sounds like a philosophy, not a small brain."

His father considered it. "You could be right."

She'd met a grasshopper and didn't know what to do about it. She pounced, it sailed away; she galloped after it, pounced again, it floated off from between her paws, she tripped over her own feet and fell in an untidy chestnut-coloured heap.

"She always falls on her left side," Ian said. "You notice that? Could her legs be shorter on that side or something?"

"Unlikely," his father said.

She was on her feet again, spinning around after the grasshopper, who'd rashly returned to tease her. She snapped at the air and then ate something, crunchily.

"Was that it?" Ian said.

"Yup. She's quick."

"Are you kidding? That was luck."

"Nonsense," his father said. "She's a born hunter—she's going to be a great gun dog. That reminds me, where's the rabbit?"

"Around the back in a cardboard box."

"A strong enough cardboard box?"

"Yeah," Ian said. "I think so. I'll have another look at it before we go in."

He wanted to sit right here on the step forever. It had been hot as a bread oven all day, but now the heat was easing and the air was so heavy it was like sitting in a bath.

He wondered how many more times he would sit like this with his father. Not many.

The puppy gambolled up to them. His father stretched out his hand and she licked his thumb and then began chewing it vigorously.

"Ow!" he said. "No, no, no—your teeth are sharp." He gently prized her jaws apart, removed his thumb from her mouth and stuck it in his own. With his free hand he smoothed her ears and she licked him rapturously, then galloped off.

Old Mr. Johnson appeared, shuffling around the corner, heading their way.

"It's Saturday," Ian said, though without rancour. It no longer bothered him as much as it used to that people took advantage of his father. In the process of correcting Jake's view of his father's relationship with the people of Struan he'd corrected his own as well. The truth was his father wanted people to take advantage of him, if that was what they were doing. He needed them as much as they needed him, and that didn't stop at five o'clock on a Friday afternoon.

"He's old. He forgets."

"Like everyone else in this town," Ian said. "A town full of old people with lousy memories."

The old man had reached the gate and half-opened it, but now he'd seen the puppy and he paused to watch her.

"A puppy," he said after a minute or two.

"You got it in one, Mr. Johnson," Ian said.

"Bitch or dog?"

"Bitch."

"Whatcha gonna call her?"

"Molly."

The old man thought about it. "Wasn't there one called that before?"

"It's tradition, Bert," Dr. Christopherson said. "It's such a good name we're using it again."

"Oh," the old man said. The three of them watched the puppy behaving like a puppy.

"Not very good on her feet, is she?" the old man said.

"She's young," Dr. Christopherson said. "You weren't very good on your feet at that age either."

"I'm not much good on them now," the old man said. "And that's a goddamn' fact."

"You don't do too badly."

"Did you see the sign on the gate, Mr. Johnson?" Ian asked.

"What sign?"

"The one on the gate."

The old man looked down, then bent stiffly and peered at the sign. "What's it say?"

"It says, 'Please close the gate.' We were kind of hoping everybody would see it."

"Nobody reads signs," the old man said. "And anyways, she'll find another way out."

"We've checked the fence all the way around," Ian said. "There aren't any gaps big enough for her to get through."

"I'll betcha a quarter."

"Okay," Ian said. "Done."

"Anyways," the old man said. "Now I can't remember what I'm doin' here."

"Waterworks?" Dr. Christopherson suggested.

The old man thought about it, then shook his head. "Nope."

"Constipation?" Ian offered.

"Nope."

"Your toes?" Ian's father said.

"Nope."

"Maybe you're just out for a walk," Ian said. "It's a nice evening."

"Nope. I came for a reason."

"Heart leaping about again?" Dr. Christopherson said.

"Nope."

"Memory?" Ian said. His father frowned at him but the old man thought it was funny.

"Ha!" he said. "Nope, memory's perfect." He thought some more. "Maybe I only came for a checkup."

"You've just had it," Dr. Christopherson said. "You're in better shape than I am."

"Where's Molly?" Ian said, suddenly realizing that she wasn't there.

"She went around the back of the house," the old man said. "Probably dug a hole under the fence, miles away by now. You owe me a quarter."

But as he spoke she came galloping around the corner of the house. She'd found an old grey sock and was killing it savagely. They watched her shake it violently back and forth. It flew out of her jaws and into the air and when it landed she crouched down and waited, panting and delighted, hoping it would move so that she could kill it again.

"Wonder where she found the sock," Ian said. He didn't recognize it as one of his or his father's.

As if she heard him Molly pounced on it again, seized it in her jaws and brought it proudly over to deposit at his feet. It was only then that they realized it wasn't a sock.

"That's pretty damned quick," Mr. Johnson said

grudgingly. "Catchin' a rabbit at her age—even a little 'un. Pretty damned quick."

~

"You two have to get a move on," Mr. Hardy said. It was Monday morning and he had summoned both Ian and Pete to the school to see him, despite the fact that they were now on vacation. "You need to get your university applications in now. By the time the exam results come out it will be too late. I want both of you back here tomorrow morning—you, Christopherson, at nine; you, Corbiere, at half past—decisions made, pens in hand."

They cycled back to the reserve, went straight down to the dock, got into the *Queen Mary*, puttered around to Hopeless Inlet, and tossed the anchor overboard. It was raining, a quiet, gentle rain, dotting the surface of the lake with a billion tiny circles.

Pete picked up his jigger, stuck a bug on the hook, and dropped it over the side. Ian attached a lure to his line, cast it out across the water, and began slowly reeling it in.

"So," he said.

Pete nodded.

"Decision time."

"Seems so."

They fished. Pete caught a trout. He dropped it in the bottom of the boat and said, "Thought you'd made your decision. Thought you were going to be a pilot."

"I am," Ian said. "It's your decision we're talking about."

"Why didn't you tell Hardy?"

Ian didn't know the answer to that one. "I will. Tomorrow."

The rain was trickling down the back of his neck. He looked around for a hat, or something to use as a hat, but there wasn't anything. The rain was warm, though, and not unpleasant. Pete was twitching the jig up and down in the water. Ian said, "If you don't tell me what you've decided to do in three seconds flat, I'm going to throw you overboard." He felt nervous, and didn't know why.

"I'm not going on," Pete said.

Ian looked at him, sure he must have heard him wrong. Pete let out a little more line from the jigger.

"What?" Ian said.

"I'm stayin' here. Me and a couple of the guys are going to set up a little fishing business for the tourists. Make sure they don't catch all the good fish. I think we can make a pretty good thing out of it." There was a tug on his line; he hauled in another trout and knocked it on the head. He glanced over at Ian and said, "You better keep reeling, man. You're gonna snag your hook."

Ian's line had sunk down into the water. The hook would be down on the bottom, wrapping itself in bits of weed and water-logged driftwood. He didn't care. He put down the rod, let it drape over the side of the boat. "When did you decide this?" he said.

"A while ago."

"How long is a while? A month? A year? Ten years?"

"Why does it matter?"

"I'm just curious."

Though he wasn't curious, he was angry, and getting angrier as it sank in. Angry, and somehow betrayed. He knew Pete was smart, maybe smarter than any of them, though mostly he kept it hidden. Smart in ways both broad and deep. He thought for himself, questioned things, took nobody's word for anything. And though Ian had never been able to imagine exactly what Pete might end up doing, he had always been sure that it would be something impressive. He would show them all; Ian had been certain of that.

Pete shrugged. "I guess quite a few months."

Something big grabbed Pete's line, then spat it out again; Ian thought he saw a long dark shape drifting away. "Shit," Pete said.

"Why didn't you tell me?" Ian asked. That was almost as upsetting as the decision itself. Neither of them was given to talking about personal things, but this was different; there was no reason why they couldn't have talked about this. And they should have. They definitely should have.

"I guess 'cause I knew we'd end up having this conversation," Pete said. "I was putting off the evil day." There was, at least, a note of apology in his voice.

"I don't get it," Ian said. "Why did you take the exams?"

"My grandfather wanted me to."

"Doesn't he want you to go to university?"

"Yeah, but he understands."

"Well I don't," Ian said. "I do not understand."

A pair of Canada geese flew low over the water and skidded to a landing twenty yards away, feet turned up like water skis, then settled, shuffling their feathers.

Pete said, "I can't leave this place, man."

Ian looked out across the lake, to the rocky shore and the woods behind. The rain had stopped and the surface of the lake gleamed like pewter. He said, "Okay. Sure. It's going to be hard to leave, I know that. But it will all still be here. It isn't going anywhere. You can come *back* to it, if you want to. But you can do other stuff *first*. I don't see why you can't do other stuff first. I think you're making a mistake. A big mistake."

Pete hauled in his line. He dropped the jig in the bottom of the boat and sat, his elbows on his knees, looking down into the water. After a while he said, "I don't know how else to put it, man, except to say that everything I care about is here. Everything that matters to me is right . . . here."

"But that's because it's all you know!" Ian said. "Jesus, Pete! You don't even know what else is out there!"

"No," Pete said. "But I know what's important to me. And I know I don't have to go anywhere else to find it."

They sat in silence. It passed through Ian's mind that it was the first time he had ever seen Pete sitting in the boat but not fishing. He supposed it showed how seriously Pete was taking the conversation, but that did not mollify him. He was too frustrated, too disappointed, to be mollified by anything.

He said bitterly, "People are going to think you're scared to try. You know that, don't you? They'll think you're scared you can't make it out there."

Pete turned his head and looked at him. He said mildly, "You care too much what people think, man. That's your biggest problem. You think I'm making a mistake? At least I'm not doing something I don't want to do just to prove a point."

"What's that supposed to mean?" Ian said, hot with anger now.

"You know what it means." Pete picked up the jig and dropped it over the side again.

"No, I don't."

"You're dumber than I thought, then," Pete said, still mild as milk. "Go work it out."

~

He dreamed of his mother again, the second time in a week. They were sitting in the living room, just the two of them, and she was looking through an Eaton's catalogue and suddenly she looked up, her eyes wide, and said, "Listen!"

He listened, but there was nothing to hear but the faint dry rustle of the wind in the trees. He said, "I can't hear anything."

She said, "That's right. That's because there's nothing to hear. Nothing! That's what I can't stand about this place. I can't stand the nothingness!"

He said, "I'm here, Mum. It isn't nothingness if I'm here, is it?"

She smiled at him and for a moment he almost thought she was going to say. "No, you're right, of course you're right." But instead she said, "Go work it out."

~

On Tuesday morning he had his appointment with Mr. Hardy at nine o'clock, so he was late getting to the farm. Jake and Carter were in the farmyard when he arrived. They were standing beside Jake's car; the hood was up and Carter was headfirst inside the engine. Jake was looking as he always did when he was dealing with Carter—half bored, half amused. He liked the fact that Carter was so impressed with the car, though; you could see that. As for Carter, he was a different kid nowadays. It was as if he had been waiting his whole life for someone to talk to about cars. Or maybe just someone to talk to, period.

"So what's the news?" Jake said when Ian got off his bike. "Hear you were called in to the school."

"Just some paperwork," Ian said. "Nothing important." His mind was still on his conversation with Mr. Hardy and he didn't feel in the mood for chit-chat. Hardy had smiled his know-it-all smile when Ian told him what he'd finally decided to do, and although Ian had known that he would, it was still extremely annoying. Pete had been waiting in the hall when he came out, but Hardy had summoned him in straight away, so there hadn't been time to talk. Given how they'd parted last night, maybe that was a good thing.

"What's this thing do?" asked Carter from half-inside the engine. Jake went over to have a look, so Ian was spared further questions. He went to the stable and harnessed up Robert and Edward and when he came out, leading the horses, the car was pulling out of the drive with Jake in the passenger seat and Carter behind the wheel.

Ian took the horses out to the fields. It was oats they were harvesting; Arthur cut oats early and let the grains ripen in the sheaves. It was heavy work and by noon both they and the horses were in need of a break. They unharnessed the horses and left them to graze on the long grass at the edge of the field while they went back to the farm for dinner.

Jake's car was just driving into the farmyard as they arrived, Carter still at the wheel, his face flushed and happy. "We got her going a hundred and ten!" he said as he got out. He was aiming the comment at anyone in sight. "Boy, you should have seen us! She goes like a bomb!" Jake smiled tolerantly.

They all washed at the pump and filed into the kitchen and sat down and waited for Laura to serve them, which she did. Carter was still going on about the car, asking

Jake endless questions. "So if the road was paved, how long would it take her to get from zero to sixty? And if it was downhill? Say it was paved and downhill, how long would it take?" Julie and March were bickering, as they always did at the table. Arthur was silently plowing through his dinner. Laura was trying to help her father get the food from his plate to his mouth without spilling it all down his front.

Ian wasn't paying much attention to any of them. Random thoughts were floating in and out of his mind. He was thinking that when he reached the stage where someone had to help him eat he'd shoot himself; and that Jake was surprisingly patient with Carter, given that he wasn't a patient kind of guy; and that last night it had taken him almost an hour to reassure his father that he was not going into medicine only, or even partially, because he thought it would please him. He was thinking about Pete's decision, wondering why it had felt like a betrayal, and whether he just wanted Pete to make the same choices he did; and about his own decision, wondering whether he had, in fact, made it, or whether everything was decided for you at the moment of conception and there wasn't a thing you could do about it. And he was thinking that it was since his mother's letters had stopped that he'd started dreaming about her, and the dreams were worse than the letters because you couldn't chuck them away unread. The sick anger left over from the last dream was still lying in the pit of his stomach. He knew it was irrational to be upset about something someone said in a dream, but the fact was, even if she had never said it, the gist of it was true: he and his father hadn't mattered enough to her, when weighed against the "nothingness" she hated so much. Given the choice between them and some other life, she had chosen some other life.

He was thinking all those things when suddenly Julie took a break from tormenting March and said, loudly, "Mummy, you keep dropping things."

Ian glanced at Laura. She was retrieving a serving spoon from the floor, and when she straightened up her face was flushed. He saw her look at Jake, just a quick look and then away. Ian looked at him too and saw that he was watching her. That was when he remembered what he'd seen on Friday night. He'd forgotten all about it until then.

"I know," Laura said. "I seem to be clumsy today."

"You must have something on your mind," Jake said.

She gave a little laugh, not looking at him. "No," she said. "Not really. I'm just clumsy." She took the serving spoon over to the sink and rinsed it under the tap.

Maybe if the shadow of the dream hadn't still been with him, Ian wouldn't have thought anything of it. As it was, though, a whisper of suspicion drifted into his mind, just enough to make him wonder if there might be another interpretation of what he had seen. He wouldn't put it past Jake, but Laura? No. He rejected the thought, and the normal to-and-fro of dinnertime washed over him again and carried it away.

~

Afterwards, when he looked back on the events of that afternoon, it seemed to him that there was an inevitability about them, as if fate had arranged a number of trivial little incidents—a series of them, like stepping stones—without any one of which everything would have turned out differently. After dinner, for instance, when he and Arthur settled down in the armchairs for their post-dinner digestion time, March came in from the farmyard. That was the first stepping stone. The children were supposed to stay out of the way while the men rested, but Laura had gone outside to bring in the laundry (so maybe *that* was the first stepping stone) and March slipped in. He was carrying what turned out to be an old billhook, which he announced he wanted to sharpen. Probably he had seen his father and Ian sharpening the scythes that morning and thought it looked like fun.

"That looks kind of dangerous," Ian said, frowning at the billhook. "Let's have a look at it." March handed it to him. It was old and rusty but still sharp enough to be a bad idea for a not-quite four-year-old.

"Where did you find it?" Ian said. Tools were never left lying around. He glanced at Arthur to see what he thought of it, but Arthur's eyes were closed and his mouth was open and a faint sighing snore was drifting out with every breath. He was having a proper post-dinner break for once, like he used to before Jake arrived, which Ian suspected had something to do with the fact that Jake had gone outside after dinner, instead of joining them.

"I was digging a hole," March said, anxiously hauling his T-shirt up and down over his belly, afraid that all these questions meant that he was going to be stopped, as usual, from doing anything that might be fun. "Out by the barn. I was going to bury my truck, and it was there."

"Well, I'll tell you what," Ian said. "This is your dad's and it's a tool for cutting things, so it wouldn't be a very good toy"—a huge sigh of exasperation from March—"Hang on, hang on, what I was about to say is that we can sharpen it

337

together, if you like." He dug around in his pocket for the sharpening stone. The scythes needed frequent sharpening, so the stone lived permanently in his pocket at the moment.

"Can I do it *myself*?" March asked, stretching his T-shirt down to his knees.

"Yes. I'll show you how and then you can do it yourself. I'll just hold it and you can do the rest. You see the billhook has one flat side and one rounded side? Well, you don't sharpen the flat edge, you just smooth the stone over the rounded edge like this. . . ."

So he showed March how to rub the stone over the bevel of the blade, and March had a go at sharpening the hook himself, and then in the middle of the task Julie burst in, highly excited because there was a huge bird—a bald eagle, as it turned out—sitting on the top branch of the white pine at the corner of the hay barn. March rushed off to see it and Ian put the sharpening stone and the billhook down on the kitchen counter, thinking that they'd come back and finish the job in a minute, and followed them out. Then Laura came around the corner of the house with the laundry basket and a minute later Jake appeared from the same direction. And then Arthur, presumably wakened by the excitement, came out as well, and they all stood around with their heads tipped back, gaping up at the eagle, who was looking down at them in utter disdain.

How many stepping stones? Laura going out to collect the laundry, March finding a billhook where a billhook shouldn't have been, a bald eagle sitting in a pine tree, the billhook and sharpening stone on the kitchen counter. Such small, unimportant events.

After a while the eagle flew off and Laura told Julie and March she wanted them to come in and wash because they were going to play with friends straight away. Arthur said, "Might as well get back to it," and he and Ian set off down the track to the fields.

They were starting on a new field and it was Ian's job to scythe the edges so that Arthur and the horses could get the binder around. It wasn't until he picked up the scythe that he remembered he'd left the sharpening stone on the kitchen counter. Arthur didn't have one with him, so there was nothing for it but to go back to the house and get it. That was the final stepping stone.

They were in the kitchen. Laura had her back to the wall and Jake was standing directly in front of her, very close. He had one arm against the wall beside her and with the other hand he was lifting her chin. She had her arms up, hands flat against his chest as if she were going to push him away, but she wasn't pushing him away. That was what Ian noticed. That and the look of horror on her face when she saw him in the doorway.

If she'd been trying to get away she would have looked relieved when he walked in, not horrified—so Ian reasoned, if he reasoned at all. Jake had his back to him and Ian didn't wait to see his reaction. He turned around and walked out.

He went directly back to the field where he'd left Arthur. He did not debate what he should do, the rights and wrongs, the possible consequences. He was filled with an intent so furious, so ungovernable, that it left no room for thought. When he reached the field he walked straight across it, straight through the tall uncut grain, trampling it, sweeping it aside with his hands. Arthur brought the horses to a stop when he saw him coming and then came to meet him, looking puzzled. When he was still a few feet away Ian said flatly, "You'd better go back to the house."

"Somethin' the matter?" Arthur said.

"Yes. Your wife and Jake."

For a second or two Arthur stared at him and then Ian saw understanding hit him. It was as if it hit him literally: Arthur almost staggered. Then he pushed past Ian and started walking, fast, back to the house.

Ian followed him. He left the horses standing in the middle of the field. He followed Arthur, still not thinking, still focused solely on the image in his brain: Laura and Jake. He felt breathless with a kind of excitement, a violent excitement, made up in equal parts of rage and retribution. He was almost dizzy with it.

He saw Arthur reach the steps to the kitchen and fling open the screen door and go inside. He knew that something was going to happen, that there were going to be consequences. He was glad. There should be consequences, the worse the better. When he entered the kitchen Arthur was just disappearing up the stairs. Laura was standing at the foot of the stairs, her hand on the banister, looking up. Jake must be up there, packing, probably. Packing in a hurry, thinking that he would get away. Ian heard Arthur's footsteps crossing the landing, and then Jake's voice, light, falsely cheerful. There was a scuffling sound, and Jake said, almost laughing, "Hey, Art! Hey! Calm down! What's the matter?"

Laura looked at Ian and he saw she was shaking. She said in a whisper, "Ian, what have you done?"

Ian stared at her, his mouth open, speechless with disgust. When he could find words he said, "What have *I* done? What have *I* done? What have *you* done?"

"Yes," she said. "Yes. But oh, Ian . . ."

Upstairs Jake was talking fast, still sounding amused, but then there was more scuffling, crossing the landing, and they heard him say, "Jesus, Art! Jesus! Take it easy!" And then he came hurtling down the stairs, Arthur right behind him. At the foot of the stairs Jake fell and before he could get to his feet Arthur reached down and grabbed him and hauled him upright. Jake tried to brush him off, he said, "Okay! Okay!" still trying to make light of it, trying to sound amused. He looked across at Ian and gave an embarrassed laugh as if in apology for the unseemly behaviour of his brother, but Ian saw that he was scared, which was good. Laura looked terrified; she'd backed away from the stairs and was standing in the middle of the room with her hands pressed against her face, and that was good too.

It wasn't until he saw Arthur's face that Ian began to feel uneasy. Arthur hadn't said a word but there was something in his eyes that Ian hadn't seen before in any-one, far less in Arthur. It was the look of someone who had reached the limit, the end of the line—as if he were teetering right on the edge of a cliff within himself, and if he went over, there would be no telling what came next. He propelled Jake across the kitchen towards the door and when they were still a few feet away he gave Jake a shove, and Jake cannoned into the screen door so hard that it slammed open, right back against the outside wall, and he flew out into the yard. Laura gave a cry and ran to the door and Ian came after her. They saw Jake scramble to get up and Arthur reach down and grab him by the back of his shirt and stand him on his feet and start pro-pelling him towards his car. Jake was saying, "Okay, Art.

Okay. It's okay," but his voice was breathless, there was no pretense of amusement anymore. Laura ran after them. Ian followed hesitantly, apprehensive now, but not yet scared, or not yet admitting that he was scared. He approved of what was happening: it was more serious, more violent than he had expected, but that was okay.

Arthur and Jake had almost reached the car and Arthur, pushing Jake towards it, spoke for the first time. He didn't shout and his back was to Ian but there was such force behind the words that Ian heard him clearly. He said, "Go. Go now."

Maybe Jake was emboldened by the fact that Arthur had spoken; maybe he thought he could reason with him now, that they could have a civilized discussion, which he, of course, would win. Arthur had let go of him, expecting him to get into the car and go, now, this minute, but Jake turned to face him, his back to the car, and smiled and said soothingly, as if to an overexcited child, "Okay. Okay, Art. I'll go. I'll go right now, but my stuff is still up in the bedroom; just let me get my things, okay?"

He shouldn't have done that. He should have got into the car and gone. Instead he gave a little laugh as if it had all been just a joke between them and now it was okay, it was over, it was fine.

He said, "You're kind of overreacting, brother."

Was it the laugh that did it, or the patronizing tone? Arthur reached out and took hold of the front of Jake's shirt with both hands and lifted him into the air, right up into the air, and then slammed him against the car, slammed him so hard the car rocked with it. "Go now," he said.

Ian, scared now all right, seriously scared, saw the colour drain from Jake's face from the force of it. Laura cried out and ran towards them and grabbed Arthur's arm, but it was clear that Arthur didn't even know she was there; he lifted Jake and slammed him against the car again. "Go now," he said again. And lifted him once more. "Go *now*."

It was the thud of Jake's body against the metal of the car that was so terrifying. Running towards them, appalled, Ian saw that the force of the blows would kill him. Maybe that wasn't Arthur's intention, maybe he just wanted Jake to go—wanted it so badly that there were no words to describe it and so in the absence of words he was urging Jake on his way. Maybe that was all he thought he was doing, but he was going to kill him nonetheless.

Ian reached them and grabbed Arthur's arm, yelling at him to stop, but Arthur pushed him away. Ian staggered, regained his balance and flung himself at Arthur again, wrapped his arms around his neck this time, and heaved backwards. Arthur lost his balance and toppled over and they both ended up on the ground. But in falling Arthur did let go of Jake, and Ian, fighting to keep his arms locked around Arthur's neck, managed to yell, "Get into the car!"

Out of the corner of his eye he saw a figure running towards them. Carter, still too far away to help but coming fast. He saw Laura help Jake into the car and slam the door behind him, but he couldn't hold Arthur any longer and as the engine roared into life Arthur broke free.

From where he lay on the ground, what happened next seemed to Ian to take so long that at any stage he should have been able to reach out and stop it. Jake, finally inside the car, his face stiff with shock; Arthur, scrambling to his feet and lunging for the car, one hand stretched out to grab the handle; Carter, racing towards them; Laura, reaching for Arthur, trying to block his path—and then the car, lurching as Jake slammed it into reverse, taking off from a standing start and roaring backwards in a great plume of dust and gravel, travelling so fast that Carter had no chance whatsoever: his face, as it hit him, frozen in astonishment, his body pitching forward, head hitting the rear windshield with such force that his legs were flung up and over, straight up and over, so that his body somersaulted right over the top of the car, and then, slowly and finally, down. And after that: stillness. Silence.

~

Strange, the way the mind works. The way it protects itself from things it cannot face. Grief, for instance. Or regret. Guilt. It finds something else, anything, to draw between it and what cannot be looked at.

What troubled Ian most, in the days following the accident, was that he couldn't remember whether or not Carter had been with the rest of them earlier that afternoon when they'd gone out to look at the eagle. He would call up the scene in his memory again and again, trying to recall where they'd all stood, where within the little cluster of them Carter might have been. The others he could see quite clearly. He himself had stood directly behind March, because the little boy was craning his head back so far he was in danger of falling over backwards. Laura was to his left, with Julie beside her. Jake was a few feet behind them. Arthur was beside the water trough. But he could never quite see Carter.

He worried about it constantly. He wanted to be able to see him, there with the rest of his family, head tipped back, looking up in awe at the magnificent bird.

EPILOGUE

~

It was five in the morning when the phone on the bedside table rang. When he answered it and heard her voice, for a moment he was back at the farm, watching the car roar backwards, the cloud of dust fly up. But then she said, "I'm sorry to call you at this hour, Ian, but it's Arthur," and he was back in the present again.

"I'll be there in ten minutes," he said. He switched on the light and swung his legs out of bed, feeling shaky and slightly nauseous from the vividness of the memory. It was like malaria, he thought. Like a virus that lingers in the body and returns to haunt you.

"Who is it?" his wife said, her voice muffled by bedclothes.

"Arthur Dunn." He reached out and rested his hand on her hip, rocked her gently. "Go back to sleep."

She rolled over and looked at him, her eyes screwed up against the light, but then she nodded, and turned over, and drew the covers up around her. She did her fair share of night visits.

He drove to the farm with the windows down to clear his head. Dawn was just breaking, a pale slit of light dissecting the darkness. When he turned in to the farmyard he saw that the lights were on in the kitchen and in the bedroom upstairs.

Laura was waiting for him at the kitchen door. She was wearing a dressing gown and her hair was loose—she must have got up in a hurry, alarmed and frightened—and silhouetted against the light she could have been a girl again, younger than he had ever known her. As she opened the door for him she said anxiously, "I'm not sure I should have called you, Ian. He seems better. I think he's asleep."

"Don't worry," Ian said. "I'd rather you called."

Six months previously, just before his fifty-ninth birthday, Arthur had had a heart attack, and then a month later, another one. He refused to go into the hospital so there was very little Ian could do for him, but he visited him every day, twice a day in the past few weeks, to ensure that he was comfortable. Whenever he had time he sat with him. Mostly in silence, of course, Arthur being Arthur, though occasionally Ian would pass on some bit of local gossip or ask how things were going on the farm. March was running the farm now; he and his wife had built a house a couple of hundred yards down the road. They had just had their first child, a son, delivered by Ian's wife.

He went upstairs on his own. Arthur was asleep—Laura had been right about that—but his breathing was noticeably worse than it had been the previous day. Ian stood looking down at him, his fingers on the faint, irregular pulse, feeling the heavy ache of loss. His own father had died two years ago and the weight of that was still with him.

Laura was at the foot of the stairs when he came down. She asked how Arthur was and then said, not quite looking at him, "I wondered if you would have time for a cup of tea, Ian? I know you must want to get back. . . ."

"Of course," he said. She must know that the end was very near for Arthur, and he supposed she had questions.

And that was so, at first. When she had poured the tea she sat down opposite him at the table he had once known so well and asked all the painful and inevitable questions that attend the ending of life: how long did Arthur have left, would he suffer at the end, was there any way of easing his passing. Questions that Ian had been asked so many times, in the course of his professional life, that giving the answers should have become easier. But it was never easy, and particularly not today. Laura was struggling with tears, and Ian was not far off himself.

When she had run out of questions they both sat for a minute or two, and then Laura said, "You have been a good friend to him, Ian."

He looked at her uncertainly. In the years since Carter's death they had never spoken of what had happened. In fact, they had scarcely spoken at all. Where do you start, when something like that lies between you? What words, what topics of conversation, do you use? After the funeral he had written to her, apologizing for what he had done—for his criminally stupid action in telling Arthur what he had seen, an action that over the years had caused him a thousand sleepless nights. He'd been desperate to know how much she blamed him. She had not replied, and somehow, over time, his need to know had become a need not to know; given the choice now, he would have avoided the subject forever. But it seemed he no longer had the choice.

"I've always admired him," he said. If they were going to talk about it he would be as honest as he could.

She nodded. "Yes. I know."

"And you," Ian said. "I admired you very much."

"Not always," she said, looking at him. Despite her directness, she looked very fragile in the early morning light. Bruised, almost, as if her emotions lay just beneath the surface of her skin.

He hesitated. "No. Not always. But I was just a kid, Laura. I thought in black and white, back then."

Black and white. For a long time after Carter's death it had been more like black and red, the colours of rage and loathing–of her and of himself. Rage, loathing, and overwhelming guilt. He had left for Toronto at the end of that summer and had spent the first two years of his medical degree in a haze of exhaustion and despair. During the day he was able to distract himself with his studies, but at night, Carter would come to him. Ian would see him sitting at the dining table, questioning Jake about the car, his eyes alight, his whole body animated with interest and enthusiasm. Or he would see him at the moment the car hit him. Or on the ground, staring sightless at the sky.

In the darkness of those nights, it seemed to Ian that he was guilty not just of an act of jealous rage, but of murder. Sleep became a place to avoid at all costs, and at the end of his second year at medical school he had a nervous breakdown. Even with his father's help, the climb back to health took a long time, and it was more than a year before he was well enough to return to Toronto and continue his degree.

During all the years of his training he was sure that he would never return to Struan, but in the end it pulled him back. His wife, Helen, whom he'd met during his third year in Toronto, was a city girl, but her family had a summer cottage on Lake Nipissing and she loved the North. She was a general practitioner too—until his father's death there were three Dr. Christophersons in the town.

There being three doctors meant, of course, that there was no need for him to see the Dunns professionally, so apart from meeting briefly at church or in the town Ian was able to avoid them, and to avoid what lay between them. And so it went on, and time passed, and although the ghost had not been laid, it tormented him less often.

And then, six months ago, at eight o'clock on a bright Monday morning, Laura phoned the doctors' office to say that Arthur was lying on the ground and couldn't breathe, and it was Ian she asked for. He didn't know why—perhaps it was Arthur's wish—but whatever the reason, he was grateful to her now, because it had forced him, finally, to re-establish his relationship with Arthur, and gave him the opportunity in some small way to make amends.

Still, though, when he looked at Laura, what he saw was the events of that day, and he knew that for her it was the same. They could not get around it. If he stayed to chat with Arthur she would bring tea up to them, but she never stayed herself. Before he left, Ian would step into the kitchen to tell her how Arthur was doing, and then he would go. That was the extent of their communication, up until now.

Laura was looking away, across the kitchen, focusing on nothing; he studied her, looked at her properly for the first time in many years. She was still beautiful, in his opinion, but her face was thin and lined, and her hair had faded to an uncertain grey. Perhaps she had never been quite as beautiful as he imagined. He had laid his absurd image of womanhood upon her and required her to live up to it, and when she failed—when she failed, how devastating his retribution had been.

She turned and looked at him, and he was afraid she had felt his gaze and guessed his thoughts, but she said, "There is something I want to say, Ian."

He nodded, and braced himself for what might come.

She said, "I want you to know, now, while Arthur is still here, that I love him. And that I loved him then."

He was startled. It was not what he had expected her to say. He had expected her to tell him how much she still held him to blame.

She went on, her voice unsteady but determined. "You said yourself that you thought in black and white back then. Young people do. So probably you would have assumed that I didn't love him. That I couldn't have."

He remembered Jake's hand, lifting her chin. Her hands on his chest. Yes, he had assumed she did not love Arthur.

"After the funeral," she said, "when Jake was finally leaving, Arthur asked me if I wanted to go with him. I said no. He said, was I sure." Her face suddenly flushed. "That question, Ian! That question! Was I sure! Next to Carter's death, that question has been the hardest thing I've had to live with. The fact that he had to ask it."

Ian saw the scene so clearly he might as well have been there. Arthur standing in front of her, his hands hanging empty at his sides, *desperate* to be sure of her. Preferring her to go, rather than stay and be unsure.

Unable to endure the thought of any more doubt, any more deceit.

Ian had a question too, one that he could never ask, a question that next to Carter's death was the hardest thing he had had to live with. It was this: had she been sleeping with Jake that summer? Because if she had not, if the scene he had walked in on was all that had taken place between them, then how much greater was his guilt? He remembered Jake as he had been at the inquest, his face ashen, looking straight in front of him, meeting no one's eyes; it was when he saw the state Jake was in that it came to him, in a sudden, shocked moment of clarity, that Carter was Jake's son. The verdict had been accidental death, but that had been no comfort at all.

He turned his mind back to what Laura had said. "What did you say to him?"

"I told him I was sure," Laura said, her face still flushed with the pain of remembering.

"I said I wanted to stay with him. I told him that I did not love Jake; I loved him. It was true, it had been true for years. I knew what sort of man Jake was—how could I not know? And I knew Arthur was worth ten of him. I think I'd always known that."

She lifted her hands, fingers spread, as if she were trying to hold something, or understand something. "I don't know how to explain it, Ian. There was something about Jake . . . excitement, I suppose. I remember the first time he spoke to me, the feeling that he had singled me out—me, out of all the world! I thought he was the most exciting, fascinating person I'd ever met. I was very young, and of course I fell in love with him, and didn't see how little else there was."

She stopped for a moment, and looked at her hands. Then she looked back at Ian and said, "The incredible thing is, Ian, when he came back, all those years later, he still had it. Whatever it was. That . . . spark. I didn't love him—in fact, I almost hated him by then—and I knew exactly what he was. And yet, *still*, he had it."

Listening to her, seeing her distress, her urgent need to explain, Ian suddenly found himself thinking of his mother. He wondered if she had ever regretted what she had done. Over the years he had come to understand her a little better, but he had been unable to forgive. He feared it meant that he had an unforgiving soul.

"I wish . . ." Laura said, her voice unsteady again. "I wish I knew that he believed me."

"Arthur?"

"Yes. I wish I knew for certain that he believed me, when I said that I loved him. And that he still believes me. I can't stop thinking about it. I hope he does. I think he came to, over the years. I've told him so, many times. But after all that happened . . . maybe he doesn't. It worries me so much now, when he's close to the end."

"He does," Ian said. Here at least was one question he knew the answer to. "He believes you."

She gave him a strained smile. "That's very kind of you, Ian, but you don't need to say that. I wasn't . . . you don't need to say anything."

"It's true," he said. Her smile made him feel sixteen years old again, and foolish.

There was silence. She studied his face.

"It's true, Laura. I know, because in spite of . . . everything, that is not an unhappy man up there. I've spent enough time with him lately to know."

She was searching his face. "Are you sure?" she said at last.

"Yes," he said. "I'm sure."

~

He went up to see Arthur again before he left, suspecting that it would be the last time. He thought at first he was still asleep, but he opened his eyes as Ian came in.

"Hi," Ian said. "How are you feeling?"

"Okay." A trace of the old shy smile. He was a big man still, not reduced by his illness. A big, powerful man, with a heart that was on its way out. From long habit Ian touched his fingers to his pulse, felt the faint, uncertain heartbeat, weaker now than even an hour ago.

He sat down in the chair by the bed, turning it slightly so that it faced Arthur more directly, and as he did so, suddenly he saw the two of them, sitting on burlap bags at the side of a field, scalding themselves on hot tea, the horses beside them, cropping the grass. The image was astonishingly clear and strong. It made him wonder if maybe, given time, an image like that might come into his dreams, instead of, or at least alongside, the ones of Carter. So that he could look back without such pain on the time he had spent on the farm; set the peacefulness of those days against the tragedy that brought them to an end.

They sat in silence, comfortable apart from Arthur's laboured breathing. Once, looking out the window, Arthur said, "You reckon it's gonna rain?" and Ian turned and looked and said, "It could, all right. Did March get the oats in?"

"Yeah."

"That's okay, then."

Arthur nodded and they settled back, Arthur thinking about the harvest, Ian guessed, and he himself thinking that he was lucky—unimaginably lucky—to have had this time with him.

Finally he said, "I should go." He badly wanted to stay, but the morning was progressing and he had other calls to make. He got to his feet, resisting the impulse to check Arthur's pulse yet again. He knew what it would tell him. "Is there anything I can get you?" he said, fighting hard to keep his voice light.

Arthur shook his head. "I'm okay. Thanks."

"I'll see you later, then."

"Yeah." The smile once more. "And Ian . . . thanks for comin'. Not just now. All those times, back then."

By the time he had finished his calls and got home, it was late morning. He and Helen divided the office hours between them and it was her morning for the baby clinic, but she must have seen the car pull in because she stepped out into the hall to see him. It was a weekday, so their daughters were at school.

"How was Arthur?" she asked.

"Pretty bad."

"I'm sorry." She studied his face. He smiled at her, and she said, "It's quiet this morning. Do you want to go out for a while?"

"Are you sure?"

"Yes, I am. Really."

"I will, then. Ring the dock bell if you need me, okay? Or if Laura phones."

"I will."

He went down to the dock and slid the canoe into the

water. It was full daylight now, but quiet and still. He paddled slowly around to Hopeless. The *Queen Mary* was there as usual, Pete bent over his jig like a patient vulture.

"How's it going?" Ian said. There was a fair-sized pike sloshing around in the bottom of the boat, teeth grinning wickedly.

"So-so," Pete said.

"Any sign of him?" He tied the canoe to the rowboat and climbed in.

"Nope. But he's down there, man. He's down there."

ACKNOWLEDGMENTS

~

The town of Struan is an invention, but in my mind it is located at the northern edge of the vast and beautiful area of lakes, rocks, and forests known as the Canadian Shield, in Northern Ontario. I imagine it west and a little north of the real—and much larger—town of New Liskeard, and I would like to thank the people of New Liskeard and the surrounding area for their help and advice about how things were "up there" in the past. In particular, thanks are due to George Dukovac for answering many questions and for parting with a rare copy of *Northern Doctor* by Clifford Hugh Smylie, MD.

For sharing his knowledge and memories of what it was really like to be a family doctor in the Canadian North in days gone by, I would like to thank Dr. Jack Bailey of Manitoulin Island, Ontario. The reality of such a life lies in the details—the bell on the dock, the volunteer system for person-to-person blood transfusions—and those details I could have obtained only from someone who had been there.

For further help with medical information, my thanks go to Jane Bremner, of Lakefield, Ontario, and to Dr. Oscar Craig and Drs. Alison and David Elliman, all three of whom live in England. Any errors, medical or otherwise, are my own.

I found the following books particularly helpful: *Ten Lost Years, 1929–1939: Memories of Canadians Who Survived the Depression,* by Barry Broadfoot; *Six War Years, 1939–1945: Memories of Canadians at Home and Abroad,* by Barry Broadfoot; *Up North: A Guide to Ontario's Wilderness from Blackflies to the Northern Lights,* by Doug Bennet and Tim Tiner; *The Way It Was,* by Dave McLaren; *In the Beginning: The Story of New Liskeard,* by Edna Lillian Craven, MBE, and its twin publication, *Now,* by Nora E. Craven; and *Home Farm: A Practical Guide to the Good Life,* by Paul Heiney.

The "Paper of Record" website, surely one of the most useful research tools for authors ever devised, provided access to back copies of the *Temiskaming Speaker* dating back to 1906. The title of the newspaper changed over the years, but for the sake of simplicity I have referred to it as the *Temiskaming Speaker* throughout the book. I am grateful to that newspaper for its headlines, as well as for providing much information and a wonderful picture of life in the Temiskaming area.

Thanks are due to my agent, Felicity Rubinstein, of Lutyens & Rubinstein, and to my publishers, Alison Samuel at Chatto & Windus in London, Louise Dennys at Knopf Canada, and Susan Kamil at the Dial Press in New York, for their patience and encouragement.

Gratitude also to Amanda Milner-Brown, Norah Adams, Hilary Clark, and Karen Solomon, for their insightful comments and many heartening words along the way.

And, above all, huge thanks to my family: To my brothers, George and Bill, for their help with all things relating to the North; without their knowledge and assistance I would not have attempted this book. To my sons, Nick and Nathaniel, for their unwavering support (and thanks for finding the "Paper of Record," Nick). And finally, to my sister, Eleanor, and my husband, Richard. For both of them, thanks are not enough.

Mary Lawson, 2006

MARY LAWSON was born and brought up in a farming community in Southern Ontario. She moved to England in 1968, is married with two sons, and lives in Kingston upon Thames. This is her second novel.